AMERICAN SKY

AMERICAN SKY

JAMES GRADY

PEGASUS BOOKS
NEW YORK LONDON

AMERICAN SKY

Pegasus Books, Ltd.
148 West 37th Street, 13th Floor
New York, NY 10018

Copyright © 2025 by James Grady

First Pegasus Books edition July 2025

Interior design by Maria Fernandez

Library of Congress Cataloging-in-Publication Data is available.

ISBN: 978-1-63936-921-8

10 9 8 7 6 5 4 3 2 1

Printed in the United States of America
Distributed by Simon & Schuster
www.pegasusbooks.com

This Is for All of Us

We all *grow up*.

You.

Me.

America in the years after WWII made it a "superpower."

These are two future-forward sagas united by that era's blue sky.

Fictions. Tales set in a fictional heartland town with fictional characters.

But the time and forces of that era are real. The cultural and muckraking references are real. That era's language, humor, heroisms and horrors are real.

Before this *American Sky* volume came my novel *The Smoke in Our Eyes*.

Smoke reveals our childhood awakening.

American Sky reveals what we did with our opening eyes.

As Ziggy Marley sang: *"Don't know your past, don't know your future."*

Or where we are right now.

James Grady

SOMETHIN'S HAPPENING HERE

RUN

Luc fought to calm his hammering heart as he faced the wall of windows to the world outside the Thriftway grocery store that early September Saturday afternoon. His white shirt and clipped-on black tie held no incriminating stains as he scanned the blue sky horizon of his Montana prairie valley hometown.

The treacherous thirteen-year-old gray Dodge smirked in the parking lot.

He stood near the checkout counters of two chatting cashiers who he'd worked with those months of 1967 that the news was calling The Summer of Love.

Dennis, the other box boy, snuck onto the empty elevated office platform where local AM radio station KRIP filled the store with nightclub crooners and country and western wailers, *not* the rock 'n' roll music sought by teenagers like *just-graduated-from-high-school* Luc. Two-years-younger Dennis spun the radio dial to a hundred-miles-away big-city Montana station. Landed on them playing an oldy-goldy that was still the #1 hit song for American troops in Vietnam.

That song title rocked Luc to his bones: "We Gotta Get Out of This Place."

Hell yes!

Especially after what happened last night with Cherie.

And what he'd done about that today that nearly got him . . . *um* . . . crucified.

Now all I've got to do is make it to tomorrow's road outta here!

Then *right now*'s wall of windows showed him white-uniformed Cherie getting out of a car in the parking lot.

And heading into the grocery store.

Luc flashed on how maybe it all went back to the murders.

DREAMERS

Luc slammed his high school freshman locker door shut on a November 1963 Friday morning four years before that desperate grocery store afternoon.

On one end of that new "Big Pink" high school rose a gymnasium that could seat all 4,029 beating hearts populating this town called Vernon with seats left over for out of town crowds who came for the hallowed basketball games.

Two pancaked floors of windowed classrooms stretched between the grand gym and the music and arts auditorium with its fold-up wooden seats for twice the number of the school's 401 students.

The black hands on the wall clock above Luc's locker read: 8:53.

He had seven minutes to find Buffy.

Casually walk up to her. Talk to her. See her smile.

Maybe she'd let him walk her to their first class. *Maybe. Maybe. Maybe.*

The thick lenses of Luc's glasses scanned the gray lockers' corridor teeming with students in collared shirts and skirts below their knees.

Blink/FLASH:

Everyone shimmers in their own shaft of light!

Sure, he knew their names. Vernon was Small Town America.

But that *flash* made Luc realize how little he knew of their actual lives.

There was Wendy from his class. Wide eyes, dusky curls. Not a mean bone in her body. Headed to an ambush in their senior year that exploded her world.

Wendy waved at her best friend, blonde Alice, whose savvy smile betrayed nothing of The Boogeyman.

There's Walt walking steady to be who "they" said he wasn't cut out to be.

There's Tod, a scared stranger in his own skin.

Luc saw classmate Donna's dusky blonde head swaying with her polio limp. Her high school classmates dodged that virus until science came through and stood all those lucky kids in lines at their elementary schools to get a vaccinating hypo needle stuck in their arms and become safe. Parents cheered. Cried. But all that came too late for Donna. And Luc's Gramma Meg.

Luc heard a burst of laughter from a crew cut boy in his class named Mike Jodrey. His glasses held far thinner lenses than Luc's.

Luc saw his buddies Wayne, Kurt, and Marin going their own ways.

But not Buffy.

Luc wedged his way through the streaming hall. Hurried down switchback stairs to the first floor. To the right waited the auditorium and music rooms. To the left was the gorilla's cave. And by the bathrooms past the stairs—

—stood Buffy.

Talking to Steve.

Steve. A year older than Luc and Buffy. Taller than Luc. Better looking. Cool. Luc and Steve were only just "*Hi!*" friends even though they were both tight with Marin, who told Luc that Steve was *deep smart* and, like them, read books.

A few weeks before, Buffy'd taken Steve to the annual formal gowns and suits Co-ed Ball when the rules reversed and high school girls "got to" ask out the boys.

Bobbi Jean'd asked Luc to go. He had to say *yes.*

Bobbi Jean told him: "My dad'll drive us because we live at the refinery west of town."

He'd been friends with Bobbi Jean since fifth grade.

But she wasn't Buffy.

Who he fell for *hard* when northside her and southside him merged in the junior high that held all the town's kids—

—except for the red brick St. Jude's Catholic School kids where that November '63 Friday morning, a girl Luc didn't know named Cherie was dodging nuns' rulers in her last year before ascending to the Big Pink public high school.

During his date with Bobbi Jean, Luc blinded his eyes to Buffy and Steve. Teenagers gyrated with no-touching fast dancing, not early rock 'n' roll's holding-hands jitterbug. Three years earlier, a Black eighteen-year-old New

Jersey singer who made a suit look *fine* triggered that change with his song and dance "The Twist."

No Black people lived in Vernon.

And except for military bases, few lived in the whole state of Montana, even though many cowboys *back in the day* had been Black and the Army's Buffalo Soldiers left hoofprints on those yellow prairies.

Bobbi Jean insisted on dancing the first slow song.

Luc was careful not to wrinkle her ball gown or hold her too tight.

"Huh," she said after that dance.

After their properly arms-length second slow dance she said: "Oh."

Chaperone and music teacher Mr. Bundy smiled his way toward them.

"Good to see you out there, Bobbi Jean," he said. "You've got music in your soul. Music you want to live. Set you free to be."

Blood rushed into Bobbi Jean's face. She had no words.

So Luc helped her out: "She plays good. We took piano lessons together."

"My guess is you quit," said Mr. Bundy.

Luc nodded.

Mr. Bundy told the blushing girl: "You're just getting started. I can feel it in your heart. I hope you get it right. Figure it out. Live it."

Teacher Bundy was a muscled six feet with thick black hair.

Luc glanced across the dance floor.

Saw a sad-eyed, too-thin senior girl staring at Bobbi Jean.

Bobbi Jean rode in silence as her dad drove them home from the dance.

That dad idled the car out front of Luc's house. *Oh so obviously* stared at the car's hood ornament—*not* the rearview mirror reflecting two nervous teenagers sitting side by side in the backseat.

Luc's heart thundered: *Am I supposed to kiss her?*

You're fourteen, he told himself. A freshman. *And never been kissed.*

Bobbi Jean whispered: "It's OK."

Shrugged her bared shoulders: "I'll see you in school."

Now on a month's later fall Friday, trapped Luc hurried his steps down the stairs to the first floor where Buffy stood with *not* him.

He whirled left to charge through that first-floor corridor. That hallway held mostly upperclassmen—

—like the junior star jock named Daryl, who spotted Luc.

Daryl's smirk reminded his prey how after yesterday's football practice, he'd ordered freshman JV Luc to kneel, use his fingers to clean Varsity Daryl's cleats because the *real* rules said—

Gorilla in the office doorway!

Stabbing his meaty pointer finger at Luc: "*You!*"

GORILLA RULES

Principal Harris's gorilla thumb ordered Luc into the office.

The office had a counter. The secretary's desk. The principal's private lair with its desk covered by papers creating The Permanent Record to Decide Everything Forever in the lives of Vernon's high school inmates.

Harris's gorilla forefinger drilled Luc's chest: "You're supposed to be smarter than this!"

"I . . . I don't know what I'm supposed to be smart about—*Sir!*"

"Why did you sign that damn petition?"

Luc blinked.

"The one some of the not so smart senior girls passed around. The one to make it OK for girls to wear pants to school."

"I figured that was something that should be up to them."

"You *figured*? You didn't *figure* what that kind of stuff leads to!"

Huh?

"You and those kind of kids, damn near two hundred of them, you better *figure* this is *my* school. *Mine!* While you're here, you do what I say, how I say. Or else."

Disgust shook Harris's bullet-shaped bald head.

"Your sister Laura was a star here and you're off to this start? What would happen if your dad found out? Did you *figure* how much trouble that would cause him because he's on the school board?"

"I told him about the petition!"

"You told your father? About this?"

"And I heard him talkin' 'bout it on the phone with Mr. Makhem!"

"So now your School Board Dad *and* Superintendent of Schools Makhem know about that damn petition?"

Luc nodded yes.

Last Bell rang.

Principal Harris stared at the boy backed up against the office wall.

Leered: "Well, now *figure* you messing with the way things are made you late for class and got you after-school detention."

"But . . . the football game! I get to ride the bus! Dress out with the team!"

"Nobody will miss you. Now get a hall pass and *get*," said Harris.

"Remember," growled the gorilla, "I got my eyes on you."

PUPPET MASTERS

Two classes later—

—*detected, inspected, rejected, dejected*—

—Luc stepped into Study Hall at 11:03 that Friday.

Shuffled to his desk. Spotted his buddy two rows away reading a novel.

"What's that?" said Luc.

"*The Puppet Masters*," answered Marin.

"So *finally* we get to find out who they are!" said Luc. "Is it any good?"

"Yeah." Marin gestured with the book: "From there."

There: the school library behind a glass wall. Tables. Bookshelves. A rack with magazines, the town's two weekly newspapers, a big city daily newspaper. Mrs. Dawson leaning back in her librarian's chair. Staring through the high school windows at nothing.

The Vision seized Luc.

He hurried to the Study Hall teacher's desk where twenty-four-year-old Miss Casey reigned. Filled out the sign-in sheet. Grabbed his gear. Headed to the library.

The *school* library.

Not the two blocks from his house *county* library.

Where four days before, he'd witnessed America's freedom chained.

After football practice and dinner, Dad went back to work. Luc dried dishes. Mom told him to take a stack of books back to the *county* library.

He walked through that moonlit eve lugging crime and science fiction novels he'd devoured. Mom's heaving-bosoms romances. Dad's book called

The Grapes of Wrath. Luc shuffled past the hospital/nursing home that caged Gramma Meg. Climbed concrete steps to the county library.

Luc pulled open its glass door—

—stumbled into a raging battle.

Mrs. Sweeny. Widow's black dress over her hunchbacked flesh. Gray hair. Wrinkled flesh. A blooded maw expelling tobacco breath as she screamed at the public librarian with her back pressed against the wall under the sign:

QUIET PLEASE

"—telling you that filth, that . . . un-Christian, un-American, subversive, has to be Commie, degenerate filth has no place in *my*—in *our* public library!"

"But Mrs. Sweeny," said the librarian. "Please listen to reason!"

Luc eased into that palace of bookshelves plus a display of arrowheads from governments who ruled this valley before: Blackfeet like his classmate Sheila Stiff Arm and 2024's breakout Hollywood movie star Lily Gladstone. Crow. Gros Ventre like Marin.

"Stands to reason I don't need to listen to anything else 'cause I'm already right!" said Mrs. Sweeny. "You get that filth out of here. Don't let nobody see it. Especially not kids like this four-eyed skinny teenage trouble!"

"What aren't I supposed to see?" said Luc.

"It's just a magazine!" said the librarian. "*LIFE* magazine! Millions of people all over the country get it every week! That issue . . . We got it three weeks ago!"

"And we gotta fight to stop this right now!"

"The cover picture is just—"

"I refuse to see it!" said Mrs. Sweeny. "Lord don't burn my eyes! Radio's Reverend Carl told me. Righteous people are outraged! Took a while for the news to spread, but now thousands of crusaders all over the country marching into libraries and schools. We demand you lock up the magazine that dared to print such a subversive *un-American* picture!"

"What's wrong with that picture?" asked Luc.

"That . . . girl! Her bathing suit. It's a two piece! You can see her belly button! Staring right out at you. That obscene, sacrilegious *naked* belly button!"

A belly button? thought Luc.

When he graduated from eighth grade the year before, his college big sister Laura gave Luc a four-year subscription to a hefty magazine called *Playboy* that featured pictures of women naked from the waist up *plus* a hint of Everything Else. Maybe Laura wanted to help him slip the reins of their hometown. Maybe she wanted a good laugh. Whatever, Laura flummoxed their parents. You can't take away a graduation present from a big sister.

Now every month, wrapped in a green paper mail sleeve, *Playboy* showed up at Luc's house and his parents had to let him have it.

But they made him keep it in his bedroom.

Darn.

That November's "centerfold" color photo showed smiling Terre Tucker sitting on a crimson-sheeted bed. Black hair sprayed into an upward curl. Draped eyes welcoming you above naked breasts. Her bare left leg demurely crossed over her "private parts."

She'd been an "airline stewardess."

Comedian Lenny Bruce encouraged her to audition to be a centerfold.

Luc remembered reading about Lenny Bruce being a "sick comic." Being blacklisted from TV shows. Arrested on obscenity charges in Philadelphia, Chicago, Hollywood and Greenwich Village. Banned from several American cities as well as all of England, God Save the Queen.

One of Lenny Bruce's "sick" routines had Christ and Moses coming down from heaven to the gilded wonders of St. Patrick's Cathedral in New York and being dismayed seeing poor people who had nowhere decent to live and not enough to eat when the church's cardinal wore a ruby ring worth $10,000.

New York City's district attorney prosecuted Lenny for that.

And Mrs. Sweeny's yelling about a belly button.

I mean, thought Luc. *What the hell?*

But he saw the county librarian surrender. Take the belly button magazine into the back office so no one else had a chance to suffer its corruption.

Now on that following Friday morning at 11:09, *high school* librarian Mrs. Dawson stared at the outside world as The Vision gravitated Luc into her domain.

What's the worst that'll happen? he thought. *A gorilla's steel finger?*

Luc *casually* walked to the librarian's desk: "Um, Mrs. Dawson?"

Her eyes focused beyond the windows as she mumbled: "So they tell me."

"Can I get on the list for *The Puppet Masters?* Marin has it out now, so . . ."

The brown-haired woman lined by four decades swiveled the sunlit chair to face the thick-glasses freshman boy standing across the desk from her.

"*Really.*" Her eyes bored into Luc. "Ask Marin to tell you when he's through with it. Then come get it. Not much of a rush in here for you to worry about."

The two juniors huddled at a far table cribbing term papers from a five-year-old encyclopedia where you could find everything you needed to know.

"Oh," said Luc. "OK."

"*Naw.*" Mrs. Dawson's smile curved like a sword. "Something's not OK."

"No—honest! It's just . . . I was just wondering . . . *Um* . . ."

Luc swallowed. Released *The Vision.*

"I was wondering if we have any *LIFE* magazines."

"*Ahh,* the big fuss issue. Principal Harris told me to do something about it," said the librarian. "Tell me what our First Amendment says."

"Freedom of speech. And the press. And being—doing free."

"Did your teachers ever tell you we all have to protect that?"

Luc nodded.

She pulled *that LIFE* magazine out of the center drawer of her desk.

"Look at this," said Mrs. Dawson. "Safe and sound.

"I bet you're interested in it because of its story on the Italian dam disaster. *No!* Wait: You want to read about the movie they're making about that book *Lord of the Flies.* Boys just like you turning from good guys into monsters."

"I . . . I haven't read that book."

"So I'll put it on your list with the one from your buddy Marin. Read both of them, then come back and tell me 'bout 'em."

Luc carried that weight to a blonde wood table.

What a perfect name! thought Luc. *Life is what it's all about.*

His family subscribed to the smaller-sized weekly magazine: *TIME.*

LIFE mostly published pictures.

TIME explained the news of the world.

His dad read *TIME* every mailbox Monday along with every dawn's daily newspaper *thunked* on the front porch so he could know what was going on.

How much more "timely" information could anybody need or want?

The price on *LIFE*'s cover was twenty-five cents—no more than a large Coke from the Tastee Freeze or Uncle Johnny's drive-in with its teenage girls as carhops.

The magazine's length ran from inside Luc's elbow to the bottom of his middle finger. The magazine was about two-thirds that wide with 122 pages.

On its front cover loomed The Trouble.

A smiling wet-blonde-haired woman holding an orange surfboard.

Orange like her two-piece swimming suit that was not a *wow* bikini.

Her navel was a shadowed dot.

That's why all of this LIFE *is being censored?*

He looked around his high school library. Out its wall of windows to his hometown in 1963. Through the glass partitions to the Study Hall.

Where are we? Somewhere like George Orwell's way-off 1984?

The clock on the library wall that 1963 November Friday read 11:07.

Luc looked down at *LIFE*'s cover. The dangerous navel. The damp blonde hair and honest smile of the movie star holding the surfboard:

Yvette Mimieux.

Whispers of California and Paris in one heaven.

He opened that magazine.

THAT LIFE

O h, the glories of that *LIFE*!
   Full-page color ads:

> *Top picture*: A fisherman with a jaunty cigarette in his lips admires his dangling trout catch as his buddies behind him look on with admiration.

> Lucky Strike separates the men from the boys . . .

> *Bottom picture*: His pretty but demure wife holds a pan with that fish she's fried for him as he smiles down at it with a cigarette between his fingers.

> . . . but not from the girls.

A four-paragraph news story opposite that ad headlined:

A WEIRD INSULT FROM NORWAY

The story noted the one-year anniversary of the Cuban Missile Crisis, then:

> Caltech's chemist Dr. Linus Carl Pauling has denied under oath that he is a Communist and has occasionally criticized some aspects of Soviet tyranny. But it is hard to quarrel with the verdict of the

Senate Internal Security Subcommittee, which has called him "the No. 1 scientific name in virtually every major activity of the Communist peace offensive in this country."

Pauling's main subversive activity was opposing testing nuclear bombs.

Last fortnight, in an extraordinary insult to America, the Nobel Peace Prize Committee conferred its prize for 1962 on none other than Linus Pauling . . . However distinguished as a chemist, the eccentric Dr. Pauling and his weird politics have never been taken seriously by American opinion.

Cigarette ads flowed past Luc's eyes.

Marlboro's cowboy-hatted "man's world of flavor in a filter cigarette."

Newport's blonde woman crimson-smiled at her man and held her cigarette that he no doubt lit.

Luc flipped pages with ads for bourbon. Puppy treats. Encyclopedias to "wake up" underperforming *boys*. Catsup and color TVs. Cars newer than his parents' still-innocent gray '54 Dodge. Ads showed happy families. The women wore trim hair. Proper dresses. The men were tall. The children adoring. Everyone was White. An ad from the all-powerful monopoly phone company proclaimed: "Long distance. It's the next best thing to being there."

Luc pictured the corded rotary dial telephone hanging on his family's kitchen wall. To save money, Laura called from college person-to-person collect for "Meg Conner." Whoever answered truthfully told the operator that person wasn't there, so the call ended with no cost to Laura or their parents.

No one mentioned that Gramma Meg had been committed to the nursing home since 1959 when rock 'n' roll pioneer Buddy Holly's plane crashed.

Their parents always called Laura back by cheaper "direct dialing."

Now sitting at a library table, Luc read the "Life Guide" to what was going on that didn't tally the 171 American soldiers *killed in action*—"KIA"—so far in the Vietnam war that got zero mention anywhere in that *LIFE*.

He lingered through the black and white photo story about that movie being made from the novel *Lord of the Flies*.

Those black and white photos showed a cast of pale boys younger than him. Luc tried to imagine himself, Wayne, Kurt and Marin in those images. *Had we been like that?* Scruffy little kids about to become monsters?

Luc flipped past a story about pro football player Jim Brown. Luc paid no attention to sports. The only reason Luc bled on the high school football team was he refused to be seen as *just* a thick-glasses skinny geek.

Jim Brown was the only Black face reported on in those 122 pages of *LIFE*.

Nowhere in that *LIFE* were pictures of three girls Luc's age of fourteen—Addie, Carole and Cynthia—*who shared Luc's birthday!*—plus Carol, who was eleven. Back in September, White Christian Ku Klux Klanners bombed a Baptist church in Alabama and murdered those four Black girls.

Page 119 revealed the horror that galvanized Mrs. Sweeny.

Black and white photos captured a twenty-ish blonde actress learning to surf for her guest role as a patient on a popular TV doctor series.

The blonde actress rode ocean waves on a surfboard, stood tall and balanced and *again* with her belly button shockingly visible.

Luc looked up at the clock on the wall: 11:43 on a sunny November Friday.

Carried that week's *LIFE* toward Mrs. Dawson's desk.

Laughter burst open the door from the library to the outside hall.

TRIGGER

The library door burst open to let in laughing Mr. Egan who taught social studies and was an assistant football coach.

The head coach was Mr. Moent. Moent's grandfather decades before brought a horse to sell from his Sioux lands to the Blackfeet reservation coincidentally on the day the cavalry showed up to sign up every *obviously* eligible body onto the tribal roles that legalized their wheres and whens and whys.

Moent's grandfather signed where the White men with guns told him to. Realized that meant he now had to live on the Blackfeet reservation. He snaked a path through the army-patrolled golden prairies and mountain clusters for more miles than between Washington, DC, and New York City to get his wife and children—and then snuck them all back up to the Blackfeet reservation where they were accepted *but* not blood of that nation.

Now the grandson of that flight couldn't walk down Vernon's Main Street without someone buying him a drink for being a winning football coach. Nobody cared that his students insisted that he was also a savvy history teacher.

That Friday his assistant coach Egan strolled into the library *laughing*.

"You're never going to believe this!"

Gray-suit and tie Mr. Egan lifted his glasses off to brush away tears of mirth.

That gave Luc the chance to flip the magazine on the librarian's desk front cover down. He sidestepped in front of that now hidden contraband.

Not gonna get caught! he told himself. *I'm going to get away with it!*

"Just come on the radio in the teacher's lounge. Kennedy's down in Texas on LBJ's ranch. They're out riding around, come up on some deer hunters who was shooting and all hell broke loose. Some Secret Service guys and Kennedy got winged, and Johnson—you know him, vice president, Texas boy who knows about huntin', he skedaddled it real fast up over the hill."

Mrs. Dawson wide-eyed her colleague: "*Someone shot the president?*"

"Well, how bad could it be? JFK fought in WWII and today is just Texas."

A cold wave swept Luc to the table where his school gear waited.

He flipped open a notebook to a clean sheet of white, blue-lined paper.

Used his blue ink pen to write it down.

Didn't know for who. For somebody else. For him. For tomorrow's true.

Egan just said somebody shot Kennedy!

YOU BLINK AND . . .

Grab your gear off the library table.

Walk back into the Study Hall. Check in at the warden's desk.

Miss Casey frowns as she sees your face: "Is everything OK?"

She holds up one finger for Luc to wait as she turns to deal with the geometry teacher hurrying toward her through the open doorway.

Luc floated to his desk.

To Luc's left sat sophomore Linda who presided in the glass booth of the cashier ticket seller at the Roxy movie theater where Luc often worked.

He passed her his notebook open to the page he'd scarred.

She blinked. Looked at it. Shook her head. Read it again.

Turned to her left where another sophomore girl named Becky sat.

Becky'd moved to town last year. Now she stared at the notebook page Linda showed her. Becky and Luc locked eyes.

He saw Becky believe him. Why wouldn't she?

That autumn, Luc's parents were still puzzling out how Luc'd get to the Big Pink across the railroad tracks on the northside from their southside home on the low hill above Main Street. He could walk the two miles there. Or Dad had to leave earlier for work at the trucking firm on the northside to drop Luc off.

But the Ross family got relief via a family who moved to Vernon from exotic Saugerties, New York. Their sandy-haired son Zack dominated basketball courts. Got nicknamed Surfer Z: *Saugerties was on the East Coast, so it had to be near an ocean—right?* Because he helped at his dad's used car lot, Surfer Z had a special driver's license. Zack took a shine to Luc. They were both freshman.

Zack liked showing up as Luc's morning ride. Liked talking to Luc's mom and dad. Liked when they listened to him. Talked about wanting to be a doctor.

Noon Bell rang.

Luc hustled to his locker.

Heard voices: *"Oh my God!"* and *"What?"*

He grabbed his jacket. Slammed his locker closed as he scanned for—

"Zack!" Luc shoved his way to his buddy. *"Please give me a ride?* Not to my house, the trucking company where my dad works!"

They plowed through the crowd to Zack's car in the parking lot.

Luc shook his head: *"What the hell happened?"*

Zack shook his sandy-blonde head. "My old man says get it while you can 'cause you never know. Even if you're president."

Blocks of dreams-painted family homes slid past the car.

"Goes to show he's right," said Surfer Z. "Get it while you can."

THE VISION OF

Luc stood staring at the open garage bays of Marshall Trucking.

His dad had worked there as the manager for Luc's whole life.

Luc spotted his dad, two mechanics and three truck drivers huddled around the shop radio.

Dad saw his son.

"Head to the car, Luc. I gotta phone the border."

Canada waited thirty miles north of Vernon on a border guarded by yawning gatekeepers who waved everyone back and forth between the two countries—including truckers hauling oil from the refinery where Bobbi Jean's family lived in company houses enveloped by the stench of sulfur and methane flames routinely blasting out of the top of a giant burn-off chimney.

A black station wagon with white letters reading MARSHALL TRUCKING waited outside the gray clapboard house turned into the company's office that Luc's dad hurried into. The cigarette in his hand trailed wisps of smoke.

Head mechanic Harry McNamer limped to Luc, every step a victory over the shattered leg freedom's enemies left him with on D-Day's Normandy beach.

Harry put a steadying hand on Luc's shoulder.

Stared into his eyes.

Told the just-a-teenager: "We got this."

They shared a nod.

Harry's steel-braced leg clanked him back to the garage bay and voices coming out of the radio. Harry listened to the *what's what*. Listened for the *what to's*. Harry clumped to the garage to stand with his men. To *stand*.

Luc walked to the dark shadowed back of the garage where the watch light bulb dangled from the ceiling. This was the first year he was tall enough to reach that teardrop bulb shining down on her.

She's the glory of that calendar celebrating Luc's birth year—1949.

She's forever.

She's naked.

The first naked woman Luc saw pictured or in the flesh.

Forget all the Playboys, Luc telepathed to her. *You're always the one.*

That noon Luc worshipped in the flowing light of a dangling-down bulb. Where *she* was. Not walking away. Watching you be worthy to walk to her. Not a photograph. Not a fantasy. A prayer.

She ruled a bright red world.

History says the radio was on when she posed for that immortality.

Nobody knows what song was playing.

She sits facing you over her heart with her legs pressed together and bent at her knees. Her back is arched. Her breasts are nature true with wondrous pink tips feared by Mrs. Sweeny's crusaders. Her face leans into the crook of her left arm curled behind her head of blonde hair.

Not the color she was born with. The color she chose as a rebel.

Her heart-side eye hidden by that protective arm.

Her right eye blue and honest, open to what was really there.

Her red lipstick smile whispers her name: *Marilyn Monroe.*

Movie passes Luc earned by door-to-door passing out handbills had let him see many of her Hollywood productions at the Roxy on Main Street.

His family's TV in the basement recreation room outside of Laura's pink bedroom let Luc see Marilyn's last black and white film that made him feel . . . *yes*, she was beautiful in that role, her white blonde hair and lipstick smile, but . . .

But Luc sensed she was more and less than herself in that news clip.

What a grand affair! A political fundraiser for President JFK. Madison Square Garden filled by 15,000 black tuxedos and big-bucks suits there to throw money into the coffers of a millionaire politician in celebration of his birthday.

His wife, Jackie, did not attend.

Marilyn Monroe performed.

Sang "Happy birthday, Mr. President" in breathless tones.

Murdered herself less than three months later.

The newspapers headlined that she was found nude.

Pills, they said. Booze, they said. The blues.

That 1962 summer led Luc to a drugstore rack holding a movie fans magazine with her picture on it and the headline:

SCANDALOUS SECRETS YOU DON'T KNOW ABOUT MARILYN.

She had to be sewn into the shimmering with rhinestones and nearly translucent gown. The JFK night, they kept giving Marilyn champagne and pills to prop her up to perform. She'd been a problem on the movie set of *All About Eve*. The director had to tell her to stop reading an autobiography of Lincoln Steffens, who was one of those nasty muckraker journalists. The studio public relations executive had to keep crossing off questionable names like Steffens from a list of her favorite books. A New York photographer caught her shopping in a bookstore and paying attention to a book critical of big business. Worse, she signed on as one of the founders of a suspiciously left wing group called SANE—The Committee For Sane Nuclear Policy.

When asked why she was who she was doing what she famously did, the dyed blonde actress confessed:

'The truth is I've never fooled anyone. I've let men sometimes fool themselves. Men sometimes didn't bother to find out who and what I was. Instead they would invent a character for me. I wouldn't argue with them. They were obviously loving somebody I wasn't. When they found this out, they'd blame me for disillusioning them—and fooling them.'

She also shockingly revealed:

'I never understood it, this sex symbol. I always thought symbols were things you clash together. That's the trouble, a sex symbol becomes a thing. I just hate being a thing. But if I'm going to be a symbol of something, I'd rather have it be sex than some of the other things we've got symbols of.'

She died as a pill popper. Someone who abused doctor-ordered helpers for stressed mothers and office workers. She didn't even have the decency to put her clothes on to kill herself.

But THE BIG QUESTION is:

Did Marilyn have an affair with our President JFK or with his brother Robert Kennedy, who's our attorney general?

Luc stared at her that November 1963 Friday morning in the shadows of a trucking firm's garage in a nowhere small town:

Do you know what's going on?

MAD WORLD

Dad drove them through their small town of shut doors.

Cleared his throat.

"We didn't vote for the man."

Luc knew his mom, sister Laura and he were in that "we."

"Nixon should have won," said Luc.

Dad shook his head. "Still bothers me that . . . Well, JFK's Catholic. People worry he takes orders from the pope. Give away our secrets in his confession."

Dad stared at empty Main Street as he drove toward where the sun rose. "I never wanted anybody to harm him. This is America! We're not like that!"

Luc saw the Roxy movie theater's marquee announcing that night's movie:

IT'S A MAD MAD MAD WORLD

In the time it takes to soft boil an egg, the car Luc was in parked in front of the two giant pine trees in front of the small white wood and blue-shingled house.

The two Ross men hurried through the front door that was never locked.

"I was watching my soap opera *As the World Turns*," blurted Mom. "A bunch of *News Bulletin* words came across the screen plus the voice of that Walter guy saying somebody shot three times at a motorcade in Dallas, probably the president'd been hit. Then TV cut back to *As the World Turns*, but . . ."

They tromped down to the basement and its live black and white TV images:

A newsroom with clacking manual typewriters. Rotary telephones. The TV camera centered on a starting-to-lose-his-hair, mustache and black-rimmed glasses announcer named Walter Cronkite.

They watched that man in a cinched black tie on a light-colored shirt.

At thirty-eight minutes after high noon in Luc's western hometown, Walter put his glasses on to read a white sheet of paper he'd been handed. Took those glasses off. Trembled as he stared into the camera:

"From Dallas, Texas, the flash, apparently official, President Kennedy died at one P.M. Central Standard Time."

Walter looked past the camera at an off-screen clock on the wall. Spoke the *when* calculation for the president's death in Eastern Standard Time.

Walter's face fought for control. His eyes closed.

Beat.

      Beat.

            Beat.

                  Beat.

                        Beat.

Walter put his glasses back on his face.

Forced out words about What Else.

RING!

Dad ran to Laura's pink bedroom's phone.

Pressed the receiver to his face: "Hello?"

Mom and Luc stared at him as he listened to words they couldn't hear.

Dad hung up.

"Luc, I'm going to the high school and you—Hurry!"

Dad and Mom charged up the twelve steps out of the basement.

Luc stayed behind to run into Laura's bathroom with the house's only shower and its second toilet that let him *Ahhh!*

When you gotta go, you gotta go—even when it's the end of the world.

He zipped up and ran up the stairs.

Found Dad cinching on a tie.

Dad never wears a tie for regular days, thought Luc as the two of them marched out the front door. A sport jacket, *sure*, that was what a boss was supposed to wear and wearing one made sure everyone knew who was a boss.

Who now drove the two of them in the company station wagon.

Two blocks from the high school:

"*STOP!*" Luc pointed out the windshield. "You gotta stop! Pull over there!"

Where *she* marched the sidewalk to the Big Pink. Shoulder-length milk chocolate hair stirred in the wind and the wind she stirred.

"Buffy!" called out Luc. "Come on! Ride with us!"

He watched her sitting in the backseat as his dad drove on.

"Mr. Ross, I—sorry, I mean thank you!" said Buffy. "My parents, back to the floral shop and I—we—right, Luc? Have to go to school because . . . because . . .

"This isn't how it's supposed to be! *What's going to happen?*"

Buffy burst into tears.

Luc handed her a clean handkerchief from his right hip pocket.

Buffy took it. Wiped her eyes. Blew her nose.

Blushed with embarrassment as she looked up from the snot-filled white rag. Saw Luc giving her a sad smile. Almost cried again.

The black station wagon drove past the Big Pink's gym side parking lot that should have been full instead of half-empty of kids' cars. The station wagon stopped in a row of cars in the other-side-of-the-school teachers' parking lot.

Getting out of a parked car was Superintendent of Schools Makhem. Another member of the school board waited on the sidewalk.

"Luc," ordered his dad, "you gotta find your own way home."

Adult public servants hurried into the Big Pink.

GOD BLESS AMERICA

Luc and Buffy drifted apart in high school corridors of murdered beliefs.

Kurt stared into gone. Alice walked with her arm around shaking Wendy. Marin watched the windows to blue sky. Nowhere could be heard Mike's laugh.

We're all strangers now, thought Luc. *Even to ourselves.*

The clocks on the walls said ten minutes to First Bell for afternoon classes.

Algebra, thought Luc. *How to make sense of equations. X is the unknown. What X is this right now?*

Teachers rippled through the hallways.

"Homerooms!" shouted the teachers. "Go to your first period homerooms!"

"Had to come back," Zack told Luc. "Coach Hopper—not Moent—gave me a pink slip to get out of class so he could see if I needed help for basketball, but . . ."

"Yeah," said Luc. "*But.*"

Surfer Zack wove away through the shuffling crowd.

Steve hurried to Luc.

Said: "Have you seen her?"

Luc nodded.

"How's she doing?"

"About like all of us. Maybe more."

"We gotta take care of her," said the guy who was to the guy who wasn't.

Whispering out of Luc came: "Yes."

"This summer," mumbled Steve, who wore glasses, too. "Sitting on the living room floor at Danny's. The TV was on. That Martin Luther King reverend-guy back in DC. Huge crowd. Talking about how he has a dream."

Luc shook his head: "This is a nightmare."

The bell rang.

Luc sat in his first period English class/homeroom.

Mrs. Davis cowered behind her desk. Taught no lessons in diagraming sentences that dominated her classes from first to last days when she'd finish each teaching session by reading out loud from the quartet of novels about a man who woke up to find himself naked on Mars.

Gorilla Harris blared from loudspeaker boxes above blackboards:

Attention all students and teachers!

President Kennedy was shot and killed in Dallas. All schools in Vernon are closed. Country kids, buses for you are on the way. After school detentions are canceled. Our football game in Shelby tonight is canceled. We don't know about school Monday. Tell your parents all that will be announced over the radio, KRIP.

Now get your stuff, then get on out of here. Go home.

And God bless America. Remember that: God bless America.

School books floated from Luc's arms into his locker. His windbreaker wrapped itself around him. He flowed down the stairs toward the first floor's gym and glass doors to the students' parking lot.

The corridor by the gym doors made a vast room with benches and folding chairs for bus kids and other sack-lunch bringers like Luc. The same tiles hosted post–home game dances during football and basketball seasons.

Now in that rec corridor, Luc saw bus kids guided into waiting herds by Mr. Bundy with freshman Bobbi Jean waved to his side to help him orchestrate.

The roar of engines. The smell of exhaust smoke. The concrete sidewalk beneath Luc's feet as he stood by the student parking lot.

"You need a ride?" asked Linda, who'd been the first to see his blue ink shock. "Becky probably got a ride from somebody else, you know, like you do."

Like we all do, thought Luc. *If you don't stop for someone who needs it, nobody will stop for you when. That's how it's supposed to be. We all need a ride.*

Luc dropped into Linda's shotgun seat as she put herself behind the steering wheel. They joined the parade of student cars leaving the parking lot.

Linda turned away from crossing the viaduct. Drove toward the train station and the block of northside bars. The Oasis with its fenced-in bullpen out back where they threw the drunks to sleep it off or fight it out. On the corner stood the Bucket of Blood, whose real bar name nobody from Vernon used.

Linda said: "I usually take a left instead of crossing the tracks."

"'S OK." Luc pointed to the station's wooden platform where travelers could wait for one of the two daily passenger trains. "You can let me out here."

Luc watched her car glide away.

He stared at the backs of Main Street buildings. The train tracks. Wind skittering yellow and brown autumn leaves.

Thought: *Everything looks the same, yet . . . not.*

Blinked: *Now I don't have to go to detention.*

FOR YOU

No," said Mom that Sunday into the bedside phone in Laura's pink basement bedroom. "She's not coming home from Chicago on 'count of. Costs too damn much even w' her scholarship . . . So that'll be another thing she tells that shrink.

"Besides, Dory," said Mom to the youngest of her three sisters, the baby she'd helped raise in a clapboard house that held eight Conner kids and a polio crutch-swinging wife named Megan with a husband/father who was gone cowboying from spring roundup to slaughterhouse sales or dealing cards for a winter-warm saloon: "Those kinda doctors always say it's the mother's fault."

Luc sat outside of the pink bedroom staring at his pick of the four black and white "live" TV channels. JFK's funeral was tomorrow—Monday. No school.

He checked his watch: 11:17.

Dad was sleeping in. He'd worked nonstop since JFK's murder. The school board. The trucking company. The upstairs toilet that kept running.

Now Mom sat on the bed in Laura's pink bedroom. The cord dangled down from the phone's receiver pressed to her ear as she talked.

"She says Johnny's not sleeping. Something's on his mind."

They're talking about Aunt Beryl, thought Luc. And Uncle Johnny who runs the northside drive-in and the blue taxi and the two-story red whorehouse.

Never been there, thought Luc. *And now that I, you know, can . . .*

The whorehouse.

He didn't want that—*that* that.

But *sure*, Luc was *dying* for *that*.

The calendar's true love dream or the dreams that, *well*, wet his nights.

Beyond what Marin blurted to him in fifth grade and a sixth grade kitchen table explanation from his dad that was so *Huh?* that Luc'd asked if a doctor needed to be present, most of what Luc knew about sex was fantasy. Movie trains racing into a tunnel. Novels where *Bond, James Bond* swooned every woman with one touch rocketing her nipples hard so she cried out in orgasmic ecstasy.

That sounded *great* to Luc.

But paying $10 to have a strange woman let you do it to her—*with her?*—when she wouldn't care about your name and would tell you lies . . .

That wasn't what Luc wanted.

Even though his mom told everyone she'd give him the $10 "to go get it out of your system once and for all" so he wouldn't get some girl pregnant—

—as if geeky him could get some girl to *want* to let him even come close to getting her pregnant! And as if "once and for all" would be enough.

Uncle Johnny might let him ride the blue taxi to the house for free.

You had to take the blue taxi to the red two-story house on the gravel road north of town. That's how Uncle Johnny kept control. Kept busybodies from seeing his customers' cars and knowing whose wife to call. Plus, taxi dollars rolled in to his out-of-town associates and paid for the girls getting driven into town twice a month to get a VD check by the county doctor—

—not ex-mayor Doc Nirmberg with his Main Street upstairs office where *everyone knew* most of his patients were women seeking illegal abortions. A shotgun leaned against his wall so he could stop anyone from interfering with his patients. They came from as far away as a train ride from Seattle or Chicago. Those women, girls even, some with their mothers, brought *Oh yeah!* dollars into town by staying at a local motel, buying local meals.

That Sunday, the pink bedroom's phone pressed to Luc's mom's ear:

"—saw her when I was taking out the garbage. Come down Main Street in her fancy *Thunderbird* car . . . Yeah, well, good thing for her, he'd rather spend time workin' the rigs, livin' in the oil field trailer . . . Yeah, *no shit* a weird duck. Lucky he hit a gusher on his family's old homestead before the bank come for it . . .

"You're telling me. All the men. Fancy clothes. Big city lipstick. Tryin' to be more than who she's stuck being because—*because Mister Hit-It-Big spotted a pretty high school girl 'n' figured he oughta drill her, too!*"

Mom's laughter drowned out the black and white TV replay of what Lee Harvey Oswald was saying to reporters in the Dallas police station.

"Nora Fields," said Mom. "Most days you gotta be glad you ain't her."

"Mom!" yelled Luc. "They're bringing him out!"

Light gray walls of a cramped corridor in the Dallas police station.

Hard-faced men wearing white cowboy hats.

A barred jail door opening to bring a prisoner into their flow.

He was ordinary. A laundromat guy. A warehouse guy. The quiet neighbor. A husband whose wife mocked him. Who wouldn't fuck him the night *before*. Dark hair. No glasses. Wore a light-colored shirt. Collars winged out over his dark sweater. His hands were cuffed in front of him. His arms relaxed even though he had a bear wearing a dark suit with a police detective's hat holding on to his left elbow while a pale Stetson and light-colored suit detective gripped the prisoner's right elbow. The prisoner's smooth, square-jawed face with set-back eyes seemed to know right where he was.

A TV man's voice talked over the prisoner being led through a path waved between two hordes of cops and reporters and cameras. Mutterings. A car horn honked. The lawmen led the prisoner through the crowd.

"There he is, Lee—"

Dark suit man charging the prisoner—*BANG!*

Echoes off the jail's brick walls! Shouts!

A crowd of men pull down some guy in a suit and businessman's hat to falling with the prisoner to the ground.

"He's been shot!" yelled the TV. "He's been shot! Lee Oswald has been shot!"

Murder for the whole world to see.

TOUCHDOWN

Friday is *Yes!*

You made it through the week of *got–to's*.

Now it's time for the *get–to's*.

And that Friday, the school is making a Big Deal about it because of last week's game with Shelby being called off *and* to show that Life Goes On.

Football coach Moent decreed that if you'd survived his brutal hot August pre-season, three-a-day practices, you dressed out with the varsity.

Surfer Zack picked Luc up early for school that Friday morning.

They went straight to the men's locker room. They and their teammates pulled maroon and gold game jerseys on over their shirts.

Luc strode through the second-floor corridor.

Big smile and dark waterfall curls Wendy walked past him.

"*Yay!*" she called out to the universe. "Luc is on the team!"

She kept *a–walkin'* and *a–talkin'* but she *witnessed*.

Saw Bobbi Jean give him some strange smile.

Saw blonde Alice notice him as *more than* but her look was surprise, *not*.

First period. Homeroom and English.

Buffy turned around from her desk and gave Luc a *see–you* grin.

But he knew it wasn't the *special* one she smiled at Steve in his game jersey.

Marin caught up to Luc in the hallway. Marin wore jersey 44. Was handsome. Black hair. Lean. Coffee-with-cream skin. He handed a book to Luc.

"*The Puppet Masters*. If you turn it in to the library, it'll save you time."

Third period Study Hall.

Luc headed to the librarian talking on her desk's black rotary dial telephone.

Mrs. Dawson told the phone. ". . . leaving the TV staring into me or me falling into a book."

She sensed *student* standing across the desk from where she sat.

Hung up the phone like good-bye didn't matter.

She took the book from Luc. Pulled out the checkout card. Picked up a metal date stamper.

Said: "Careful what you sign on for."

Wa-CHUNK!

That cold November Friday night.

The football field across the gravel road from the Big Pink.

Helmeted and dressed-out Luc stood beside Marin at his team's bench.

Tie score, 14 to 14 with 129 seconds left to play.

Whistle on the field!

Vernon's senior speedster halfback limped off the field.

Coach Moent stalked the time-out sidelines—

—*toward Luc!*

A puff of coach's breath glistened the night air with a whiff of whiskey.

Coach Moent grabbed Marin's facemask. "Tell Daryl run fullback through the middle. Head left. Then quick-snap run the right sweep with th' other halfback."

Coach growled at Marin: "You're our speeder. Race around the end. Run interference. Cut down anyone in the way!"

Marin rushed onto the green grass field.

The crowd in the white wooden bleachers roared. The hometown cheerleaders stamped and chanted, "Let's go, Cougars, let's go!" *Clap-clap.*

The visiting team's cheerleaders chanted: "Push 'em back harder, harder!"

Vernon's team huddled.

Down . . . Set . . . WHAM!

Vernon's senior fullback crashed into a mob of players—

—picked up a few yards and moved the action to the left. Like Coach said.

A minute to go. Fourth down. Goal posts in reach.

The Vernon Cougars break out of the huddle.

Quick snap! A flurry of charging players!

Marin spins through the air tangled up with a guy from the other team! Vernon's other halfback dodges their collision—

—races into the end zone!

A ref snaps both hands straight up: Touchdown!

The crowd roars!

BANG! The game-over gun!

Luc and his teammates shout and leap with joy!

TWEET!

A lone yellow flag floats up into the night air.

That ref shouts as his hand waves behind his legs: "Clipping! Number 44! No touchdown!"

Marin, thought Luc.

Quarterback Daryl rips off his helmet as he races to Coach Moent, yells—

—remembers who he's talking to. Pivots and hides shooting the *Fuck you!* middle finger at shuffling-toward-the-team Marin.

The white wood grandstands started to empty. Cars parked around the field turned on their engines. The other team headed toward their yellow bus.

Marin stood straight. Walked through the huddle to the coach.

Loud enough for everyone to hear: "Sorry."

The players ringing their coach heard him tell Marin: "Next time."

"Now let's get out of here!" roared the coach.

His team ran toward their locker room in the Big Pink.

A man wearing a topcoat of a suit and a Russian-style fur hat quick-walked through the end zone to intercept Marin with Luc running two steps behind him.

Fernell Powell, thought Luc. *The town's insurance man who spends his days going from café to café. Nurses a cup of coffee as he tells anyone trapped listening to him about this, about that, about it all.*

The field spotlights glistened on Fernell's pale face and gold-filled teeth as he surged toward fourteen-year-old Marin running past in the night.

"*You!*" yelled Fernell. "What the hell is Moent teaching you, you dumb Injun son-of-a-bitch!"

Fire consumed Luc as he ran past Fernell:

What—Why—What am I supposed to do? To say to . . .

But all he could do was chase after Marin.

The locker room. Bright silence. Then someone farted. Somebody else laughed. Everyone lightened as the showers steamed.

Marin dressed in his street clothes instead of lining up to take a shower.

"Hey, you did good," said Luc. "Bad luck. We still got a tie."

"Who's *we*?" Marin walked out the door to the night.

Through the locker room door into the school came sounds of the dance setting up—fifty cents to look/see/do whatever courage and the rules allowed as a DJ from KRIP spun 45 rpm records.

Luc knew the record being played: "Walk Like a Man" by the Four Seasons.

Not gonna get a better entrance song.

He hurried past the glass door of the coach's office. Glanced in.

There sat Coach Moent. Alone. With long gone eyes. Cradling a mug.

Luc pushed open the door to music and prayers.

BE COOL

D im lights in the corridor rec hall outside the gym.

The pine scent of the mopped floor. Wisps of perfumes and nerves.

Luc stood with Wayne and Kurt. Scanned the dancers.

"Can't believe they're playing a song as old as this," said Kurt.

"If you run the machine, you do what you want," said Wayne.

Buffy put both arms around Steve's neck to dance to a slow song.

Luc's heart sank.

Blonde Alice talked with sophomore and junior boys while Wendy danced with innocent glee and a friend of her one-year-older sophomore brother Ed.

Luc spotted Bobbi Jean standing near the DJ.

She turned away from him.

Kurt noticed that exchange: "How's she getting home? Are her folks waiting to drive her back to the refinery?"

"Some teachers volunteered to give country kids rides home so they could come to the dance," answered Wayne, who'd made sure to talk to the chaperones. "I think she's riding with the going-west kids in Mr. Bundy's car."

Luc glanced at the huddle of girls in his freshman class who'd grown up going to St. Jude's Catholic School. Catholic girls were a bigger mystery than—

Whoa!

Suddenly, *there she was.*

Wearing a snug dark blue dress.

Close to but *not with* the Catholic girls. A newcomer. Moved to town this year. Short-cropped black hair. A lean face, a smile that seemed . . .

Seemed *what*, Luc didn't know, but her eyes didn't look away from his.

Her name was Marla.

Luc left Kurt and Wayne staring at him as he marched through the crowd.

Marla brightened her smile as Luc stepped close.

He swallowed. "Wanna dance?"

Her grin said *yes.*

Made it to the dance floor without tripping or bumping into her/anybody!

Whirled. His glasses didn't fall off. She laughed at his dorky move. They sought the rhythm of dancing, *not* touching because this was a fast song.

That ended.

The DJ played a slow instrumental.

Marla.

Luc.

Still on the dance floor.

"Want to do another?" he said.

She slid into his hold and *oh*, she came in close, so close he felt her heat.

That dance ended. They dropped each other's arms. Stared at each other.

Out of the DJ's speakers came chording guitars' *bump-bump-bump * Bamp Bamp * Nuh-Nuh-Na* . . .

"*Louie, Louie*," thought Luc. The version by The Kingsmen.

Nobody understood its bone-shaking lyrics.

"*Woo!*" Marla whirled in the same kind of circle Luc made when they'd hit the dance floor. Hit him with a smile and a *what-do-you-see* stare.

Dancing, he was dancing with her as only a thick-glasses, crew cut, unco-ordinated skinny dreamer could.

Ten weeks later, J. Edgar Hoover's Federal Bureau of Investigation launched a thirty-one-month secret investigation into whether the mumble-jumbled lyrics in that song were politically subversive.

"OK, kids!" announced the DJ. "Last dance!"

The needle dropped onto a slow song.

Marla faced Luc. Draped her eyes. She fit them body to body. And instead of their intertwined hands "properly" angled out from their pairing, she laid them above his heart. Not her arms circling his neck for Officially Together—

—*but damn!*

His cheek touched her head. The scent of her shampoo. The warmth of her flesh. The brush of her breasts.

Luc felt a spotlight beaming down on them. Knew she felt that, too.

That song ended.

Ceiling lights rippled on.

They let their hands drop. Stepped apart.

Luc swallowed his fears: "Um . . . Can I walk you home?"

Her lips curled a smile.

ON THAT ROAD

Ah . . . I don't know where you live," confessed Luc as they found their coats. "On the southside. Up Main Street to the swimming pool hill."

Or as his dad would say, more 'n' a couple miles away as the crow flies.

That crow's route led out the Big Pink's glass doors. Into the night. Past the parking lot where teenagers now gunned cars. Across the gravel road. Past the football field and over sprain-your-ankle gopher holes prairie to the railroad tracks, then through the lines of waiting boxcars.

Two juniors named Mel and Clancy walked that way to school.

One morning when Luc strategically showed up early, he found Mel standing outside the locked science lab. Mel had his father's WWII gas mask bag full of rocks at his feet.

Luc knew most teachers had decided Mel was *um*, not so smart. Quirky. In his own mind. He mixed around the letters in words he seemed to know but was not able to spell. They didn't flunk him—and thus be stuck with him—*but*.

Mel smiled at the kid he'd known his whole life: "You here early because you got caught or because you're catching?"

"I got nowhere better to be," fibbed Luc.

When Buffy comes to school, I'll be here waiting!

And now since I'm standing *with* someone, it's more natural.

The two of them leaned against the wall of other people's lockers.

And Mel told Luc about talking to hobos amidst the boxcars. Luc rarely heard anyone talk about those men riding the rails unless it was to warn about them. To scorn them. Most people looked away from the lines of boxcars so as not to see. *Don't want to know, just want them to go.*

"What do they say?" asked Luc.

Mel shrugged.

"Ask what we've got that they can have. About jobs. But my dad just uses me at the gravel pit. A guy with a thick bedroll asked Clancy what's playing on the radio these days. One guy said he'd seen both oceans. 'Nother guy in the corner of a boxcar mumbled about how they'll catch us if we don't keep moving."

The science teacher turned the school hallway's corner.

Sighed.

That guardian of this lab far below Frankenstein's standards told Mel: "You can use the big magnifying glass but don't go leaving dust and pebbles for me to have the janitor clean up."

Mel picked up his bag of rocks. Kept his head down as he entered the lab.

"You with him?" the teacher asked Luc.

"*Naw,*" said Luc.

Now on that glorious night, Friday night—*naw*, no way was Luc taking blue dress Marla *anywhere* on Mel's route through the boxcars and bums!

"This is great!" said Marla. "Now I don't have to payphone my dad."

Two steps together toward the EXIT—

—then she said: "Plus, you know. This is not about me saving a dime."

Cupped his hand in hers as they passed through the glass doors into the chilly night.

Two blocks of houses from the high school. A car rolled up from behind them. The front seat passenger rolled down her window.

"Hey!" called out that older teenage girl. "You two wanna ride?"

"No thanks!" said Marla. "We're doing fine."

"Looks like it," said their would-be rescuer as she rolled up her window. The car drove off.

A second car of teenagers chugged alongside them on the viaduct. Rolled down windows to offer a ride out of the cold and risks.

"We're OK!" said Marla. "This is safe."

That car's red taillights turned left off the viaduct to Main Street.

"We go the other way," said Luc.

"Yes," said Marla.

Out of the bright lights of downtown Main Street. Up that road past the Catholic church. Between the next block with Luc's junior high to their left and his elementary school to their right—neither school ever walked by Marla.

Marla led him to a white painted, L-shaped apartment building like a two-story motel alongside the steep swimming pool hill. The streetlight shadowed the second story's balcony where they walked hand in hand to the corner door.

And then . . .

. . . oh THEN Marla's *kind of like* . . . leaning closer to him!

Turn face which way/don't bump—

Luc closed his eyes.

Pursed his lips and leaned forward.

His cold lips met a warm cushion pushing firm line of *OH!*

FIRST KISS!

He leaned back from his Remember Forever.

Marla whispered: *"Bye!"*

Opened the door/slid inside with one smooth motion/*clunk.*

Luc stared at the closed door.

Not what would have happened to *Bond, James Bond.*

Luc, just Luc, turned to face November's dark sky of time's twinkles.

What came to him as he was walking home: *Was it her first kiss, too?*

Naw, Luc told himself. She's pretty. Why would she pick some not-cool, nerdy guy like me to be her first?

He hurried home through that cold night she called *safe.*

Luc and Marla never spoke again.

Luc ignored the *Huh?* of all that.

She moved away in the spring.

STOP WORRYING

Fat flakes of a February '64 Sunday afternoon snow swirled outside Luc's kitchen picture window as he stood talking into the wall phone.

"But what if you miss it?" said Buffy's voice.

"Then you'll tell me all about it."

Yes, and then I'd get to—Have To—*call you again tonight!*

"And your dad set this up?"

"Sort of. Mr. Tom asked my dad if it was OK."

Please, Dad! Luc'd argued. *It's the only way I'll be able to keep going there!*

"Yeah," said Buffy. "Soon as I get my driver's license, Dad'll have me making deliveries for our floral shop."

He told her: "I gotta go catch the bus."

"Don't get on it!" she joked and hung up.

He zipped into his parka.

On that February Sunday, 1964, when our Vietnam war KIA tally was 214, weather reports in the newspaper, radio and TV failed to predict the blustery change to high noon's whirling wet snowflakes blizzard.

Icy splotches papped Luc's face as he hurried down the front steps. A flake hit the glass lens over his right eye.

Luc tromped past the hospital across the street where America's flag flew atop a pole that blizzardy afternoon.

He cut through the passageway running past the gray cement sheriff's office and county jail to Main Street. The bus station was two blocks away.

Three blocks past there, a silver Greyhound bus turned onto Main Street. *Who's dodging across Main Street in front of the bus?*

Luc shook wet off his glasses. Shoved them back on.

Becky!

That sixteen-year-old girl hurried through the blizzard toward the viaduct.

Luc reached for the bus depot's door—

—looked back to Main Street.

No Becky.

"You made it just in time!" Mr. Tom waved Luc through the snack shack where the cook had the Sunday newspaper color comics laid out on the counter.

The silver bus waited through a door under a sloping roof open at each end.

Two anxious-eyed women in no-nonsense coats stepped down from the bus.

The bus driver grabbed two suitcases from the cargo hold. Put them on the cold pavement. Reached inside the cargo hold and got what brought Luc there.

Three silver steel film canisters. Those eleven-inch wide, fifty-two-pound steel cans held two-feet-tall reels of 35mm film. A reel held up to twenty-one minutes of movie. The third can held a reel for Previews of Coming Attractions and a reel for a color cartoon: The Roadrunner outwitting Wile E. Coyote— pronounced "*Ki-oat*" in Montana but "*Ki-oh-tee*" everywhere else. Until the year before, a third reel held the week's Movietone News. Now people watched the nightly news on TV.

"You'll like being a projectionist," Mr. Tom told the now tall-enough high school freshman who'd delivered Roxy handbills door-to-door since fifth grade.

From the depot waiting room behind that theater manager came whispers of the two women travelers asking the cook about "the doctor."

"You'll get to see every movie comes through town," Mr. Tom told Luc. "Well, the ones that aren't out to the drive-in. *And OK*, you miss seeing about three, four minutes every twenty when you do the changeovers, switch projectors."

Luc could only muscle one heavy can at a time up the red carpeted stairs to the Roxy's projection booth with its five box windows.

Mr. Tom set up reels so the film ran across a workbench behind the two black steel projectors the size of stallions. Showed Luc how to use a steel rod and the tap of a small hammer to put a dot in the upper right-hand corner of four consecutive frames that flashed past moviegoers' eyes at twenty-four frames per second.

"Changeover marks. Warning bell dings. Your projector is re-loaded. Carbon rods burn for the light to go through the film. When the four dots fly past in the screen's upper right-hand corner, you switch without missing a beat—*if you're good*—and the movie keeps playing like nothing ever happened."

Mr. Tom showed Luc how to splice two reels of film with glue and soldering iron. How to cut one frame out of the whole movie to make the splice work.

Or, as Luc later discovered, splice frames of a naked woman stolen from some kind of special movie into the "leader" of the film the audiences never saw but projectionists all down the line did.

"What say you stay for the five o'clock show?" Mr. Tom told Luc that Sunday. "You can see the movie from up here, get a feel for what you gotta learn."

Then I'll have to—yes: get to—*call Buffy to find out what I missed!*

Even with every nineteen minutes' dings of bells, lifting reels and Mr. Tom threading film through the projectors with pupil Luc at his side, Luc's vision flowed with the light beams the machines freed. *And what a movie he saw!*

DR. STRANGELOVE
OR
HOW I LEARNED TO STOP
WORRYING AND LOVE THE BOMB

A clock-ticker in black and white. American Air Force fliers on a routine Cold War mission. A madman who flipped a switch because of a conspiracy he realized after he'd been unable to "perform" with a woman. A British officer prayerfully coaxing him toward reality. Buck, the belly-slapping American warrior. The drunk Soviet Russia Premier. No fighting in The War Room. The cigarette-holder-gripping, Germanic wheelchair spinner whose hand spasmed *Mein Führer!* The Doomsday machine that triggered ICBM nuclear warhead missiles like those in the five Minuteman missile sites ringing Luc's hometown. A musical "*Yee-haw*!" of mushroom clouds flowering earth.

Luc left the Roxy. Stepped out onto Vernon's Main Street.

Quiet stillness filled that snow dusted neon darkness.

He started to tromp home to call Buffy—

—then came the sound of the opening door of the Alibi Club.

Mrs. Nora Fields stepped out to the icy sidewalk. Snowflakes vanished on her dark red hair. She pulled her coat around her like she was *the dame* in some Roxy *noir* movie. Saw no one except a teenage boy with thick glasses seeing her.

"You're the Ross kid."

Luc nodded.

"I know your folks." She shrugged. "Good people."

Out of her purse came the cigarette with a lighter that clicked flame to life. A white cloud puff mushroomed between them. Luc couldn't tell if it came from the breath she'd been given or the breath she'd lit.

"I got a kid," she said. "Little girl. Guess what? Now I get to go pick her up at another of her Gramma's *special dinners* for just the two of them. Her in her pajamas. Maybe a new doll. Ready for sleepy time in her *daddy's* house."

She looked at the teenage boy standing in the cold night.

"Maybe some night she'll be where you are now. I'll ride you home."

In her famous actual sports car? With HER? Hell, yeah!

The brown Thunderbird's doors clunked closed. The engine purred on.

Nora jerked the steering wheel hard to the left. The car careened a 180-degree spin over the slick pavement. A whirl of Main Street filled the windshield. The car rumbled toward where the traffic light glowed red.

The radio filled the car with the *wa-Wah-wa* theme song for the cowboy justice movie *The Magnificent Seven.*

She mumbled: "Men and their guns."

The traffic light turned green. She took a right. Another right. Pulled over in front of his house with its two spruce trees sagging with snow.

Stared straight through her windshield. "Get out of here, kid."

He barely had time to shut his door before she drove away, her taillights glowing red and her headlights—

—her headlights illuminated three huddled figures shuffling down the sidewalk from the hospital doors to a beat-up pickup at the curb.

Becky!

It's Becky. Her mom on one side, dad on her other, the two of them *damn near carrying* Becky. Luc swore he heard sobbing in the wind clacking the chain for the drooping frozen American flag.

That family clumped into their pickup. Drove away through the storm.

Luc hurried inside. Called Buffy.

Whose phone buzzed busy. Busy still fifteen minutes later.

So he didn't have a chance to find out from Buffy what he'd missed or if something was up with Becky, who was the first thing he mentioned to Zack the next snow-covered morning as they drove away from Luc's house.

"You're not supposed to know about that!" yelled Surfer Z.

"*What?*"

"That damn Becky's caused enough trouble."

They drove past the red brick bowling alley.

"What are you talking about?"

"*Not. Supposed. To. Talk. About. It.* Harris called all of us on the basketball teams, *because*, you know, lesson had to be learned and has to protect the team."

"Becky," said Luc.

Surfer Z braked the car at a red STOP sign.

"OK, *maybe* they shouldn't have given her a ride in the first place."

"Yesterday! The bus station. I saw her headed toward the viaduct!"

Zack mumbled and leaned on the brake so its red lights glowed back through the snow smeared streets.

"So yesterday. Daryl and two other guys from the A squad. Riding around, digging the storm. Daryl spots her. Asks if she wants a ride, she says *yes*."

"That's what we all do. Why wouldn't she?"

"That's right! Daryl was just doing what we all do! That must have made Becky wild happy 'cause they're, *you know*, and let's just call her F squad.

"And then she . . . She did things with them."

"What things?"

"She fucked them all, OK? She wanted it. The guys all said so. But she gets pissed when they drop her off. Calls the cops and her parents and up t' hospital.

"Sheriff calls in Daryl, his parents. The other guys' parents. Principal Harris shows up. Says it's a case of *he says, he says* and *he says* versus *she says.* Gave the guys hell for putting themselves in a mess everybody had to clean up."

"What happened then?"

"The guys went home with their parents. Harris called us guys on the team, told us *what's what* so we can crush down any gossip 'bout it."

Beep! A gentle car horn in their mirrors.

A mom taking her kids to fourth and fifth grades.

Luc shook his head as Zack motored past the four stories of tan bricks Rainbow Hotel where confirmed bachelors lived.

"Why would . . . Becky . . . Why would she do . . . ?"

"Well . . . For guys like that . . . All women *wanna.*" Zack clicked on the *going right* turn signal to drive over the viaduct where Becky'd walked yesterday.

Luc shook his head: "I don't get it."

Surfer Z blinked at the doubter sitting in his car's passenger seat.

"All that STOP sign talking might make us late. Hell, I oughta always come in early, shoot a few hoops. So . . . Don't think I'll be picking you up no more."

First period Study Hall.

Miss Casey tapped Luc to pick up morning attendance slips.

Which way to go? thought Luc as he stood in the second-floor corridor.

To the right: Linda and a black rubber garbage can at an open locker.

"Good," she told Luc. "He sent you to help."

She dumped schoolbooks into his arms.

"What are you doing?" said Luc.

"It's Becky's locker. Principal Harris told me to clean it out."

"*What?*"

"I'm just doing what I'm told." Linda threw notebooks into the garbage can. Hesitated, threw a red wool scarf in there. "Those schoolbooks go to the office."

No one looked at him as he sat those official texts on that hard counter.

Walked out and started knocking on classroom doors to collect attendance slips. Got a smile from Buffy in Home Ec class. Circled back to the Study Hall, turned and started down the switchback stairs to deliver the slips to the office.

That black rubber trash can stood empty back outside the office door.

Becky's family vanished.

The A squad basketball team won the B Division state title.

And that Monday as Luc started down the stairs, out of the bathroom marched a junior boy patting down his water-slicked short hair.

The bathroom boy celebrated What Luc Had Missed:

That Sunday's broadcast through TVs in a record seventy-three million American homes. An English bar band from Hamburg, Germany, in snazzy black suits and ties and down-over-their-ears, mop top hair.

But you couldn't rewind the band's appearance or find it on some other kind of screen than the one in your family living room, plus the record was not yet dominating America's AM radios, so the bathroom boy who'd slicked his hair down with sink water got the lyrics wrong in their hit song "She Loves You" as his singing echoed down the corridors of the Big Pink:

". . . *yeah-dah, yeah-dah, yeah-dah YEAH!*"

THE AMERICAN WAY

The flood roared out of 1964's early June rains through snow-packed Rocky Mountains. Exploded dams. Killed thirty-one people. Whooshed out of prairie ravines. Turned Vernon's northside where Buffy lived, where Aunt Beryl and Uncle Johnny lived and had their drive-in, into a brown shit-stinky, thigh-deep lake that lapped from the Big Pink high school through block after block of houses all the way to the Thriftway grocery store and the viaduct.

But even that spring cataclysm couldn't, *wouldn't* stop now fifteen-year-old Luc from joining the battle for Truth, Justice and the American Way in the state capitol of Helena at Montana's 1964 Republican Party convention.

From a car's front passenger's seat, he stared at the river-flooded bridge sixty-three miles south of Vernon that his crusade had to cross.

We'll get through, he told himself. *Somehow. Someway.*

Hope The Secret Plan coming tomorrow gets through, too!

Luc turned his eyes from the windshield of What Was Stopping Him to the steering wheel hands of Who Was Getting Him There:

Mrs. Nora Fields.

"Just call me Nora," she'd told the two dozen Teenage Republicans—"TARS"—who met in her living room with paintings of places *so* not-Vernon. She'd let them talk. Led them without bossing. Smiled at their teenage nonsense. The high school senior boys stayed behind as long as they could in her house where no one ever saw the alleged husband or the mythical child.

And now I'm riding alone in the car with Nora for FOUR HOURS to Helena!

She stared out her Thunderbird's windshield at the flooded bridge. Her rust hair curled at her shoulders. Dawn shaded her lips. A taut crimson dress fit her lean legs up past high school rules to a finger width above her knees. Red fingernails left the steering wheel for her purse. Pulled out a cigarette.

She glanced at Luc.

Rolled the driver's window down. Let in the sunny June Thursday afternoon and let out an exhale from the cigarette her lighter flamed.

"Three choices," she told him. "We can turn around and go back to Vernon. Or 'bout a mile back, I saw two gravel roads. One going east. One going west. Good chance one of them loops around on high ground."

She took a slow drag on the cigarette.

"So what do you think?"

Doesn't matter if she's really asking or just being polite. Tell the truth.

"Don't go back. I say go west. That's more the way Helena is."

She took a deep drag. Grinned: "Man after my own heart."

Tossed the cigarette out her window to lay on the ground and wisp its smoke up from the too wet to burn yellow prairie.

Punched the gas.

Luc learned about *just Nora* a month after she'd given him a whirlwind ride the night of Becky's sobbing. He was walking through the living room to the kitchen where he heard Dad say:

"I think it's the right thing for Luc to do."

Luc stopped silent in his shoes on the gray living room rug.

"Must be right for her," said Mom. "Heard she joined the Republican Women's Club to keep her mother-in-law happy. *I mean*: they're them and she's who she is. But they said *yes* to her idea for Teenage Republicans. Made her the sponsor. Good for her, I guess. Gives her something of her own."

"The country isn't about her," said Dad. "We've got to get the right man in the White House. Luc should be part of that."

Luc strode into the kitchen with pride swelling his heart.

Who wouldn't want to be a Republican? thought Luc as the T-bird rumbled on the detour's gravel road. Especially that year, when the Democratic president who rode with a coffin in the plane from Texas back to Washington, DC, was clearly mumble-jumbling about Vietnam where 266 Americans had died fighting Godless Communism because of the Domino Theory that was *of course* the *only* cause of that war and the forces shaping the world.

Wayne and Kurt joined TARS.

Marin shook his head *no* when Luc tried to recruit him.

He's just a loner, Luc told himself.

What saddened Luc was when Buffy told him *no.*

She'd smiled: "We're Kennedy people."

The T-bird's loop to the west worked. The highway through red walled Wolf Creek Canyon pulled Nora and Luc into Helena before sunset that Thursday. They parked in front of the eleven-story-tall convention hotel near Wong's Restaurant on that capitol city's Main Street called Last Chance Gulch—the tallest building and only Chinese eatery Luc had ever seen.

The idea hit Nora at a TARS meeting. She spotted the paperback "conscience" book by conservative candidate Senator Goldwater in Luc's back pocket as he walked out to his family's gray 1954 Dodge with his two-month-old driver's license. Nora told him her idea. Called his parents for the OK. Called whoever in the State Party with *her* idea for keeping future voters in the Party.

I'm on the State Platform Committee! Luc still couldn't believe it.

I'll get to help write Big Ideas about what it means to be alive. What to do in Vietnam. About Russia. China. How to make sure all Americans stay free and get to see Yvette Mimeux's belly button.

The convention was due to gavel-in at noon that Friday.

The Platform Committee meeting was Friday morning at nine. Luc had to get to Helena a day early to be there on time. Nora didn't mind.

She checked them in to their hotel rooms. Starting the next night, she was chaperoning the lone TARS girl, sharing her suite with her while Luc was sharing his hotel room with one of his two fellow about-to-be sophomore class guys—

—and The Secret Plan.

Nora made sure he got settled in his room. Told him to lock the door. Meet her downstairs before nine o'clock the next morning at the registration table. Get a good night's sleep because tomorrow was going to be A Big Day.

She closed the door.

Walked away on the other side to wherever.

Luc leapt into the hotel room air—

—whomped flat on his back on the hotel bed.

Stared up at the pale ceiling screen flickering with imagined movies.

Next morning at 8:40—teeth brushed, white shirt, black clip-on tie, black suit—Luc stood in the bustling, laughs and shouts and smoke-filled lobby.

At 8:50, he realized Nora *must be* tied up with convention business, so he asked the woman running the registration table where to go for the Platform Committee meeting. She raised an eyebrow but gave him a room number.

He walked into a room of chattering adults. Men in shirt sleeves. The only two women wore vacation dresses. Moved like they were chaperoning each other.

A sports-coat-wearing, balding man with a stack of mimeographed papers hustled into the meeting room.

"OK," said Sports Coat. "Let's get started."

One of the adults gestured for Luc to take a seat at the long table.

Fourteen of us. Plus, Sports Coat passing around stapled sheets of—

Prose bullets.

Sports Coat announced: "So what we were thinking—"

Guess "us" at this table aren't part of that "we," clicked in Luc.

"—the quickest way for us to get the platform right is to type up some ideas and then I'll sit here, read 'em out loud. Sound good?"

Everyone at the table shrugged. Nodded yes. Paid respectful attention.

Except for one guy with hooded eyes who slumped far down the table.

Luc scanned the eleven pages for Abe Lincoln Gettysburg Address–worthy prose or grand visions like Dr. King's *dreams* speech. Found none. Found "in favor of" and "support" or "oppose" this or that of one town's or one set of wallets' wants or woes. He figured that easy stuff was just the start before *Real Politics.*

Twenty minutes later, hoarse Sports Coat read from the list: "We strongly support emergency flood relief for the Sun River valley."

That's only by the big city of Great Falls, thought Luc.

His hand shot up.

Startled the room like a lightning bolt.

Because I'm a teenager, thought Luc. *Not because questions are startling.*

Sports Coat blinked. Nodded *Yes?* to the kid in thick glasses.

"Um, how 'bout flood relief for places like Vernon, too?"

Hooded Eyes blinked at the questioner.

"*Ah,* thanks for the suggestion." Sports Coat shrugged. "Good idea."

Droned on from the mimeo sheet.

Nobody else raised their hands as the voice read to them.

What should I do? worried Luc.

On the one hand, the right thing to do was to get the platform to talk about prostitution. Like the fake Marilyn he'd failed to help escape the whorehouse in Vernon back when he was ten.

On the other hand, it was his Uncle Johnny's whorehouse.

Totally illegal yet totally protected by the badges and righteous in Vernon.

How can we write what to do about all that into the platform?

Sports Coat read the last bullet on the suggestions list.

"So," he said to the faces around the table, "does all that sound OK to you?"

Everyone politely nodded *yes.* Mumbled ascent. Luc shrugged *sure.*

Luc's shrug also said: *Now let's get to the important stuff!*

"OK then." Sports Coat slapped his hand on the table. "Platform adopted!"

BEHIND CLOSED DOORS

Numbed, Luc drifted back to his hotel room.

And The Secret Plan.

The Secret Plan recruited him the week before when his fellow now-sophomores and TARS companions Kyle and Gideon offered to let him join.

"Our guy out at the Outpost has a rule," said Kyle.

The Outpost was a restaurant and bar eleven miles east of Vernon on the two-lane highway. The food was acceptable. The jukebox took dimes. The bar floor welcomed dancing cowboy boots. The only other nearby shelter was a shoddy motel where patrons parked their cars out back and away from driving-past eyes.

Gideon said: "He sells us a case of beer if we buy a bottle of whiskey, too."

Booze was illegal for teenagers.

Back in 1959, a beer-fueled car wreck killed one of Laura's high school friends, almost cost her the college scholarship that let her escape Montana, and made Luc into a (secret) outlaw.

Now in 1964, Luc didn't care about any scholarship.

He worried about the high school Key Club that all the best nerds—well, all the best nerd *guys*—belonged to. *That* was a crew he figured he belonged in. But Key Club also had a no-drinking pledge and would *definitely* kick you out.

But I'm not in yet, reasoned Luc. *So . . . Yes! I can be one of the cool kids!*

Kyle and Gideon drove The Secret Plan down to Helena.

"Free ice machine on every floor," said Kyle as Luc stared at the case of beer beside a brown bottle of bourbon on his hotel room bed. "Fill our bathtub."

They agreed they should wait until after dinner to crack the cold cans.

Wandered around the convention hotel. Through a flood of adults. Voices of certainty and power. Red, white and blue Goldwater for President buttons. Cigarette smoke. The stench of cigars.

Their teenage trio grabbed a dinner burger at 4:20.

Pop! went the tab on the first illegal beer Luc ever drank.

Kyle passed around the bottle of bourbon.

Yucky! Burning fire! Pop a new can to cool it off and wash it down.

Then . . .

Things got hazy for Luc.

Until The Incident.

Turned out they weren't the only TARS with illegal booze. Room to room calls were made. Adult chaperone Nora wasn't in her suite with the TARS high school girl, who *was* there and said come on up, plenty of room.

So when did chaperone Nora come back into the suite?

She was smiling there in the easy chair of the suite's living room where the radio was playing 'n' kids were laughing.

Why am I down on the carpet doing push-ups to show Nora I'm not drunk?

The phone rang.

She told whoever called: "Soon as I can."

Blink.

Luc was standing in the hotel lobby. *Why did I come down here? How?* Luc slumped into a chair facing the doors of a flesh-packed-against-flesh hotel bar.

That room surged. Tingled. Women and men far from their hometowns, spouses and neighbors. In that bar, they were Important. They were Power. Cool.

Luc's drooly face flopped toward the other parlor chair set against the wall facing the bar: *Hooded Eyes sitting there.*

Hooded Eyes nodded toward the uproarious bar: "The only place busier getting it on tonight is Big Dorothy's."

"I know 'bout that!" slurred Luc.

"And now I know you know."

"Wan'd talk 'bout prostitution like that platform thing's morning."

"Bet you did."

"Wha's politics gonna do 'bout that? Seen 'em be bad, not gonna tell, but . . ."

"Yeah. *But.*" Hooded Eyes laughed. "And I don't mean *butt.* Only the lucky never need to go to some Big Dorothy's one way or the other. Man or woman."

He beckoned the drunk teenager closer.

"Politics is about sweat and blood. Being, buying and being bought. The Bs. And the Ds. About doing and getting done to. About you *do*. About your *dues*. You gotta figure out the Ds of *you*. Or somebody's going to decide your *Bs*."

Hooded Eyes leaned back.

"You got some fire or wouldn't've thought about bringin' up whorehouses."

Luc slobbered: "Other stuff like doctor. Does abortions 'n' everybody in town knows. Law says he can't. Town says he can 'n' oughta. Ev'body pretends."

The full-grown man leaned closer to his reflection in Luc's glasses: "Society runs on people *pretending*."

Luc nodded like he got it—and he did *get it*, but that night in the hotel lobby outside the laughing and lusting bar, still he slurred: "What's society?"

"Yeah," answered Hooded Eyes.

Stumbling down the corridor. Kyle's got my left. Gideon on right. Door opens.

They dropped Luc on his hotel room bed.

Door, closing door, they're goin' I'm goin' swirly . . .

. . . *"Luc?"*

Mouth blanket *muha* go back 'sleep.

"Luc."

Bright eyelids.

Radio bares—*Oww!*

"Time to get up," said Kyle. "We gotta watch the convention."

Luc found himself wearing his black suit, white shirt. Kyle wore a nice shirt and pants. Gideon met them in the hall wearing his good clothes.

Kyle pushed the button.

Silver elevator doors slid open to let them into its cage.

Luc turned with his glasses *katty-whompus* on his nose.

Pushed a button.

"You hit eleven, not one!" said Gideon.

Whirring up from six went the elevator.

Luc slumped onto the railing.

DING!

The elevator cage jerked to a stop. Luc's stomach sloshed.

A convention-tagged couple stepped into the elevator: "Busy as the elevators are, might as well ride up so we can be on it when it goes down."

Luc closed his eyes. Gripped the railing. His skull *bong bong bonged*.

The silver doors slid open on the suite-city eleventh floor.

"Oh my God!" said the husband. "Governor Babcock!"

And there he was. Hero-handsome. Blue-suited. Smiling as he and another Powerful Man stepped into that cage. Ten years after he got into Luc's elevator, the law nailed then-former Republican Governor Babcock for illegal campaign cash schemes to steal the presidency in Watergate.

That elevator morning, Governor Babcock shook hands with everybody.

Even the limp hand of the wobbly teenager clinging to silver rails.

The elevator dropped.

Stopped at every floor. People climbed aboard. "*Governor! How are you!*" Luc jostled off the wall. Silver doors whooshed. Fall. Bump. Stomach surged. Repeat until the elevator was at capacity. Luc got *smushed* next to the silver doors. Stared at his blurred reflection.

History has hazy recollections of the snapshots Luc's glasses caught next.

Gideon and Kyle jerking him out of the elevator.

Their trio stumbling into the lone TARS girl from Vernon wearing her band uniform sweater emblazoned with a *V*.

Gideon seeing that *V* witnessed by the gaping-mouthed angry crowd of adults in the open elevator. Yelling: "*We're not from Valier!*"

An honest denial heard as an obvious lie as those teenage boys and girl ran and whirled French movie style through the hotel's spinning glass door to sunshine.

But in the opening elevator slamming heartbeats before *that* . . .

Luc doubled over and threw up all over the governor's shoes.

EVERYBODY SAYS

An early August sunny Thursday morning.

A breeze dusted Main Street as Luc leaned on Mr. Tom's pickup parked across from Vernon's bus station. The truck's radio played the news:

"Authorities have found the bodies of three civil rights workers forty-four days after the night when they'd been released from the county jail in Philadelphia, Mississippi, just down the road from where they'd been murdered."

Murders, thought Luc. All he could do was shake his head.

Luc let his eyes close. Deeply breathed the wondrous scent of free air.

If the law wanted to catch me, I'd have been badged by now.

He let his eyes open—

—and spotted a dream: *"What are you doing here?"*

"Getting out of town!" answered Buffy.

They laughed as she walked toward him. Blue shorts. Lean tan legs. A short-sleeve shirt embroidered with the name of her folks' floral shop.

Somewhere a police siren wailed.

"Wow," said Buffy. "What are you doing here?"

"I'm working."

"Oh *sure*, looks like it." Her blue sky eyes twinkled.

"I'm waiting," said Luc. "Waiting is work."

The breeze floated her milk chocolate hair. She looked one way down Main Street. Luc looked the other.

He scooted down the pickup's side to make a space for her to lean.

The radio played the slow guitar blues riff opening of a British band.

Luc angled his head toward his dream girl.

Impress her.

"This song," he said, drawing on folk music records that once ruled charts but now were his sister's left-behinds. "'The House of the Rising Sun.' The Animals. They're not the first to do it."

Buffy shrugged: "They're who's doing it now."

The road beneath his feet fell away.

Tried to be savvy. Came off like a snob. And a fool Who Doesn't Get It.

The volume of the pickup's radio faded.

"You better turn the music off or turn your pickup on," said Buffy. "Your battery's running low."

He switched off the keys.

"Look!" Buffy stepped away from the pickup as the silver Greyhound bus turned the far west corner of Main Street toward the bus station.

But then *WHOA!*

Whooshing faster past Luc than it should:

That's Mom in the gray '54 Dodge! Barreling toward—taking a right over the viaduct to the northside. Blew right past me and didn't wave or honk.

Where the hell is she going?

"Are you coming?" Buffy crossed the street toward the bus station.

He hurried after her to the platform alongside the bus station where he'd earlier heaved three heavy leaving-town cans of film out of Mr. Tom's pickup.

They stood beside the hissing-brakes silver bus as it stopped.

"I haven't seen you—*any* of your guys since school got out," said Buffy.

"Kurt's a counselor at church camp. Wayne's working at his dad's hardware store. Every summer, Marin goes to his family's ranch on the Rez."

Luc didn't need to tell Buffy "the Rez" was "the Reservation," that Gros Ventre federal allotment two-plus hours' highway drive away from Vernon.

"Takes me all day to janitor the drive-in," said Luc. "Five nights a week, I'm up in the Roxy's projection booth until after eleven. I barely see anybody."

The bus driver folded the bus's undercarriage cargo doors open and up.

"Lucky me," said Buffy. "I get to see you here and now."

The bus driver loaded her outstretched arms with long boxes of flowers destined for a wedding of a girl who'd been in Luc's big sister Laura's class.

Laura was home from the university in Chicago. Working at the phone company as one of the operators ordered to wear "proper" dresses and makeup in a locked room sitting in front of a switchboard with wires to plug, keys to click, headsets nestled in their combed and sprayed hair. She'd volunteered that week to take the late-night shift so she could have the wedding event off to help her friend walk down the aisle to a guy Laura hoped was good enough for her.

Luc smiled at Buffy with her arms full of flower boxes.

"I can walk you back to the flower shop. Be there to catch any you drop."

"That's OK, I got it. See you later!"

His glasses screened Buffy walking away, smaller, smaller, *gone*.

Luc checked the metal cans the bus driver unloaded. Saw the right movie. Lugged them up into the projection booth.

Walked home as usual as the noon whistle blew.

Looked through the kitchen's picture window:

Mom and Dad, Laura in her puffy should-be-in-bed robe—

—and Aunt Dory! In from the farm. She's not supposed to . . .

Luc hurried inside.

Laura pulled him close to her. Held up her hand so he knew to shut up.

"Iona said it was just *awful*," wailed Mom. "She and Beryl sitting at Beryl's kitchen table smoking cigarettes. Johnny's at the drive-in next door having coffee with some business guy from out of town. And just as Iona's getting up to go, Johnny comes in, kinda looks at her, says something or gurgles *BANG!*"

Dad and Aunt Dory, Laura and Luc jumped in their skins.

"Johnny falls down flat on the floor. Writhing around and puking and shuddering and then just . . . stops."

Absolute stillness held that yellow-walled kitchen on an August day, 1964.

"Heart attack," said Mom. "Dead."

Dory closed her eyes. Pushed her hand against her own chest.

Opened her eyes to ask her sister: "Where's—"

"Iona's up with her now. Up to the undertaker's."

"We gotta figure the place for Beryl to stay," said Dory.

"Wait!" said Laura. "*WHAT?* A heart attack?"

Big sister Laura. Her bags unpacked from Chicago where she rode elevated trains clattering through that city filled with Al Capone ghosts.

"He's *Johnny Russo*! The cathouse! The whatever else! A business cup of coffee then spasming and puking and—And that's supposed to be a heart attack?"

"Enough, Laura," said her father. "Your uncle is dead and everybody says it was a heart attack."

"Everybody?" said Laura. "*Huh*."

"What else could it be that would let everybody make sense of all of it."

Not a question from The Man of the House.

Aunt Dory took Beryl out to the farm. Luc's mom paid to clean up the home and drive-in café Beryl owned. The blue taxi's business moved to an odd-jobs guy.

Nobody in the family mentioned the red stucco two-story whorehouse.

But from then on, cruising teenagers spotted cars they knew out back where Uncle Johnny's waived rules let customers park. No taxi necessary. Losing that money was offset by more customers at the red house.

Luc went to work at the Roxy that warm August night.

"What are you doing here?" said Mr. Tom as Luc walked into the projection booth. "Your uncle just died!"

"They ran out of things for me to do. Laura, too. She's working her night shift at the phone company."

"You don't need to be here," said Mr. Tom as he loaded film into a projector.

"Just sitting in my room . . . Mom with Beryl and Dory . . . Dad, he went to work, too. Everybody had to just . . . keep going on. Me . . ."

Luc stared at the kind man: "Feels like I know what I'm doing here."

Mr. Tom *got it*. But said:

"There's gonna be a good crowd. We don't want you . . . distracted. If you don't wanna go home, stick around for the first show. Take your mind off . . . you know."

Luc found a lonely seat high up in the balcony.

The lights went down.

The red curtain rolled up.

The studio logo faded to black screen.

Then came the most globally famous movie opening sequence for the era from JFK to Donald Trump: A white circle like a moon flows across the blackness. The circle becomes the inside of a rifled gun barrel, a tube for all the eyes in the movie theater to watch through as a business-suited man with a face you can't quite see walks past the lit gun barrel tube . . . whirls/shoots—

—at you.

At Luc sitting in the Roxy watching *Goldfinger*.

That *Bond, James Bond* adventure was the kind of movie that thrilled him. Secret identity—007. Saving the world. A beautiful blonde yearning to be his.

But the images from that screen only flashed on Luc's face.

Uncle Johnny. Dead. Was he a bad guy? Was he a good guy? *Does it matter now?* Squirting nieces and nephews with the hose. Laughing when they squirted him. Sending a smile to Aunt Beryl she couldn't help but send back if only in a scowl. His only son Paul. In the Air Force. Flying home. *More alone on a night plane than me sitting here in the flickers of a movie theater.*

The Party platform. Hooded Eyes. The red whorehouse on the edge of town. The Rising Sun in New Orleans. Three civil rights workers in Mississippi. The blue taxi. Church bells on Sunday and four bombed Black girls who'd heeded their call. The time Uncle Johnny saved ten-year-old me and Marin from getting whipped by vigilantes on the dark prairie outside the county fair's glow. All the times he showed up. Sat down and stood up as family. Us. His wife. His son. A cup of coffee. A heart attack.

How do you judge the dead—or hell, the living? And then do WHAT?

007 discovered his last night's sexual conquest lying murdered on the bed—her naked body completely painted gold.

That scene flickered on Luc's tear-scarred face.

THE RIVER

The Grady River runs its crooked way seven miles south of Vernon. A silvery blue crease in the rolling yellow prairie carving a valley of purple hills. Trees line the banks. Lewis and Clark named the river for White settlers to come. History doesn't know who Grady was. The river doesn't care.

The river tumbles down from the Rocky Mountains. Many places you can wade it to the other side. The river bends flow around gravel beaches.

Luc drove the '54 gray Dodge south from town on a September '64 Saturday. Vernon lost a home football game the night before. Luc sat on the bench.

The next afternoon, Mom said: "Why do you need the car?"

He didn't lie.

He *was* going to see Kurt's new reel-to-reel tape recorder.

He *was* going to see if Marin was home from his aunt's funeral on the Rez.

He *was* going to see if Wayne had the afternoon off from his family's store.

But where Luc was really "going with the car" was . . .

Going.

Wrap your hands around the steering wheel. Turn the key. The gray '54 rumbles on. The radio turns on. KRIP reports the Vietnam tally of dead American soldiers not much older than Luc stands at 323. Spin the radio dial. The big city station comes in almost static free. Back out of the driveway and You Are *Going!*

Going nowhere. Going somewhere. Going everywhere.

Burning up dead dinosaurs from the Bobbi Jean refinery west of town via Dad's oil-hauling trucking company.

Sure, he dragged Main to Kurt's house where Kurt puttered around his suitcase-sized reel-to-reel tape recorder on that great Saturday afternoon. After twenty minutes of watching, Luc said he had to go.

Sure, he dragged Main a couple more times before he saw Wayne working in the hardware store where Luc'd been pretty sure he would be.

Sure, the gray '54 crawled past Marin's house and *maybe* somebody could have gotten home from the out-of-town funeral, but those lights were dark, *so*.

Got a car. Got my license. Half a tank of gas. Driver's window rolled down. Radio on. Thick-lensed glasses instead of cool wrap-around shades, but what the hell: I'm here and I'm going!

He drove past Buffy's house.

Hoping to see her. Hoping she'd see him. Hoping she wouldn't. Hoping.

He drove past like he would a thousand times more.

Drove to the Big Pink.

Luc'd gone to the dance last night.

Buffy wasn't there.

Neither was Steve.

Luc danced a few friendlies. Thought about asking Alice to dance, but she'd been too cool for him the moment her parents moved here in seventh grade. Now her smile to him didn't say *no*—nor did it say *come on over*.

The DJ dropped the needle for a song that Luc didn't like.

Plus, he had to pee.

A guy from Luc's class washed his hands at one of the sinks below the BOYS bathroom wall of mirrors.

"Hi, Tod!" called Luc as he hurried to a urinal, pulled down the zipper . . .

Ahh.

Finished. Fastened.

Faced the sinks. The wall of mirrors. Tod still washing his hands.

Luc stepped to a sink two sets of faucets away from Tod.

Turned on his faucet. Stuck his fingers into the stream of cold water. Looked into the mirror at the reflection of the boy standing two sinks away.

Luc told their mirror reflections: "I hope they start playing better songs."

Tod muttered: "Me, too."

Tod's dad was a milkman. His mom was a clerk. He shut the faucets off.

Asked Luc's reflection in the bathroom mirror. "Do I look like I should?"

"Sure," answered Luc. "Why not?"

The reflection down the mirror from Luc's was an average guy of fifteen. No glasses. Short hair, not a taboo Beatles shag. A pimple threatening his forehead.

Luc frowned: "Are you OK?"

Tod answered: "Why wouldn't I be?"

"*Ahh* . . . OK, then. See you out there."

Luc left Tod staring into that mirror.

What was up with that? thought Luc that sunlit Saturday as he drove toward the Big Pink's auditorium and teachers' parking lot.

Where three parked cars waited in the afternoon sunlight.

And four girls stood on the sidewalk saying good-byes.

The three girls wearing pants got into one car. Drove past Luc coming the other direction. Waved. Left the fourth girl in their rearview mirrors. Alone.

Bobbi Jean stood on the sidewalk.

Wearing a dress on a Saturday. Waving goodbye to the other girls. Staring at Luc as he cruised into the teacher's parking lot. Giving his windshield her back. Walking into the band entrance door she jerked shut.

Luc didn't know one of the two parked cars.

Could be Bobbi Jean's. She must have a license by now, too. Country kid.

The second car belonged there: Mr. Bundy's. He directed Girls Chorus that the three girls who'd left were in. Bobbi Jean sang with them. Played the piano.

Luc drove away from all that on the fine Saturday afternoon.

Drove past Buffy's house again.

Drove across the viaduct over the railroad tracks and the hobo jungle. A lost seagull skimming over the lines of parked brown train freight cars.

Had to drag Main again even if he was going home.

Dragging Main.

Driving past stores. Neon bars. The Roxy. The west end turnaround was a national chain grocery store parking lot. The east end turnaround was a gravel lot at the peeling white-painted, X-crossbars that would *ding-ding-ding* bells and flash red lights to stop cars from crossing a spur line railroad track.

That car coming Luc's way: Alice driving. Wendy riding shotgun.

Alice honked her car's horn.

Luc honked back.

That's what you're supposed to do when you're dragging Main and drive past another car of high school kids. Honk your horn to say *I'm here*. Honk to say *I see you*. Honk to say *Can you see me?* Honk to tell the world this is *our* town.

He watched the girls' car recede down Main Street in his rearview mirror. Long-brown-curls Wendy chattered to driver Alice how much better it was when her traveling salesman dad was home with her mother, brother Ed and her.

But blonde Alice heard the voice in her own head: *Will I ever get as goofy for a guy as Luc is goofy for Buffy? What about The Boogeyman?*

Luc looped around the east end of Main Street. Cruised back the way he'd come, hoping to catch another honk from those two cool girls.

But they'd driven onto some other road.

He gripped the steering wheel and took the highway south out of town.

Drove past the chain-link fence around gray concrete slabs of doors for the atom bomb Minutemen missile silos poised for *Dr. Strangelove*.

Drove down the hill to the river park exit. The gravel road bounced him through scrub prairie to the line of trees, the city park with picnic benches, outdoor toilets and a gentle beach by the silvery blue flow.

Luc parked the gray '54.

Stepped out into the warm autumn river breeze *because he could*.

"*Whoa!*" yelled some guy's voice far downriver in the trees.

"Stop yelling!" cried another guy's voice. "You're scaring them!"

Luc walked through the trees toward the voices.

Clancy. Standing on the gravel shore. Whipping a fly rod back and out to send a hook and line skimming out to the river.

Mel. Squatting in a gorge at the far end of the beach. Hammer in his hand. A pile of rocks by his boots and WWII army bag.

Clancy flicked his fly rod back behind his right shoulder—

"Hey, Luc!" Clancy flicked his cast into the river.

Mel whirled: "You guys gotta come see this!"

Clancy sighed. Reeled it in. Propped his rod on a battered wicker case.

Winked at Luc: "We better look or he'll keep scaring the fish."

The three of them squatted on their haunches on the gravel beach. The river sang behind them. Mel held out a palm-sized, hammered-open rock.

"That white swirl of lines!" said Luc. "It's a fossil!"

"It's Jurassic," said Mel.

What the hell is Jurassic?

"It's a keeper?" said Clancy.

"Oh yeah." Mel eased the fossil into his khaki bag.

Put his smiling eyes on Luc: "What are you doing down here?"

"Getting out!" escaped from Luc before he could think.

Clancy grinned: *"Hell yeah!"*

Nodded to Mel. "I'm out here fishing and he's out here banging on rocks. Like we do. Getting out when the getting's good."

"You want to stick around?" asked Mel.

"Don't scare the fish!" warned Clancy.

"No I . . . I gotta go."

"Gotta or oughta or wanna?" said Mel.

"Yeah," said Luc.

They all laughed.

Mel nodded to Luc: "You better hammer that out."

Turned the hammer in his hand to the riverbed slab of rock.

Luc walked Clancy back to his waiting rod and reel.

Clancy said: "Do you like to fish?"

"Nope," said Luc. "Why do you like it?"

Clancy's arm flowed from the center of the earth with a soft swing of the rod that was part of him as its line flew out a fly to skip on the rippling river.

"Out here," he said, "nobody to scare the fish. Being able to bring something home for family's dinner table . . ."

He reeled the fly hook in slow and steady.

"This is me getting to throw the line instead of getting hooked."

Luc walked toward the woods and his ride home.

Will I get to throw the line instead of getting hooked?

Will anybody ever look for our fossils?

The river flowed on.

THE GAME

March '65.

America launched Operation Rolling Thunder—the first *official* aerial bombardment of enemy North Vietnam—and sent 3,500 Marines wading ashore in South Vietnam for the TV cameras.

On Bloody Sunday, two hundred Alabama state troopers with tear gas, bullwhips and garden hoses wrapped in barbed wire attacked six hundred peaceful civil rights marchers.

A Friday afternoon in Vernon, Montana's high school.

A brown-haired freshman girl sailed through the Big Pink's deserted second floor corridor of in-session classes. Her right hand held a pink hall pass.

White sneakers carried her down to the first floor entryway with its doors out to the students' parking lot and into the vast gymnasium where the janitor was mopping the shiny blonde wood basketball court for that night's game.

Some boys were setting up tables as one of their community service stunts for Key Club. She knew two guys from St. Jude's. Recognized sophomores she'd never talked to: *nervous* Kurt, *weird* Luc and *wound-tight* Wayne.

She put them all in her shadow. Trod the gray tiles. Saw the red fire sign that was her final chance to flee. Swung the other wooden door open.

The girls' locker room.

"Nnnnh."

That brown-haired girl's eyes darted through the locker room. Saw no one.

"Ahwwa!"

The last gray metal bathroom stall door stood closed.

She stepped to that stall: "Hello? Is anybody in there?"

"*No.*" A weeping whisper.

"Are you OK?"

Sobbing/laughing/wailing.

"Look, you have to unlock the door and let me in." *Use any bullshit that works!* "If you don't, we'll both get in trouble."

Heartbeat. Heartbeat. Heart—

Click! The gray bathroom stall door swung inward and open.

A girl slumped on the toilet with her panties and skirt circling her ankles.

"Too late," she sobbed.

Her bloody hands rose in front of her blood-smeared, tear-wiped face.

The blooded girl was Sarah. Also a freshman. Italian movie star sexy.

"I'm already in trouble!" sobbed Sarah.

"No, hey, it's OK. It's just your period. Aunt Flow. We'll get you—"

"I already got *got!*" Sarah slumped on the toilet. "This blood . . . 'S supposed to mean now it's OK. That it's over. That I got . . . got lucky! Got away with . . .

"I didn't want to!" she cried. "Saturday. Kept telling him I didn't want to. I was so drunk. Everybody was. Him, too. Somebody's parents not home. Garage couch an' why wouldn't I go out there? 'S a star on the basketball team. Handsome, just a sophomore . . . just . . . Just Zack. Thought he liked me. Kissing like everybody does but . . . Tried to push him off, I did! *I did!* Told him no, *no*, and he . . .

"'*You know you want it.*' He kept saying that. Over and over. And he . . . he . . ."

The brown-haired girl whispered: "He did it to you anyway."

"It hurt! Hurts all through me. My head, heart, my stomach oh my . . . And everybody will know! Even if he doesn't tell them. He said I didn't wanna get in trouble. Said Daryl, 's senior 'n' basketball star too, told him . . ."

Sarah snapped into a *wow* of what and how and now.

"Look." Sarah raised her bloody hand in front of her face. "Isn't this funny? Came in here to do what I'm 'posed to and felt it and . . . And so . . . And it came so he . . . we . . . I got away with it."

Sarah shook her head.

"But tonight. The crowd out there. Everybody looking at me. They'll see. They can tell I'm not a virgin anymore. That . . . I . . . I can't go out there tonight!"

The other girl grabbed Sarah's shoulders: "*Listen to me!*

"Nobody . . . You can't see. Can't tell. Nobody knows. And you've got to go out there tonight! Otherwise he takes that from you, too. Can't let him. Don't let him."

"But all those eyes looking at me, I don't—"

"Miss Casey told me to pick another flagbearer. If you carry the American flag, that's what everybody watches. Or carry the Montana flag. You choose."

"I . . . I get to choose?"

The brown-haired girl pulled Sarah up from the toilet: "We've got to get you cleaned up and out of here."

Sarah froze: "What about Zack?"

Never would the brown-haired girl mean what she said more than then: *"Fuck him!"*

Sarah whispered: "I already did."

"No you didn't."

They walked out of the girls' locker room as Final Bell rang through the Big Pink and the do-good Key Club boys hurried outside to their cars.

Luc slammed his door on Kurt's car as Wayne settled into the shotgun seat.

Luc couldn't help but be happy.

Tonight he'd see people. See Buffy sitting on a bench like him in the under-classmen upper rows of the courtside bleachers. Knowing she was seeing Steve on the bench of the basketball A squad.

So what, I'm used to it.

Besides, there's the game. Library novels. That murderous truck driver fantasy yelling at me to write it down. Movies at the Roxy I get into for free even though my job doesn't start until after school gets out. My Beach Boys album with "I Get Around." Even if I don't. The radio in my dark bedroom. Snuggle under the covers. Play it low so Mom won't yell: "Turn that damn thing off!"

And now I'm in the backseat of a car going.

"You know," said Kurt as he steered the car. "Key Club. We—next year when we're juniors and then—We could really make it into something. Earn points and maybe get way up there in the state—Hell: *national* listings."

"That'd look good on m—on *our* record," said Wayne.

"And we'd be doing some good," said Kurt.

Wayne watched Main Street stream past his shotgun window.

They dropped Luc off forty minutes before 5:00.

Why is Dad's work station wagon here this early?

He was sitting at the kitchen table.

"Sit down. I want to talk to you."

I didn't mean to puke on the governor!

Dad said: "There was a school board thing. Me, Superintendent Makhem, Mr. Schenk, plus those two. Not a formal thing."

Dad's mouth made a grim line: "Coach Moent. Has he been OK lately?"

Blink.

"What I mean is, you ever see or hear or know something like how he maybe has liquor on his breath? Having a little trouble with it?"

The game when Moent grabbed Sid's facemask right beside me. Him sitting alone in the office with a mug in his hands that epic night of My First Kiss.

"Why?"

"The bottom line is it might just be about two bulls in the same corral." Dad sighed. "Principal Harris . . . He insists it's his school. But Coach Moent was the big man out there until you football team guys started losing—sorry, Luc."

Luc shrugged.

"Moent's been butting heads with Harris for a long time over stupid things like Harris not wanting you guys to get an *S* letter for a school jacket for just getting to play in a couple quarters. Harris wants to be sure only the stars like he was in high school get credit. Moent is more of an everybody earns it kind of guy.

"All this stays between us," said Dad. "Today, Harris made a crack about how he's hearing Moent has a problem with booze.

"Moent stayed cool. But shook. Said: 'I do my job.' And Harris told him *sure* and that it was Harris's job to make *sure* he did."

"What's going to happen?"

"I don't know."

Luc's Key Club crew picked him up early to set up for the ticket takers.

An adult ticket taker wanted to set up a row of folding chairs along the wall for old people to sit in while someone stood in line to buy their tickets.

"I'll get them," volunteered Luc.

He headed into the boys' locker room with its storage recess.

Coach Moent stood on a stepstool pulling something from a box. Dropped it into a black rubber garbage can. Luc heard a *clink* of glass on glass.

Their eyes met.

"You're a Ross kid. School board dad. Your mom is a Conner." Moent smiled: "And that don't make one God damned bit of difference to me."

Moent stepped down to the floor. Held the garbage can behind him.

"Gotta tell you, Luc. You're never gonna be an athlete. But you try. That's worth . . . Well, that's worth what you make it."

The coach walked past.

Luc didn't turn around to see him go. Heard him stop.

The man Luc couldn't see said: "Don't let them just take it away from you."

Came a pause, then the invisible man said: "Don't go and lose it either."

The *clink* of glass. The locker room door opened. Closed.

Luc grabbed the handle on the dolly stacked with gray folding chairs. Had them set up way before the games started.

He sat in the bleachers with his buddies as Vernon's B squad lost.

"Ladies and gentlemen! For your between games entertainment . . . The Vernon Tumblers and Twirlers!"

The Vernon band struck up a brassy song.

The school chorus sang.

Luc spotted Bobbi Jean standing front and center as Mr. Bundy waved his hands. Saw Tod in the chorus. His face showed happy to belong there, not the lost gaze Luc'd seen in a bathroom mirror.

Into the gymnasium marched the flags of democracy, justice and freedom.

Everyone stood as they should.

Luc saw Italian movie star Sarah carrying the red, white and blue.

Wait! Who's that with the Montana flag?

Was *the way* of her white legs.

Muscular. Not movie actress legs. Solid. Smooth.

The flagbearer's mid-thigh white skirts awed Luc with more of her legs than he would have seen walking the school's hallways. More than he would have glimpsed if she were crossing them under her desk in Study Hall behind him when he dropped his pencil and slyly turned to look. Those legs marched firm. Her brown hair cupped her tight-jawed, trembling face.

Lucas *got it.* Absolutely *of course* knew *why*:

She's fighting to not cry at the beauty of this moment as the band plays.

Like her, he fought tears when music and majesty merged into poetry.

The tumblers whirled and twirled through their routine. The band played. The crowd shuffled. Luc nudge Kurt sitting next to him in the bleachers.

"Who's that girl holding the flag? Not Sarah. The other one."

"She's a freshman," answered Kurt. "Went to St. Jude."

"What's her name?"

"Cherie."

THE TUNNEL

May Day '65.

A newborn Saturday in the darkness after the bars closed.

Four high school boys crouched where the bus depot used to be.

No cars moved on Main Street.

A few random vehicles slumbered by lonely sidewalks.

"Hold up!" whispered the leader.

"Come on!" whispered Fred who was a junior. "What are we waiting for?"

The cherry-topped cop car rolled down Main Street past their hidden faces.

"I told you," said their black-framed-glasses-wearing leader. "He heads to the truck stop café every night this time. My sister waitressed there."

"Tick-tock," said Fred. "Come on! Let's go, Steve!"

"Go smart," ordered Steve. "Eyes open."

"There better not be anybody to see," said Mel.

"Or to see us," said his buddy Clancy.

Fred grinned: "I can run like a motherfucker!"

"You better hope you're not a motherfucker," said Clancy. "Though that might be one way to get out of the Draft."

In that late night/early morning darkness when the Americans killed in Vietnam tallied 551—a procession built by the federal government "drafting" certain males over eighteen to serve in the Army—Steve counted ten heartbeats after the cop car turned the distant corner toward the highway truck stop.

Whispered: *"Now!"*

Led the charge across Main Street. Down the side street. Edged along the back of businesses to concrete steps down into a recess between two buildings.

Four flashlight beams revealed metal double doors on that concrete floor.

Fred squirted oil on each of the four hinges for the steel double doors.

Wiggled the pins out from one door's two hinges.

Levered that door up. The locked-together doors groaned out of their frame. Rose. Tilted back. Mel caught the doors so they landed *quietly*.

Steve followed his flashlight down the uncovered stairs.

Then came Mel.

Clancy.

Fred eased down the stairs. Pulled the doors closed down over him.

Patted his pockets: *Got the pins. Nobody's gonna lock us in that way.*

Three flashlights watched Steve find a wall switch.

Ceiling bulbs blasted on. Four teenagers stood in a canyon of boxes.

"Smell that?" said Steve. "Moldy cardboard. Dust. Must."

"'*Must*' what?" said Clancy.

"Hey!" Fred pointed into an open trash can. "Look at this!"

Toy rubber soldiers. Green rubber. Maybe three inches tall if they were posed standing, firing a rubber gun or arched with extended arms to throw a grenade.

"Why'd they throw them away?" said Fred.

Steve picked a handful of the toy soldiers out of the trash.

"That one got twisted," said Mel. "That one, too. Maybe got drove over."

Steve checked his watch: 2:47 on Saturday morning.

Fred led the two first-timers to a set of stairs on the right wall.

Steve stared at green rubber little men in the palm of his hand.

Let all but one fall back down into the trash.

That soldier was crawling. He carried no weapon. Legs scurrying. Arms bent at his elbows so his raised head could see where he was going.

Steve slid the trashed crawling toy soldier into his jeans pocket.

Didn't know why.

Hurried up the stairs after Fred, Mel and Clancy.

Fred whispered: "No flashlights! The streetlight shines through the front windows into here."

Here spread out before them like a box. Store aisles. Shelves stacked with board games and rows of toy trucks. Cap guns. Toy revolvers in holsters to strap young gunslingers into cowboy myths in a town where their grandfathers knew or like Luc's grandfather had been the real thing.

The outside world's eerie pale light grew brighter as the teenagers crept into the cubicle checkout counter with its hawk's view of the locked glass doors.

Fred's head rose above the cash register's countertop: First his black hair that pushed the Big Pink's new *keep-it-short* rules. Then his pale forehead. Rising over the counter's edge came his hunting eyes. He jerked the cash register's arm.

DING!

The cash register drawer popped open—

—got shoved back into place by Fred as he dropped into the cubicle.

Headlights from a car slowly driving Main Street flashed through the store's wall of windows to illuminate a deserted cubicle and drove on.

"Could be the cops," said Steve.

"Well," said Clancy. "It ain't the robbers."

He nodded at Fred: "Was there money in the cash register?"

"Who knows?" said Fred. "Ain't about money. It's about that *Ding!* I made it. Love that sound. Some days I come in here to hear it for real. Makes me smile."

Steve crept them out of the cubicle. Back down a different aisle—

—into horror.

Shelves of demon dolls. Bold pink faces. Hungry wide eyes that made you look and wouldn't look away. Lips painted as bloody leers. Eager rubber arms.

"Hey, Fred!" Clancy gestured to the dolls. "Need a Prom date?"

"Naw," said Fred. "I got Kitty. But you know Ellen? Year older than us, a senior like you and Mel here, but I'm telling you, she's been giving me the eye. This is her last Prom. Maybe she wants to go out with a bang."

Clancy groaned: "How long did it take you to think of that one?"

"I've been thinking about it a lot," said Fred.

"What you better be *'thinking about'* is nobody crosses Kitty," said Steve.

"You got it easy," countered Fred. "You're taking Buffy."

Steve said: "We gotta move."

They trooped back down the stairs to the basement.

Fred walked to the basement's east side. Grunted a fire-charred wooden bookcase with broken shelves away from the brick wall—

—and a door so broken it hung loose and cracked open.

He led them into another basement. Flipped another switch of lights. Led the way up to the sales floor of Butwins' clothing store.

Flashlights caught mannequins of women and men trapped in poses. A fancy-aproned housewife. A secretary. A businessman in a respectable suit.

What am I going to wear in my someday? wondered Steve.

Fred's flashlight flicked to Mel's and Clancy's faces.

"Hey, maybe you two could pick up graduation suits," joked Fred.

"What are you guys doing after graduation?" Steve asked Mel and Clancy.

"You should have seen Stern," said Mel of the Big Pink's guidance counselor. "I told him I—Clancy, too—that we're gonna try college over in Missoula. He looked at me like I was crazy. Burst out laughing."

"So all in all," said Clancy, "a pretty positive wrap-up interview."

"Hey, guys!"

They swung flashlights to the sound of Fred's voice.

Illuminated him standing by a table in the women's section.

Holding a white bra across his chest.

He grinned: "Don't you love it when they reach around to unsnap it?"

Let go with one hand. The white bra swung down. Dangled.

"You're always thinking about that, aren't you?" said Mel.

"And you aren't?"

Back down to a door in the cellar that led them further.

"The basement of Teagarden's Bar," said Fred.

Like most of the town, he didn't know the bar was named for a jazz star.

Fred snapped on the lights in that night's basement.

Stacked cases of beer. Of gin. Vodka. Bourbon.

"Can't take a bottle without them knowing." Fred sighed.

Mel shook his head: "If I drink at this hour, I'll wake up down here."

"Be a shame to leave you behind," said Clancy.

His buddy laughed: "Like you ever would."

"Come on," said Fred. "This is the cool part."

He shoved aside a wooden panel in the opposite wall to reveal a dark cave.

Mel and Clancy shone their flashlights into that circle of darkness.

"It's a tunnel under the side street off of Main," said Steve.

"Secret tunnels under Main Street," said Mel. "Who knew."

Flashlight beams found places for teenage boys' shoes in that dark tube.

Then they were out of the tunnel. Back in an upstairs business. The sweet smells of shaving soap and aftershave. Tonics to lacquer an Elvis sweep.

"Not much in here," said Steve. "Just the corner barbershop."

Clancy sat in the barber's chair closest to the Main Street wall of windows. Spun the chair around. The world circled him like scenes from a carousel at the county fair. His friends in the shop's shadows. Chairs where no customers sat. Two walls of windows. A glimpse of the side street above the tunnel. Teagarden's bar. The swirl of businesses across Main Street. Capitol Café. A women's clothing store. The unlit Tap Room neon sign in the bar's window. The barbers' back mirror that showed him spinning in a throne he couldn't keep.

Steve said: "Come on."

The barbershop basement door to *further* opened with a skeleton key Steve bought at the hardware store.

Metal shelves in a row. Neat rows of boxes. No smells of dust or must—tile floor-mopping ammonia. A railing on the stairs leading up into the business floor.

They wandered into an aisle with labels: Salves. Vitamins. Bandages.

Clancy reached onto a shelf for a palm-sized bottle.

"My mom can't shake her work backaches," said Clancy. "And these cost."

Steve said: "Go on then. But only take one bottle."

Fred nodded toward the drugstore's pharmacy counter:

"Wonder if they have any of those new birth control pills back there?"

"They don't work like that," said Steve. "A girl can't just pop one *and then*."

"A fellow can dream," said Fred.

Steve risked being close to the store windows to visit the shelves of magazines. The town's grade school kids ranked the comic book selection in this magazine rack as barely worth your time and didn't dare reach high to the adult eyes' shelf for the latest issue of *Playboy* no customers admitted buying as each issue sold out. The drugstore kept paper sacks behind the cash register.

Steve kept his flashlight wedged into his back pocket as he lifted down that month's *Playboy*. Held the magazine out from him and turned so the glow from the streetlight outside hit the centerfold page as it flipped down and open for his eyes to see. Miss May's sprayed-stiff red hair curled up at her shoulders. Her bare breasts sloped like twin swollen footballs with pouty pink tips. The yellow bath towel wrapped around her back covered everything but her clean-shaven legs.

"Let me see," said Clancy.

Steve handed him the magazine with that *her* in it who got 1,114 votes while running for Honolulu City Council in 1992.

That streetlight '65 night, Steve turned to the rotating metal rack of paperback books. Saw the same book he'd gotten from the school library.

As I Lay Dying by William Faulkner. A comic farce about a rural family in the yesterdays survived by the parents of that night's Main Street burglars.

Steve shook his head.

Is my tonight worth somebody writing a book about?

"Let's get out of here," said Clancy with guilt bulging his front jean pocket.

Another skeleton key door to *next*.

"Oh, man!" whispered Fred as the four of them stood in the café's kitchen. "The Chat 'N' Chew. Bacon sizzling on that black stovetop. Or a burger. Usually sit at the counter. If I'm with my folks, we take a yellow booth."

"We don't eat out," said Mel.

"Well," said Clancy, "you and me after our rabbit hunt last winter. Came back with a truck full of dead Bugs Bunnys with pelts for Mr. Jensen to skin 'n' sell. After bullets and gas, didn't make much more than our dinner here."

"All this eating talk is making me hungry," said Fred.

"No," said Steve. "Mrs. Dumas needs the pennies from every slice of pie."

"What kind of pie?" said Fred. "Apple? *Don't tell me cherry!* My favorite!"

"Of course it is," said Clancy. "Me, I'm a pumpkin kind of guy."

"I'm American," said Mel. "Give me apple. What about you, Steve?"

He stood there in the dark café kitchen. He wasn't the tallest of the group—that was Clancy, lean as a fishing pole. Wasn't the smartest. Mel was, though his hows and whys puzzled Steve. And Fred . . . Well, Fred radiated pure energy.

I'm just Steve, he told himself.

Answered the pie question: "I take the best I can."

"Come on then," said Fred. "Time for the best."

Flashlights lit dark basement turns and twists, shoves of boxes, a big step up into a canyon whose vastness they could sense but not see in the darkness.

Steve found the switch. Flicked it on.

"Where the hell are we?" whispered Mel.

"Behind the movie screen at the Roxy," said Steve.

Steel girders braced the back of a white screen as tall as eight men.

Slumped against the back wall was a chest of drawers that the last of the boon-docks vaudeville troops used back when these four boys were learning to read. A mustached barker with a hatful of magic tricks and a ventriloquist's dummy. A strong man who acted like a clown. His wife who flounced and bounced in showgirl costumes. The bowling pin comedian they called Midget Mike. They'd strutted their stuff on the stage in front of the red-curtained movie screen.

Fred pointed to a set of stairs going down from the far wall.

"Use your flashlights. Walk up the aisle to the lobby."

Mel and Clancy followed the stairs out.

Fred frowned at Steve: "You flinched when I said Prom."

"They hired that old guy group to play," said Steve. "Not my kind of thing."

"You're pissed off because they didn't hire your cousin's band!"

"They're good when I'm not trying to sing with them," insisted Steve. "My cousin rocks lead guitar. Sings. The drummer pounds it out. And Andy, the freshman from the northside, he plays a mean bass guitar."

"I heard they don't know enough songs."

"They can fake it." Steve shrugged. "*Yeah*, maybe not for Prom."

"But I still don't get it," said Fred. "Buffy's crazy about you."

"Nobody ever said luck wasn't part of the deal."

The deal, thought Steve.

Being ten. Sitting on his parents' sofa staring at black and white photos of what *LIFE* magazine said was a "regular American family." In fancy summer clothes. All White. Mom and Dad, Sis and Junior. A mown lawn in front of their house. Everybody happy in What Was Going On.

That's how things are, thought Steve. *That's the deal to believe. Hope for.*

You are here echoed in his head like in that new TV show called *The Twilight Zone*. But *here* might be something else someday. Maybe you find out about tunnels under Main Street. Maybe *Dr. Strangelove* wins.

Buffy and me, thought Steve. *Maybe the deal means we'll . . . we'll . . . We'll get married. We fit. Even with what she won't do 'n' how she gets nervous 'cause I roll out with my guys after I take her home. But she's . . . she's the real deal.*

Fred frowned: "Hey! Did you ask Buffy . . . and she turned you down?"

Steve started down the stairs into darkness.

"She's waiting for me to ask. Alice told me she's dodging Luc in school and on the phone so he won't get to ask her before I do."

"What are you waiting for?" said Fred.

They flipped through the red curtain under a red sign.

Fred's flashlight flowed over rows of empty movie seats. "Look at all those people who aren't here to see us."

He led the way up the faded and filthy red carpet's sloping aisle.

"You go on ahead." Steve sent his flashlight beam up the balcony's steep stairs to the closed projection booth door. "I'm going up there."

Fred shrugged. "I'll make sure they don't take more popcorn than they should or bloat themselves with the Coke machine."

Steve turned his flashlight to the stairs and climbed.

He opened the projection booth door. Snapped on the lights.

Knew: *Luc works up here.*

That wasn't why Steve was there. Was something, though.

He stared at the two giant delivery machines for celluloid dreams.

Lying across the back of the workbench behind the two projectors was a shelf of tiny rooms like a doll's house. Junk filled some slots. Some were empty, like the one behind a radio pointing its long antennae toward invisible stars.

He imagined Buffy's searching eyes.

Can't call her on her home's only phone until hours from now.

He pulled the toy soldier out of his blue jeans pocket.

Positioned him so he was crawling out of the empty slot behind the radio.

Getting out. Getting away. Going somewhere better. Doing. Choosing.

Steve left the toy soldier there not ever to know if Luc would see it.

He snapped out the projection booth's lights. Closed its door behind him. Stood high up in the balcony's darkness of that vast auditorium of escapes.

We came here because we can. We came here to do. We came here to be.

His flashlight beam cut through the darkness.

Couldn't reach the distant red-curtained big screen.

YES YOU CAN

Buffy caught Luc that Monday in the hallway outside of first period class. Blurted: "You're going to Prom—right?"

"*What?* I—"

"I'm going with Steve and you gotta go," babbled Buffy to *obviously* a friend. "After this one, you and I only get two more before we graduate. It'd be sad if you don't go. If you don't have a date, get one fast. She needs to get a dress."

RING!

Last Bell hurried Buffy into the classroom.

Gutted Luc shuffled in behind her.

Least I didn't get a chance to make a fool of myself asking her, he thought.

Heard his teachers *blah blah blah* in front of his first two morning classes.

Heard Wayne and Kurt as they walked together between classes.

Wayne said something about the new rules that let boys wear collarless shirts and let girls wear "*dignified*" pants—but only on Fridays.

Kurt babbled about some Key Club thing.

Luc slouched into Study Hall.

Marin had a permanent Study Hall pass to run all-alone miles on the crunchy gray loop around the football field for the track team.

Inertia drifted Luc into the empty school library.

A woman's urgent whisper: "*Give me the keys!*"

Behind the checkout desk for the school librarian was a glass-walled office.

The office door hung a hand-width open. The angled door glass made a translucent mirror, so Luc saw reflections in the office windows to the world.

Those windows trapped phantoms of Mrs. Dawson and Coach Moent huddled in the office. Mrs. Dawson held her demanding hand palm up to the shrunken man backed against the school's inner wall.

"Come on!" she said.

"I could go home and—"

"*Home* means the basement where you probably got bottles stashed. *Yeah,* your wife told me she threw you down there. Tonight, probably tomorrow night—hell, maybe all week—you're staying with Bart and me. And I know all the hiding places there, believe you me. He's cleaning our booze out now."

"Can't stop trembling. Feel like shit."

"Oh, you look it, too. Got the dead pallor. I'd make a bad joke, say now Indian *you* looks like a paleface but this ain't no joke. Give me the damn car keys."

Coach Moent filled her waiting hand.

"My history class—"

"Miss Casey and I worked up a pop quiz for you to give them this afternoon. She typed the mimeo pages. I fit each page on the ink machine and rolled out the test papers. All you gotta do is pass 'em out. Say *ready, set, go.* We'll figure out what to do about tomorrow. She had a father who . . . He fought what you got."

"Did he win?"

"This is about you. You do this or Harris wins. It's twenty-nine days before school's out," said Mrs. Dawson. "Hang in there."

Luc flashed on Coach saying: *"Don't let them take it away from you."*

Scurried to the far corner of the library. Stared at the world globe on a low bookcase. Spun its rainbow ball.

Wendy would be an easy-going ask but he was pretty sure she'd "OKed!" to somebody else. Alice . . . A *wow* ask he'd never get to say *yes.* Bobbi Jean . . . Bobbi Jean . . . Luc had this sense that his friend he'd known since grade school didn't want him to pay her back for their freshman Co-ed by asking her to this Prom.

A curving wind cupped him in its hand of *maybe.*

RING!

Noon Bell.

Luc ran out of the library.

Dodged through the second-floor hallway filling with his fellow students.
Scrambled down the stairs.

Dashed to the glass doors leading to the students' parking lot.

Slammed his brakes at that only way out for teenagers headed to lunch.

Coming past him. Mike laughing. Mel walking beside Clancy. Kitty, who'd drunkenly turned at the New Year's Eve dance where an out-of-town rock band swayed her to *what the hell* give that *just happened to be standing there* four-eyes, year-younger "good boy" named Luc his first deep *Happy New Year* kiss. Now Fred walked her to his white convertible. Kurt called out to Luc: "Come on!"

Not yet. Not yet. Not yet. Not—

Here she comes.

Luc edged through the streaming crowd. Startled her to a stop, her back to the wall, her nervous smile a *What?*

The first words he ever said to her:

"Would you go to Prom with me?"

Cars in the parking lot outside revved their engines.

The ivory-legged flagbearer freshman girl went wide-eyed.

"*Yes!*" said Cherie.

THE WAY THINGS WORK

Saturday morning four days later.

Dad taught Luc to tie a black tie into a knot named after British royalty.

Mom pressed the black suit that he wore to Uncle Johnny's funeral.

He shined his black dress shoes.

A boxed corsage from Buffy's family's store waited in the refrigerator.

The sun warmed that May Saturday afternoon back in '65.

Luc pulled the green garden hose to the driveway.

Sprayed water all over the gray '54 Dodge.

Used a dirty dishtowel to dry the car windows.

The flap of a sparrow flying to the trees in Luc's backyard.

A vision of plopped-from-the-sky bird poop.

Luckily, Mom had just been to the Thriftway grocery store.

He ripped strips of clear toxic plastic food-wrapping from a steel-toothed rectangular box. Saran Wrapped all the car windows to keep them clean *until*.

Prom doors opened at 7:30.

At 4:30 he'd showered, shaved and *Yes!* didn't cut himself.

Mom made him have an early bite to eat.

"Not so much so you won't be hungry for that dinner you're paying for after Prom. You were lucky to get a Sports Club reservation this late."

Prom night customarily required paired-off teenagers to make a reservation at one of the town's better restaurants for an after-dance meal.

At 6:30 he perched on the living room couch.

Glasses cleaned—*check*. Black suit—*check*. Knotted black tie—*check*. Teeth brushed three times—*check*. Right Guard underarm deodorant slathered all over his pits—*check*. No water or milk or Coke since Mom's mini-dinner so he wouldn't need to go pee—*check*.

At 6:51 he peeled Saran Wrap off the gray car's windows.

At 7:09 he slowly backed down the driveway.

Cherie's house rose on a hill eleven blocks away and facing a steep street sloping down to the highway bordering the train tracks.

Luc scouted that house five times during the week. Clocked it as a four-minute one-way journey. And every time after driving past Cherie's house, Luc drove past the balcony of his First Kiss. *For luck.*

On that *Prom date* journey, no cop pulled him over for driving below the speed limit. No bird shit on the windows. And no one else was parked on the steeply sloped street facing Cherie's house.

That meant he could legally park his car so the front passenger's door faced a curb above a sloping-down dirt lot where walking wasn't easy.

Yes!

If the girl liked the guy, she'd use the driver's door. Slide in past the steering wheel. Settle herself on the flat continuous front seat facing the rearview mirror and riding shoulder to shoulder to the lucky guy. Cherie probably wanted to avoid walking on the dirt lot's slope to the passenger side, so . . .

Luc parked the gray '54. Shut off the engine.

There were thirty—*No: forty!* There must have been a *ga-jillion* high steppin', sweat-makin', deodorant-breakin' concrete stairs he had to climb slow and easy to her front door.

And knock.

"He's here!" came through the wood a heartbeat before the door flew open—
—and there stood her father.

"Come in, Lucas," he said, using the teenage boy's full legal name.

The father looked the boy up. Looked him down.

"Least you didn't have to drive out to our farm to pick her up."

He disappeared down a hallway.

The mother and older sister raced in from the living room.

Cherie came down the stairs in a Prom gown that flowed with frilly puffery. Step by careful step down until she stood an arm's length away from him.

"Hi," she said.

"Hi. I . . . I got you this." Handed her the white-boxed corsage.

Cherie had time to open the corsage box before her mother and big sister swooped in and pulled the corsage out of the box to push it first onto one side of Cherie's chest and then to the other in the legendary *"Which tit?"* dance.

Settled on pinning the corsage on her heart side.

Handed her a thin coat "in case it turns chilly."

Cherie's eyes pleaded with Luc.

"We better go," he said.

From the depths of the house came her father's voice: *"Home by midnight!"*

"Yes sir!" yelled Luc.

He opened the front door for his date like a gentleman should.

Followed her out to the front landing where she stood to one side.

The door slammed closed.

He felt a hundred pounds lighter.

Saw her grin. Knew she felt that relief, too.

Cherie said: "Is that your car?"

She noticed! All that work washing it! The Saran Wrap! She likes it!

"Yes," said Luc with a proud smile.

"It's rolling down the hill."

HERE WE GO!

And we're off!

Rollin' under a pink sunset sky straight down the street where Cherie lives came the gray '54 Dodge. No motor sound. Sparkly clean glass windows showed *nobody's holding the steering wheel.*

But look!

Here comes Luc! Black suit and tie a-floppin'. Glasses bouncing. Face gone crazy. Running like never before. Running down thirty—*No: forty!* There must be a *ga-jillion* high steppin', sweat-makin', deodorant-breakin' concrete stairs he was pounding his way down!

Bam! His shined black shoes hit the street—

—same thundering heartbeat as that gray '54 rolled into the intersection headed down and picking up speed toward the killer railroad tracks.

Luc grabbed the handle/jerked the door open and jumped inside. Stomped the brake. The '54 shuddered/stopped.

WANG! The front passenger door flew open!

Cherie jumped in, coat and all. Slammed the door.

She damn near beat him there. Dashed down thirty—*No: forty!* No: a *ga-jillion* high steppin', sweat-makin', deodorant-breakin' concrete stairs. In high heels.

Now instead of anger or fear or *Why did you do this to me you loser?*—excitement *wow'd* her wide-smiling pink rouged face.

She shoved her coat onto the shotgun seat—

—plopped beside him, her Prom dress billowing toward the dashboard.

Luc checked the transmission. In neutral. The silver metal handbrake under the dashboard: *Must not have pulled it out enough. Or it's broken.*

He turned the keys in the ignition.

The engine roared on.

He turned the steering wheel. Pushed the hand brake *all* the way off. Put his foot on the gas and *oh so slowly* drove them down a gentler slope five blocks to the curb outside Blackhawk Elementary where *he'd* gone to grade school and one block 'cross the street to St. Jude's where *she'd* been schooled.

Parked the car. Luc's right hand lifted the automatic transmission stick on the steering column so the indicator needle went from D to P.

They held their breaths as he lifted his foot off the brake . . .

The gray '54 Dodge didn't move. Settled. He turned the engine off.

Faced the sparklingly clean windshield: "We better go inside."

Opened his driver's side door, stepped out—

—and Cherie slid behind his steering wheel to join him on the street.

Told him: "I'm leaving my coat."

He slammed the car door shut.

Walked beside her toward the crepe-paper-streamered glass doors into the grade school auditorium and the sounds of a band warming up.

SOMEBODY'S SOMETHING

Buffy wobbled on a ten-foot ladder as six blocks away, the windows of a '54 gray Dodge got covered in Saran Wrap.

You got yourself up here, Buffy told herself. *Get yourself down.*

"I should have been taller!" she joked down to Wendy, Alice and a dozen other high school girls hustling around Blackhawk Elementary School's student gymnasium, some of them with scarves over the curlers in their hair.

Now just don't fall off this wobbly ladder!

She reached . . .

. . . and YES! Scotch-taped a pink paper streamer high above the stage.

Stepped down to Wendy's reaching-up hand.

"Do you think they'll even notice that streamer?" said Alice.

"Who?" said Buffy. "The old guys' band or our school chorus?"

She shrugged: "I don't know why the chorus is even playing. But lots of them are going to be here anyway, so . . . what the hell."

"Yeah," said Wendy. The three of them sat at a white tablecloth covered card table to fold red paper napkins into hearts. "Mr. Bundy's in the band. He must have figured it would be a chance for the chorus to sing for a crowd."

"He kinda gives me the creeps," said Alice.

Buffy shook her milk chocolate hair: "He's just another teacher."

Alice sent Wendy a wink, smiled as she stared down at the red paper napkin she was folding. "Well, one thing's for sure: He's no Steve."

Steve.

There was something about Steve. Something that made Buffy tingle. Some sense. Smell. Something when he looked at her with eyes that saw more of her than any other boy in school. Except for maybe Luc, and that was . . . *well* . . . was Luc.

Steve's something pulled her like a magnet. Puzzled the hell out of her. Pissed her off sometimes. Yet she knew—

Knew!

—she knew that this was just high school. Today's Buffy. Knew Big Words to come for Future Buffy. Maybe a bigger *Who* she'd find over some far horizon. Like in college. Or like when Future Buffy did whatever she would do. She shook her head back to Today's Buffy and this Prom that was just one night, not forever.

Still, whenever Steve came toward her . . .

She snapped back into that afternoon reality. A radio played on the long table where the punch bowl stood empty beside stacked paper cups:

The Supremes sang their hit: "Where Did Our Love Go?"

Everybody *knew* The Supremes.

Their trio of sparkling dresses swaying to the music in front of black and white TV microphones softly singing stories of heartache and hope.

Buffy *loved* The Supremes.

Stood in front of the mirror on her bedroom closet door. Swayed in that glass pane in a rural Northern Montana town as those three stars from Detroit sang on the radio. Mouthed the words, wishing she could be cool like them.

She *grokked* how ironic it was that rural Montana White boys found their hearts tugging for three big city Black girls. Only once did she hear a White junior sneer at them. Use that *nigger* word that made her want to slap him. Buffy wished he could see. Wished they all could be in the same song.

"Did you hear they almost couldn't find enough chaperones?" said Wendy.

"Mrs. Dawson canceled," said Alice. "Miss Casey said she couldn't either. Mr. Pulaski, the English teacher, suddenly he's helping with something, too."

"Get this," said Alice: "Over there, Janice is bragging 'bout how next year, she's going to be a varsity cheerleader."

"*No!*" yelled Buffy.

Other girls working in the gym turned to look.

Buffy dropped her gaze to working the napkin in her hand. Whispered:

"OK, I didn't want to tell but . . . In school, Donna walked past—and Janice smart-assed something about: '*We should have a special Prom for gimps.*'"

"Oh my God!" said Wendy.

"Bitch," said Alice. "What did you do?"

"Went after Donna. Babbled about I was sorry. *'What for?'* she said. *'Who'd wanna go to some little kids' dance anyway?'* But . . . you know: she gave me kind of a nod and a . . . a sad, pissed-off smile."

Wendy shook her head: "Janice shouldn't be cheerleading us."

"Most of the boys will vote for her," said Alice. "Big tits."

"Somebody ought to try out, beat her out of winning." Wendy sighed. "Standing out in front of everybody . . . I'd freeze up!"

"I'm too much of a smartass," said Alice. "What about you, Buffy?"

"I just want it all to work—you know?"

She shrugged: "Besides, my tits aren't big."

"Big enough for Steve," said Alice.

"For Luc, too!" added Wendy.

Nobody laughed.

The radio played The Byrds singing "Turn, Turn, Turn," a guitar rocked-up song with lyrics from the Bible about "a time for every season."

Luc, thought Buffy.

I know I know I know I know I wish but no I don't yet he's—

There when I need him. Cares about me. He's who he is, not somebody else. Smart. Funny. Kinda cute. But dorky. Crazy like she didn't quite get. He could make her laugh and—but he didn't make her feel the *something* that was Steve.

The Bible and the radio said: *"To everything there is a season."*

Buffy folded another red heart.

BLUE VELVET

Luc and Cherie sat by themselves at a white-clothed table amidst Prom. Trapped in their silences.

Revolving lights spun hues of blue and green and red.

Scents swirled. Perfume. Aftershave. Pheromones and hormones.

The band played on the stage. Five adult men, four with kids of their own. They played gigs in local bars. Took turns singing. Piano player Bundy twice left his bench to sing into a lone microphone rising in front of the band.

Luc and Cherie danced to a few fast songs.

Danced to slow songs. Held each other polite.

Two freshman girls led their dates over to say *hi* to Cherie.

Wayne wanted to sit at Luc's table but the girl he brought didn't want to get stuck talking with Cherie while Wayne and Luc jabbered about their *whatevers*.

Kitty let eager Fred think he was driving this white-convertible evening. She noticed gawky Luc who she couldn't quite remember something about . . . *New Year's Eve?* Hell, gave him a grin as he and his date sat in silence.

Wendy waved as her date walked her past.

Blonde Alice led her dazzled senior date behind them.

Buffy swirled by in Steve's arms.

Luc stared across the white-clothed table to Cherie.

Figure out what to say! kept screaming in his skull. *Say something!*

"OK!" yelled band member Mr. Bundy. "Let's make this a real show!"

Onto the stage marched two dozen teenagers. Most of the girls wore dresses for this Prom. Half of the teenage boys wore suits that carried them here with dates. The rest of the *showed-up* teenagers wore "good" school clothes like Andy who was in Cherie's class and played bass guitar in Steve's cousin's band.

Mr. Bundy wore a shiny sports jacket. He beckoned the school chorus into rows. Bobbi Jean left the table where she was alone to stand in the front.

Something about her made Cherie frown.

The chorus sang two songs.

Bobbi Jean stepped from the chorus.

Joined Conductor Bundy at the tall, lean, hard steel silvery microphone.

He smiled. Lowered the mic so it pointed up to her pink-lipsticked mouth.

Stepped aside to where both the chorus and the band could see him. Out to where he could watch Bobbi Jean at the mic and everyone could watch him.

Luc blinked:

Bobbi Jean's not wearing her glasses. We're all blurred images for her.

She leaned into the microphone.

The whole room heard her inhale.

As she slowly, sultrily sang the song "Blue Velvet" that was first a hit for a male music icon way back in 1951 when Bobbi Jean was two years old and now was again popular with a different generation's male star singer, but . . .

But that Prom night Bobbi Jean sang that "standard" in the fashion of a *noir* movie created twenty-four years later by a Montana-born *auteur* three years older than Luc. That cinematic experience rocked Luc in his movie theater seat as actress/singer Isabella Rossellini purring that song confirmed what Luc hadn't realized that Prom night as outside that 1986's palace of dreams movie theater, the "neat idea" murderous political scandal known as Iran-Contra rocked America and a devastating nuclear accident rocked Chernobyl in Ukraine.

Prom night, Cherie whispered across the white paper tablecloth to Luc:

"Bobbi Jean's wearing the blue Cinderella dress! They keep it in the band room with the other costumes. Mr. Bundy must have gotten it for her."

Makes sense, thought Luc. A blue dress for a blue song. Plus, why would her folks spend money to buy a Prom dress if she didn't have a—

Wham!

Realization blew Luc away from Bobbi Jean's song of rapture.

Money, he thought. He looked around the spinning lights rainbowing the teenagers watching one of their own woo the mic. Gowns and suits. Tickets to the Prom. The post-dance dinner. Having a car. Gas. The corsage.

So many *don't*s if you *don't got* the *dues.*

Bobbi Jean dramatically closed her mascaraed eyes at the end of that song.

Applause. She bowed. Walked off stage with the chorus. Went to a table where her purse gave her back her glasses. She sat all alone.

The drummer called: "Last dance!"

Thank God! Luc's relief crimped when he remembered they still had to go to the Sports Club after-dance dinner reservation shouldering their heavy silence.

He and Cherie waltzed like two ventriloquists' dummies.

The lights came up on a grade school full of formal-clothed teenagers.

Luc and Cherie joined that exodus to the night.

Blue-gowned Bobbi Jean sat at her table. Watched them go.

The gray '54 Dodge waited where they'd left it.

Luc pulled open the driver's door.

Cherie slid past the steering wheel. Fussed as he scooted behind the steering wheel to hurry toward the end of this night.

"Aren't you going to help me put on my coat?" said Cherie.

Oh great! I screwed up again!

She leaned forward. The coat she'd left behind lay bunched behind her.

Luc raised his arm along the back of the front seat to spread her coat wide.

Whump went her head onto his right shoulder to nuzzle in and drape his right arm across her shoulders to cuddle her close.

MAKING IT

Every heartbeat changes the stars.

One beat you're sitting behind the steering wheel staring through the windshield trying to race to the end of this dark night of *no*.

Next beat she's leaning into you with *yes*.

They kissed. Kissed again and again.

But Luc knew the Rolling Stones' song was wrong: Time is *not* on your side.

"Home by midnight!"

That executioner *tick tick ticked* ever closer.

How can I turn the car on without losing my arm around her?

She saw where he stared *not* at her.

Cherie turned the ignition key.

The gray '54, automatic-transmission Dodge roared to life.

Cherie turned the stick shift to D.

Luc spun the steering wheel. His shined shoe put the pedal to the metal.

STOLEN TIME

Riding the night streets of their lives. A kiss. Streetlights and porchlights. Parked cars. Dark houses. A dog trotted across the headlights. A nuzzle. She spun the knob to turn on the radio.

The radio announced it was 10:47 on a Saturday night in 1965's May.

What can I do? Where can we go to? How much time can we steal?

Never occurred to Luc to blow off the dinner reservation at the Sports Club. They had his name. They'd know. There'd be trouble. Because. *Right?*

He turned into Main Street's parking lot by what was left of the bus depot.

The '54's headlights swept over an empty brown Thunderbird.

Luc turned the steering wheel and slid into an empty space like a pro.

Cherie put it in P. Turned off the key. Turned into their embrace.

Oh, this, THIS is how you kiss her!

Headlights flashed over them. A car horn honked. Teenage laughter.

He pulled back from her burning lips: "We better go. *I mean*: to the dinner."

Cherie grinned. Slid out his side. He slammed the car door shut. They held hands. Walked the sidewalk amidst streetlights and neon glows from bar signs.

Wait! Across the side street from Teagarden's Bar:

Is that Coach Moent kind of . . . kinda like shadow boxing?

Every heartbeat tumbled thoughts through Luc.

I don't know where kids go to park and make out! Her! Me! MIDNIGHT!

The Sports Club. Tables of Promgoers filled the dining room and spilled into the bar where late night adults perched on stools. Held glasses of fire and forgets. Stared at the teenagers. Saw their own *might have beens.*

The white uniformed waitress gave Luc a blank stare:

"Can't find your reservation. Put you there."

A table of upperclassmen made room for them. Kitty pulled Fred's hand up from under the table and put it on his own white plate.

"They got fresh shrimp," Kitty told the cute underclassmen. "Flown in from Seattle yesterday. You gotta get it."

They told the waitress they'd go with that. She waddled into the kitchen.

"You guys!" said the other junior class girl. "I can't believe she's dead!"

Luc blinked behind his kiss-smudged glasses: "*What?*"

The disbeliever named a girl who'd graduated the year before.

I know her! thought Luc. *She's the really skinny girl who stared at Bobbi Jean way back last year when we were freshman at the Co-ed.*

Kitty looked Luc straight in the eye: "She killed herself."

"*How?*"

"You don't wanna know," said Kitty. "Dead is dead and nobody knows *why.*"

"Heard she'd dropped out of college," said Fred. "Came home up to her mom's place up on Knob Hill. Never left the house. Then yesterday . . ."

"*Stop!*" snapped Kitty. "This is Prom. It's dumb. It's goofy. We get all dressed up when all we really want to do is get undressed. But in some damn way, it makes me happy and that's what I want. What I paid for. Happy. And I don't want to . . . to let what she did today be all I remember tomorrow.

"So start talking about something else. Like why hasn't Mr. Bundy made a move on Miss Casey? And has Clancy really been *fishin' around* with the married woman next door? Who farted in English class? The dumb joke you heard from who-gives-a-shit *BUT I CARE* about having fun tonight!

"So everybody," said Kitty: "Say a prayer if you gotta, but start laughing because you oughta."

The waitress bumped her way out of the swinging door to the kitchen. Put steaming plates in front of four teenagers.

Saw empty-plated Luc and Cherie staring at her: "Oh shit!"

Charged back through the swinging door into the kitchen.

Four teenagers consumed a meal.

Luc sat at that table with Cherie. Waiting. Waiting.

The two older couples left their *good-byes* and *good-lucks* on the table. Walked out to their cars with backseats.

The waitress at the kitchen door: "You kids wanna share a burger instead?"

"Whatever!" yelled Cherie.

Four minutes later, the waitress plopped an already cut in half steaming hamburger in buns on plates in front of them, said: "You want catchup?"

They'd scarfed the burger down before she got back with that bottle.

The waitress waved away Luc's grab for his wallet.

"Don't worry. The boss says it's on the house *'cause*. It's your lucky night."

The Sports Club door sprung open into Main Street's neon night at 11:47.

They dashed toward midnight.

Hand in hand. A frilly Prom dress and high heels. A flapping suit and shined shoes. They raced to the parked gray '54. She jumped in the passenger door because it was quicker—wrapped herself around him in a hungry kiss before she broke away and yelled: "Go!"

They whipped out of the parking lot.

Surged toward the green stop light three blocks away.

"Faster!" cried Cherie.

The light turned orange as they shot past the bachelors' Rainbow Hotel.

The light turned red—

—the gray '54 blasted under it.

The '54 flew up Main Street's slope up swimming pool hill. Careened left at the corner onto the steeper street where she lived. Roared past her house to the level top of that hill. Slammed to a stop. Luc put it in P and jerked the damn handbrake to heaven. Pulled Cherie out of the car, coat bunched in her one hand.

They grabbed each other for their first hips-to-hips kiss.

Ran down the steep hill.

Thirty—*No: forty!* There must have been a *ga-jillion* high steppin', sweat-makin', deodorant-breakin' concrete stairs they raced up.

Stood under the porch light. Catching their breath. Grinning at each other.

Through the wooden front door came: "*Bong! . . . Bong! . . . Bong!*"

They snatched a kiss.

She shoved open the door. Stepped over the border into her father's house. Called out for all to hear: "Goodnight, Luc!"

One last "*Bong!*" and "*Wonk*": That door shut.

Luc turned around on that concrete stoop to face his *now*.

Told those stars above his sleeping hometown:

"Good night? *Oh yeah!*"

REALITY

*F*inally! thought Luc. *Time IS on my side!*

That Monday morning put him last in the line of three boys waiting outside the closed door of the guidance counselor, Mr. Stern.

It's the last period before lunch *when.*

Yesterday's Sunday morning after *good night* Saturday.

Mr. Tom called him from the Roxy.

"The weather turned warm," he said. "Gonna open up the drive-in theater Friday. Got that old black and white one: *The Thing*, that flying saucer from outer space. *Do you think people really saw one of them flying saucers in the night sky south of town?* Folks love *The Thing* 'cause they shot lots of it up on the Hi-Line. Makes us feel like we're worth being in a movie.

"Thing is," said Mr. Tom, "you're not supposed to start running the projectors until *after* school gets out, but now I'm in a real bind. Need you to work the Roxy Saturday night. What do you say?"

Yes! The drive-in theater is open! Double feature in your own dark car!

With only the actors on the screen watching you and who you're with.

And where I get in free! My folks can't say no. Friday will be my only chance to go to the drive-in—hell, maybe to go anywhere!—all summer long.

Luc shouted *Yes!* to working the Roxy Saturday night.

Now on Monday morning *before*, he leaned against the wall, third in line.

Second came Walt from his class.

First came their fellow sophomore Tod standing outside the closed door.

Our turn to have Guidance Counselor Stern tell us what classes we're supposed to take our junior year, thought Luc. Like a butcher knife chopping carrots.

A steel blade shoving some chopped pieces one direction for the soup, other pieces into the salad.

The glass door swung open.

Short dirty-blonde-haired Donna limped past the three boys in her class.

Behind her moving-on, out of the office came Stern's voice: *"Next!"*

Tod stepped inside that office and pushed the door closed—

—yet didn't: The glass paned office door slowed, snugged into the door frame but its latch didn't click into the metal slot.

Walt and Luc heard snatches of someone else's conversation.

Tod pleading: *"No . . . I want . . . take chemistry . . . not a mechanic, I . . ."*

Counselor Stern: *". . . be realistic."*

". . . some days it's just hard to . . . And that's why . . . so . . ."

"Well, it's your funeral," said Stern loud and clear.

The door opened as Tod fled.

Wouldn't look at his two classmates. Disappeared into the Big Pink.

"Next!" yelled Stern.

Walt whispered to Luc: *"Wanna bet how this will turn out?"*

He walked into the domain of power.

Made sure he shut the office door behind him.

Walt settled in the chair in front of the file-folders-stacked desk. He was stocky with a chest and shoulders that came from working fence post diggers and whatever else needed doing to help out his uncle or to get some cash. His dad drove trucks for the Highway Department. Walt knew that defined who he was to The Powers That Be. His smile puzzled the man sitting across from him.

The guidance counselor. Mr. Stern. Taught trigonometry to juniors.

Mr. Stern said: "VoTech track has you in junior auto shop half a day in the Quonset garage out back of the school."

"Yeah, I figured I'd be on that sine."

"What sign?"

"You know, *sine*: It's one of the angles of a triangle."

"How do you know that?"

"The trig textbook upstairs in the library. I was curious."

"You don't need to worry. No trig for you."

"I guess that all depends on my cosine."

The counselor/teacher shook his head and gave a grudging *got it* smile.

"At least you're doing what you're supposed to do, unlike some students."

"Like Tod?"

"Yes. Exactly. Science and chorus—*ha!* Someday soon he's going to look in the mirror and realize he's on the wrong track."

The Man in Charge scribbled something in Walt's file folder.

"Send in whoever's next out there in the hall."

Walt walked through the door—politely closed it behind him.

And out of sight of the door's glass pane, leaned close to Luc, whispered: *"If you figure out what's going on in there, don't let him know."*

Mr. Stern was a friend of Luc's family. He helped Laura get a scholarship to a famous Chicago university. Helped Honor Society students figure out college. He'd already picked Luc's schedule of classes to take next year when he was a junior—the kind of class schedule an obedient, white-collar middle-income family, college-bound White male would *of course* punch in the Big Pink.

Luc pondered what Walt said: *What's going on that I haven't figured out?*

But more important things pressured Luc that Monday morning.

High noon would make it all happen *if* he got there in time!

Inspiration snipered Luc as he sat in that guidance chair.

Next to the chair at home in his bedroom was a library book:

The Green Berets—the Army's new Special Forces who *officially* used community building projects combined with sneaky guerrilla strategies to stop Communist forces from taking over a country like Vietnam. The Green Berets were heroes. A song praising them was climbing the radio hits chart. They were the kind of smart and savvy soldier Luc pictured himself being. Creative. Tough. Spotting a chance and—

Wham!

Green Beret savvy rocked Luc. He joked with Stern. Told him Laura was fine even though he hadn't talked to her in weeks. Stern didn't blink when guerilla Luc *casually* asked for a pink hall pass. Signed it with no destination or purpose filled out, unlike the pink hall pass in Luc's blue jeans pocket that restricted him to Guidance Office and Study Hall.

The black hands on the white background clock pointed to 11:43.

Took a Green Beret chance. And now I'm pink-slipped safe.

Like he was *supposed* to be doing that, Luc walked upstairs to his locker. Left his books. Grabbed his jacket. Hurried through the second-floor hallway and down the stairs on the gym side of the Big Pink.

Stood with his back to the MEN's locker room door beside the glass doors to the student parking lot where everyone would head to lunch. He made it. He had nothing to worry about. Nothing. *Really*, nothing.

Shifted from leg to leg.

Not now! Why now! I can't go to the bathroom now and miss . . . !

But he had to. He *really* had to.

The black hands of time pointed to 11:53.

Luc whirled to the locker room three steps behind him—

Unlocked!

Swept through the door. Eased it closed so no bangs echoed down the first-floor hallway to the ears of a gorilla. Jumped into the cinderblock recess in the shower stalls' wall where three white urinals mawed at him as he unzipped—

Unseen Man One's Voice: "Did it help?"

Unseen Man Two's Voice: "I don't know. I don't know."

I got a hand full of gotta go! Can't splash sound!

The Unseen Men's Voices came from benches between the rows of lockers.

Unseen Man One's Voice belonged to Mr. Pulaski, the English teacher.

Unseen Man Two was Coach Moent.

Mr. Pulaski said: "You've only got until next Monday."

"Guess I'm lucky Harris won't let me on the platform for graduation." Moent sighed: "You think they give cured diplomas at Warm Springs?"

"You're still shivering. I'm gonna turn the hot showers back on."

AAAH! Luc couldn't hold it any longer. Sprayed the urinal with his yellow stream. Aimed at the white porcelain wall where he wouldn't make a splash.

Can't flush. They'll hear me. He tucked himself back into his jeans. Zipped up. *Can't wash my hands: the sinks are by the showers and they'll see me.*

He heard the hiss of spraying water.

They're in the showers stall! Go!

RING!

That Noon Bell's blare covered the locker room door slamming shut behind Luc as he raced to The Spot.

Lunchtime high schoolers streamed past him.

And there was Cherie. Grinning at him as he walked to her just like before. *This is poetry. This is a great song. This is how it's supposed to work!*

He didn't even wait for her *Hi!* before he said: "Will you go to the drive-in theater with me Friday night?"

Oh, Wow went her face as she said: "I have to ask my parents."

He walked her toward her carpool. Got back to school as early as he could. Stood in the May sunshine outside the glass doors into the Big Pink.

Cherie walked away from her carpool.

Stopped in front of him with a shy grin and a happy whisper:

"My parents say I can't go to the drive-in but . . . something else?"

Luc stood there stunned like a puppet whose strings got slashed.

The song. The poem. The chance. The precise plan.

All gone.

He couldn't think. Couldn't speak. Couldn't imagine.

Walked away like a gunshot fool.

Left Cherie standing there watching him *just leave her* as First Bell rang.

THE TICKET YOU GOT

L uc zombied the rest of that week.
       Studied so finals would score him high enough for Laura's brother.
    Tuesday—as a Key Club service gig—he, Kurt and Wayne helped set up
the year-end Science Fair exhibit graduating senior Mel would blue ribbon
with his multi-part exhibition of fossils. Clancy drew Hollywood dinosaurs
on his buddy's white poster boards.
    Wednesday Luc watched Buffy walk into English class with Wendy.
    He just couldn't take a chance on Buffy *too* telling him *no* for the drive-in.
    Besides, taking anyone else except Cherie just didn't feel right.
    Wasn't the poem he imagined.
    Thursday was Aunt Beryl's birthday. No one wanted to let her spend it alone.
The Conner sisters' families gathered for dinner at Aunt Iona's. Luc rode with
his aunts to the nursing home, a run timed to get there near the end of visiting
hours so Gramma Meg couldn't hold them hostage. They brought her a slice
of birthday cake. Sent Luc across the street and home while they went "riding
around" this town they'd watched rise from prairie winds.
    Friday electrified the Big Pink with the last real day of school.
    Sure, come the next Monday and Tuesday, all students had to show up to
turn in their textbooks. Get their final grades. Clean out their lockers.
    And Wednesday would be graduation where Mel and Clancy would wear
robes and mortar boards. Turn their tassels to the other side after An Important
Person gave a speech the graduates ignored as they sat in rows on the floor of
the basketball court. Kurt had come up with a Key Club project to give the club
one last batch of points in the state and national ratings: He and Luc would

pass out programs. The band would play and ninety-one still-not-able-to-vote American citizens would walk out of the Big Pink into a world where they'd been told the sky was the limit for them and the news said 627 of their peers had graduated from their lives in the jungles of Vietnam.

Friday the drive-in theater opened.

Luc knew he wouldn't be there—not even with his buddies.

He sat in his bedroom after school. Stared at nothing. Listened to nothing. Knew Mom would put dinner on the table at exactly 6:00.

He exploded at 6:17 when dinner ended with Dad rushing to work because an oil tanker overturned on the highway west of the refinery where Bobbi Jean lived. Mom scrubbed dishes in the sudsy-hot-water sink. Luc stood next to her holding a white dish towel. She had the radio turned to KRIP and the Reverend Carl because she knew it drove Luc crazy to listen to that blend of *I Know Who Jesus Is and You Don't* plus *Keep America's Politics Mine* with Reverend Carl's God plus *gimme dollars* and the co-host voice named Amen Charlie.

Luc blurted: "I'm going to the movies! The Roxy!"

"Hell, you'll see that movie tomorrow night when you're getting paid for it."

"Yeah, but . . . There's things."

Mom looked at her son Luc with Conner sisters' wolf eyes.

"*These things*: Are they some bad come around?"

"I almost wish so."

"*Don't you ever say that, young man!* You don't know *nothing* about bad. Polio like Gramma Meg. The Spanish Flu your dad near died from. The Depression. This place like the dust bowl. You were lucky if you had a Sears catalog for the outhouse. Then the war that could have killed your father."

"Mom, don't worry. This is just the same old same old."

"But tonight you want to go to the movie you're going to see tomorrow?"

"Yeah."

"Antsy as you are, might as well go now. I'll dry the dishes."

"*Thanks!*"

"An' let me guess. It's a short walk to the Roxy. But you need the car."

He stared at her. The picture window behind her showing the yellow hills.

She sighed. Nodded to the glass ashtray beside the radio.

Luc grabbed the keys to the gray '54 and was *gone*.

Looped the block to head west on Main Street.

Chugged the gray '54 toward the pinkening sky. Curbs full with maybe ninety parked cars. Flat-faced stores and neon bars made a canyon he drove through. He saw faces he knew on the sidewalks of the warm May Friday evening. Drove past the Roxy where people were standing in line to buy tickets.

The marquee read: THE SOUND OF MUSIC.

He drove on.

Cherie lived on the west end of Main Street. That steep hill.

Luc turned right to drive over the viaduct.

That road would have let him turn left. Drive past Buffy's and the Big Pink.

But instead, he followed its two-lane blacktop highway north out of town past the canyon in the low slung prairie hills that'd rushed water in '64's flood.

He turned left off the highway. Parked the '54 on a graveled lot.

Stared down at the North Star Drive-In movie theater. Cars already parked in rows facing the waiting sixty-foot white wooden screen backed by the setting sun. More cars waited their turns to drive past the ticket seller booth.

He loved that movie *The Thing*: *"An intellectual carrot? The mind boggles!"*

Drove back to town.

Slowed at an intersection to let a car turn onto the out-of-town road. The driver was a man he didn't know. English teacher Mr. Pulaski and school librarian Mrs. Dawson sat in the backseat on either side of Coach Moent.

The movie'd already started when Luc walked through the Roxy doors. Linda sat in the cashier's booth in a swivel chair that made her taut dress slide up her sleek thighs. He tried to not look there as her eyes smiled at his struggle.

He got a free "company Coke" from the candy counter girls his age.

Quietly padded into the movie theater's gangland turf.

High school students claimed the left side of the auditorium. Junior high students owned the rows halfway down the middle section of seats. Kids younger than that were either with their parents or as close to the right section of seats as they could. Adults ruled the balcony that cost fifty cents extra to sit in. Little kids sat in the front rows. Gawked at the moving images towering above them.

Flickering Technicolor darkness showed Luc no empty seats amidst the heads in the teenagers' section. The grandmother he sat next to kept turning to see awe on her daughter's face, the only movie Gramma cared about.

Luc watched the crowd as the same rainbows lit their faces as his.

All of us got broken songs, he thought. *Break some, too. I'm not special.*

He sensed the end of the movie. Slid out of his seat before the final crescendo of sound. Stood by the concession stand where he could watch the coming crowds stream out of the auditorium's two doors.

People! I want to see people! I like people! I'm here! Glasses and goofy smile and yeah, so what, I'll spot somebody who'll like that, go say "Hi!" and—

Out of the moviegoers' exiting stream appeared Cherie—

—holding hands with her fellow just-promoted to sophomore Andy who played bass guitar and had watched her as he sang in the chorus at Prom.

Andy let go of Cherie's hand.

Strode toward Luc.

Cherie stood in the streaming moviegoers. Tried to beam up to Mars.

Andy grinned. Stepped straight up to Luc.

Reached up with his guitar plucking hand to *pat-pat* Luc's left cheek.

Went back to Cherie. Used that same hand to take hers.

They walked out into their warm May night.

THE BOOGEYMAN

Luc drove the gray '54 over the two-lane blacktop highway heading east of town through that last evening of July 1965, the week when the world changed.

The breeze through his rolled-down windows brushed his bare arms. Dried the summer sweat but left the summer heat. He spun the radio dial off KRIP as the news reported the tally of Americans killed in Vietnam's war had reached 871. A distant big city station crackled The Four Tops' "I Can't Help Myself."

The Grady River Four County Fair & Rodeo was in town.

"And what I'm thinking," Mr. Tom had told Luc, "all the hours you been janitorin' the drive-in, five nights every week in the projection booth, figure you need a break. It's the last night, so why don't you go out t' the fair? I'll projector first show, you run the second. Get to the booth at say . . . by a quarter to 9:00?"

Hell yes!

Wasn't the fair or a blue ribbon won by a sobbing 4H girl as Mabel the cow she'd bred with evolution and raised from a wobbly calf was led off *Sold!* to the slaughterhouse that pulled Luc onto the highway that night. Wasn't pens of snorting pigs. Rows of farm machinery. Wasn't the arts and crafts, sewing and baking contests. Wasn't the white grandstands where sun-leathered ticket buyers watched horse races or a rodeo or some bandstand night show of Broadway razzle-dazzle by troupes from as far back east as St. Paul.

Was the carnival.

Luc drove the '54 two miles east of town past towering gray grain elevators and brown railroad cars parked on side tracks to the fenced-in fairgrounds to see those bright lights of lies and sighs, screams and dreams.

There's the Tilt-A-Whirl spinning laughing kids. There's the Merry-Go-Round with moms or dads holding wide-eyed children onto their first wooden horse. There's that year's "special attraction" to wow thrill seekers spinning around in a rocket or splashing through a roller coaster spectacular. Over there are the carny cons—"Just one thin dime gets you the chance of a lifetime!"

That year boasted a sword swallower and a fortune teller who prophesized blindfolded. Luc walked the packed oiled midway earth to see if the geek who'd trapped him and Marin the summer when they were ten had returned.

Past, present, future, thought Luc. It's all right here, right now.

Carnival lights twinkled. Glowed the night. Let him see the crowd of people strolling with him. He was alone. But he was there. Someplace special. Not in his own head or at work. Was like being in a movie or novel or a song. Being part of the guitar strum. The changing scene. The turning page.

There was TARS sponsor *Mom* Nora coaxing her pouty elementary school daughter to stop frowning, to see—*see*—how they were having fun.

There was Donna taking a break from waitressing at the Elks Club's burgers and beer stand. Her short blonde hair brushed her blue eyes as she leaned her polio leg's side against the stand's white wall and listened to an oil-slicked black-haired man.

There was Bobbi Jean solo walking toward the parking lot.

Over there by the Tilt-A-Whirls:

Alice. Curled blonde hair and white blouse. Standing with her crew for that Saturday night. Wendy but not Buffy. Fred but not Kitty. Linda, night off from the Roxy, too. Mel and Clancy with their leaving-town eyes.

Alice waved at Luc.

Watched him wave back.

Turned to the crew she'd met up with, said: "So what's gonna happen now?"

"Nothing here," said Fred as he met her restless gaze: "Let's go."

"Where would we go?" said Mel.

"And what would we do when we got there?" said Clancy.

"I want to go on some rides," said Wendy. "Why else go to the carnival?"

Alice smiled at her friend: "Go. I can catch a ride with Fred."

"I've got the white convertible," said Fred.

"Of course you do," said Clancy.

They chattered. Waved. Went their separate ways.

"Promise me one thing," Alice told Fred as their shoes crunched over the prairie earth of the parking lot.

The crimson sky lit Fred's grin: "Sure!"

"Promise you'll keep the top down."

They were out of the parking lot in two minutes.

Stopped at the dirt road intersection with the two-lane blacktop highway.

Fred did a movie star turn from behind the steering wheel to show her and see her. White blouse and black shorts with *just-so* curves. Tanned bare legs. Her blonde hair curled and falling to her jawline and its smiling pink-glossed lips.

"Where to?" he said.

"Right down the middle of Main Street."

The open white convertible carried them into town where no one was on Main's drag to see them drive by: the fair was in town.

"Let's get out of *just here*," she said.

Fred gunned the white convertible north past the drive-in theater with its sixty-foot-high screen filled with Technicolor tiptoeing images of a bumbling Paris police inspector and a beautiful blonde who was *mais oui* innocent of murder.

Alice sank into the shotgun seat of the white convertible. Draped her eyes as the sultry summer night air flowed over her being driven ever faster, ever further into that rising full moon night.

She watched Fred turn off the highway to a gravel road.

Let him park the car on a prairie plateau miles from any human eyes.

He reached for the ignition keys—

"Leave it on," she said. "For the radio."

"You're listening to KOMA Oklahoma City," came the scratchy broadcast from nearly two thousand miles south of the white convertible. "Fifty thousand watts of rock 'n' roll coming straight to you."

The radio played "I Got You, Babe," a love song duet where the savvy woman had long black hair and the goofy man died in a skiing accident while serving as a Republican US congressman thirty-three years after this Saturday night.

Warm wind brushed the white convertible bathed by the full moon. Alice and Fred watched each other in the glow of the idling car's dashboard lights.

Alice sat all the way over there by the passenger's door.

Fred scooted out from under the steering wheel and closer to her.

They'd been alone and close before. Wrapped around each other in a closet at a parents-gone house party. In a parked car where their necking filled the front seat while Steve and Buffy's embraces filled the back.

Now Fred stretched his arm along the back of the front seat.

"You know you've always been special to me," he told Alice.

She laughed: "Every girl you get like this is special to you."

"Well . . . Yeah. But maybe you're—"

"I'm not anybody's *maybe*," said Alice. "I'm *me*."

They leaned together in the familiar kiss of *for sure* friends.

Six minutes and a mile of tongues later, his hand cupped her breast.

Panting, can't take his eyes off her, Fred said: "Let's go in the backseat."

"Is that what you want?"

"Don't you?" asked Fred.

THE BOOGEYMAN & Alice Is in Fourth Grade.

Nine years old. Neighbor boy—fourteen. Knock-knock.

Let him in. You know him. Where are your parents?

At work.

He grabs the little girl. Slobbers all over her face.

No! No!

Slams her into the living room rug. Arm pressing her down.

Under her skirt pulls off panties, hand pushing her face down through carpet to where Daddy says Hell is.

Can't scream! Barely breathe. He's down there—

Owww Ahh nn . . . nn . . . nn . . . HURTS!

Dead bear on her.

Tell anyone what we did and you'll get in big trouble!

And I'll get you. And no one will believe you. And they'll send you away and lock you up.

And he's gone and she's sobbing on the living room rug. Clean it up 'fore Mom comes home and he's gone and never let him see you and he's gone and family moves to Vernon in seventh grade and he's gone, he's gone, he's The Boogeyman who keeps showing up, laughing in her skull and . . . and . . .

"*What I want*," whispered Alice.

She jerked open the car's door. Fred fell out face first onto the prairie. She bent the front seat down to clear the way. Shoved him into the backseat of the top-down white convertible as the radio played.

"Promise me two things!"

Fred frantically nodded.

"Don't make me pregnant."

"You won't! I won't! I've got—I know how! I've done this before!"

"Even with all you guys' bullshit brags, *yeah*, I know. Kitty told me."

Alice stood in the open door of that white convertible.

"One more thing. Promise me this. You won't push me down to do it."

"We can work it that way!"

Alice stared at the boy who was one year older than her sixteen as he hovered and throbbed in the backseat of a white convertible.

She tossed her white blouse into the front seat.

Reached around. Undid her bra. Tossed it—

—saw it drape over the car's steering wheel.

She slipped out of her sneakers.

Pushed her shorts and panties off in one *whoosh*.

Stepped into the backseat.

Stood there—one foot on the floor, one foot on the cushion.

Naked.

She felt the breezy heat of this night in July. Glanced over the white convertible's trunk and through its flashy fins.

The Boogeyman.

Shimmering there.

She yelled so loud the stars shook: "*FUCK YOU!*"

Then she—*she*—lowered her naked self to where she chose to be as the KOMA DJ broadcast: "Have you out there in radio-land heard about the controversy that exploded Sunday night? You know, at—"

Then panting-breaths and thundering-heartbeats Alice and Fred tuned out what was coming from the engine-purring car's radio.

The ghostly Boogeyman shimmered away from Alice.

As the moon watched.

And Luc stood in the deep heat projection booth of the Roxy theater.

Stared out a slot window toward the big screen.

A heroine kissed the man who was worth it after all.

What does it take for me to be that guy? thought Luc.

Thoughts of Buffy shimmered through him.

This year, couple months, we'll be juniors. Upperclassmen.

Steve will be a senior. Still here, but maybe. Maybe.

"Maybe" is what gets us up in the morning.

He turned from the slot windows of the movie he worked. Walked to the workbench. Turned the radio there on, already knowing its volume was set so low he had to lean close to hear its sounds from the world beyond.

The long antennae brought in scratchy KOMA rock 'n' roll:

"—out there in radio-land heard about the controversy that exploded Sunday night? You know, at the Newport Folk Festival when Bob Dylan gets up on the stage . . . and plugs in an electric guitar! At a folk music festival!

"Some of the crowd booed him. That's right: *Booed!*

"And then he plays like a rock 'n' roll guy. With that song that, well, *you* tell *me* what it's about. He shook things up. Guess now instead of just rock 'n' roll, we're gonna have some new kind of rock. And while the Stones and Beatles and like them have already been pushing Buddy Holly and Elvis, plus Motown and the Beach Boys' California sound, after Dylan plugged in electric in front of a booing crowd, guess now we got some real rebels.

"Give a listen. Here's what he played: 'Like a Rolling Stone.'"

Through that moonlit night from some faraway place in the universe . . .

. . . to a sixteen-year-old, glasses-wearing dreamer in a white T-shirt and blue jeans amidst the colors and celluloid smells of the movie playing behind him . . .

. . . came the *Ba-bump* of a drum. The *Scree* of an organ. Guitars. The nasal twang, unpolished voice of a future Nobel Prize for Literature winner stepping out of a classic opening from hundreds of stories from our childhoods into *NOW*:

"*Once upon a time . . .*"

For five minutes and fifty-nine seconds, Luc was in that Once Upon a Time. Not just *here* working in a hot projection booth in a nowhere town.

He was *there*. In the song. In the whole of it. The hole of it. Surrounded by guitars, organs and one lone voice sharing stories Luc recognized but couldn't always *grok*, stories with him *in* them and *outside* of them in the same heartbeat.

The song ended.

Luc leaned back from the workbench to—

Hello! Who are you?

A green rubber army man commanded a slot above and beyond the radio.

The toy soldier was on his stomach. No rifle in his hand.

Luc's fingers and thumb lifted the toy soldier out of his slot.

Played with guys like you for hours when I was a kid, thought Luc. *You must belong to one of Mr. Tom's grandkids. And now you're here.*

He tilted the toy soldier so they were face to face.

You're looking up. Looking to see where you're going. Crawling to get there.

Luc smiled: *Me, too.*

The Change Projectors warning bell went *ding ding ding*.

Luc put the soldier back in his slot.

Whispered to the soldier like the song they'd just heard:

"How does it feel?"

AMBUSH

Now is—has got to *be*—*a brand-new everything*, thought Luc as he walked down the morning sun's front steps of the house he'd lived in for his whole life.

The keys to the gray '54 Dodge dangled from his right hand.

His left hand carried virgin spiral notebooks and a paperback book.

He wore no jacket that warm early September 1965 Monday morn. The Marine Corps cut the number of its boot camp training weeks from twelve to eight to churn out more warriors at a faster rate for the Vietnam "conflict" that now claimed 1,067 dead American soldiers. Protestors filled the streets of Ukraine because Russian secret police locked up their intellectuals and artists who might have been triggered by a movie called *Shadows of Forgotten Ancestors*.

Luc ached from football practice.

Glanced across the street to the hospital.

Told himself: *Aches are just part of life*.

Now it was Registration Day, when you were told where you were supposed to be.

And he was a junior. An *upper*classman. Him and his buddies Wayne, Kurt and Marin. Alice and Wendy. Donna with her limp. Buffy with . . . Buffy.

Luc settled behind the gray '54's steering wheel.

Rolled down the driver's window. Smelled the day. Autumn leaves. The pine trees in the front yard.

The engine chugged to life.

On his way to be the *who* everybody'd decided he was back in fifth grade: College, then lawyer school.

Maybe a tour in the Army via Reserved Officers Training Corps in college.

The gray '54 Dodge rumbled down Main Street. Past the Roxy movie theater. Past the second-story office where Doc Nirmberg leaned his shotgun. Past where a metal parking meter pole proclaimed "Taxi Stand" for the blue taxi.

Part of Luc's channeled way mandated Key Club, the service group of nerd boys who kept a B average and swore never to break the law or drink.

I gave my word, thought Luc. *I gotta make that mean something.*

Luc parked in the student lot.

Stepped into streams of teenagers in the sunlit September halls.

After he picked up his class assignment slip signed by the speech teacher—*Debate Club, here I come!*—Luc strolled through the halls, looking for Buffy.

Spotted Tod.

Who stood at the railing above the open view, long fall down to the ground floor. Faced the wall of windows that bathed him in changing seasons' sunlight.

With closed eyes.

Luc called out: "*Tod! What are you doing?*"

Tod turned toward the sound of the name he'd been given.

Flashing through Luc came: *He's got fugitive eyes.*

"You OK?" said Luc as he stepped between Tod and gravity's railing.

"OK?" said Tod. "Why wouldn't I be?"

Luc made a soft shrug and a safe sigh.

"Yeah," he told fugitive eyes. "No big deal now. Just Registration Day."

"So this is when they tell us who we are." Tod's smile was an obvious lie but Luc didn't know what to do about that. "I guess I better get to it."

His fugitive eyes brushed the streaming crowd of hormonal teenagers. Those eyes never lingered where The World said they shouldn't.

Tod turned to march down the switchback stairs.

Whatever that was, thought Luc, *I can't do anything else.*

He swung his way down the stairs to his own locker, 152.

Spun the combination on the slip of paper issued him by the office. Three easy spins. Jerk the handle up/pull back . . . and *voila*, like he'd learned in French: That locker's empty space was his for that year.

Well, his and Danny's, who was a jock and thus one of the cool kids.

Luc stacked his two new spiral notebooks on the top shelf.

Weighed the notebooks down with the paperback book.

Backed away to close the door—

—and there stood Steve.

THE REAL DEAL

Two teenage boys stand by an open locker in a high school hallway.

They both hear Mike's infectious laugh somewhere down the hall.

They both wear glasses, one set like windows, the other like Coke bottles.

They both wear front-buttoned short-sleeve shirts. A muscled chest strains one of the shirts. One male is taller but they still look eye to eye.

Steve said: "Ahh . . . *Hey*."

"*Hey*," echoed Luc, staring at his bushwhacker.

Steve's nervous gaze flicked away from Luc and into the open locker. Nodded toward what he saw: "What are you reading?"

Luc handed the drugstore paperback to Steve.

"*The Man with the Golden Gun*," said Steve. "A James Bond book. I've seen some of the movies."

"Only the book is out now," said Luc.

"Is it any good?" said Steve. "I've never read any of them."

"Ian Fleming, the author, he's the real deal. He was a spy."

"The real deal." Steve shook his head. "Good to know."

Luc frowned: "What are *you* reading?"

"*Catch-22*. It's not just about World War II where it's set. There's . . . You know, how a good story gives you more than its plot."

Then—four decades *before* it became a National Security Alert—Steve changed his voice to quote that novel: "*Where are the Snowdens of yesteryear?*"

What Luc thought was: *Catch-22! Gotta get it!*

What Luc said was: "Where are any of us?"

"Ain't that the truth." Steve shrugged. "The truth is, we do the best with what we got and find what's new to get."

Luc's brow furrowed as he answered: "Guess so."

"And that's what you 'n' me do," said Steve. "Neither of us are bad guys."

He stepped away from Luc. Joined subtle-smile blonde Alice walking past with curly-haired Wendy and her big brother Ed who was a senior like Steve.

Their quartet of *cool* walked down the hallway away from Luc with his open locker and his open mouth that went: "*Huh?*"

WHO WE GOTTA BE

Steve felt Luc's eyes ride his back as he walked away alongside Alice.

"Didn't see much of you this summer," said Steve.

Alice smiled. "My family went to the lake."

"Fred said you two went out a couple times."

"Once or twice," she said. "Neither of us wants to get tied down."

Alice's eyes twinkled: "I didn't see much of you either."

"Working for my dad fixing up houses."

Wendy grinned at Steve: "Are you and Ed in any classes together?"

Wendy's brother Ed answered: "Senior English. The B class."

"They say that's who we gotta be," said Steve.

"Yeah," said brother Ed. "Yeah."

Alice told Wendy and her brother Ed: "You two go on ahead. See you in the car. Steve and I gotta talk about something I saw."

Wendy and Ed had only gone three steps before the curly brown-haired sister of the crew playfully snatched her big brother's registration card from his hand. Pursed her lips in a movie's exaggerated smile—

—that blinked into a frown:

"How come there aren't any college prep classes on here?"

"You're kidding me," said Ed. "College is money and we aren't. You know that. If Mom didn't cut and sew last year's dresses from Dad's samples case, you'd be wearing the same thing every day. Hell, money's what had Mom and Dad all worried about this morning at the breakfast table with his suitcase packed for him to go out on the road again for sales calls."

"Was that what it was?" said Wendy. "They were saying nothing when I walked in. Just looking at each other over cups of coffee."

"Must have been," said Ed.

"I miss him when he goes on the road. We laugh more when he's home."

"You always got a smile going on, Sis."

"With all we got, why wouldn't I?"

Her enthusiasm made her brother smile along with her.

"I'll meet you in the car," Wendy told her brother as he headed toward the students' parking lot. "I've got to check my locker stuff for Tumblers & Twirlers."

Wendy sailed into the women's locker room. Said "*Hi!*" to her and "*Hey!*" to her and "*Yay!*" to her before she reached the locker the same time as . . .

It's sophomore-now Cherie!

"Hey, how are you?" said junior-now Wendy.

She leaned in: "Are you still dating Andy?"

Cherie sighed.

"We're off, we're on, we're who knows where," she said. "He spends nights in a garage. Bass guitar in the *gonna be so great* band that keeps breaking up. Plus, I had to spend *weeks* all summer living out at the farm."

Cherie shook her head: "I gotta get a town job."

"Maybe get a new guy," said Wendy.

"Either they don't see me or I don't see them," said Cherie.

"Somebody told me you dated Luc."

"For *one* date," said Cherie. "Prom. Then he just walked away."

"But oh well," she said: "Andy walked up."

Cherie and Wendy checked their white-uniforms women's locker room.

"I gotta run!" said Wendy. "See ya!"

Cherie checked her wristwatch. Her family—*her dad*—insisted she had to be on time for everything from Catholic Church Confession to cleaning the barn.

But now it was Registration Day. An open schedule day.

She could stroll around the school. See her friends.

Cherie walked past the first-floor girls' bathroom near the school's exit.

Heard: "*Bwhalacckgrr!*"

Push that door open.

"Hello?" she called out. "Is everything OK?"

Whoosh! went the flushing toilet inside a closed gray metal stall.

The stall door swung open and out shuffled chopped-blonde-haired Donna.

"I'm just sick," said Donna.

She turned on a sink's faucet. Cupped the stream of water into her hands and gulped as much as she could from that pool trapped in her grasp.

Spit it out and did it again.

Donna raised up from the sink. Stared into the wall of mirrors.

Cherie said: "It's Registration Day. You don't have to stick around until tomorrow. You could just go home."

Thought: *Why do I keep running into girls in trouble in toilet stalls?*

"Yeah," said Donna as she faced herself in the mirror. "Just go home."

Donna pulled a coarse brown paper hand towel from a white box dispenser.

"Well," said Cherie as she backed outside. "Long as you're fine."

The door to the world outside closed behind her.

Just-starting-to-be-a-junior Donna dried her hands.

The wall of mirrors trapped her reflection.

She threw up yesterday morning.

Wondered if she'd puke tomorrow.

Remembered working the food stand at that summer's county fair where she *met*. Where a guy finally took a shine to her. Where she did what she could and wanted to do. Sort of. Obviously. *Oh yeah*, she thought. *Obviously.*

Donna shouted to Cherie's getaway from the empty women's bathroom of the Big Pink high school: *"AS LONG AS I'M FINE?* Why wouldn't I be *FINE!"*

WHAT DO YOU KNOW?

Luc steeled himself for football practice that Registration Day.

I just gotta make it through this season, Luc told himself in the locker room as he strapped on his shoulder pads. *Moent's still head coach, so he makes sure everybody on the team steps onto the playing field for at least two quarters so they'll get gold V letters for a letterman's jacket like I already bought. Then everybody will see I'm not just who they think I am.*

The gold helmet's cage mask kept his metal athletic glasses fitted with last year's less-thick lenses from getting smashed. He was the geekiest guy on the team. Finished last in all the sprints. Held heavy stuffed-canvas blocking dummies for his teammates. He knew his place. Who he was. Who he wasn't.

But that Registration Day practice—

—even beyond Luc's heartbeat of counterfeit glory—

—ranked as strange.

School librarian Mrs. Dawson sat in the white wooden bleachers.

Why is she here? thought Luc.

He stood with other third string players on the sidelines beneath her steady gaze. A book waited on the seat beside her.

Principal Harris marched onto that field across from *his* Big Pink.

Harris lumbered up to the man holding the whistle of command. Loomed so close to the coach that they could have kissed. Harris's lips rolled questions.

Then came *movie magic.*

Coach Moent's mouth *slow motion* opened cartoon-wide. Answers drawled out. Bathed his boss with their *wa–wah–wa* and scent.

The smile Moent gave the principal said *fuck you.*

Got back Harris's gorilla sneer.

Coach Moent turned his back to what had been done.

"You guys on the sidelines!" he yelled. "Get in here! Your turn."

They all charged toward where the first two varsity squads stood.

Principal Harris marched through them going the other way.

Luc heard Harris yell up to the woman sitting in the bleachers: "Your husband must be wondering where you are!"

Coach Moent sent Luc and other third string players on opposites sides of the brown football. The coach waved varsity stars to fill any empty positions.

Luc found himself on his hands and knees at the line of scrimmage.

Defensive guard.

You get hit every time that brown football is snapped.

"*Hut!*"

However many *huts* each of those first two plays called didn't matter.

Luc was always the last to surge when the ball got snapped.

Each snap of the ball crashed Luc into faster, bigger, stronger, combat-armored guys. That scrimmage's second play left Luc sprawled on his back. He rolled over to his hands and knees. Didn't care who saw him. Crawled like a baby back to his place on the line of pain.

He lifted his gold-helmeted head. His off-kilter glasses filled with the laughing boxer-like image of a new kid in school.

Who was his cousin.

"Third cousin," said Luc's mom. "My—our Conner side. He needed a place to stay, so other family closer to him took him in."

"He could stay in our basement. In Laura's pink bedroom."

Luc's mother who burned with anxiety if library books on the living room end table were stacked crooked shuddered with the thought of anyone besides the four members of her marriage-made family staying overnight in her house where everything must always be as it was supposed to be.

"He's better off there." Luc's mom wiped the kitchen table. "Thank God he doesn't have to go live with strangers like some kids."

"Why can't he stay with his own family up in Shelby?"

"You never know the *cans* and *can'ts* for any family."

Luc's mom fussed around the kitchen. Kept her back to him. Stood tight and tall so her kids and husband would be alright. Be safe. So everything will be fine.

"If they're lucky, a family gets a chance. 'Specially for a good kid like him."

Him was Gene Pezzani.

"Yeah," confirmed Gramma Meg Conner in the after-dinner visit to the nursing home. "But he's blood Montanan, not *Eye*-talian. Just like our other Pezzanis up their house on Knob Hill."

Gramma Meg's steel eyes filled with grandson Luc standing beside her bed. Told him: "Names don't tell you no more 'n a place to start seeing."

That Registration Day football practice, crawling on his hands and knees, Luc saw his "new" cousin Gene laughing as he huddled up with the other team.

They broke their huddle. Trotted to their places across from Luc's team.

WHONK/SLAM! Two blockers blasted into Luc. Flipped him into the air. Crashed him into the packed grass so hard that he rocketed back up—

—*WHAM!* The ball carrier leapt over the pile of blockers and defenders. Accidentally kicked Luc's face cage. Steel cleats knocked Luc back to the grass even as that collision tripped and flipped the ball carrier flat on his face.

Luc lay there dazed.

"*Nice tackle, Luc!*"

The yell of cleats-kicker and ball-carrier Gene.

Heard by everybody.

A hand pulled Luc to his feet.

Someone on his team said: "Good job."

And *whoa*, Luc knew the compliment was meant for him.

Praise for randomly and unwittingly getting kicked in the face.

Nobody saw the *cause*, only the *effect*. And made their call.

Luc settled his gold helmet into place.

His counterfeit moment of glory was over.

Tweet!

Moent yelled for everyone to "Bring it in!"

Luc heard words from the coach. Clapped with others. Turned with the team to run the lap around the goalposts and head to the Big Pink's locker room.

He saw no sign of Principal Harris.

Mrs. Dawson stood in the white bleachers holding her book.

Luc popped the chin strap on his gold helmet. Used both hands to lift that protection off his head as he loped toward a steamy shower. Realized:

There's always more happening on the field than you know.

THE FACE IN THE MIRROR

*W*here is he? thought Buffy as she searched the high school hall swarming with fellow students on Tuesday's first real day of classes in her junior year. *Hell, WHO is he? Who am I looking for?*

That's. Not. Funny.

Last Friday, she'd turned the pages of *TIME* magazine while working the counter at their family floral shop.

Saw pictures and words about that August's "race riot" in a place called Watts somewhere close to Los Angeles where Hollywood ruled and the Beach Boys surfed. The article said the final tally for the Watts Riots meant thirty-four people died and the cost was $40 million in property damage *plus* whatever it cost for the 14,000 fixed-bayonets National Guardsmen to "put down" the riots.

She stared at pictures of Watts's sad and sullen Black faces staring out from the ashes of the lives they'd been allotted. Imagined her idolized trio of The Supremes walking those sidewalks.

Not fair, thought Buffy. None of that.

She turned the page of *TIME.*

Spotted a story that said the war in Vietnam had so far cost 1,074 American lives, but we were winning the hearts and minds of—

DING! went the bell above the floral shop's Main Street door.

In walked her dad.

Now as she walked the halls of her high school on the First Day of her junior year, OMG: *She still couldn't believe it!*

"Got a delivery for you," Dad'd said. "There's a bouquet on the table in back. Take the van. Run it up to . . . you know, the . . . the red house north of—"

The whisper blew out of her: "*The whorehouse!*"

"Watch your language, young lady!"

"Watch my . . . But you want me to go to . . . No. No! NO! *NO!*"

"This is business," her father told his horrified daughter. "It's what we're supposed to do. Sell—and it's all legal! Money don't care where it comes from or where it goes. It's up to us to take it for the honest work we do and what we sell them fair and square. Just like the grocery store gets. The laundromat."

But Buffy still refused to put her fists on the van's steering wheel for *that*.

What happens between men and women can't be BUSINESS! I can't be any part of THAT! What's between us 'n' guys has got to be, should be, will be—

Buffy blinked: *Keep walking. Keep searching for him. Gotta do this right.*

Check the mirror for how you look!

Put her hand on the flat blonde wood door into the GIRLS room in the same heartbeat as Donna's straight-arm push.

Something about Donna's surge told Buffy to let her burst into the GIRLS bathroom first.

Buffy flowed into Donna's wake: *She's hurrying so fast with a crippled leg!* Then . . . *Oh then!*

Two steps into the bathroom they both froze at the sight of *bizarre*.

A girl bent over a rushing-water sink in front of the wall of mirrors dunked her face into the filling-up sink's lake.

The dunked girl whirled up:

It's Sandi Khoury! A junior with Donna and Buffy, neither's close friend.

Water sheen dripped over her teenage girl's face that had been scrubbed hard with bleach and thick bristle brushes.

One glance of lava-faced Sandi and Donna ran into the gray metal stall. Puked.

She can't stand the horror, thought Buffy.

Sandi grabbed paper towels she'd stacked by the sink to wipe—

"Oww!" whispered Sandi as coarse brown paper brushed her raw red face.

Donna puked again in the gray metal stall.

"*Hey-hey-hey!*" Buffy rushed to Sandi. Turned off the sink. Took the paper towels from the sobbing girl's hands. "It's going to be OK."

She dabbed the paper towels over Sandi's red cheeks.

"It hurts so bad!" whispered Sandi. "My face's on fire, had cool it down!"

The toilet flushed in the gray metal stall.

Donna appeared. Hesitated. Walked to the sink. Grabbed brown paper towels. Helped pat dry Sandi's bright pink First Day of School blouse.

"Don't worry," Buffy told her whimpering classmate Sandi. "Won't lie to you. Your face is bright burning red. But it'll go back to regular in a few hours."

Told this girl she *sort-of* knew: "There's better ways to get rid of pimples."

Sandi . . . *Burst out laughing!*

"Pimples!" said Sandi. "I wish I had pimples!"

She shook her head.

"My parents," she told these two girls she seldom spoke to. "They scrub my skin. They want . . . My dad's Lebanese. Came over as a refugee after fighting with us—with the Americans against the Nazis. Now my parents are afraid my *olive skin* will . . . that I'll be . . . That people here will hold it against me."

Donna with polio's limp said: "It's only part of you."

"Besides," said Buffy, "nobody's ever noticed it's . . . that you're . . ."

"*Not White.*"

"You're *American*," said Buffy. "That's who you are. Who we all are."

The three of them saw their reflections in the mirror of here and now.

Sandi sighed. Closed her eyes. Opened them:

"But what will I say if anybody asks why my skin is so . . . burned?"

"Stick with the pimples story," said Buffy. "People will believe that. We all do stupid things and get caught."

Sandi whispered: "*Thank you!*"

Hurried out of the GIRLS room so they wouldn't see her cry.

Donna faced the same sink. Turned those faucets back on to rinse out her just-puked mouth. Used the last of Sandi's paper towel stack to dry her own face.

"We all do stupid things," repeated Donna. Trembled like she was scared.

Puking a couple times will do that to you, thought Buffy.

"Let's keep all this between us," said Buffy. "We don't want to embarrass Sandi even more. This is America! She's supposed to have a choice!"

"*Supposed to* isn't *always.*"

"No shit." Buffy sighed. "But what are you going to do."

"Yeah." Donna's eyes fell into the mirror. "What am I gonna do?"

Buffy blinked:

Doesn't Donna know "what are you going to do" is just what people say?

Buffy sent her another cliché: "Guess we just keep on keeping on."

The girls' reflections in the wall of mirrors stared at each other.

"You're nicer than I thought," whispered Donna.

Buffy blushed: "*Naw.* I'm just like you and everybody else."

"Like me," mumbled Donna. Shook her head, not knowing all that she felt.

RING!

First Bell. Five minutes to Last Bell and Better Be in Your Classroom.

"*Aaaa!*" said Buffy. "I still gotta find—*Bye!*"

She dashed from that GIRLS room's scent of vomit and tears.

Left Donna alone staring at her own reflection in that wall of mirrors.

WHERE YOU ARE

L uc steered the gray '54 through that same Tuesday morning's streets.
Felt like he was in a movie.
Does anybody else ever feel like they're in a movie?
In this movie, I'm driving an old gray car through my hometown.
His buddy Wayne rode shotgun as they motored to their junior year's First (real) Day of High School. The car radio crackled with the Rolling Stones' throbbing-guitars and pounding-drums song "(I Can't Get No) Satisfaction."
No shit, thought Luc.
Forced a grin: *This year is going to be SO different!*
Right?
Then came the question that had puzzled him since kindergarten:
How old are the heroes in movies?
How old do I have to be? When will I get to be? Will I get to be? And get . . .
Get what the hero gets.
The special smile of that dream woman when Everything Is Swell.
Luc flashed on guys about his age fighting in the jungles of Vietnam.
Next year I register for the Draft, thought Luc. His mind blanked.
The gray '54 turned onto the viaduct to cross over the railroad tracks.
"I don't get it," argued Wayne.
"I don't get *you*," said Luc. "This'll work fine for us, too. We all got football, so we need a ride home from practice besides getting to school every day.
"And those guys: *Kyle,* whose mom is my mom's best friend, their family cars broke down. He gives my cousin *Gene* and *Gideon*—I hung out with Kyle and Gideon when we went to the convention in Helena—Kyle is their ride. So least for a week or so, we carpool with all of them 'n' I drive.

"Starting tomorrow."

Luc shook his head as they drove past the drive-in restaurant Aunt Beryl had owned since coffee murdered Uncle Johnny.

"What's . . . Why are you all pissed off?"

"Kurt's coming back to ride with us after we're done with football and . . . We're the kind of guys who don't . . . I won't get in trouble. Those guys . . ."

"They're our friends," said Luc.

The car hummed to the student parking lot at the Big Pink.

They rolled out of the car. Books in hand. Slammed the doors.

Luc couldn't help himself:

He whipped off his thick-lens glasses like they were cool sunglasses.

Saw a blur.

Wore a smile as he put his glasses back on and saw the Real World.

Told himself to walk it like he was new and Everything Was Different.

Luc and Wayne strode together into the Big Pink.

Wayne broke away from Luc: "I gotta pee."

Luc frowned amidst streaming teenagers. Wayne's retreat toward the BOYS room door looked calmer than the urgency his assertion implied.

First Day grins and "Hi's!" greeted Luc as he walked down the corridor to his locker. He heard Mike Jodrey's happy laugh. The wave of stocky Walt's hand pulled Luc to lockers where Walt stood beside nervous Tod.

They said their "Heys"—

—though while Tod's face said he was hearing them, Luc saw Tod's gaze flow away through the hallway of streaming teenagers.

Walt's voice said: "You two ready for what they signed us up for last spring?"

"Would it matter?" said Luc. "I don't care about trigonometry or chemistry.

"I mean *I do*," he added. "We gotta know enough about everything to know what's going on with anything. But . . . *um* . . . You guys, you . . ."

"*Us guys*," said Walt, "Stern—*Good name for a guidance counselor, right?*—him and Principal Harris think guys like me and Tod and most girls don't need to know what they obviously can't understand because of who their parents are."

Walt shrugged. "Guess I'll get it on my own. What about you, Tod?"

The sound of his name jerked the nervous teenage boy.

Tod's eyes pulled back from watching someone further down the hall.

Luc glanced that way—

Saw Steve.

Of course it was Steve who Tod was staring at! Looking cool. A hunk of a guy. Who every guy wants to be. Who fills girls' eyes and throbs their hearts.

Tod whirled back to Luc and Walt.

Blurted: *"Ah* . . . Chemistry. Yeah. I mean, I hope I get it."

"You got the brains for it," said Walt. "So be who you are."

Todd blinked.

Flicked his gaze back to Steve.

Luc looked, too: Steve was heading up the stairs to the second floor where Luc needed to go. And—he was pretty sure—so did Buffy.

Get to her first! triggered Luc: "Gotta run, guys!"

Luc raced to his locker. Spun that gray metal door open. Glanced to his left.

Saw Bobbi Jean walking out of the Music Department's double glass doors leading back to practice rooms and music teachers' offices.

There's Marin standing near the stairs Steve'd climbed!

But not just "standing there."

Marin, who'd been Luc's buddy since fifth grade. Who Luc saw the insurance salesman curse *"son of a bitch Injun"* at. Who shared novels with Luc. Who ran long distance races for the high school track team that bought him some freedom. Marin with his brushed-flat, home-barbered black hair and tan skin.

Marin stood there at the bottom of stairs leading up to the next level.

Holding hands with a freshman girl named Barbara.

Beautiful Barbara. Golden dawn hair. Heavy fullness in her white blouse. Strong lean legs covered by a black skirt the principal's ruler would measure as just barely at the required no-higher-than-knee length.

Luc blinked: *Wait, when—how—did that happen?*

You're so lucky! Luc wanted to (but didn't) shout to his buddy Marin.

That could be me this year, too! thought Luc. *If I can just get Buffy to see—*

RING! First Bell.

Luc grabbed what he needed from his locker. Scurried toward the stairs.

Saw Donna limping up them ahead of him. Falling behind other hurrying students who zigzagged around her ascent.

Luc's two-steps-at-a-time search for someone else hurried him to her side.

But he dropped his pace to hers. Gave the girl he'd known since fifth grade a smile: "Hey, you figure we'll be sitting next to each this year?"

Donna's face went from trembling to rigid: *"What?"*

"You know, our last names. They sit us alphabetical, so . . ."

She shook her head as they navigated the switchback turn.

"You think you're in the same class as me?" said Donna.

They turned to start down the hall.

Blonde Alice and curly brown-haired Wendy hurried their way, saw Luc—
—quickly looked away like they knew some *Oh-oh!* he didn't.

Down the hall behind them, Luc saw Buffy.

She's standing in the open door of our trig class! Like she's waiting for . . .

"Gotta run!" said Luc to Donna as he fled from her toward the dream.

Buffy on that new school year morning. Soft pink gloss. A waterfall of milk chocolate hair falling down along her lean face. She clutched her schoolbooks and cinnamon cover binder across her chest, her breasts, her heart.

Was an awkward way she'd positioned her arms to hold her burden.

Her white-bloused left arm strained to cup her schoolbooks stuffed helter-skelter behind a faded cinnamon binder.

Her right arm rose up the middle of that binder's shield to hold it close so her still summer-tanned hand spread wide and flat against the cinnamon.

No one could miss seeing the back of her splayed-open right hand.

She'd blurted at Luc when he was still three steps away from her stance with her back to the open trig class door: "Hi! I haven't seen you for—"

Blink and Luc saw it all.

Her right hand displayed on the cinnamon cover for the world to see.

For him to see without any awkward words needing to be said:

Steve's class ring wrapped with yarn so it wouldn't slip off Buffy's finger.

Her friendly patter faded into echoes in the hallway of everybody's high school as Luc saw and knew exactly where he was:

They're going steady. Nobody else. Now I'm for-sure just some "friend."

He felt himself go hollow and sink as Buffy babbled on.

RING!

Final Bell!

Buffy whirled her retreat through the classroom's open door.

Yesterday's ghost of Steve's sincere alert whispered: "*We do the best with what we got and find what's new to get.*"

Final Bell's echo faded in the high school hallway where only Luc stood.

He took a breath.

Stepped through that new era's classroom door.

BLINK

Tod drove the rickety pickup into a new world of trouble.

Was the Wednesday morning of that first week of school his junior year. September 1965.

The pickup's radio played Vernon's AM station KRIP loud and clear.

Loud and clear, thought Tod as he turned onto the street where Luc lived. *When has that ever happened?*

He focused on the white church up ahead just past the hospital.

At least driving past that Lutheran church was an understandable and acceptable route to the high school across the railroad tracks—

—though not so direct as turning right after he passed the Baptist church.

But Tod drove a sly road whenever he turned left at Fourth Street to roll past the Methodist church where a quick glance through its front windows might show him the bare golden cross on the altar.

And when Tod overshot any legitimate route to cruise past the Catholic church, that was plain goofy.

Tod always left early for school.

Some days that meant after dawn milk delivery runs with his dad, instead of getting dropped off early at the Big Pink, Tod got to solo drive the rickety pickup away from the family's rented house on the far east side.

But those days weren't lucky. They only happened when Dad was sick or hadn't picked up a second job working for building and carpentry contractors or painting jobs. Those *no work* days he'd stay home. Help Tod's mom before she left for her clerk job. Collapse onto the narrow bed those parents shared while Tod got the curtained-off end of a hall for his room.

Still, those solo pickup-driving days gave Tod a slim chance.

Or so he told himself:

If there is a God, maybe driving past where He's supposed to be will tell me what the hell is going on and what the hell am I supposed to do about Being Broken.

So far, that hadn't worked.

Not that Tod really expected it to. His family didn't go to church. His dad said it was because they didn't have enough to put anything in the collection plate, and while that was true, Tod knew the real reason was his parents just didn't know what to make of religion or which church to trust with their souls.

But as he neared the white-walled Lutheran church, Tod remembered his mom blurting *"Thank God!"* last night as his parents sat Tod down to tell him that Dad had lost his phased-out milkman route.

Then Tod's beloved Old Man grinned.

"Burt'd clued me in 'bout an opening at the county crew," said his dad. "It ain't the top-of-the-heap State Highway Department crew or the utilities' crews, but it's a step up above the city crew. And I got the job!"

That was the moment his wife praised an ill-defined deity.

"Hey," said this dad whose paycheck would now be 19 percent heftier. "End of next week, you'll be going to high school on time like all the other kids."

Like all the other kids. When have I ever been like "all the other kids"?

Maybe tonight, thought Tod.

Maybe I'll keep it together if *so*-rugged Gene shows up at Luc's dad's trucking firm's garage with dozens of other juniors to stuff colored napkins into the squares of chicken wire fence for our Homecoming parade float.

He reached the red STOP sign.

Looked to his left.

The road thataway ran past the county library.

He'd never found a book there that told him what he yearned to know.

A giant four-story sandstone castle with a shiny aluminum roof claimed the hilltop behind and above the library, the prominence in this prairie valley town called Vernon that was the county seat of Martin County, Montana.

The Works Progress Administration built the courthouse with federal money that gave jobs to local victims of the 1930s Great Depression caused by Wall Street's crash and compounded by the Dust Bowl environmental disaster catalyzed by unscientific farming methods. The WPA grew out of President

FDR's successful strategy to save America by "bubbling up" dollars from the ground rather than "trickling down" dimes from the skyscrapers and mansions.

Tod's eyes drifted beyond the windshield of his STOP-sign-idling pickup.

The courthouse flowed to a raised road bordered by stone walls arced alongside and above the sidewalk for the street Tod waited to drive on.

Facing that concrete path for pedestrians, halfway down the twenty-five-foot-tall arc "bridge" was a narrow flat earth strip with a wilding of bushes and trees.

Three fourth grade kids crunched their way toward their grade school along that narrow strip of glory thirteen feet above the concrete sidewalk.

Two blue-jeaned boys and a girl in a flouncy skirt.

The girl walked between them with a grace possessed by neither the leader nor the boy who'd been last to climb over the wall to—

Last Boy *TRIPPED*/crashed into Girl!

She flipped/rammed into his wobbling scramble/rocketed them—

—crashing over the edge down to the merciless sidewalk.

Tod gunned the pickup to that sidewalk. Two kids screamed and writhed on that sunny September morning's concrete flecked by crimson rain.

Tod blasted out of his ride.

Graceful Girl somehow sitting up on the sidewalk. Bleeding nose. Dazed eyes. Whimpering. Scrapes and cuts on her bare legs and arms blossomed red.

Last Boy screaming in pain on the sidewalk.

A broken bone speared through the blue jeans over his right leg.

Leader Boy freaked out on the rock wall's scrub brush thirteen feet above his friends and Tod: "*No no no no!* What—I don't know what—"

Tod squatted/grabbed gravity-smashed Last Boy.

Tod whipped the belt out of his own blue jeans' loops.

Between the blood-beating heart and the wound.

Cinched his belt high up on the boy's thigh.

Tod yelled to the screaming boy:

"Grab down by the knot. Opposite ends of the belt in each hand. Now pull! Yes, that's right. You'll be OK! If you fall back, just keep pulling on the belt."

He yelled up to Leader Boy: "Run to the hospital just down the block! Run *screaming*. Grab every nurse or doctor. Any adults. Bleeding wounds. *Got that?* Tell them all '*bleeding wounds.*' Now fucking *RUN!*"

Tod cupped the back of the dazed girl's skull. Slid his hand down her back. Found no wounds. Scanned bruises and scrapes on her arms and bare legs: *Not dangerous.* Stared into her widening pupils:

"How's your head?"

"Don't feel so—*BWACK!*"

Tod whirled away from her spraying vomit.

"You've got a concussion! Don't move, alright? Just stay there."

Tod whirled back to tourniquet-holding boy.

He's going pale.

Tod grabbed the ends of the belt tourniquet. Pulled them tighter.

A white-uniformed nurse with a black bag raced toward him.

Behind her raced a doctor helping another nurse charge a clanging stretcher over the sidewalk. A plastic bag dangled from the stretcher's frame.

Hurry up! Tod wanted to scream.

Knew they were coming as fast as they could.

Knew that his screaming might dangerously rattle his . . .

His what? Responsibilities?

*These two kids who fell, they're Who I Got To—*GET TO *Help. Be ME!*

Flicking through Tod came a crazy feeling that if he could've put it into words would have said: *"Helping somebody else helps my hurting, too."*

A blur of white uniforms and Tod *"Easy! Easy!"* laid the splintered-bone boy onto the stretcher. A nurse slid a transfusion needle into the pale boy's arm. The stretcher clattered away to a future where he had a story and a scar to warn his grandkids with and an ache in his leg bone when the weather turned cold.

That morning the first nurse stood with her gentle knowing and certain hand on the dazed-eyed, vomit-covered little girl while they waited for a wheelchair.

Tod's beltless blue jeans hung loose on him.

A cop car red light and sirened to a stop next to Tod's pickup.

Tod knew other cars of curious eyes crawled past or stopped to see What's Happening. He feared for the two hospital-bound kids.

But what crept into Tod were *could bes*—for himself.

SECRETS

Luc stared at what was happening behind the grinning swagger of Kyle marching out of his westside house toward the idling '54 with Luc behind the steering wheel that autumn-leaved Thursday morning. Gene rode shotgun.

Kyle yelled: "Least you two aren't late like yesterday!"

"Hey!" said Luc. "Yesterday I had to see what the cops were doing to Tod."

The car's backseat door slammed behind Kyle.

"No cops today," added Luc.

Riding shotgun beside him, Gene said: "Don't worry, they're coming."

They all laughed.

Luc caught Kyle's eyes reflected in the rearview mirror.

"What's going on in your driveway?" said Luc. "I thought both your cars were broken. But isn't that Mrs. Markham loading boxes in the backseat and tying a mattress on your car's roof?"

"The Chevy isn't broken," said Kyle. "Mom just didn't know when . . . Last night when he was out t' the Dixie Inn was the first time Mrs. Markham had a chance to get back into her house 'n' grab what she could. Been a few nights on our couch. Plus, her face and arms had to heal up before she could drive."

"Where's she going?" said Luc. "Why?"

"Nobody's supposed to know *where*. You figure out *why*."

Luc drove to Gideon's.

Gideon lived on an alleyway in front of a thick wall of bushes.

The Catholic church rose on the other side of the bushes and across the street. Next to the church rose the rectory.

Luc parked the gray Dodge in front of Gideon's house.

Gave no thought to letting the car engine idle fumes of gas in the warm autumn morning to keep the radio playing songs of what is and what could be.

Kyle said something about tomorrow night's Homecoming football game.

The radio played a commercial for relief from common constipation.

"No shit," said Kyle.

"That's what the man's saying," cracked Gene.

They all laughed as the idling car trembled their youthful bodies.

Where's Gideon? thought Luc. *He's usually standing there waiting for us.*

Luc glanced down at the watch on his left wrist below where that hand held the steering wheel: *Not late yet, but . . .*

"I'll go get him," he told the other two guys in the car.

Was one step away from the ground-level concrete-slab front porch when the white-painted wooden door swung open. Gideon charged through it.

Luc saw through that closing door into the shadowed house:

A looming hulk. A man, hands down by his sides.

And beyond that stepfather figure: *Was that intertwined shadow Gideon's mom wrapped around his younger sister who was a cute junior high girl even though she walked hunched over with her eyes cast down all the time?*

Gideon grabbed Luc's arm. Propelled them toward the idling car.

"Come on," muttered Gideon. "Let's go."

Luc glanced down at the hand that held his arm:

Gideon's knuckles are scraped.

He jumped in the back behind Gene in the shotgun seat.

Gideon tried a joke: "What the hell, Luc! You give any bums a ride?"

Nobody laughed as the car drove away from that house.

First period sent Luc to Study Hall.

He walked to the librarian's desk to ask for other books like *Lord of the Flies.*

Spotted Mrs. Dawson standing with another woman teacher in the glass-walled office behind the librarian's desk. Heard Mrs. Dawson's hushed tone.

"What we're doing . . . just people trying to save a friend and colleague. Men, women, why does there always have to be . . . Him and I, there's nothing . . ."

A breath filled her. Let her go.

"I am who I am. Being here. Living here. But I gotta be me when the other choice is to ignore what's going—"

She spotted Luc standing in front of her desk.

That made the other teacher turn her head and see him, too. She mumbled to Mrs. Dawson: "Later." Walked past Luc with a *Watch it!* warning of authority.

Mrs. Dawson stared at Luc: "Of course it's you standing there."

He asked her to recommend another mind-opening book.

"We don't have a copy," she said. "Principal Harris and Old Lady Sweeny. But the county library, they have a copy of *East of Eden*. John Steinbeck."

"My dad read another book of his about workers in the Great Depression."

"Good for him. Good for you *if* Steinbeck won the Nobel Prize last year."

A Nobel Prize, trembled Luc's soul. *For writing the shimmers in your skull.*

He thanked Mrs. Dawson. Turned around to—

—Buffy stood five steps away anxiously staring at him.

She held her ring-heavy right hand low by her waist.

Frantically used it to beckon Luc to her.

HOMECOMING

H omecoming Day. September '65. Vernon, Montana.

The Friday ending the first week of Donna's junior year in high school.

She blasted awake. Ran to her home's bathroom. Puked.

Flushing that white toilet swirled her into a blurred terror of time.

Monday . . .

Registration Day. The day she heard Cherie's *"Long as you're fine."*

Tuesday . . .

Buffy and the scrub-it-away Sandi in the high school GIRLS bathroom.

Luc *choosing* to shuffle upstairs with her. Talk to her, even if only for a few heartbeats before he ran to Buffy only to find out he was a loser. A loser *too*.

Home after school. Sitting on the bed she'd made. Heart pounding.

Her father and mother griping in the kitchen.

"Oh look," said her father. "In slumps our daughter with her face full of trouble. What'd you do that's gonna cost me money now?"

Her mother snapped: "So you got money you ain't spent on some floozy?"

"Ain't no floozy ever stuck me in a place like this."

"Oh yeah? What about the floozy you moved us here 'cause of?"

"You said where we were was no place for the kid."

Like I'm not even here in the kitchen with them, thought Donna.

"Wasn't this that I figured on getting when you baby bumped," said he who everyone back then would have called the man of the house.

"Life's shit for you, ain't it?"

"I bring home the bacon. And I put up with your bullshit."

His wife glared at their daughter: "Some school thing you gotta tell us?"

"School, *hah!*" snapped her father. "She can read damn good. Write. Do sums. What the hell more is she gonna get out of there besides a piece of paper? Law says she's old enough. She should get a job."

"What could she do?" snapped his wife. "She can't stand all day on that damn leg like a waitress or a salesgirl. She barely made it couple hours a night at the Elks Club's burgers 'n' beers stand during this summer's fair."

Screams rocketed in Donna's skull as she limped away.

Wednesday . . .

Everyone in school talking about Tod and the bloody kids.

Tod did what he could with what he knew when he had to, thought Donna.

That night her father announced that he had to go back to his shop on Main Street to figure out how to fix the tubes on a customer's TV set.

Her mother'd sat out back on a lawn chair with a six pack of beers. Lit the backyard's autumn darkness with her glowing cigarette under the stars that'd dropped her there.

Donna snuck through their next-door neighbor's front door.

After dinner, old Mrs. Kelly hid in her bedroom where pictures on the wall gave her faces she knew wouldn't hurt her even if she forgot their names. She'd play KRIP radio so she'd know she was still here. And not alone. Even if she couldn't hear the radio so good anymore. She'd fall asleep and "*Damn it!*" wake up in sunshine to sounds of music she knew *she knew* yet didn't.

And she never missed the keys from the hook on the wall for the old car in her driveway she'd give to "hired girl" Donna to run errands for her.

Donna found slick-black-haired Jerry ruling a barstool at the Oasis.

"You got ID?" yelled the bartender who loved to give someone the bounce.

Jerry turned to see Donna staring her way toward him.

"She's here for me." Jerry kept his eyes on Donna. "Won't be staying long."

The bartender grunted. Polished glasses.

Donna whose driver's license said she was sixteen hissed at Jerry: "Where've you been?"

"Workin' the rigs." Jerry lit his cigarette. His driver's license said he was twenty-seven. "Not lookin' for you."

"We've got to talk!" whispered Donna. "I've got to . . . to tell you . . . And we—"

"Who's this '*we*' you're talking 'bout? Summer's over."

"The hell it is."

"Is for me and them few *legal* times we had 'round the fair."

Tears she couldn't stop scarred her cheeks.

"I thought you . . . you liked me. Thought I wasn't . . . Thought I was . . . Even after you dumped me three weeks from the first time we . . . I thought at least you . . ."

"I liked what we done," said Jerry. "You must've had a good teacher."

"You're the only . . . !"

"Now who'd believe that? Easy once, easy always."

Always steeled Donna as she stood in that northside bar. Knew she *always* was going to be who she was. Vibrated the resolve she'd clung to since fifth grade after the school's principal made her shuffle in front of the class to show the other kids how polio survivors walked so they'd be glad they'd been lucky to have gotten the new vaccines:

FUCK TEARS!

"I need money." Her tone chilled his glass of beer.

"Who don't?"

"I said: *I. Need. Money.*"

"And I ain't the kind of guy who has to pay for it." Jerry looked at the swell of her blouse as she stood there on the barroom floor with eyes full of him. "You might could grab a few bucks up t' the house on the hill.

"Course," he soothed in a voice of charm, "if you're just looking for a free ride, *well*, I know a gravel road you'd like. Just for old time's sake."

"This is now. Fuck your road. I need money."

"You ain't got no *or else*. But hey, I hear *ya*. I feel for *ya*."

Mister Slick Black Hair scooped silver coins scattered on the bar beside greenback dollars and his glass of tap beer.

Grabbed her heart-side hand as smooth as a snake. Dropped the silver coins in her palm. Closed her fist for her so the coins wouldn't fall out.

Grinned when she closed her other fist.

"Just 'cause this is the toughest bar in town don't make you tough enough."

He let her blink.

Then raised his hands open palms out to her for anybody to see: "Hey, don't ever let it be said that I ain't a good guy."

He scooped up the three $1 bills from beside his beer mug on the scarred brown wooden bar. Slid them into the pocket on her faded white blouse. Let his fingers linger feeling her warm flesh there.

"Now you got all I got for you," he said.

Leered and loudly said: "What's your name again?"

Donna felt the sawdust floor beneath her white sneakers. The juke box playing somebody else's song. Scents of sweat. Of cigarette smoke. Beer. Fear.

She leaned toward the man on the barstool.

Saw his brow wrinkle with wonder and just a whiff of worry.

Spat *Plop!* into his beer mug's pool of gold.

Marched/limped out of the bar into that warm September neon night.

Didn't look back. Wouldn't look back. Couldn't, she just *couldn't* look back.

Drove her stolen car through town.

The radio was off. The front windows were down.

Donna drove past the Big Pink. Drove back over the viaduct. Rumbled the old car up to Knob Hill. Drove through the open gates of the plateaued cemetery.

Saw the lights of Vernon below her.

Saw the twinkle of stars in the giant blackness above her.

Sat there and . . . and . . . and.

Drove back down Knob Hill.

Turned right onto Main Street past the Catholic church.

The lights were on in her father's radio repair shop. The golden lit marquee of the Roxy proclaimed a movie about heroes and women who got the good ones. Her windshield twinkled the neon bars: Teagarden's. The Alibi. The Tap Room.

What Donna fixated on were two side-by-side, second-story dark windows.

Thursday . . .

Buffy and Luc stood on the second-floor landing outside the gym's far end after lunch and before First Bell that Thursday afternoon.

Donna saw them and trembled with none dare call it hope.

She'd pulled Buffy into the GIRLS room before First Bell. Checked to be sure the stalls were empty *before* she whispered.

Buffy blinked. Her gaze widened. Her pink-slicked lips quivered: "*OK!*"

Jesus, thought Donna, *how pitiful is it that the only name I had to give Buffy was Luc's! Now we're all "just talking" here at the end of a hallway where people seldom come. Plus, people look away from me, so they won't really see us.*

"I grabbed Luc in the library," said Buffy.

Luc handed Donna an envelope.

"I only had less than three bucks stashed in my room and jeans pockets," said Luc. "All the money I earn working at the Roxy goes into my bank account to save for college like my sister Laura, and my parents—"

"*Luc!*" urged Buffy.

He softened his face to teenage Donna who was his snide friend ever since she'd been his blackboard eyes before he got glasses in fifth grade. Told her:

"You should know I asked—*No, I did not tell anybody 'who'!* Just told them the truth that Buffy told me—didn't say her name either, never will. Said:

"'*A friend of ours is in trouble and needs money and it's a to-die-for secret.*'"

"A secret we don't know," said Buffy. "Unless you want to tell us."

Donna shook her head from side to side and DID NOT cry.

"And it all had to happen before classes this afternoon," said Luc. "When I could catch 'em, some of my guys who I *totally* trust threw in. Marin only had a nickel and Gideon beat him with a pocketful of four pennies. Gene had a spare dollar from unloading a railroad car after football practice. Kurt pitched in a couple bucks. His dad's a CPA, so good money."

Don't tell her Wayne said no, thought Luc. *Don't wonder why.*

"Kyle's mom needed all his paper delivery money to help—but he had a coupon for a dollar off at the grocery store, he threw that in," said Luc.

His deep exhale said he was done.

Buffy inhaled. Let it all out.

"I've only had $3.55 because I wouldn't deliver—never mind. I said I needed more for cheerleading at Homecoming. My folks gave $5. And $2 from . . ."

They all knew that "from" was Steve.

"Wendy is always broke," continued Buffy, "but Alice came up with almost $2 for the two of them. And Sandi from the GIRLS room when . . . When I caught up to her in the hall after American History class, she just handed me her whole purse. She had $3 and change."

She handed Donna a pink Hallmark card envelope she'd bought at the drugstore on Main Street. Buffy'd imagined writing a real through-the-Post-Office letter to Steve. She didn't know what she wanted to say that she hadn't said yet. Or say everything again so it all made sense. But conflicting visions of Future Buffy haunted her heart and got in her way of putting pen to blank pink paper.

"That's all we got," said Buffy. "If we had more time . . ."

Donna shook her head *no*.

Buffy and Luc believed her barely-holding-on face.

"Thank you!" whispered Donna. "I can't . . . You . . . Everybody . . . Thank you!"

"Just doing what you're supposed to do for a friend," said Luc.

Nods from him and Buffy filled Donna's glistening eyes.

She watched them retreat down the corridor past the gym. Scurry out of sight into locker-walled hallways filled with student chatter. Mike's laugh.

RING! First Bell.

She hurried to the three payphones on the wall near the entrance to the gym's upper levels. Kept the two envelopes closed on $15.93.

Used her own dime.

Dialed the number she'd memorized from the phone book.

Ring.

Ring.

That voice she knew said: "Yes?"

Friday.

The black hands on every clock in every classroom that Friday afternoon hammered Donna's head as her eyes clung to their red *tick-tick* second hands.

Homecoming has gotta make it all work!

Donna's heart flip-flopped between frozen and thundering.

Act like everything is OK!

She sat through lunch hour without opening the brown paper sack she'd packed with a peanut butter and jelly sandwich just in case her mother noticed before she ran off to her job. Her father left for work before she left for school.

Her father was The Main Danger.

She had to get there before he walked outside of his radio repair shop to stare at the parade's cheerleaders and twirlers.

Booming out of the schools' loudspeakers came Principal Harris's voice:

"Listen up! School buses in the teacher's parking lot. Marching band, you're in one. Cheerleaders, twirlers, cram in there or the next bus. Pep squad, fill up that one along with other groups marching in the parade. The team will catch its buses out of the gym side. So that means . . ."

Silence filled classrooms through the whole Big Pink.

"That means," continued a snide Principal Harris, "Coach Moent says all you guys out there wearing team jerseys gonna ride that bus. Even JV and third stringers. Riding in the back of the trucks. Waving at everybody."

"And no funny business by anybody!" boomed the loudspeaker. "Or else."

RING! The Dismissal Bell.

Donna risked falling on her bad leg's side from too-long strides. Hurried through the hallway teeming with excited teenagers.

She was not in Pep Club like most girls. But who would say *no* to her getting on the bus when they barely ever noticed she existed?

Made it!

Got pressed against a window in a seat beside a senior girl named Kitty.

"I lost my baton," said Kitty. She wore a twirler's uniform, short white skirt and women's athletic top. "Oh well, what the hell."

The yellow bus surged away from the Big Pink.

Donna stared out the bus window at the town she'd lived in since she was ten. The bus rolled across the viaduct over railroad tracks taking her nowhere. Followed Main Street past the Catholic church. Stopped at the playground curb of Blackhawk Elementary school where she and Bobbi Jean became friends until 'bout halfway through their freshman year when Bobbi Jean . . . drifted away.

Donna peeked at Kitty's watch: twenty-seven minutes left *before*.

Three o'clock.

Then is when.

The bus doors *whooshed*.

A crush of teenagers pulled Donna to the world waiting outside.

Where Donna became The Hunch.

The Hunch curled her shoulders in. Bent her at her waist. Her eyes seemed downcast but saw everything in this world where she knew nobody wanted to see her. The Hunch made her even more invisible and *oh* that Homecoming Friday, invisible was what she had to be.

She eased into the crowd of teenagers. Adults yelled and gestured orders. Donna saw Principal Harris being In Charge.

The marching band's maroon and gold uniformed mob shuffled in her way. Slide trombones. Silver flutes and black clarinets. Hanging from white-shoulder-strapped drums and one *Boom! Boom! Boom!* bass drum. Polished gold trumpets.

Donna spotted Tod smiling with other chorus members climbing into the back of a grain truck. Chorus coach Bundy gave Bobbi Jean a helping hand.

The Hunch knifed her way through the marching band.

Passed floats from each high school class.

The chief of police stood at the curb talking to one of the volunteer firemen who'd be riding the polished red fire trucks in the parade.

The Hunch walked her right past those unknowing badges.

Walked her toward where tomorrow's sun would rise over Main Street.

Donna rose up through The Hunch.

Can't be late!

She walked past the red-and-white-walled Conoco service station.

Committed to the quickest route *to*.

Donna glanced ahead at the newly built bank's tall clock tower with a clock that flashed the time as yellow electric numbers changing every minute.

The clock read: 2:49.

She had eleven minutes.

Marched as quickly as she dared. No falls. No bumps.

Made it to under the big clock.

Only three doors from the wide shortcut passageway past the Tap Room.

Her dad's radio repair shop was two storefronts further down that sidewalk. Past the men's fancy clothes shop and the Cinderella women's clothing store with its picture windows full of dead-eyed female mannequins.

NO! Dad's stepping out of his radio repair shop! He'll see me! Catch me!

He bent his face down to light a cigarette.

Donna's right arm pushed a glass door closest to her and jumped into—

The Capitol Café. A horseshoe counter. Booths against the wall.

Nobody in there except a white-uniformed, grumpy-faced sixty-ish waitress who everybody knew and knew everybody. She made people laugh when she suction-cupped customers' coffee cups to their saucers for A Big Surprise.

Grumpy Waitress stared at the high school kid who she damn well knew.

Sunlight streaming through the Capitol Café's smudged front wall of windows filled Donna's eyes. Made her flesh burn. Her body tremble.

"Bright out there," said Grumpy Waitress.

She stared at this kid with low-ass parents.

"You're in some kind of hurry. And some kinda *Don't see me*. You know where you is. You know where you're going. You gotta get there and get outta of my damn gray hair. So go through the kitchen 'n' out the back way to get gone."

Donna nodded frantically. *Thankfully.*

Grumpy Waitress yelled at Donna's retreating back: "'N' don't you go telling anybody I let you go thataway! We can't get my wrinkly old ass in trouble!"

Donna never saw the smile Grumpy made behind her hurrying away back.

The café's back door launched Donna into the alley of the long way she should have taken instead of the "shortcut" to the front doors on Main Street.

And that's kind of a lie. The alley route she declined to take was only half a block longer to where she had to go in the ticking clock.

But the alley route took her past the two-story county jail.

Donna shuddered every time she imagined those gray cement walls.

The alley's switchback of weathered gray wooden slopes built for wheelchair patients led her to the thick brown door: Unlocked!

Donna ran down the hallway of empty offices.

Froze in front of an office door with a black lettered, fogged glass door.

Just for a second. A second of hope. Of fear. A second of *Please!*

Came her knock on that door.

"Cheer, cheer for old Vernon High!
Cheer for us Cougars up in the sky!"

THE BIG PINK'S SCHOOL SONG

Come in," said the old man's voice behind the door.

Donna swung open that portal entrance.

"Pull the door closed behind you. Give that lock a twist."

Donna saw the shotgun. *And if that was true . . .*

"Am I on time?" she asked.

"You're here now," answered the sixty-ish man behind the desk.

"*Whoof,*" went a shedding hairy sheepdog.

"So," said the watchdog's master: "What's your problem?"

"You know," said Donna to the man she'd talked to while she swept the sidewalk in front of her father's store. She knew what he did once he climbed those stairs to his office on the second floor overlooking Main Street.

"Are you sure you got a situation?" said Doc Nirmberg.

"I don't need to get any surer."

"Well," said the Doc. "We could do the blood test. That'd take time."

"I've got no time."

"So I guess I gotta believe you. You're a minor but that's no never mind to what you need, so . . . We're already here."

"But for my peace of mind," he said. "Say it out loud nice and clear."

Donna stared straight through the glasses over his eyes.

"I want you to give me an abortion. I need you to give me an abortion."

"And what do you think *I* need?"

"How much?"

"Well, the usual rate is $35. Plus, if we use laughing gas like at a dentist's, that's another $5."

She put the $15.93 from Buffy and Luc on the desk in front of him. Added $7.42 she didn't feel one bit guilty about stealing from her father's pants.

"This is the *usual* I've got," said Donna. "I can pay you the rest later."

Doc Nirmberg looked at the steel-eyed teenage girl.

"I believe you will."

He scooped the money into his desk's middle drawer.

Gestured for her to lead the way into the next room.

"Before we get started, the hospital needs another clerk to rustle files, but for now they only got part-time money. Long as you can kinda type, you can earn a few bucks a week."

What Donna saw overwhelmed her as she stepped into the next room. The inclined and padded gray chair that rolled down into a flat table. The stirrup rods to hold/trap legs. She didn't hear the words she whispered: "I can type."

"Good. I'll put in a word with the clerk up there. Behind that white screen there's a hospital gown. Drop all your clothes. Put it on and come back out here."

She did.

Obeyed him to lie back in that inclined seat.

Put her feet in stirrups he locked.

He changed his white smock. Scrubbed his hands. Dried them with paper towels. Told her what to do Now and After. Snapped on surgical gloves: "Moment you called, figured gonna need the gas."

Doc Nirmberg wheeled a handcart carrying a tall metal gray cylinder.

A *thunk!* A *wunk!*

Donna's flat on her back. A flat gray nylon strap folds across her chest. And thus her arms. Snugs them not *too* tight.

Doc Nirmberg fits a black mask tubed to the gray cylinder over her face.

A hiss—

"*Wee-Ooooo!*"

Outside in the street below! Police siren! Gonna catch me!

Groggy Donna shoves against the straps. Jerks up off the operating table. Shakes her head from side to side. The hissing black mask twists off her mouth.

"*Shh*," says Doc Nirmberg as he comforts her back down. Adjusts her hissing mask as the room spins. "Police sirens always start the Homecoming parade. They're going to march and play, hoot 'n' holler right outside that window giving us the good afternoon light in here. Right out there down below us on Main Street. So don't worry. It's just Homecoming."

Rat-a-tat snare drums. *Boom booms.* Golden horns blasting out brass band songs. Whoops of teenagers Donna knew flowing past below where she lay strapped down breathing swirling colors. Hearing shouts, clapping *and and and* . . .

Darkness.

Donna never forgot that passing parade she never saw.

Luc riding down Main Street in the truck with the *"Woo-whoing"* football team—including Steve. Buffy pom-pom strutting with the other cheerleaders. The *oom-pah-pah* marching band. Twirling batons. Class floats. Police cars. Fire trucks. They all paraded past and below that second-story window never knowing what they never saw.

Homecoming Day. September '65. Vernon, Montana.

THE MATCH

That next Monday afternoon after school.

Donna sat on a folding chair. Faced a gray metal desk. A gray-haired woman peered at Donna through a valley between mountains of file folders. Cigarette smoke floated its way to the white tiled ceiling. There was no window. The one door held clouded glass for black letters: HOSPITAL RECORDS ROOM.

The woman's cigarette voice said: "You OK?"

Donna blinked. "I'm fine."

"Maybe yes, maybe no, maybe later. Doc Nirmberg sent you here for minimum-wage work. Your parents'd have to sign off on your hour a day or however much school and the hospital budget gonna give you."

"Everybody will sign anything to get rid of me."

Donna heard a stubbing ashtray crush of a cigarette. Saw a radio on top of a gray file cabinet. Hoped it worked.

"Look around," said the woman named Zelda. "You think you can stand being *in here*? Working *in here*? Nobody *out there* seeing you *in here*?"

"I've spent every day since I was seven not being seen even when I was stared at. Being *in here* and out of those blind eyes sounds pretty OK to me."

"You're something, aren't you?" Zelda shook her head. "If people only knew."

Zelda's hands rose in a V above the plateaus of stacked files.

"This is the twentieth century. Screw satellites. Banging up houses. Lawyering or banking. Selling bras. *Nah*. Life now is all about pushing paper.

"Paper pushers make it all happen. Maybe that ain't the kind of life anybody wants, but it's the kind of life you and I can hold on to."

A pack of cigarettes with matches tucked in its cellophane wrapper flew through the manila file folders' valley to land on the desk in front of Donna.

"Might as well get used to the smoking—if you're coming here."

Kids don't smoke, thought Donna.

Took a breath of the air that surrounded her.

Was I ever a kid?

She stuck her first-ever cigarette between lips seared by a lying asshole.

Lit a match in this office crammed with paper.

Chose what to burn.

THE GREAT DISAPPEARANCE

Shh!

The second week of October 1965. A crisp Saturday afternoon.

Luc walked to the county library to return *East of Eden* that *wow*'d him, plus his family's usual load of mystery and historical novels.

He chose a couple novels for his mom from the adult fiction section. Pulled *To Kill a Mockingbird* off the shelf to read. The movie had been great. What the story showed "regular" White people doing to people who weren't blew Luc's mind.

Had to be fiction, right? he thought.

He walked into the L-shaped nook reserved for mysteries and crime fiction.

Books in that nook crammed on shelves in alphabetical order by author's last name. The first shelf ran down from A to G on the bottom. H books started on the next-row-over's highest shelf—too high for pre-teens to reach.

On that top shelf stood a thick white-jacketed book with a spine lettered:

The Novels of Dashiell Hammett

What the heck is a "dashiell hammett"? had wondered fifth grader Lucas.

"Oh, you wouldn't like any of that," his dad had told ten-year-old Lucas when he mentioned the *couldn't-reach-it* book. "Just . . . forget about it."

"Dumb stuff," said his mother. "Boring stuff too adult for you. You'd hate it."

But now it's 1965, thought Luc. *And I'm not a little kid anymore.*

He glanced at the mystery shelves. Saw cherished names: Westlake. McBain. The MacDonalds. Chandler. Christie. Rex Stout. And way up there . . .

The Novels of Dashiell Hammett

Now an easy reach for teenager Luc.

He pulled that book off the shelf.

Wait! thought Luc when he saw the titles of the five novels in that thick anthology. This guy Hammett! They made great movies out of his books. *The Thin Man*: black and white comedy and killers. *The Maltese Falcon*, one of Luc's favorite *ever* movies: *"The stuff that dreams are made of."*

Why would my parents think I wouldn't like this book? thought Luc.

He added that Hammett to his checkout pile.

Walked that pile home.

Didn't notice until Tuesday that Hammett'd moved to the bottom of the library books' stack. He put it on his bedtable under a new *Bond, James Bond*.

Didn't notice until Thursday that Hammett had been replaced by one of the library's murder mysteries. Glanced into his parents' off-limits bedroom.

Spotted the Hammett volume under one of his mom's library novels.

His life tick-tocked. Schoolwork. Football. Key Club with Kurt, Wayne. Catching Marin to *"S'up?"* whenever he found him in the hall without blonde Barbara. The debate team. The school newspaper. *Not* with Buffy (except phoning her at night about trig homework and laughing at everything else, *really*, that was all *that* was).

So he didn't realize Hammett had completely disappeared until Saturday morning, the day before 1965's Halloween.

The house was empty.

Dad was at work where *Oh, Marilyn!* hung in the light of a bare bulb.

Mom was with her sisters in the nursery home that caged Gramma Meg.

Luc hunted for Hammett all through the house. The shelves used for World Book Encyclopedias and an eight-volume, gray hardback Encyclopedia of Science, his family home's corner of all the knowledge he was supposed to need. *No Hammett.* He hunted in the downstairs "rec" room where the TV and ironing board stood. *No.* Laura's shrine-like pink bedroom. *Nope.*

He opened his parents' closet. Dresses. Suits. Shirts. Pants. Rows of shoes. A top shelf where a few of the hats businessmen wore way, *way* back in the 1950s waited alongside hats Mom wore when she had to be church-proper.

Their bed.

Don't even think about no don't no STOP THINKING!

TIME magazine waited on Dad's table, but Mom's held nothing to read.

Their bed had a headrest of shelves and private cabinets.

A quick glance in Mom's bedside cabinet showed tubes and jars and lotions and no secreted volume with its white cover emblazoned by a Maltese falcon.

Luc hurried around the bed to his dad's side.

Slid open Dad's cabinet—

—found a book.

But not Hammett. A drugstore paperback novel Dad had bought and read long ago and—*evidently*—hung on to.

Luc had found ways to not be seen reading that novel his mother couldn't hide until after his father had officially finished reading it the first time. Luc memorized Where Those Pages Were.

That Saturday morning before Halloween, 1965, Luc couldn't help himself.

Flipped open the cabinet book to a page number he'd memorized:

"*. . . she raised his hands to cup her naked—*"

"*I'm home!*" yelled Mom, turning to close the front door behind her.

Turned back to see Luc looming in the living room doorway to the bedrooms. Caught something in his breathless look.

"Hey," he said. "What happened to my Hammett book?"

"I took it back to the library."

"But I haven't read it yet! And you never go to the library, so why—"

"It was overdue. A couple of mine, too, *so.*"

"It's due *today.* Like the others. I was gonna renew them."

"Now you don't have to."

The fire tower's noon whistle blew through that Saturday's autumn air.

Mom hurried into her kitchen.

Left Luc standing there in the gray-walled living room.

He heard the car door slam outside the front door as Dad got home.

Bologna sandwiches with catsup for lunch.

Luc dried the dishes. Asked for the gray '54's keys: "*Gotta do stuff.*"

He drove the gray '54 Dodge two blocks and invisibly around the Lutheran church corner to the parking slots alongside the library.

The librarian waved at him as he walked in. Disappeared. Came back with a book she'd just re-shelved.

Luc asked her: "Do you know about this book or this Hammett guy?"

"*Ooo!*" said the librarian. "I don't *know,* but I *saw.*"

She led Luc to the magazine racks.

"Your Mrs. Dawson," said the county librarian. "She's so good to us—and I don't just mean as school librarian to county librarian. She subscribes to a weekly magazine from New York. One after another, they keep coming. *Plop, plop, plop* on your doorstep. '*I try,*' she says. '*I keep trying.*' When she's done with 'em, she brings 'em up here for everybody.

"I never *really* read them," she confessed. "Except for the cartoons."

She plopped a magazine on an empty round wooden table. Flipped through the pages: "But when I was going through this one—*There!*"

Her red fingernail tapped a small black and white picture on the white inked page of that magazine. A lean man. Mustache. Gray suit, white shirt and dark tie. Left hand in his front pants pocket. Right hand dangling a lit cigarette.

"That line under the picture says he's Dashiell Hammett."

She walked away to help another library user.

Luc skimmed the prose around the picture of a hard-eyed man:

> . . . of course is Lillian Hellman's decades-long *relationship* with troubled and once popular crime novelist Dashiell Hammett, who some critics credit with creating the fictional genre called *noir* and who confidants say Hellman believes was triggered in 1917 when then-Pinkerton detective Hammett turned down a corporate murder contract to assassinate left-wing political leader Frank Little in Butte, Montana—

WAIT! thought Luc. *Our—MY—Butte, Montana?*

> —a city on the richest hill in the world that's bled with violence and struggles for power since its "War of the Copper Kings" in the late 1880s when the US Senate refused to seat William Clark because of his bribery to win that Montanan *and* American chair of power. Clark later said: "I never bought a man who wasn't for sale."
>
> By the time the Pinkertons sent Hammett to Butte, the big battles were between big money and bulldog labor unions being buoyed by left-wing groups like the Industrial Workers of the World who at one time were a major officially subversive group.

The IWW sent Frank Little to Butte where Hammett was then offered a $5,000 fortune to kill him.

Hammett refused. A few nights later, he watched masked thugs drag broken-legged Frank Little out of his boarding house room, tie him to the bumper of a car that drove to a downtown Butte railroad trestle where they lynched Frank Little.

Hellman said that beyond the horrors and injustice of the lynching, what haunted Hammett was that "the big money" thought he would take their cash to do their killing.

Little's murder and the impact of Butte triggered Hammett's shift to left-wing politics—and to writing detective fiction that made him Hollywood bankable until he went to prison in 1949—

The year I was born! thought Luc. *The year of Marilyn's calendar!*

—for refusing to name names to government communist hunters. Volunteered for WWII, veteran Hammett's mandated prison job was cleaning toilets. He got out—then later also refused to name names to Congress's House Un-American Activities Committee investigating Hollywood.

That earned Hammett an official blacklisting of cultural troublemakers from Tinsel Town to tiny magazines.

His dreams vanished. His conscience canceled.

Blacklisted. Banned. Broke even as his books still sold while movie theaters and late night TV re-ran his major Hollywood hits. TB and tobacco coughing. Thanks to Hellman, living by America's dawn sea. Hammett died in 1961.

Luc's skull exploded.

Because he *got it.*

His parents didn't want him to read anybody who'd been blacklisted.

They worried . . . Who knows what all they worried about.

Maybe that he'd be seen with the book. Which he would be for the weeks it took him to read all five novels in Study Hall after he drove Hammett to the safe haven of his school locker that afternoon with the excuse to the janitor that he had to pick up something for Key Club.

Or maybe his parents were afraid that there was something in those novels that would suck Luc into Wrong Thinking that could draw the fire and fury of J. Edgar Hoover's FBI and destroy their beloved son.

He got that.

But what he didn't get . . .

A Montana senator made by bribes. Blood shed by Big Money in Luc's own backyard of Butte. Politics and power lynching a man from a railroad trestle.

Luc got As for the whole of eighth grade's year-long Montana history class.

Never once had he been taught, heard or read anything about any of that.

That discovery Saturday he sat at a round table in the county library.

While waiting outside . . .

Ghosts. Goblins. Grinning jack-o-lanterns of horror. Laughing. Waiting to claim their due outside the Vernon, Montana, library that October '65 day before Halloween when America's KIAS in Vietnam rose to 1,407.

Luc shook his head:

What else aren't they teaching me in school?

THE V

A virus came to town in November.

Hitched a ride to Vernon with Wendy's salesman father.

Some people said that the *V* as in *V*ernon virus was a cold. Some said it was the flu. Fever. Yucked noses. Sneezes erupting from sluggish sleep. Coughs.

The town's docs had miracle antibiotics like penicillin to prescribe and the town's two drugstores never ran out of pills. But those pills only vanquished bacteria like strep. Aspirin could help ease the yucks of the virus, but not stop it from running wild. Such science didn't exist in 1965.

The salesman's daughter Wendy heard her brother Ed sneeze as he climbed into a carload of his buddies to go to school. Wendy felt a slight tingle.

V kissed Mrs. Dawson when she stamped the checkout card for Marin in the school library. She walked into her glass-walled office. Closed the door. Stared out at the horizons of Vernon. Screamed. Didn't cough until the next day.

Took two more days for V to slap Luc. He spent that time with Kurt who kept doing most of the Key Club work and Wayne who was there.

V nailed Buffy the week before Thanksgiving after Steve kissed her *oh so just right* in his car parked on a gravel road under the autumn moon. He felt bad about that as V put him in bed the next day. Steve figured V'd gotten him the night before he gave it to Buffy when he secretly met up with year-younger-than-her Lizzie who thought she knew how to claim his heart.

Wearing-his-ring Buffy didn't know about any of that. Then. Walked into the GIRLS room the next morning after that *oh so just right* kiss to fix her dress.

Bobbi Jean stood in front of those bathroom mirrors.

Unsnapped her black purse.

Pulled out a tube of lipstick—

—and Buffy heard herself say: "What a great color!"

"Ruby Midnight," said Bobbi Jean.

She smiled at the girl she hadn't talked to in a while.

"Here," she told Buffy. "Try it."

She handed Buffy a Kleenex tissue to wipe off her own soft pink gloss.

"*Oh my God!*" whispered Buffy as she rubied her lips in that high school bathroom mirror.

Bobbi Jean's reflection smiled at hers.

"You've gotta hold on to your man's eyes," said Bobbi Jean.

"Wait!" said Buffy. "I didn't know . . . You're going with some guy?"

Bobbi Jean painted that just-shared ruby lipstick over her own lips.

Put her tube of power back in her black purse. Snapped it shut.

Turned and walked out of the GIRLS room without another word.

Oh wow, I wonder who? thought Buffy.

Should I use a tissue on my lips to go back to who I'd been?

But the hell with that: *Try something new. See if . . . See who likes it.*

Bobbi Jean's guy has gotta be Luc, thought Buffy. Those two had gone out once. *Must be more now. Good for Luc. He deserves Ruby Midnight.*

Buffy walked out to the Big Pink hallways where Mike Jodrey laughed and where, in days, the V infected most of the chorus and music teacher Mr. Bundy.

The V caught Walt in the Big Pink's auto mechanics garage classroom as he solved puzzles his classmates couldn't imagine.

Tod got tapped at the nursing home where he'd grabbed a job as a nurse's aide that usually went to a high school girl. For some reason, V missed nursing-home-bedded Gramma Meg and her polio legs. Luc's aunts and his folks got it.

After-school clerk Donna's boss Zelda left the hospital records room to deliver file folders to the nurses' station. She got so sick she could barely get a cigarette to stay in her lips for the coughing.

The hospital boss got Principal Harris to excuse Donna from classes to "run our whole damn show" for days until Zelda came back.

Mel and Clancy got the V in their university dorm. They were over it by the time fall quarter ended and they came home for Christmas. They rode the four hours to Vernon in silence. Couldn't talk anymore about What To Do.

Laura rode the Empire Builder train from Chicago to the Vernon valley of the V. She got it. Shrugged. Gave Luc the new Beatles album *Rubber Soul*.

Christmas with the pine tree strung with lights and silver strands of tinsel in the living room meant he gave Laura three paperback mysteries for her train ride back to Chicago. Like always, he and Laura chipped in and bought a box of cigars for their dad. They all chipped in and bought Mom a night out for dinner with the family so she wouldn't have to cook one.

The V faded from town as people took down their Christmas lights.

New Year's Eve.

Mel's house after dinner.

Came a knock on their front door.

Mel swung it open . . .

There on the front porch stood Clancy. Snow fell all around him. On him. He'd never knocked before. Always just walked right in. But now . . .

"Just gotta say it," he said as he stood on that concrete front stoop.

"I told my folks and I already did it, so . . . I threw the hook. Dropped out of the U. Went down after Christmas to the Draft Board office. Volunteered. Mrs. Theen stamped V for volunteer on my file so's up the line they'll know and maybe that'll help. I was gonna flunk out come spring anyway. So the Army'd have grabbed me up then. This way . . . It's like I chose."

"It's . . ." said Mel, a catch in his voice and a lump in his throat his best friend Clancy sensed as he fought all that in himself. "Now it is what it is. So come in."

The door closed behind them.

And 1966 started with 2,267 Vietnam KIAS.

VALENTINE'S DAY

A snow-just-melted February Sunday afternoon in 1966.

The day before Valentine's Day.

Buffy slammed the door shut on her parents' square house at the corner of *"What the Hell!"* and *"Right fucking now!"*

Rocketed the family's floral shop van away from the curb.

The Big Pink bounced and shrank in her rearview mirror.

She obeyed the STOP sign because *You Do What You Swore to Do!*

Gunned the van down Main Street past the car driven by Alice with Wendy riding shotgun. Didn't honk back. Didn't see their faces wonder. Knew *that house* waited past the southside Blackhawk Elementary school where he'd gone to—

There!

The flower shop van crunched *full stop* in front of that faded brick home.

Buffy didn't see its side mirror reflect a blue car braking behind her.

She charged from the van. Pounded on the brick house's front door.

That door swung open.

There stood sophomore class, tight-sweater Lizzie. With a *Gotchya!* smile.

Lizzie stepped out of her house and into the big chill.

A '57 Chevy with FOR SALE signs in each back window double-parked beside the blue car behind the van.

Buffy felt herself backed away from the house by Lizzie's emergence.

Heard herself yell at that leering year-younger *bigger boobs* teenager:

"Only reason he sneaks off to . . . to you is 'cause what you let him do! He doesn't give a shit about you. He's . . . He's mine! I'm the one who . . . who . . ."

"The one who's standing out here in the cold with him and me?"

Buffy whirled:

There stood Steve.

She saw his blue car behind him.

Saw his hands rise up: *Don't shoot!*

Remembered the phone call with him she'd just hung up on.

"*Is it true?*" Buffy'd demanded.

"*Look*," said across-town-in-his-house Steve. "*I was gonna tell you—*"

"*Tell me WHEN? Tell me WHAT?*"

"What did—"

"Sue called to tell me she heard *WHAT* Lizzie is saying about you two! Saying you're cheating on me! On us! With her!"

"It wasn't so much cheating, it was just—"

"*Just!*" Buffy had yelled into the telephone. "Like in *justice*? Well maybe somebody better go make sure little Miss Lizzie knows what's *just!*"

She'd slammed the phone down.

Grabbed the van keys and . . .

. . . now stood on the cold front porch face-to-face with arms-crossed Lizzie.

"You!" snapped Buffy. "I came here to tell you he only gives a shit about what you let him . . . whatever it is you let him do! He loves me! He . . . we . . ."

Lizzie smirked.

Steve yelled: "BUFFY! *STOP!* You can't just go crazy!"

Buffy whirled toward Steve—

—saw Zack from her class standing behind Steve/didn't care. Shouted:

"We're going steady! I love you! We can't . . . I . . . You say I '*can't*' . . . You say . . ."

Then her voice turned to ice: "I *can't*, huh. Well, this is something I *can*."

She twisted off Steve's class ring. Threw it at him.

Athlete Steve caught it against his chest.

"Happy Valentine's Day!" screamed Buffy.

She roared the van away.

Didn't look in the rearview mirror.

Sobbed toward the van's windshield.

The car drove her up Knob Hill past the balconied, blue-roofed, white-walled house where *he*, where *Steve* lived. *Where . . . Where . . .*

A bouncing gravel road *bonked* her sobbing forehead on the steering wheel.
Buffy slammed on the brakes.

Blinked away her tears.

Looked out of the vehicle that'd brought her here.

I'm in the cemetery.

The poetic perfection of her arrival *here now* made her mind whirl.

She collapsed. Tears. Sobs. Wails. Shaking with sorrow. With anger.

The van's KRIP radio station played a finger-snapping song by her folks' New Jersey crooner Frank Sinatra and then a lament by a Texas country guitar twanger named Willie Nelson. The news came on. The number of Americans like her who'd died in Vietnam now stood at 2,844.

Whatever else was in the radio news, she didn't hear it.

The chilly breeze rocked the van.

A van, she told herself as she looked at this field of the dead. *Not a hearse.*

She used paper wrappings for bouquets to blow her nose.

Breathed in the scent of roses.

Dried her eyes.

Drove herself home.

One block away from her bedroom where she could hide—

—Buffy spotted the FOR SALE '57 Chevy parked across from her house.

She parked the van in front of her home. Charged across the street.

He climbed out of the used Chevy.

Met her in the middle of the road.

Buffy hissed: "What the hell are you doing here, Zack?"

Surfer Zack's sandy hair matched the stubble on his cheeks this no-shave Sunday afternoon. He wore the maroon and gold winter coat for basketball players.

"Take it easy, please, Buffy: *Take it easy!* I know you saw me at Lizzie's and—I was up to Steve's. He's helping me cram for English 'cause I blew off readin' the books. You phone 'n' he races out of there like a bat out of hell!"

"Knew he was in trouble. Caught up with his car. Got out. Heard."

"He sent you here to—"

"Nobody sent me. I did it on my own like I do, long as . . . you know . . . as the team or buddies don't get hurt. Like Daryl taught me when I was a freshman and he walked out of trouble. You do what you can when you get a chance.

"You gotta give Steve another chance, Buffy. He needs it."

"He's got all he *needs* standing up there smirking in a tight sweater!"

"You gotta understand guys," said Zack.

"*What about ME?*"

"I see us standing out here in the cold talking about how you gotta give a great guy who's crazy about you a chance—"

"A *chance*? Like you get a chance, Zack?"

"Like I get?" Zack shook his head. "I get what I get from being on the A squad. Winning for the team. Hell, that got me off scot-free when a whiskey bottle rolled out from under my seat when the cops stopped me for running that STOP sign two blocks from here. Except for Key Club. They kicked me out."

A memory struck Buffy.

Her voice softened: "Luc—"

"He's a good guy too," said Zack. "But Steve is *Steve*."

"Luc said you used to talk about being a doctor."

"Plenty of time for that down the road for me."

Zack nodded his head like he was nailing *what he said* into *what was true*.

"Down the road," he said. "Like the '57 Chevy here. Coolest car ever made. I get to drive it around so people will see the FOR SALE signs. Come to my old man's used car lot. Buy it."

"What about you?"

The wind blew past the Big Pink five blocks to the west.

"Guess I go with the deal I got to get where I . . . I . . ."

"Where, Zack? Where do you want to go?"

The surfer-blonde basketball star shook his head: "Just give Steve a chance."

Didn't look back as he drove off toward tomorrow.

Monday morning brought *Oh no!* news to the high school yearbook's staff meeting before First Bell that knocked Buffy out of her angry blues.

Principal Harris opened the door to the room for the school paper and yearbook staff. There were layout boards. Boxes of black and white photos. Manual typewriters that *clicked clicked* zinged/clunk to *click click* another line of prose.

Principal Harris came in with a softness none of the kids on the yearbook had ever seen. *That* made Buffy even more nervous than Harris as a gorilla.

His voice actually *asked*:

"You guys got that page for Sam Smith planned out?"

Sam Smith was in Steve's class. Only Mike Jodrey could match his laugh. Sam'd gotten a job the summer before like all lucky kids in Vernon. Worked at one of the grain elevators by the train tracks east of town. Tripped over the rail around a forty-four-foot-deep silo full of wheat kernels. Got quicksanded to gone.

The senior girl who was the yearbook's ruling editor told Principal Harris: "Yes, sir. We're working on it."

"You need to figure out another page.

"Just got word . . ." Principal Harris shook his head. "Mitt O'Brien got killed in Vietnam. *Damn communists!* He was class of '64."

Principal Harris shook his head.

"Figure it out," he ordered. "We're getting his Army photo in dress uniform."

One more shake of his head and Principal Harris walked out of a classroom with layout boards and silent typewriters and eleven stunned students.

First Bell rang.

Buffy gathered her books and walked with the others out into the hall.

Ghosts of dead boys not much older than her flowed in her wake.

I knew him, she thought. Knew *them*. Kids just like . . .

Buffy floated through the second-floor hallway in the Big Pink amidst streams filled with laughing, shouting, whispering kids *just like*.

There's Wendy telling Alice: "Don't know why he all of a sudden keeps telling me he loves me, that he's my dad. Maybe it's because he's on the road so much these days." Sophomore Cherie gave Buffy a smile. Luc hurried past with his Coke-bottle-thick glasses that didn't notice her empty finger. Mike Jodrey walked past with his thin-lensed glasses. Wendy's big brother Ed who needed no glasses at all leaned against the wall of lockers. She imagined Clancy who Steve'd told her had passed his physical and was in an Army boot-camp for Basic Training. There was Kurt walkin' and talkin' something about Key Club while striding-beside-him Wayne's eyes watched for who was watching. There was Sandi who smiled at the girl who helped her stop getting scrubbed. There's Marin listening to Barbara. There were Walt and Sheila Stiff Arm. Tod, there was—

Lizzie.

Walking straight toward Buffy. No rings on her fingers.

Lizzie's eyes daggered Buffy before she disappeared behind her.

Well, thought Buffy. So . . . *something.*

She imagined the coming yearbook memorial pages for Sam and Mitt.

This is the chance Today's Buffy has.

The hallway crowd parted.

Buffy stepped to her left.

Steve stepped out of the crowd, coming her way.

Two gunfighters in a high school hallway.

She met him halfway.

Reached into her purse. Pulled out what she hadn't had the heart to throw away. The sealed envelope she'd hidden there days ago *before.* She drew smiles, hearts and different shaped "love" words around the card's Be My Valentine!

Pressed her pink lipstick lips below that ask. That hope.

Now Buffy shoved that sealed envelope against Steve's chest.

"Open it. Toss it. Keep it. Do . . . *just* what you're going to do. Me, too."

Buffy walked away as first period Final Bell rang on Valentine's Day '66.

THE CARDS YOU GET

May 21, 1966. A Saturday.

Make it 7:57 P.M. when Prom had already started.

Luc sat on his bed. Playing solitaire.

America had circled the moon but the Russians had already dropped something there. The Beatles announced they'd given their last live concert.

Another chance I never got, thought Luc.

He played Las Vegas Solitaire:

Turn over one card at a time.

Luc had the radio on and loud. A new Beach Boys album waited by his stereo, but he wanted to hear what the world would broadcast to him, not what he *controlled and chose*. He wanted to hear poetry that might sing *true* to him.

He *coulda shoulda woulda* gone to Prom *except*.

"I'm already going with Steve," Buffy'd said.

Her fingers were naked.

She said: "We're working things out."

Hurried away from Luc in their high school hallway.

That Saturday Prom night, Luc flipped over his next card:

The Jack of Diamonds.

Yes! Put it on top of the Queen of Clubs on second of seven piles.

The radio said: "It's the Top of the News!"

Our guys are shooting Commie enemies in Cambodia and our allies in South Vietnam are shooting Buddhists. Our KIAS were now 4,499.

He shook his head as he scanned his overturned cards.

He could have gone to the movies.

Seen *The Chase* starring made-famous-by-a-black-and-white-wild-teen-agers-and-motorcycles-movie Marlon Brando in Technicolor cinema as an honest sheriff in a modern Texas small town where businessmen in suits bragged about the guns on their belts. Bullied a Black man. Broke laws to vigilante a young actor named Robert Redford playing a man named Bubber who'd been falsely sent to prison and who'd that night escaped to find justice and his true love played by an actress from Hollywood royalty named Jane Fonda.

But Friday night, Luc'd seen that movie.

Gotten blown away by what unfolded before his eyes.

What if there were places like that? Towns where money made the rules despite the laws. Towns where "respectable" gun freaks battered anyone who didn't look like them. Towns where you could get away with murder *if.*

But though he loved to rewatch great movies, Luc showing up at the Roxy again *and solo* that night would've weighed him down like a cowboy's duster coat.

Better to ride the darkness alone.

Like Kurt was. Wayne, too. Prom or not, Luc knew that Marin spent that warm May Saturday night in 1966 in the arms of his girl.

Luc flipped over a card: 2 of Spades.

The wrong color for either of the two aces for the win in the top row.

Why did Donna do it?

She'd braced him in the Big Pink's hallway on an April Tuesday. Her stone expression braked him in place as other teenagers streamed around them.

"I wanted to say *thanks*," she told him. "Not just for . . . *you know* . . . but for, *hell*, since fifth grade you've been . . ."

Her hand wiggle said she was jokingly diminishing what she really meant: ". . . mostly OK. Alphabetic seating was going to plop me beside someone. Could have been a lot worse than you."

Luc's brow wrinkled: "What's going on?"

"I dropped out of school," said Donna. "Just turned in all my books."

"*WHAT?* Why? You're probably smarter than me."

Donna shrugged. "That's not enough.

"But don't worry," she told him. "A budget came through and I'm in the right place at the right time to get a real job that'll let me . . . hell, who knows?"

Her lips tightened over her words . . .

. . . *Yes*, she'd say them:

"I know you see me like a *crip*, like a *gimp*—No, *come on*: Whatever the word is, it's what you see. But unlike some people, you see more, too.

"What I got to tell you is *look in the mirror*. Whatever word you see in there, it isn't *cool*. Is some kind of a freak. I know that's who you see 'cause I can see it in the eyes behind your thick glasses. But you're wrong. Whoever you see in there like those fucking words for me, *do* like you do. Look again. Look with *feel ya* but no *sorry for yourself*. You can make someone else to see in that mirror if you make it who you wanna, gotta be. Least, I hope so."

She gave him a sad smile.

Turned and walked away *owning* her limp.

Las Vegas Solitaire only lets you go through the fifty-two shuffled cards one time.

What about the Joker? A wild card that could trump the numbers?

There was no Joker allowed in Las Vegas Solitaire.

Luc heard a train's lonesome whistle in the night.

FAITHFUL

Steve graduated, thought Luc on 1966's first June Monday afternoon of summer vacation as he stood outside the white stucco gas station that now served as the bus stop. *He's going to college come September.*

Come September, Buffy and I will be seniors. Without him around.

The silver Greyhound bus rumbled off the highway.

Luc moved the outgoing cans of film closer to the parking bus. Looked up—

—saw a friend trudging down the metal stairs off the bus.

"Hey, Mel!" called out Luc to the older boy. "What's going on?"

The traveler's dazed expression spooked Luc.

Gravity pulled the two friends together.

The bus driver scowled at Luc walking away. *Fucking teenagers. People who don't do their jobs.* The driver had a schedule to keep. He unloaded the new movie cans from the baggage bin under the bus and loaded the old ones himself.

"They put me on the bus back from Butte," mumbled Mel.

Butte, thought Luc. The Berkley Pit. A mile wide and a mile deep. All that was left of the richest hill on earth. Butte of Dashiell Hammett.

"My physical for the Draft," whispered Mel.

He shook his head. His voice became almost normal.

"Clancy, he's stationed in Germany with the Army. Got lucky. Sent there. When he found out I'd dropped out of the university like him, he paid extra to air mail me quick. Told me not to worry. He's a clerk tied into the whole worldwide Army personnel assignments division. When I got out of Basic Training, he'd've arranged for me to be assigned nowhere near Vietnam.

"So day before yesterday, rode the bus to Butte. Spent the night in a crappy motel. Come morning, they march about fifty of us into the Induction Center. Fill out this form. Stand straight. Bend over. Spread your butt cheeks. Hold still for the stethoscope. Talk to a shrink for five minutes so he can say you're not crazy and get to kill. Move it! Move it! Move it!"

Mel shook his head: "And the whole time, I'm rustling Acid Freak."

"*Who?*" said Luc with the stench of gasoline in the air.

"Some guy who figured the way to flunk his physical and stay out of the Army was to drop acid before he got on the bus to the Induction Center."

Acid.

Even Luc knew what that was.

LSD. An illegal psychedelic drug that gave you whacky and wild hallucinations the Powers That Be said were dangerous.

Luc didn't know the CIA's secret experiments had LSD-poisoned one of their own and thus triggered him to leap out of a New York hotel window or that a group of long-haired societal rebels called The Merry Pranksters were riding a bus around America with "tabs" of LSD, a Beatnik-era legend for a driver, plus an American author. A journalist made them all famous for at least a few years.

"We lined up alphabetically," said Mel. "That put Acid Freak next to me. I practically carried him through the lines.

"A few hours and we're all back in the Induction Center's room like a gym. We're standing alphabetical. Me holding slobbering and *Whoa!*-ing Acid Freak.

"An Army sergeant stands in front of us. Bellows out names. One after the other, guys get marched over to the far wall.

"The name calling comes to me . . . And skips over me! Skips over Acid Freak! Calls the next guy's name. And the next. Calls out names until it's only me and Acid Freak standing there in the middle of the gym floor. The sergeant tells all those other guys they have passed. They're being inducted into the US Army. He makes them raise their hand. Swear an oath.

"And me, I can't fucking help it. I'm grabbing Acid Freak and jumping up and down, telling him *we did it!* We beat the Draft. We're not going into the Army!

"The sergeant has his corporal march those sworn-in other guys out of the gym. Marches over to us. Grins as he shakes his head.

"You two poor dumb sons-of-a-bitches," he said. "Stay where you are."

"He marches to the gym doors. Goes through them. The doors close.

"Suddenly it's just me and Acid Freak standing there alone. I feel my heart beating. *Ba-boomp. Ba-boomp.*

"*BAM!*"

Mel's shout is so loud the service station attendant pumping dead dinosaurs into a mom's station wagon damn near drops the hose.

"The gym doors fly open. In march three United States Marines. Full dress uniforms. Two corporals and what I got *learned* was a master sergeant.

"'*Congratulations, gentlemen!*' he shouts at Acid Freak and me like we're across the gym instead of so close his spit hits us. '*You have been selected as the only two red-blood Americans from Montana to be drafted into the Marine Corps since the end of World War II!*'"

"But *Marines*," whispered Luc. "They're the toughest. And all volunteers."

"Well me and Acid Freak made history because the Marine Corps drafted us. Not the Army where Clancy could send me and my paperwork wherever."

What do I say? thought Luc.

Mel asked him: "Have you turned eighteen and gone to see Mrs. Theen at the Draft Board office behind the bowling alley up by the county jail?"

"Not until—"

"*Good!* You know how we all got told to write down anything special about us on the forms she makes us fill out so we'd get a better chance of not being just a regular grunt shoved into shitty duties?

"Once I was collecting fossils at that reservoir south of town," said Mel. "Talked the surplus store manager into letting me try a scuba mouthpiece 'n' tube, a couple of flippers, goggles. Paddled around the reservoir a few times even though I can barely swim.

"So, for Mrs. Theen's Draft Board forms, I wrote down that I scuba dived. 'Cause that'd help me stand out. Get a better assignment if the Army Drafts me."

"*Ahhh . . .*"

"Yesterday in that gym, right after they swore me and Acid Freak into the Corps, that master sergeant glances at my file. Says:

"Scuba diver? You ever hear of Long-Range Reconnaissance Patrols?"

LRRPs thought Luc. The tip of Marine Corps combats. The Marines were taking major casualties in Vietnam, and Marines like LRRPs took higher . . .

Luc swallowed: "What are you going to do now?"

"I got ten days to '*close out my personal affairs.*'"

Mel shrugged. "Clancy's in Germany. I'll hang out with my folks. Try to get laid—a real woman, not the whorehouse. A vet back from 'Nam at the bar by the bus stop gave me a joint—marijuana cigarette. I'm gonna go down to the river. Fire it up. Take my hammer out for a good long fossil hunt. Who knows.

"Then . . . *Semper fi.*"

Mel looked at this thick-glasses kid starting his last high school summer. They'd known each other since they'd started knowing anybody.

"See you around, Luc."

Mel walked away.

Please! Luc wanted to shout after him. Shout to all of space and time. *Please see me around! Be around to see me!*

But all he could do was load the film cans into the Roxy's station wagon. Drive to his own ambush.

THE WAY IT IS

L uc parked the station wagon in front of the Roxy.

Mr. Tom shuffled outside the theater's glass doors. Pulled a legal cigarette out of his shirt pocket. Snapped a flame to light the addictive toxic white tube.

That theater manager helped Luc carry the five heavy cans of movie film through the Roxy's glass front doors to the outer lobby.

"Just leave them here for now," said Mr. Tom. "You got the wagon's keys?"

Luc passed them over.

Mr. Tom led Luc into the front lobby. The deserted candy counter. The silent popcorn maker. Shelves of sugar and chocolate treats. The Coke machine. The empty cashier's booth.

Mr. Tom shoved his cigarette into a waist-high, sand-filled public ashtray.

"No way to say this but to say it," said Mr. Tom. "Luc, you're fired."

Wha—This isn't real!

"It isn't your fault," continued Mr. Tom. "You're great. You've worked for the Roxy since *what*, you were ten? Handbills. Now janitor and projectionist. Even with all this summer's got planned for you, if I could I'd keep you, but I can't.

"My grandson is fourteen. Eighth grade. Tall enough to feed the projector, so I have to let you go. Today. But fill out your card all the way to five o'clock."

"OK," whispered Luc as his mind whirled:

I need a job! College! My dad! Gotta make my own way!

"Go up to the projection booth," said his now ex-boss. "Look around in case you left anything there."

Numbed, Luc walked up red carpeted stairs he climbed hundreds of times. Opened the door where he'd spent so many teenage summer nights. Breathed in the air of oily film. Dust. Burned carbon rods that made the fire that let him project stories onto a screen for others' eyes. For *his* eyes.

Nothing in here was his. Nothing to take.

Except.

A green rubber toy soldier filled the palm of Luc's hand.

Don't know where you came from, but we've been together all this time.

Luc put the toy soldier in his front jeans pocket.

Turned out the lights. Trudged down red carpeted stairs to the lobby.

"I'm proud of you, son," said Mr. Tom. "I know you love movies. Keep coming, and maybe, from time to time . . ."

The theater manager shrugged.

"Hey!" he said. "Take a large company Coke for the road!"

Before Luc could answer, Mr. Tom had a paper cup scooped with ice and getting filled under the Coke machine's spigot. Mr. Tom popped a plastic cap with a straw for its hole onto the cup, handed it to Luc.

"Oh, hell," said Mr. Tom as he reached with his free hand and scooped ice into another cup. "Take two."

Luc blinked: *Now I'm standing on the Main Street sidewalk outside the Roxy's glass doors with an ice-cold giant Coke cup in each hand.*

Wait, WHAT? Mel said what about . . . about MARIJUANA? From a Vietnam vet? And Mel was, he was gonna smoke it! Here! In Vernon! Marijuana!

"'S one of those Cokes for me?"

His cousin Gene stood there in a torn shirt, blue jeans and work boots.

Luc gave Gene the second Coke.

Gene drank most of it in one long slurp.

"Thanks, man. I needed that." Gene grinned. "What's going on?"

Luc shrugged: "The Roxy doesn't need me anymore. I need a job."

Luc knew Gene had a job. *Gandy-dancer.* The sledgehammer swinging, heavy steel rail lifting, jackhammering, clunky brown wooden ties flopping in the dirt and sun muscle crew for the railroad. It was the hardest summer job a teenage guy could get. It paid swell and you sweated for every dime.

"Good luck," said Gene. "Don't know if it'd be good or bad if you get a boss like Leo Sisti. '*I only need you from the neck down, Geen-o,*' he told me once when I had an idea. He gets up every morning at five. Walks the tracks from the elevators out east to the new highway overpass west out of town. He ain't on the clock. That's him checking on his responsibility. Reason you see me now is he cut us loose rather than let us hang around costing the company by just waiting for tomorrow's orders. He told us he's got no spots for new guys to—

"*Wait!*" cried Gene. "You got your car?"

"No."

"Come on. I'm dropping something off for the other Pezzanis up on Knob Hill and the dad—*we're all cousins*—he says out to the farm he needs a hay bucker besides his son Seba. You know Seba: he's in the class below us."

Gene had a third-hand Chevy but the radio worked. Getting from Main Street to the Pezzani house on Knob Hill took only one song and the news announcing the Vietnam War now claimed 4,733 dead Americans on this day that was the anniversary of D-Day when America and her allies invaded Nazi Germany's occupied Europe.

"Come in through the back door here in the garage, right into the kitchen," said Gene as he led Luc up the driveway. Gene called out "*Hey*"—and walked through that screen door *without knocking.*

My mom would freak out! thought Luc as he followed Gene in.

"What the hell," said a middle-aged woman Luc's mom's age. "Set two more places at the table. Hey, Luc! Ain't see you for a while."

Never, thought Luc. *I've never been up here.*

A laughing boy and a girl in grade school dashed past Luc.

A cross with crucified Christ hung on the kitchen wall.

Catholic, thought nominally brought-up Methodist Luc.

"*Naw,* thanks, Teresa," Gene told the mother of the house. "I gotta get home."

"Me, too," said Luc. "I . . . Thanks."

"What the hell for?" Teresa grinned. Gave Luc a friendly pat on the arm.

Gene said: "I told Luc here you guys might need a hay bucker."

"Bob!" yelled his wife Teresa. "You got hay bucking for Luc Ross here?"

"Hell yes!" A man walked out of a back room with a closed paint can and a teenage boy in the class below Luc's, the same class as Luc's Prom date Cherie. They'd both been St. Jude Catholic school kids. "Can you start tomorrow?"

Luc nodded.

The son Seba Pezzani told year-older Luc: "I'll swing by your house tomorrow morning at 7:00. Get us out to the hayfield by 8:00. You got gloves?"

Luc nodded.

"See you then."

"And now you at least gotta take some breadsticks, right, Nonna?"

A tiny gray and wrinkled old woman wrapped in a housedress shuffled her clunky black shoes into the kitchen from some hole in the universe.

Teresa and the old woman—*Nonna*, grandmother—jabbered back and forth in machinegun Italian.

Nonna took the half dozen homemade breadsticks from her middle-aged daughter's offering hand. Shuffled to the counter. Grabbed a handful of fresh breadsticks from a wicker basket. Wrapped them with the others in a white paper napkin. Shuffled to Luc with them held in her fist. Thumped her fist on his chest and glared at him with ancient brown eyes.

"You don't want to piss off Nonna," said her grandson Seba.

Luc smiled and took the fistful of still-warm breadsticks.

"Thank you so much, Nonna!" he said. Heard Teresa translate: "*Grazie.*"

Nonna patted Luc's right cheek.

She shuffled to her seat at the dining room/kitchen table. Waited for whatever was boiling on the stove that summer afternoon before Confession.

Gene and Luc left through the back door out to the driveway.

Luc rode shotgun in Gene's car past the houses of Vernon. He thought of his own home that he loved. How hard it must have been—*must be*—for his parents to keep him safe and steady toward their dream of a perfect future for him and his sister Laura. How everything in his house was always in its place or vanished like Hammett. How dinner was always at 6:00. Where they usually all read books or magazines as they ate. Where everyone knew what they were supposed to do, did it and never made a fuss because making a small fuss could mushroom everything to something horrible.

He shook his head as his hometown passed by. "They're . . . Teresa . . ."

"Cool," said Gene. "If I didn't have my crew, I'd hang there. Seba's great."

Luc's parents were proud and relieved he'd landed a new job. Mr. Tom had called to tell them. Apologize. And they liked the breadsticks.

"They're good people, the Pezzanis," said Mom. "Teresa, she's damn near one of us Conner sisters like your aunts and me."

The phone rang just as Luc finished drying dinner dishes and once would have been about to leave to go to work running the movie projectors at the Roxy.

Was his buddy Wayne, who said: "Glad I caught you."

"No problem," said Luc. Told Wayne about getting fired.

"Is it OK if I drop by?" said Wayne.

Luc turned away from the phone. Asked his mom. Who said OK.

Wayne knew to come to the front door. Knock.

They went into Luc's bedroom.

Luc's dad was already back to work at the trucking company.

His mom went downstairs to smoke and watch a rerun of a black and white TV show that a month before ended its eight-year run on one of the only three national TV networks, a half-hour comedy about a comedian/singer with a whacky wife who was always getting into funny trouble and their two sons.

Wayne leaned against the headboard of Luc's bed: "So you got fired."

Luc sat in the room's chair: "Guess sometimes that's just the way it goes."

Luc saw eagerness in Wayne's face. Hunger.

"Well," said Wayne, "turns out today also shows how you can make things go your own way—*if* you're smart."

He leered: "I got them to give me a raise at the hardware store today."

"Wow, that's—"

Wayne stood tall.

"So a week ago, I started walking everywhere there like this."

Wayne's body stiffened. Like *Oh-oh.* Like *Oh, yeah!* His legs locked so his knees barely bent. He quickly strode back and forth, back and forth in Luc's bedroom. His stiff legs whipped him bent forward like a man on a mission that had to be important or else why walk like that?

Wayne whirled to face *sitting-there-stunned* Luc.

"Didn't matter!" said Wayne. "Getting something for my uncles or my dad in our hardware store. Dodging or dancing customers. Up one aisle. Down the other. In and out of the back room. Gone back there doing *not much* until I'd hear someone coming so *hup hup hup hup* I go, marching somewhere.

"Finally passed one uncle who said: 'Oughta give that boy a raise.' Maybe he was joking. Probably was. But I was lookin' and actin' like that guy. I waited a day. Asked the other uncle when what his brother had said was gonna happen. Then I quick-walked outta sight to who knows where. Today I got that raise and my dad didn't have nothing to do with it. It was the walk."

All Luc could do was stare.

Wayne gave Luc a smile. Said he had to go.

Luc's mom'd come upstairs.

Wayne quick-walked, stiff-legged past her with a very busy nod.

Looked back over his shoulder to throw a secret smile to Luc.

Marched out the front door.

Mom noticed the strange walk:

"He must have someplace he's going."

BUCKING BALES

Baking heat under the blue sky above Luc on a 1966 June morning.
A field west of Vernon.

Scruffy brown work boots. Blue jeans. White T-shirt. Buckskin rough-out work gloves last worn for post hole digging at the drive-in movie theater. Thick-lens glasses: *Please don't let them slip down my nose!*

Hustling behind a chugging flatbed truck with no driver.

The steering wheel was lashed to keep the truck rolling straight ahead. Gearshift in neutral. The choke knob kept the sputtering engine turning the black tires so the truck rumbled fast/slow enough for Luc's hustle to keep up.

Rows of hay bales filled the giant field. The hay baler machine had dropped the bales seven loping steps apart. Each bale weighed around sixty pounds.

Luc hustled to the next bale. Grabbed cinched-around-the-bale twine. Jerked with his back and his legs. Swung his knee up under the scratchy/sneezy/stinking hay bale. Muscled it tight against his chest as he stepped to catch up to the open back end of the flatbed truck. Shoved the hay bale on the ass-end platform of the flatbed truck—

—where cousin Seba would swing/lift the bale to build a stack of bales the savvy way to keep the stack from tumbling over during the ride to the unload—

—all while Luc was back hustling alongside the truck, forward past the back bumper to the next bale to buck into position when the truck rolled past.

Coming near to the end of the row, Seba swung off the back end to the driver's side door. Unlashed the wheel. Steered the truck to turn around and go back up along the next row of hay bales. Lashed everything back to the way it was. Swung up to the back end again as the driverless truck rumbled forward.

Buckin' bales row after row until they cleared the field.

Was late afternoon by the time they'd trucked the hay bales to the Pezzanis' barn. Stacked them out of fire range from the barn where the family's father Bob would keep them until a rancher with hungry cows and the right dollars would show up.

Bob rounded the going rate per-bale-bucked up to its nearest dollar. Would have done that even if Luc hadn't been family. Luc was pretty sure his hay buckin' partner Seba got no salary: It was the family farm.

Boss of the family Teresa'd brought a pitcher of lemonade to the two teenage boys for a break before they unloaded the truck.

Bob told Luc: "Sorry that's all I got for you now."

"One day's better than no work," answered Luc.

Farmer Bob shook his head.

"Won't be easy you gettin' other jobs what with all you gotta do coming up. Let me make couple of calls."

Waved away Luc's "*Thanks!*"

Luc climbed in Seba's car for the ride back to town.

Stared at the haystack as Seba keyed the car: *We did that.*

What makes *we* is in part *me.*

They dragged Main on the way to Luc's. Grinning and talking as the breeze of that June '66 open-windowed afternoon flowed around them.

The phone rang while Luc was drying dinner dishes.

WITNESS

Is now when you'll see the end of the world?

An early July '66 Tuesday afternoon.

Luc rode inside the windowed cab of a giant yellow tractor plowing a sixty-acre field south of Vernon and west of the highway to the river or Canada.

I'm one-waying, he thought. *Aren't we all?*

Government scientists helped imperiled farmers fight their way out of the 1930s Dust Bowl starvation by introducing crop rotation farming.

The big yellow tractor Luc drove plowed a sixty-acre rectangular field to lay fallow while nearby fields greened with growing wheat. A metal shaft of plow discs stretched out at a ninety-plus degree angle from below the cab on the tractor's left-hand side. Hooked to that plow, the tractor could only go straight or make well-judged left turns. Rocks could jam the plow discs. Luc'd stop the tractor. Climb down. Clear stones from between plow discs.

Watch out for rattlesnakes.

That he knew every time he stepped down to any Montana earth.

He'd seen snakes flipped through the plow discs. Gophers could run away from the plow, but were stupid. Scavenging birds circled the plowing tractor.

Turn.

One-waying. Driving the tractor across the rectangular field with overlapping left-hand turns. That ever-decreasing *turn-turn-turn* path creating ever smaller rectangles of unplowed earth until the whole field was plowed.

Or until the end of the world.

Turn.

The Apocalypse waited in the next field.

That chain-link fence rose ten feet high to be topped by a V of barbed wire. Two cement blockhouses waited past light poles inside the fence perimeter that created a flow of spotlight images for the bulletproof security cameras.

Those two *buried all the way down to hell* cement blockhouses had giant black metal square umbrella tops. Caps, if you will. Like what Luc was supposed to throw in the air at his high school graduation only seventeen-plus months away.

Turn.

The chain-link fence was behind Luc. The rumbling forward tractor crunching over sodded prairie earth trembled Luc in the driver's seat.

What filled his eyes were rolling fields and miles of golden prairie. The distant highway. The smudged glass of the tractor cab. The way ahead he had to steer.

What filled his mind were flashes of how this field he plowed now would someday be harvested for kernels of wheat to be trucked to an elevator like the one on the east end of town where a lake of grain sucked down to death one-year-older-than-him Sam before getting freight-trained back east to a factory that let the grain become the crust on a little girl's slice of apple pie.

Turn.

And the fenced-in field was back! Out the left side of the tractor cab before the sixty-mile Big Sky view of the blue sawtooth Rocky Mountains.

You'll get to be one of the first to see It, Luc told himself.

There'll be a blip on a radar screen—then a fury of them.

Buttons pushed. Red lights flashing from Air Force bases to jet bombers that were always in the air to submarines under the seas where the Beach Boys surfed and movie Gidgets in (modest) bikinis strolled the beaches.

Dynamite blows the black metal caps off the open shaft missile silos.

White smoke billows up to the blue sky above the two shafts to the center of the earth. ROAR! The ground shakes Luc's tractor even more.

Two Minuteman missiles.

Rising out of the space and time where everything had been *until.*

And Luc'll be one of the first people to see the end of the world.

Turn.

Now the calm missile site is straight ahead of the tractor's windshield.

Luc felt *Wonder when?* about the missile silo with every turn of this job farmer Bob had put in a call for Luc to get. Good pay and OK with Luc needing to quit mid-summer.

Turn.

Sweat mixed with dust on Luc's face.

He took his left hand off the tractor's steering wheel to wipe his forehead with the back of his arm. His eyes blinked him out past the tractor's windshield.

Turn.

Felt the missile silo behind him.

TOMORROW'S CHOSEN

Black and white newsreel footage of July 24, 1963, showed JFK, the thirty-fifth president of the United States of America, shaking hands with Bill Clinton, the forty-second president of the United States of America amidst a hundred teenage boys on the White House lawn.

Clinton and the other ninety-nine teenage boys wore collared and tucked-in white T-shirts with the logo of Boys Nation over their hearts.

Boys Nation.

The creation of a national veterans' organization to help their country's teenagers learn citizenship and democracy.

The tucked-in white shirts of Boys Nation were winners from their home Boys *State* conclaves. They were the guys elected to be governors and lieutenant-governors of fictitious states created by about-to-be high school seniors brought together on (usually) a college campus. Main Street civic organizations picked boys to sponsor/pay for and send the chosen few to the summer Boys State.

Boys Staters ran for elections to hold fictional role-playing political posts from city to county to state offices. They heard lectures by elected adults. By inspirational motivational speakers resounding God & Country. Montana's most dramatic and popular anti-left-wing speaker was a professor from Texas named E. Z. Daly. He got ten minutes of standing and cheering applause.

After that speech, Luc drifted around the campus of his first ever seen college . . . Spotted Wayne stiff-walk up to E. Z. Daly to . . . *To what?* thought Luc.

Montana had Girls State, too.

Luc's sister Laura had been picked and gone and won a couple of elections.

Luc ran for county attorney. Gave an impassioned "I've been training for this for my whole life" speech and fibbed about planning to be a lawyer. His opponent beat him after a shorter speech promising he'd do the best he could.

But Luc's real struggle came with what he'd learned from Hooded Eyes before Luc puked on the governor's shoes at the '64 GOP state convention.

Vernon civic groups chipped in and "picked" who Principal Harris and Guidance Counselor Stern "suggested" to send to Boys State.

Luc. And Kurt. Wayne. Gene who everyone liked. Bill, the high school's incoming student body president. Four other middle-class B-or-better grade students. But not Walt the whiz of auto shop or Tod who wore white uniforms as a nurses' aide. Not basketball star Surfer Zack, whose off-the-court antics made sponsors nervous. Plus, why would he need such an honor for his future? He was a high school basketball star. And not Luc's buddy Gros Ventre Marin because, *well*, you know. All of Vernon's Boys Staters were White, though the Montana-wide program included Indian boys from Reservation towns.

Luc drifted from the dining room after lunch his second day of Boys State when a paperback book fell out of the hip pocket of the guy walking ahead of him.

Luc scooped the book off the ground.

Caught up to pass it back to that stranger.

He was taller than Luc. Had a real smile and a solid set of eyes.

"Thanks!" he said. "I'm Vic. You ever read this?"

"*To Kill a Mockingbird*," said Luc. "It's great!"

"I'm on my second time," said Vic. "I mean, *wow*.

"The law's got to stand up for people like that innocent guy who got lynched just because he wasn't White," said Vic. "That's why I'm a conservative. *Law and order and—*"

"*Justice!*" they chorused at the same time.

"Where are you from?" asked Vic.

"Vernon. How about you?"

"Libby."

"Big city guy. Never been there."

"Our family drove through Vernon once when I was a kid."

"Next time, get them to stop. Not much there like in Libby. You've got some kind of mines and huge factory, right?"

"Asbestos," said Vic. "My dad is a manager in the plant."

Vic closed his eyes. Breathed deep.

"Damn it's good to smell fresh air. In Libby, we've got . . . Well, the company calls it *nuisance dust*. All through the air from the mines and factory. Gets everywhere. On everybody. Hell, the company even donated a bunch of it to make the baseball field. I'm a catcher. You play?"

"*Naw*," said Luc. "I'm the worst player at any sport you'll ever meet."

"Yeah, but you play great where it counts." Vic nodded to the book that shaped them, to the campus where they were practicing politics.

They talked about The Way Things Are and The Way They Should Be. Luc knew they were both right. Knew Vic was smarter than him. And true.

All of which threw Luc into his crisis of "Dues and Do's" for who he'd "Be."

Vic was running to be chief justice of the seven-member Supreme Court. So was Wayne.

Wayne worked his strut from the time he got off the Boys State bus. Stiff-walking through football-tossing, laughing and talking about girls' groups of teenage guys. He'd snap comments that meant nothing but sounded like he knew things. Then stiff-walk away with the same parting joke: "Gotta get something done but I hope we remember each other. I'm Wayne."

Wayne, who Lucas had been best . . . *well*, good friends with since first grade, even if now being buddies somehow meant being all about Wayne.

Versus:

Just-met Vic who wanted to make things that weren't about him better.

What was due to Luc's lifelong friend?

Who would he be if he didn't support Wayne?

What should he do?

Like all the other Boys Staters assembled in the auditorium with its rows of slanting toward the stage seats, Luc listened to their two campaign speeches.

Wayne stiff-walked up to the microphone. Right away made a joke: "*Am I done yet?*" Talked about being thrilled to see everyone out there from the stage. Talked about him being lucky to be the guy who they'd get to vote for.

When it was his turn, Vic walked to the microphone. Talked about justice for everybody and how we all have to work to make it happen.

Luc stared at the secret paper ballot in his hand.

Dues and *Do's* and *Be's.*

He couldn't vote for that phony walk. Marked X beside Vic's name.

Wayne won.

YOUR SCHOOL

August 1, 1966.

A sunny Monday in America.

The blonde crewcut shooter carried three pistols, a shotgun and three rifles—including a bolt action hunting rifle with a telescope sight.

He killed his way to the highest point on the school grounds.

Took aim . . .

Rained down bullets until Charles Whitman scored seventeen more kills from the clock tower at the University of Texas in Austin for his already impressive tally.

Luc shook his head six days later as he rode in the red backseat of a white, four-door 1964 Chevrolet Impala: *Still can't believe it.*

The Ross family drove with the windows open to let the wind of their ride cool their flesh in the heat of South Dakota's Badlands.

Dad reigned behind the steering wheel.

White-blouse Mom rode shotgun.

Luc rode in the backseat beside two invisible Chicago Secrets.

Stared out the car windows.

Turns out, even though he was a wide-open rolling prairie guy, something in him connected to the Badlands' defiant knobs of black shale hills with deep golden brown gorge valleys.

Static crackled in the car's AM radio station.

His family's new car hugged the Badlands' road home seven days after Charles Whitman climbed the killing clock tower.

A week ago today, thought Luc. *Seems like only yesterday.*

Why?

And why did we let it happen?

Because we didn't know, Luc answered himself. *But now we know. And now we'll do something about All That.*

He and his family didn't learn about the mass shooting until they woke up the next morning, Tuesday, day three of their trip back east to get a new car and visit Laura in Chicago. They'd never been there.

The traveling Rosses sat in the roadside diner for breakfast only hours away from the motel in Chicago.

Dad stared at the headlines on both of the newspapers his dimes bought from a coin-clinking newspaper box just inside the diner's doorway.

"This can't be right," he said as they sat waiting for Luc's orange juice and *more coffee please* for his parents.

He read the first few bloody paragraphs out loud to his wife and son.

They saw fellow customers getting hit with this news that happened barely more than twenty-four hours before.

Dad looked out the diner's windows. "This is America. We're not like this."

Then thirty-three years before Columbine high school's mass shooting . . .

And forty-six years before Sandy Hook elementary school's mass shooting . . .

. . . they ate their scrambled eggs and bacon breakfast without tasting it. Climbed back into the trucking company's black station wagon on its way to a scrap heap in some deal the company owner Alec worked out with a truck factory in the Twin Cities that meant *deserves-it* Dad got a "damn near for free" deal on a barely driven used car.

"And hell," had said Alec, jiggling spare change in his pants' front pockets: "Take a vacation like you never do. Take the wife and Luc after Boys State 'n' 'fore school. Go see your daughter Laura.

"Go be on the road," said the boss.

Go beyond the road, flashed through Luc as Dad told that story.

And then—*Oh, then!*—after they found out about the Texas clock tower—their road rolled them straight into Chicago.

The first big city Luc had ever seen.

A giant lake. Skyscrapers like in movies. Roads going every which way. Four lanes, six lanes, eight lanes everywhere with *thousands* of cars that knew where they were going and how to get there zooming past.

Dad drove the station wagon to Laura's chosen nearest-to-her-apartment motel that boasted *Air Conditioning!* in that sweltering Chicago summer.

Mom and Dad bunked at the motel.

Luc used a bed in barely-more-than-a-closet that Clare, one of Laura's two roommates "won't be needing" because she was sleeping at her boyfriend's.

Mom and Dad looked at the ceiling when Laura told them that.

Luc's jaw dropped into a glorious grin of *Wow!*

"You're here for five days," said Laura. "Leaving next Monday to miss weekend traffic. We've got things to do. I made a list."

The Art Institute of Chicago. Galleries hung with colored images framed on white walls. Edward Hopper's *Nighthawks* painting of a corner diner with three customers and a counterman seen through the diner's windows *wowed* Luc:

Paintings are stories. I already feel stories everywhere and Chicago is more everywhere than I've ever been.

Awe filled him as his family walked Chicago's streets.

There are so many people! So many faces and ways of walking. Everywhere are all of us going somewhere alone together.

He heard someone speaking *real* 1966 Spanish!

Saw faces tanned like his but not from the sun.

There's a Chinese family—*or wait*: Maybe they're Japanese. Or Korean. Could they be refugees from the Vietnam war? Who cares, they're with us now.

He saw more Black people on one downtown block than he'd seen in his whole life. Men in suits and work coveralls. Women in office dresses and waitress uniforms. Just like people back home who were all White except his buddy Marin plus other kids and townspeople from Indian nations.

Luc grinned: *There are so many kinds of people and it's so great!*

More museums. The Chicago stock exchange. A house with its own name by an architect named Frank Lloyd Wright who saw buildings' stories in his head.

The first Chicago Secret ambushed Luc Friday afternoon.

He stood near a busy downtown street corner while his dad paced nearby smoking a cigarette and keeping a protective eye on his daydreaming son. Laura and her mom were "shopping" in the department store beside him that filled nearly the whole block at this busy downtown intersection.

The traffic lights changed.

She crossed this street she owned. She was somewhere between twenty-five and forever. If her summer blouse and skirt worked in an office, she was the boss. *Wherever whatever,* her clothes were *her* choice. Her skirt ended further up past her knees than Principal Harris's rules for the Big Pink allowed. Her legs were *oh so long.* Hers was what Luc'd heard called "an hourglass waist." Her blouse trembled. Black hair brushed her shoulders. Her neck was long and lean, her jaw clean. Her wide eyes touched everything they saw. Noted his gawky teenager awe. That innocent moment birthed a soft curl of shimmering red *heavenly* thick lips in her high-cheekboned face's ebony Blackness.

She walked past Luc with a whiff of lilac perfume.

Couldn't help himself, Luc turned to watch her sway away.

She is so cool! Beyond beautiful because she made what she got into who she is. Sees other people! Has to be smart 'n' crimson smile says funny so she's like my calendar dream! Like Buffy only . . . older. With more knowing in her step.

She disappeared in the stream of sidewalk strangers.

Cough went his dad behind him.

Luc turned and tumbled into a new world.

Dad, *his dad,* the man he loved. The man who as a first generation American Irish immigrant knew about the signs in "back east" cities that read: NINA— No Irish Need Apply. Who wore a uniform in World War II's crusade for democracy, liberty and justice for all. Who everyone in Vernon respected. Who worked honest and hard and kept a roof over his family's head. Who helped save a farm widow and her two children from poverty when Luc was ten. Who read *TIME* magazine and the newspapers *thumping* on his front porch. Who read books. Listened to the radio. Watched television. That man crouched on the busy Chicago sidewalk so only his son could hear him say:

"*You like that dark meat, huh.*"

Shock rocked Luc's whole face, his spine, his heart and mind.

Blink shows Luc his father's face struggling to turn back the hands of time.

WHY DID HE SAY THAT? What was he doing? Trying to buddy up to me like some men do? Talking about SEX that she was more than and then . . . then making all that also about freedom haters he fought against like communists and fascists and evil lynching racist cowards wearing white sheets to burn crosses?

A Chicago city bus *whooshed* past the still as stones teenager and father.

What should you do when someone you love says something like that?

"Hey, you two!" called out Mom as she and *so proud of her* university student daughter Laura walked up to join them. "What's going on?"

Neither of them said a word.

"Nothing in there to buy," continued Mom in front of the downtown department store that sold thousands of items every day as the flagship of how people shopped in 1966. "Let's ride that L-train thingy back to the motel AC and walls so we know where we are and not have all these people staring at us."

"Nobody's staring at you, Mom," said Laura.

Said that even as her stare at her younger brother said: *What's wrong?*

A yellow taxi honked its horn.

Neither Luc nor his dad ever said anything about any of *that*.

Dad never said—or Luc never heard him say—anything like *that* again.

Now on that August Badlands afternoon, that Chicago ghost of *What Dad Said* rode beside Luc in the backseat of the white four-door Chevy Impala.

Rode beside the ghost of the other far more dangerous Chicago Secret.

Mom called it "a party."

Laura called it "just a little get-together."

Saturday night dozens of her friends whirled through her apartment in the all-windows-open hot August night as Luc watched.

These are "the big kids." Mostly no more than seven years older than my seventeen. Are they what it means to be all grown up?

The guys had hair too long to be allowed in the Big Pink. They were drinking bottled beers he'd never heard of in Vernon. Paper cups of wine.

The . . .

Not *girls*, the . . . *young women*—Scratch that: Just—*Yikes!*—women.

OH MY GOD! *She's not wearing a bra!* A white cloth summer swaying T-shirt with a scooped neck AND NO BRA!

Is this a glimpse of the promised land?

Everyone treated him fine. After all, he was Laura's little brother. Nobody offered him one of their *we're so cool* smoking cigarettes.

Luc wouldn't have taken one if they had and he could have gotten away with not being seen by his parents. All tobacco did was take his family's money. Make them cough and get antsy, even nasty when they couldn't light up. At least with booze, you get fun-tipsy—as long as you don't get hooked like Coach Moent.

Or throw up on the governor's shoes.

Luc's parents did their best at that Chicago Saturday night party.

Mom sat on her daughter's apartment couch. Dad played host.

Luc sat on the black iron fire escape just like he'd seen in the movies. The alley below. The clatter of garbage cans. The rumble of L-trains. Car honks. The smells of concrete. A shout.

He heard Dad talking to Clare back inside the stuffy apartment party.

Clare was Laura's roommate sleeping at her boyfriend's.

She wide-eyed watched Dad's face as he explained why they'd come to Chicago first before the Twin Cities car swap:

"Why drive the new car sooner than you have to?"

"*Yeah*," said Clare. "*Like*, why would you want to? You can always say *yes*."

"I mean," said Dad, "this way, fewer miles between there and home for the new car to get dinged. Nicks and scrapes, you know."

"Nicks and scrapes. We keep getting them."

"I know," said Dad. "Let the old car take 'em. Gonna get scrapped anyway."

"I like the old car! Don't get it scrapped!"

From the night's fire escape, Luc saw his dad shrug.

"Well," said Dad, "things change. But you know what they say."

"They never shut up."

"*Ah* . . ." said Dad. "You know: 'The more things change, the more they stay the same.'"

Clare's eyes widened: "Time bends!"

Yes! thought Luc: *Weird ideas grab other people, too!*

He swung himself back into the apartment.

Edged his way through the crowd toward the beer cooler for a Coke.

Walked past whispers between two of Laura's women friends:

". . . and so if he's got a thing for her, why isn't he here to meet her family?"

"*Neh*, she really doesn't care. It's *who else* didn't show up."

"But I thought now they'd gone back to just being friends."

Luc squirmed past these two gossipers—

—as wide-eyed Clare drifted into their conversation, said: "It's not what you go back to, it's where you go next."

By eleven o'clock it was time for everybody to go somewhere else.

Laura's last leaving friends hung with her parents outside in the street waiting for the taxi Laura'd called to take them back to their motel.

Clare drifted down the street with the guy she'd sleep beside that night.

Laura's other roommate headed out "to see what else is going on."

Luc helped Laura clean the apartment.

Breakfast in the open kitchen meant leftover nuts and potato chips.

The other roommate's bedroom door stayed closed.

"Is she in there?" said Luc, soft and low.

Laura shrugged: "Who knows? Taste some coffee."

Yuck!

"So do you think Mom and Dad had a good time?" asked Laura.

Luc shrugged: "I think Dad liked that Clare listened to him."

"Oh. Yeah. She was stoned."

"What? Who?"

"*Who* is Clare and *what* is stoned?"

"You mean drunk?"

"Clare doesn't like drinking. I prefer it. Pot doesn't do much for me."

BLINK!

Luc leaned closer to his big sister. Whispered: "You mean . . ."

"Marijuana." Laura said it right out loud in a normal voice, like: *So what?*

"You go away to college next year," said Laura. "My guess is you're gonna see pot show up even in Montana. By the way, don't go to Montana U, come here.

"And *yes*, Baby Brother: I've smoked pot. Gotten high. And *no*, I'm not hooked on it. And *no*, it doesn't make me want to do heroin. It's OK, can be kind of fun, but I'm more of a feet-on-the-ground person. I like alcohol's smooth."

Laura blinked.

"Oh, *damn*," she sighed. "That reminds me."

Laura walked to the coats hung on hooks in the front hallway.

Stuck her hand in a pocket of her coat.

Walked back to sit with her brother and her cup of coffee.

She held a small yellow manila envelope the size of Luc's palm.

She bent back the metal tabs holding the envelope closed.

Looked in—sighed.

"Just like Clare said. I told her I didn't want it, but . . . She was raised on the Upper East Side—and *believe me*, that's 'a thing.' You never show up to a party without a gift like flowers or whatever and the *whatever* Clare had last night was an envelope of pot. Only about five bucks' worth, but it's the thought that counts."

She held the envelope for Luc to look into.

Green dust. Luc smelled.

He peered down into the small envelope like it was a mine shaft. Saw buds and stems of green *bomped* down to a mix of agriculture he'd never imagined.

"You want it?" Laura asked her baby brother for whom she'd bought an eight grade graduation present of a subscription to *Playboy.*

Blink.

Big Sister shrugged: "I'm not going to smoke it or bake it in brownies. Barely enough for a couple of joints."

Laura nodded her head to her other roommate's closed door.

"Since it's you and me who've done all the clean-up, I don't feel like giving it to *her* who was *oh yeah sure* gonna help.

"So . . . ?" His sister held that envelope *full of* toward him.

"What would I do with it?" said Luc.

"Figure it out. Throw it out. You choose."

"It's illegal," whispered Luc. "I mean, *way* illegal narcotics. Cops are serious. Drugs—even if they're not heroin—

"Like Acid Freak." Luc knew his sister had no idea what he was talking about. "But Vets back from Vietnam . . . them, too."

"Whatever. We've been smoking grass in America since Grampa was a cowboy. You decide. Just don't get caught with it."

She dangled the manila envelope that would fit in the palm of his hand.

He took it.

Knew only that taking it was what he *got to* choose.

Now that envelope of illegal narcotics hid in the pocket of his spare pair of blue jeans in his suitcase locked in the trunk of his family's "new" white Chevy Impala snaking its way home to Vernon through August's big heat Badlands.

And the Secret Ghost of all that rode on the backseat with Luc.

I'm a criminal, thought Luc. *An outlaw. Again.*

His eyes scanned the highway for police cars.

The car radio crackled as they drove through the knob hills:

". . . in case you missed it in all the news coverage of our Texas mass shooting, the criminal *say-anything* comedian Lenny Bruce was found dead in his Los Angeles home from an overdose of illegal narcotics.

"And finally in the news," crackled the radio, "the death toll for the American military in our Vietnam war now stands at 5,901."

THE SOLAR SYSTEM OF SORROW

We all end up here, thought Luc as he leaned on his shovel in the Saturday shade of a cemetery tree.

Getting there for Luc started with a phone call.

Luc's mom had marched into his bedroom that late August Friday afternoon the day before as he sat in the gold cushioned chair.

"Quit thinking on my time!" she snapped at him. "Football practice ain't till next week. You gotta get a quick job. Hell, I took the job at the library!"

Mom exploded that grenade at dinner two days after they got back from Chicago. The new white '64 Chevy glistened safely in the driveway. The old gray '54 Dodge hugged the curb in front of the house Mom's voice filled:

"Fran called. Her young librarian up and quit. Said she couldn't take it anymore. People like Mrs. Sweeny trying to pry our eyes away from what she don't want us to see. Since I'm a Conner girl who knows how to handle that old crone, plus Fran and me're friends, plus I can get there real quick in case there's a problem, county librarian Fran says: 'Do I want the job?'

"I'm standing here in the kitchen. Phone against my face. All the windows open and a fan on. And I remembered how great that motel air conditioning in Chicago felt and how they got AC in the library.

"So I told Fran: 'Hell yes.'"

Her stunned husband said: "You don't like leaving the house."

"So it's only two blocks away. Known 'head librarian' Fran forever. People mostly won't even see me in them aisles of books.

"'Sides," she said. "We seen Chicago. With some other round of that comin' with Luc, we could use extra cash."

Luc knew she was right about him needing—*wanting*—to get a job. He'd already called Mr. Tom at the Roxy, but they didn't need a relief projectionist.

"But don't worry," said his mom, grinning at him. "I think I fixed it."

That's when the phone rang.

Later that afternoon, he drove the gray '54 Dodge to the Big Pink. Went to the locker room to sign up for football.

The empty school hallways called out to Luc.

This is my last year here, he thought as he walked past walls of gray lockers. *And Steve's gone.*

Or would be any day now on his way to college six hours away.

Wendy's brother Ed was on his way to college, too. She'd told Luc so at Aunt Beryl's drive-in café where she worked as a car hop. Ed was headed to a junior college, two years of a 2-S college Draft deferment.

Luc drifted past the Office. The secretary behind the counter. No gorilla.

He climbed the stairs to the Study Hall—

—glanced into the library. Saw Mrs. Dawson sitting in her office.

Frozen at her desk.

Her half-curled dust hair brushed her middle-aged face and dark shadows eyes as she stared at a white envelope lying on her desk.

Flinched at Luc's *Are you OK?* knock her door.

"Of course it's you." Her voice stayed flat. "Congratulations. Looks like you win being my last student at Vernon High School. Go Cougars."

"*What?*"

"*Last lesson*: Comes a time you can't take it anymore. You're in a box that built itself into a coffin. Every day closing in on you. Sure, it boxes out lots of bad shit, but . . . But you gotta get out before you're boxed down into your grave."

"Mrs. D, that envelope . . ."

"My letter of resignation. The hell with tenure. A safe job. Bells dinging what you're supposed to be doing. A gorilla for a boss. A nice home with solid walls and windows looking out at your nowhere. A husband who does his best to *understand* and *fix* what he doesn't *get*. We have some kind of love. What we don't have is what else should be there. And on top of that, every day you walk around wishing you'd done something that *matters*."

"You mean like helping save Coach Moent?"

Mrs. Dawson blinked.

Luc jerked his head toward the windows full of their town:

"You mean like helping kids like me get real books so we can figure out what's out there?"

"*I can't keep doing this!*"

"Then do a different do!"

"That's what I'm doing!"

"Are you going to do any different anywhere else?"

"That's how growing works."

"You're already a grown-up."

"*Is that what this is?*" she whispered.

"Looks like it," Luc said. "And I'm beginning to see it isn't so easy."

She waved a hand toward the shelves: "All these books—"

"No," said Luc. "I mean, *yeah* for them to be there for us, but it's *your* book. *You* gotta write your own book best you can. *I read that in a book from here that you checked out to me!* And now guess if that means that letter to Principal Harris getting you free of him and us, then do it."

Luc shrugged. "We'll miss you."

He walked out of the *SHHH!* school library.

Hurried down the stairs toward the auditorium-office intersection.

Caught a glimpse of Bobbi Jean sailing out those glass doors.

Didn't think any more about what he just saw.

As he had when he drove here, Luc steered the old '54 past Buffy's house.

Now Steve was on his way to gone.

And the next morning, Luc was swinging a pick at the cemetery.

Gravedigger. I'm a gravedigger.

The phone call the day before came from his friend Kyle who knew Luc needed a job because their mothers checked in every day on the phone.

"We're slammed," Kyle had said. "We got a dig tomorrow morning plus a funeral in the afternoon. Bring your gloves."

Shovel that load to the pile up top of the ever-deepening hole you're digging yourself into. Swing that pick. Use the shovel to scrape flat and straight dirt walls. Laugh as Gideon tips David into a wheelbarrow and races him cursing around the headstones. Dig until the hole is deeper than you are tall. Dig more. Smells of summer grass. Of dirt. Of sweat from Kyle and Gideon and cemetery boss Mr. May who uses a frontend loader and chains to ease the coffin frame into the hole.

"Looks like we got 'er," said Mr. May. "Go grab lunch. Get back by half past noon case the undertaker needs us. Then it's our shovel."

At 2:47, the hearse rolled into the cemetery. Rolled over graveled paths to the other open grave across rows of humped grass and gray headstones.

A parade of cars rumbled through the cemetery's black iron gates.

The man who died lived in another town. Something about a family plot.

So Luc didn't know any of the mourners on that hot August afternoon.

He didn't *know* them, but he *knew* them.

They all could have come off of Luc's hometown Main Street.

Luc blinked.

The Solar System of Sorrow.

The sun is the long shiny black coffin above its waiting hole.

Then came the orbit of *Loving Trues.*

The LTs were a sobbing widow. A shaking widower. The younger brother who never. The older sister who meant to. The never understood son who never understood. The daughter who hoped she made him proud. Weepy grandchildren for whom he was their first death besides Jack the dog. A gray aunt in a wheelchair. His favorite cousins. The buddy from college. A few more-than-work buddies. Neighbors. That woman who worked with him sobbing under her black hat veil: Don't believe the rumors, because if coffin man had a secret lover, she wouldn't be in the ring of LTs, she'd be in the next ring out:

The *Silent Lovers.*

The SLs' love ached in sorrowful smiles and shakes. Shoulder-squeezes and hugs. These were the friends who now wished they'd been closer, returned all the calls, made more themselves. Here were that team from work. His bowling league, still a big thing back in 1966. Admiration and loss were the stardust of the SLs. Plus a whole lot of *if only*. And being there. Standing there. For him. For his family. For yourself.

If you were a secret sexual heartthrob lover, *known to* and *been with* or *not*, your misted eyes stare out from the SL ring of *coulda*s and *shoulda*s.

In the SLs, like everywhere in the rings of sorrow, there's a current of anger for the man in the shiny black box having to die so soon, now, *on me.*

The intensity of sorrow slackened the further out the ring went.

The *Good Man* ring were mourners who distantly knew and respected the man in the box. Thought it was a damn shame. Came to pay their respects. Because that's what you should do. You show up.

After the GMs came the fourth ring out:

The GBs. The *Gotta Be's.*

For the GBs, he was my boss. Or my boss said I oughta (so gotta) be here. We served on that committee together. He went to my church. Maybe we did business together. Our kids were on the same team. Our wives both volunteer at the voting polling center in the grade school gym in election years like this. The GBs were haunted by the *If I don'ts.*

Then comes The Fifth Ring.

The *Get Me Outta Heres.*

Oh God, why did I say yes—especially on a day like this! Now I don't owe X. I don't even remember why I came, so Get Me Outta Here!

Brace yourself at a graveside service:

Feel sexual lightning.

Especially in the outer rings like the GMOHs.

That woman brushed her fingers through her long hair and failed to hide her sideways glance. That man shifted his stance so his sunglasses reflected the woman with hips *oh so* curving her tight skirt.

Death is staring right at me. Let me live! Now. Have it. Feel it. Do it.

But I'm just a gravedigger, thought Luc. Standing here in the shade of a tree by the next grave.

He remembered murdered Uncle Johnny. The car wreck on a lonely midnight road's dead teenager who brought so much to life back in 1959. Two guys near his age on memorial pages in the Big Pink's yearbook. Numbers never coming back from someplace called Vietnam.

Winches screed across the cemetery as the coffin sank into the ground. Words were spoken. The crowd dispersed. Some consoling each other. Some talking about what's next. Some sneaking shared-or-not looks. All eyes blind to the gravediggers.

The cemetery superintendent May nodded to the coffin-holding grave.

Maybe he knew the man. Maybe he didn't. But Superintendent May said: "Gone before his time."

When is anybody's time? wondered Luc.

He looked around.

Answered his own question: *Now.*

The gravediggers trudged through the cemetery to fill the latest hole.

DO IT

T he Saturday after the first grave he dug was Luc's chance.

Once high noon had come and gone, he'd be alone in the house.

Remember to lock the doors! If anybody comes, say that was an accident.

The day before had been the last day of pre-season football practice.

Luc'd made it. Survived. For the first time ever, wasn't the last guy to cross the finish line in sprints. But this year . . .

Three years already proved I'm not just a geek, thought Luc.

Smiled as he knew that made a difference to nobody.

Except me, thought Luc as he cleated his way into the tiled varsity locker room after the last Friday hot afternoon pre–school year practice.

The clatter of lockers in the locker room made up his mind.

He walked through joshing and jostling to the open-doored coach's office.

Crew-cut Assistant Coach Egan leaned over the desk where Moent sat scribbling notes.

Luc knocked: "Can I talk with you, Coach Moent?"

The two adult men frowned. Egan mumbled: "I'll go check on that." Kept his eyes to himself as he walked past Luc and out to the raucous locker room.

Moent gestured for Luc to take a chair.

Watched the thick-glasses, skinny boy swallow before he said:

"I, *ah*, I'm going to—quit. Quitting football. See, it's my senior year and I'm in like *everything*—the newspaper, student council, debate team, Key Club—we're going hard this year—and I don't think I have time for football."

Coach Moent's voice was soft as he sat behind his desk in the noisy locker room's glass-walled office where the door was open.

"And what else?" he asked this teenage boy who was holding something back behind his thick glasses. "What else are you going to do this year?"

BUFFY! was what Luc wanted to scream but didn't/wouldn't.

What came out of him was the twin serpent to the Marilyn Monroe romance snake, the two of them coiling around the center pole rod of his moral soul like what Luc'd learned was the symbol for medical doctors.

The second serpent whispered to Coach Moent:

"*I want to . . . I've been . . . I gotta try to write more stories.*"

Moent leaned closer to a co-conspirator.

"One thing you shoulda learned getting banged around out there on my field: Don't *try. Do.* 'N' keep getting back up to do it again."

Luc floated back out to the steamy locker room.

Behind him, Coach Moent stepped out of the office.

Yelled to the teenage boy's walking-away back:

"Luc, I think you're right, it's a good idea for you to leave the team. You got too much going on!"

And now everybody in the locker room and thus the school knows I quit on my own. I didn't get cut for not making it. Thank you, Coach Moent!

Luc went home. Told his parents. About quitting.

They grunted relief that now he wouldn't be coming home on a stretcher.

He said nothing about writing.

Retreated to his bedroom, his cave.

The Green Monster waited atop his childhood desk. Fifteen-plus pounds of metal manual typewriter with the brand name Royal. Four rows of stiff-to-press clattering keys. On the left side, the L-shaped silver space bar Luc'd slap/hit every time he reached the end of a line that would fit on whatever margins he'd set—DING! He was pretty sure the ribbon would last a few dozen more go-rounds before he'd have to replace it. He could smell the ink.

Luc's machine was nowhere near as fancy as the new IBM electric typewriters from something the news had started calling "technology." He'd taken turns using the school's four electric typewriters his sophomore year when with just five other boys, he'd taken the year of typing class usually filled with only the school's girls who all needed to learn how to be secretaries.

A package of typing paper waited in the top left desk drawer. Luc'd fill up a page typing fifty-one words per minute as the voices in his head commanded his fingers. Scroll that page free. Insert a blank page, scroll it down and start all over again. Retype the pages to get them close to correct in spelling and appearance.

The Green Monster never told his parents about stories he'd pound into being when they thought he was creating schoolwork. You could hear him in his bedroom: clatter-clatter-clatter-*Ding! Whoosh.* Clatter-clatter-clatter . . .

And now . . .

Now it was the last Saturday afternoon before his last year of high school.

The Green Monster stared at him when he walked into his bedroom.

Not today, thought Luc. *Because now, oh now is when!*

Dad was back to work across town at the trucking company.

Mom was two blocks away working at the county library.

You're home alone.

Luc reached high up above the inside doorjamb of his bedroom closet.

Pulled the Saran-Wrapped (so it couldn't smell) Chicago manila envelope of marijuana down from where he'd taped it out of reach of his cleaning mother.

Luc'd been cast as a grandfather in a sixth grade school play. His dad bought him a cheap "costume" pipe. The pipe looked ridiculously big in an eleven-year-old boy's hands. Dad pulled off the black plastic stem. The pipe shrank to a couple inches of a brown wooden shaft into a round-cylinder yellow bowl.

Luc told himself that since Key Club rules forbid *only* drinking alcohol *not* smoking marijuana, he *technically* wasn't breaking his oath.

As for the law, *well*, he'd been an outlaw since he was ten and secretly sugared the gas tank of the sheriff's car for justice.

He eased open the tiny manila envelope. Tapped out green buds, stems and seeds to fill the pipe's yellow-walled bowl to its rim.

Still had about that same amount left in the brown envelope.

Fire was the problem.

How could he (a) hold the pipe steady between his lips like tobacco smokers do while (b) using his free hand to snap a match for its necessary flame?

He'd practiced with the empty pipe.

Burned his left hand holding the pipe while using that hand's pinkie grip to hold the match pack closed to snap the match he held in his right hand. *OWW!*

Experimented with a box of kitchen matches. Held the box on the floor with his foot while he bent over with his (empty for practice) pipe-holding left hand held high while his right hand snapped the kitchen match.

His snaps broke the first three matches.

The fourth match lit *and then* snapped off its flaming tip.

He stomped out the flame dropped on his bedroom's gray carpet.

Got on his hands and knees with a wet washcloth to wash *maybe* a perceptible ash burn off that carpet. Worried that his mother would notice the slightly cleaner spot on her son's bedroom carpet and wonder *why*.

So now how . . .

Wait.

Dad's boss Alec had a smug son-in-law leveraged into the trucking business even though he spent most of his time on personal ventures like an "advertising" hustle that sold customer pens emblazoned with their business's names. Alec gave Dad a silver cigarette lighter stamped with the trucking company's name.

Dad took it. Had to. Brought it home instead of throwing it away—*in case*.

The silver lighter lived in a glass ashtray in the parents' bedroom.

Never used.

But when Luc clicked it open, spun the wheel . . .

Fire.

He snapped the lighter shut. Positioned himself in his gold easy chair across from his bed. Held the packed-with-pot pipe between his seventeen-year-old lips.

Clicked open the silver lighter.

Lifted its business end next to the full pipe.

Spun the wheel.

Flame!

Sucked in *deep* through the pipe like he'd seen tobacco junkies do.

Crackle green smell smoke burning mouth throat chest—

Luc coughed/choked—

—blew green pot and its gray ash out of the pipe bowl!

A smoke cloud of *yuck* and *oh-oh* and *oh no* filled his bedroom.

The Green Monster laughed.

Luc got hit with a rush of *How stupid am I?*

Brushed the ashes of green dust into his hand.

Dumped all that into the toilet and flushed.

Went back to the gold chair in his bedroom.

Gave whatever it was he was supposed to feel from smoking marijuana fifteen minutes to . . . to do *whatever*.

Sparrows chirped outside his bedroom. A train whistle. He felt . . .

. . . just like he had felt before he fired up.

Luc looked at the still-got-some brown envelope waiting on his bed.

Maybe next time.

MASSACRE

This year is going to be *totally* different!" said Kurt when he picked up Luc for their morning drive to the Big Pink on the first day of their senior year. Kurt drove toward the railroad crossing route to the Big Pink.

"Go left," said Luc.

"We're right on time," said Kurt as he made that turn.

"Time is right on top of us," said Luc.

"You're so weird," said one of his best friends.

Luc shrugged.

They cruised through Main Street's horizontal shaft of flat storefronts.

"Look!" said Luc. "The bookstore's gone out of business!"

They drove past that haunted shop's whitewashed windows.

"My dad says nothing's coming in there," said Kurt, the son of a CPA. "Sure as heck not any bookstore. And he says the Whitehouse is closing, too."

The Whitehouse. A café counter and tables for cups of coffee, Cokes, all the joys of cinnamon ice cream.

"Where are people going to go for their morning jolt?" said Luc.

"They'll figure a way," said Kurt as they drove past the Roxy.

The Roxy's sidewalk-facing posters showed the figure of a man fighting the gravitational pull of an ever-smaller spiral toward *Oh-oh*. The poster read:

HALF HUMAN . . . HALF MACHINE!

PROGRAMMED TO KILL!

Luc glanced at the Roxy's high-up marquee for the name of the movie:

CYBORG 2087

Kurt babbled about English teacher Mr. Pulaski. How Kurt kept coming up with great ideas *and* how club president Wayne "let" him do them. What was Luc doing on student council? When will Teenage Republicans start meeting again?

They parked the car in the Big Pink's student parking lot.

Climbed out of it as cool as can be (for them).

Man do I wish I could wear wraparound sunglasses! yearned Luc.

But his thick clear glass lens saw one treasure:

No Steve.

That first day of school Luc walked into the library and saw—

—Mrs. Dawson.

Only it wasn't the *her* of all the years before. She'd home-scissored her middle-aged jaw-length and curled brown hair into a ragged mop then dyed it ebony black, like . . . like the fist of night. Wore no for-work makeup.

She spotted Luc.

Saw he'd used sink water and patted his mandated crew cut flat on his skull to look more like the forbidden in the Big Pink haircuts of The Beatles, The Rolling Stones, The Animals and even curly-mopped Bob Dylan.

What wordlessly passed between them Luc knew not how to name.

Friday night's first of the football games against Shelby was the first time Luc ever got to relax and enjoy that gladiators' show.

He paid his coins to enter the after-game dance in the Big Pink.

No way was he going to miss that. Plus, he had to go. Kurt had come up with a Key Club scheme to provide the KRIP DJ with something better than the local radio's songs. Kurt's reel-to-reel tape machine had four different half-hour tapes of teenage hit songs he made and not once did Kurt think about Sandi when he was recording a slow dance song. Not once.

Luc let himself wander in the dance's crowd. Saw his cousins Gene and Seba. Seba's had become Luc's hangout house. He saw Marin with Barbara. Saw Alice and Wendy and wondered how her brother Ed was doing in junior college.

Visiting team's Shelby girls filled the lenses of Luc's glasses. *They were*—

Buffy whirled him around by his arm.

Milk chocolate hair floated around her anxious face.

"Will you go to Co-ed with me?" she shouted amidst the music and swirl of that Friday night ending the first week of her senior year.

"Yes!" said Luc.

Buffy grinned: "I was afraid some freshman girl had already swooped in to grab a senior."

Wait! Was that a possibility? thought Luc.

He said: "Can I give you a ride home after the dance?"

"Um . . . OK. Let me go tell the girls I came with."

The DJ announced: "Last dance." Flipped the switch to let the tape play a *hold-me-close* slow song.

Luc stood alone on the edge of the dance floor full of holding-on couples.

Buffy made it back to him when there was only thirty seconds left in the song. Slid into his embrace—not so close but not too far away either, like Luc had been on his first Co-ed Ball date with Bobbi Jean who was nowhere to be seen.

"And we get the new car," said Buffy after the dance as she slid beneath the Impala's steering wheel—*Yes!*—and rode the middle of the wide front seat for three as Luc drove four blocks to her house.

She climbed out *again* under the steering wheel.

He walked her to her door.

They said goodnight and . . . and . . .

A friendly kiss. *But on the lips!*

Luc glided home through the small-town twinkling-stars darkness.

Somehow made it through the two weeks until Co-Ed.

When he picked her up, him suit and tied, her in a formal gown.

She let him lead her to the driver's side door. Slid under the steering wheel.

They laughed. They talked. They moved with ease and trust.

"Why are they doing this now?" said Buffy at the ball as the school chorus got summoned to the stage beside the band with Mr. Bundy. "They do it at Prom."

Luc remembered. His runaway gray car. The midnight clock. Cherie.

And after four songs from the chorus nobody danced to, conductor Mr. Bundy called Bobbi Jean to the lone standing microphone.

Mr. Bundy leaned into the mic: "We have a tradition. Let every star shine."

Bobbi Jean blinked. Stepped up to the microphone. Again sang the classic song "Blue Velvet."

Everyone applauded. Bobbi Jean graciously smiled and bowed.

Mr. Bundy angled the mic away from her.

"And tonight," he announced, "we have a new special treat."

On that cue, a shy, fighting-heavy freshman girl stepped to make a trio at the front of the stage with Mr. Bundy and lean senior girl Bobbi Jean.

Mr. Bundy positioned the mic. Stood off to the side where he could see the two girls. They could feel his eyes and everyone on the dance floor could see him up there with his protégés.

The new girl and the old pro sang a duet:

"I Got You Babe," by the future TV-comedy show star and skiing-killed congressman and the black straight-haired future movie star.

The crowd applauded.

Luc frowned: *Bobbi Jean . . . Why is her smile so tense?*

No after-dance mistakes this time, thought Luc as they marched out into the warm September Saturday night. Buffy slid behind the steering wheel. Didn't lean in, but . . . but didn't scoot away.

This time he'd called ahead to the restaurant of his after-dance reservation with the order he'd gotten Buffy to laughingly agree to let him handle.

As he figured, Luc and Buffy were thus the first to finish that meal.

The first to leave the restaurant.

The first to *go* toward where he'd scouted.

East of town.

The roadside historical marker for the Marias River Massacre where in 1870, US Cavalry soldiers charged into a camp of teepees and tents for a group of Blackfeet led by Chief Heavy Runner who waved the signed peace treaty at the charging soldiers who gunned him down and killed two hundred of his tribe, most of whom were women and children.

Behind the truth-telling sign swinging with the wind in chains was a service road that curved into a prairie gully where you can turn your car around. Park. Radio reception was good. And traffic on the highway can't see you.

But first . . .

A slow drag down Main Street.

The date couple would pass the viaduct. Then the railroad crossing. Both ways led to the northside where her house waited.

All Buffy had to do is say *"Turn left!"* and he'd take her home.

But if she said nothing when he drove the white Chevy Impala out of town toward tomorrow's rising sun and the prairie darkness . . .

They ate at the Dixie Inn on the west end of town.

She climbed under the steering wheel.

They drove to the corner of Sixth Street headed to Main Street *and*.

Turned to go past the chain supermarket's huge roadside parking lot where cars dragging main went to turn around for the next loop.

A car of high school guys parked there saw Luc's white Impala. The parked car's driver machine-gunned his lights between *regular* and *bright*.

Luc steered the Impala alongside the parked need-to-talk-to-you flashing-lights car. Rolled down his driver's side window. Stopped his car with Buffy leaning across his right shoulder to find out what was going on.

The other driver yelled across to the shiny white car:

"Hey, Luc! Tell Buffy that Steve is in town and he's looking for her!"

This good deed of message delivery accomplished, that car drove off.

WHAM! hit Luc like a punch from heavyweight champion Muhammad Ali.

He jerked the Impala into first gear.

Squealed a circle turn to Main Street.

Fishtailed over the viaduct.

Cut left, then right for four blocks past Aunt Beryl's to Buffy's corner.

Slammed on the brakes.

Buffy shoved the passenger's side door open before the white Impala shuddered to a full stop. Mumbled something. Could have been *Sorry*. Could have been *Thanks*. Luc didn't give a shit.

She ran from that night's car in her formal dance gown.

He waited to make sure she got the door to her house open *even though*.

Because he *fucking* delivered as promised, safe and done. And *done*.

Squealed the Chevy around the corner toward a STOP sign on the highway north out of town or back across the tracks to where he lived.

Knew his rearview mirror showed the string of streetlights to the Big Pink.

Glared out the windshield of a car not taking him anywhere he dreamed.

Kurt's words echoed off the windshield's glass:

"This year is going to be *totally* different!"

HEARTACHES

Buffy fled from a white car through that dark night to her porchlight door
and *why why why* POOR LUC! Didn't mean to! Don't mean to!
She rushed inside her house.
Heard her parents' bedroom light click off knowing she got home safe.
Heard her pounding heart. Her humiliated panting.
Saw the black telephone hanging on the kitchen's yellow wall.
Lost any sense of what to do or what to say or feel.
Tears trickled down her cheeks and she knew not what they meant.

CONSPIRACY

The Big Pink's hallways channeled all Vernon High School students into the auditorium for a General Assembly at two P.M. on Thursday, Oct. 13, 1966.

In Washington, DC, Secretary of Defense Robert McNamara—a corporate czar and Harvard star who years later admitted he'd known all along that the Vietnam war was an absurd lost cause for America—created Project 100,000, lowering the IQ, medical and physical requirements to serve in America's armed forces and aiming the project to recruit mostly from poverty level families. McNamara's Project 100,000's troops died at triple the rate of other Americans in the war that had on that October Thursday created 6,965 KIAS.

In Vernon, Buffy timed turning from closing her locker to fall in step beside Luc as they walked the hall.

For the first time since *That Night*, they talked.

"What's this movie?" said Buffy, avoiding talking about their real-life drama. "Kurt said it's some kind of Key Club project that's to help save everybody."

"You'll see," said Luc. "Look, I gotta hustle 'n' help with the projector."

Buffy said: "See ya!"

"See ya!" said Luc as he hurried away.

And we're back to how we were. Buffy smiled.

Teenage Republicans two nights before.

Luc was there. So were Kurt and Wayne. But Kyle and Gideon and many other TARS weren't. Luc wondered *why*.

And discovering hunchbacked crone Mrs. Sweeny preening around the TARS' sponsor Nora Fields's house stunned Luc.

Instead of Mrs. Sweeny's shellacked gray hair and black widow wraps, Nora wore a blue blouse and tight skirt like in glossy big city magazines. She'd styled her electric-rust hair into a look she chose, like . . .

Like Jackie Kennedy, thought Luc. But that comparison couldn't be right. Jackie was the widow of a Democratic president. All of us are Republicans.

When Nora asked Luc to work the projector for the surprise movie provided by the John Birch Society that Mrs. Sweeny got the Republican Women's Club to insist be shown to today's teenagers who'd become tomorrow's *whatevers*, of course he said *yes*.

The lights snapped out in that heartland home.

Luc glanced away from the screen in the living room to the kitchen. Mrs. Sweeny and Nora sat across the table from each other. Their cigarettes glowed.

Luc flipped the switch on the projector.

A cone of black and white flickering light flowed to the screen.

Movie moments of college students.

Giant black letters slammed down on those captured human sights:

A SPECIAL NEWS REPORT DOCUMENTARY:

THE INTERNATIONAL COMMUNIST CONSPIRACY INFILTRATION

OF

THE "FREE SPEECH" MOVEMENT AT BERKLEY UNIVERSITY

And for twenty-one minutes, Vernon High School TARS watched what they were told was *the real news* about faraway events from two years before that they barely understood *then* even if they'd read about the events in independent newspapers or magazines, maybe saw steady and fair Walter Cronkite factually describe on nonpartisan TV news.

Luc and his friends watched filmed college kids not much older than them:

Look! Guys have hair over their ears like Principal Harris won't let us wear! There are gir—*women* in the crowd! *Wait*: Are there . . . *Yes!* Black kids. The camera captures snatches of words like "free speech" and "freedom of choice." *People like us*, thought Luc. *Doing* something about *something*.

But the male voice-over narrator *shockingly* revealed that leaders in the evil Free Speech Movement *knew each other!* Some had Commie-linked relatives back in the great days of Sentor Joseph McCarthy's blacklist crusade that "*even*" Republican president Dwight Eisenhower had to acknowledge. How students protesting rules about what could be said on their campus were "at best" dupes of the International Communist Conspiracy *obviously* spread like a web across America through Big Government and schools that didn't teach that a correct American way was the only truth to believe and obey. How this "left-wing subversive wave" laced itself into those treacherous protestors against our anti-communist war in Vietnam and the so-called Civil Rights Movement. How the conspiracy was sucking the lifeblood out of manhood. Corrupting future wives and mothers with impure thoughts and ambitions. How people had to be told the right way to think about what was going on in order to be free. How protests against that were all being orchestrated by fiends in Russia's Moscow and yellow-skinned Red China. How true Christian Americans were all in danger.

Wow, thought Luc. *I mean, if they put it on a news screen, it has to be true. Right?*

He flashed on his sister Laura's party in Chicago.

No, he thought. None of them could be like the bad guys in the movie.

The film ran out. *Click-click-clicked* through the projector.

Someone snapped on the lights.

Mrs. Sweeny and Nora sat at the kitchen table.

One pack of cigarettes waited on the table between them.

Mrs. Sweeny sat twisted over the kitchen table. Glared a mawkish leer.

And Nora . . .

Nora stared at the crone who sat across from her at the same kitchen table smoking the same cigarettes. Stared like Mrs. Sweeny's nasty, smug, hunch-back crone like this night's vision was some horrifying mirror of tomorrow.

Kurt frantically waved Wayne and Luc to his side as the handful of other teenagers popped open Coke bottles and attacked bowls of potato chips.

"Guys!" said Wayne. "This is important. Everyone should see it. So how—"

"*We can make it a Key Club project!*" Kurt beamed excitement. "Ask Principal Harris to show it at a General Assembly!"

"That's a great idea," said Wayne. "If you think you can get him to do it."

"My dad'll help," said Kurt. "He's on the school board like Luc's."

Luc's two buddies stared at him.

He shrugged. Nodded like: *Sure, my dad will help.*

But Luc knew he'd leave his dad out of it. Didn't know why.

"OK," said Wayne. "I'll go square it with these adults. Luc, you're the movie worker. You be in charge of the film. There's a box for it somewhere."

Wayne stiff-walked to the kitchen.

And though Kurt and Luc both felt the allure of stun-faced Nora, all Wayne's charm flowed to getting Mrs. Sweeny's easy *yes.*

"Time to go," TARS president Wayne told the handful of teenagers.

He stiff-walked to the door.

They followed him.

Kurt stayed to clean up empty Coke bottles and potato chip messes.

Luc looked for the box for the reel of film.

But he really stared at the tableau of the two women sitting at that kitchen table. A pack of cigarettes filled the space between them.

". . . come next presidential election," said Mrs. Sweeny to Nora, "we got to make sure we get a real loyal American, not like that puffy, fancy high-combed hair New York City son of a sleazy landlord millionaire—*What's his name?*

"Oh, that's right. *Rockefeller Center.* Creeps like him love naming things after themselves. Guy like that, we call them the Eastern Establishment.

"Goldwater, he's our guy, true conservative. Out of the desert.

"But then Ike's ex-VP Nixon, he's a *never-gonna-stop* guy who makes things work, one way or another.

"Remember in the film we just saw? The actor? Before all this, Ronald Reagan played a gangster posing as a businessman in that movie from some stupid Hemingway story. Now he's campaigning to be governor of California and he's really giving it to those *free speech* types. Being big on a big screen means being big at the ballot box."

Nora's face didn't move. She'd seen the film. Images of "youths" who went to college like she never got to. Her generation's successors.

"Not smoking, dear?" said Mrs. Sweeny to Nora. "So I'll just take the pack home with me. After all, look around: You've got everything."

The black crone hunched her way out the door.

"You got this?" said Kurt who'd brought his own car.

"Go on," said Luc. The gray '54 Dodge waited outside for him.

The house telephones rang. Landline receivers in the kitchen and the bedroom and an office room in back Luc never saw until.

Nora flowed from the kitchen table to the distant bedroom phone.

Luc snapped the home projector into storage mode.

Shrugged into his jacket.

Tucked the boxed reel under his left arm.

Was the right thing to do to tell Nora he was going home?

Yes. That way she'd know her level of safety.

Luc padded down the hall past a little girl's empty shrine. No noise from him interrupted the phone conversation in the master bedroom. He peered past that half-open door. Saw the shadow on the wall of a woman on the phone.

". . . don't care what your lawyer Falk says! She's my daughter! Ours! But you don't give a shit about her or only do because Big Momma acts like my daughter is *hers. Hers!* Turns her against me!"

Luc froze.

"*Un-un*, no way. You can't give a shit about adultery and live out there in the oilfields in that trailer where *what the fuck* . . . She's your daughter! And I'm your wife you never loved and think is a loser 'n' I was dumb enough to believe . . . *But I'm not gonna just be put on a shelf AND THE ONLY LOVE I'VE GOT IS HER!*"

Hiding in the hall, Luc heard the tears in Nora's voice. And grit.

"No way will you and Falk get some judge to sign some order giving 'shared custodial rights' to God-damned Big Mama! . . . No . . . No . . ."

Luc crept out of that screaming house.

Now in the Big Pink auditorium, the movie he projected flashed its ending:

DON'T LET THIS BE "THE END"

STOP "THE FREE SPEECH" CONSPIRACY

The auditorium lights snapped on.

Wayne rose up from the front row to address the student body.

A wave of gorilla Harris's *I'm in charge!* hand sat Wayne back down.

"Last Period now!" yelled Principal Harris. "Dismissed!"

Luc took the boxed-up reel of film home with him.

That night he huddled in his bed with a transistor radio's plug in his ear.

Isn't free speech what America and democracy are all about? So how come that movie, Dad, Nora, the crazy crone and Gorilla Harris are against it?

He shook his head. Turned the volume dial higher on his radio. Lost himself in the darkness's songs.

Came the next day. Friday. After school.

The easy choice rode beside him in the '54 gray Dodge's shotgun seat as he dragged Main to where he was going.

He'd return the boxed documentary reel to Nora, *not* the black crone.

Whatever he'd heard that made her cry three days ago must be better now.

Luc drove the gray '54 Dodge toward her house on the west end of town.

Slowed down as he neared his Aunt Iona's house. Looked to see if he'd spot Aunt Iona or her kids through their living room picture window. The radio—

VROOMPH!

A brown Thunderbird blew past Luc!

Gone from his windshield before his slammed-on-the-brakes Dodge stopped shaking from what rushed past.

That's Nora's car! The only Thunderbird in town. Racing to her house.

He glanced toward the shotgun seat:

The movie reel box had slid off into the passenger's footwell.

Wait! I get it!

Boy, did Luc know how it felt to, need to, *got to*, rush to a bathroom!

Nora must have drunk too much coffee.

And now that he realized that, *the same urge* whispered to him.

He could wait until after he delivered to Nora, *sure*, but with her Get Out of My Way urge, *well*, the polite and right thing to do was to let her alone *until*.

Luc pulled his car to the curb.

Aunt Iona and a couple of his cousins were home.

He did his bathroom business.

"Tell your mom to get me tonight for coffee," said Aunt Iona. "I'm worried about Beryl. Working too hard. Coughing too much."

Because Uncle Orville was working his drilling rigs, Aunt Iona took a risk. Turned the fire dial on the gas stove's blue flame ring. Lit a taboo cigarette.

Smiled at her nephew Luc: "How you doing?"

Cigarette smoke floated away time.

Mark it twenty-one minutes later on an ordinary Friday afternoon.

Luc slammed the driver's door on the gray '54. Turned the key. Pulled onto the quiet residential street taking him where he needed to go.

Luc drove around the corner . . .

. . . spotted the brown Thunderbird nosedived in Nora's front driveway.

The *katty-whompus* parked car let him see its dangling-open driver's door.

Luc jerked the '54 to the curb.

Raced from that gray Dodge.

She'd left the motor running.

A woman's voice behind him: "It's been that way since she got home."

Mrs. Irvin. Luc blinked at that next-door neighbor standing at the invisible property line on her front lawn.

Luc turned back to the rumbling car.

Squirmed in enough to turn the keys off. The engine silenced.

Told Mrs. Irvin: "I got something to give her."

Fear quick-walked him back to the gray '54 Dodge.

Luc reached in/grabbed the film box. Slammed the passenger's door shut.

Hurry! whispered a voice in his skull.

Luc ran to the front porch.

Softly knocked.

Mrs. Irvin stood in the brown T-bird's driveway.

Luc *pounded* on the front door.

Glanced at Mrs. Irvin. Got the nod.

"Nora—*Mrs. Fields!*" yelled the teenage boy opening her front door. "It's Luc! I've got that film for you!"

Luc stepped into living room.

Tossed the film box on the living room couch.

Called out again.

That hallway led to the bedrooms.

Only childhood ghosts in the girl's lair for dreams.

The master bedroom where he'd seen Nora's shadow on the wall.

Someone'd torn the bedspread, blankets, sheets off the bed. Someone tried to heave the mattress into outer space but could only knock it onto a bedside table. Broke that lamp. Luc glanced to the open bathroom door. Realized the floor there held two *or was it three* dropped pill bottles.

Luc charged the open door at the end of that tunnel.

Nora.

Slouched in the padded executive's chair behind a huge flat desk where she'd shoved everything that belong there off it to the floor.

She'd wildly lipsticked her mouth so she looked like a crazy clown. Those neon red lips hung open and apart. Her eyes saw nothing.

A bottle of Scotch lay on its side on that desktop. A breeze came in through a shattered-glass window. Pills and capsules from now empty bottles lay scattered on the desktop like parachutists from a crashing plane.

"*Nora!*" screamed Luc.

Screamed louder: "*MRS. IRVIN!*"

That neighbor charged from the living room to the home office.

Luc grabbed Nora's face. Yelled her name at empty canyon eyes.

"Open her mouth!" yelled Mrs. Irvin.

Luc barely had time to open Nora's lower jaw before Mrs. Irvin jammed her own forefinger into her neighbor's throat.

Nora's body spasmed.

"*BWHACKUN!*"

The face he held between his hands blasted whiskey vomit all over Luc.

Mrs. Irvin caught Nora by the shoulders.

The phone in the office had been ripped out of the wall.

Luc ran to the kitchen. Slammed that wall phone's receiver to his face. Swung the rotary dial as far and fast as it could go.

"Oper—"

"Help! It's Nora—Mrs. Fields, at her house! By the swimming pool! She's taken a bunch of pills and whiskey and Mrs. Irvin, she's working on her and—"

"Who is this?"

"It's Luc Ross! Hurry! Get the ambulance!"

Sheriff Bill Wood's cruiser was the first to the scene. The volunteer fire department's ambulance crew raced past the vomit-stained teenager toward the room where he frantically directed them.

The ambulance tore away from the house.

The sheriff came to the Ross house the next day at dinnertime.

Sat with Luc and his parents at the round kitchen table. Twilight filled the kitchen picture window. Golden leaves filled the backyard.

"Came to tell you *good job*, Luc," said the lawman. "I wanted you to know that 'cause I . . . That family, I'm guessing neither you nor Mrs. Irvin are going to ever get much of a 'thank you' from them."

"What about Nora?" said Luc.

"She's getting' out of the hospital come tomorrow," said the sheriff. "And it turns out that just this week, she'd gotten herself some bigtime lawyer down in Billings who's some kind of political hotshot she knows from *who knows*.

"When he heard about . . . Well, next thing you know, Nora's husband and mother-in-law and their lawyer Falk got hit by Mr. Billings filing motions and court moves. So turns out, Nora's not going to get an 'involuntary commitment' down to the state mental hospital in Warm Springs or charged for trying to kill herself. He's got a private woman nurse and some off-duty highway patrolman comin' up here to take her to a hospital in that 'big-time' city.

"Figure she can afford it even after she pays her lawyer buddy off. No matter how bad lawyer Falk and her *family* make this out to be, whatever they got her for . . . for anything else, odds are if the divorce Falk's talking about goes through, all them millions, she's gonna do OK."

Luc said: "What about her daughter?"

This lawman hesitated. "That ain't my badge."

Mom said: "Why'd she do it?"

Sheriff Wood looked at Luc.

Does Wood know I didn't tell my folks any more than they had to know?

The sheriff shook his head: "Spect she can't even tell you all the *whys* herself. Only that they became too many. Too big. Too crushing."

He shrugged. "What matters now are the *why not to*s."

The sheriff drove away from their house across the street from the hospital where Nora lay in a bed under watchful eyes.

The Rosses ate a silent dinner.

Dad—just like it was a normal night—went back over to the trucking company to spend a couple hours "checking things."

Mom took the '54 to pick up Aunt Iona for that coffee about sister Beryl.

Luc sat in his well-lit bedroom's padded gold chair.

The Green Monster typewriter left him alone.

Luc didn't want to play records on his stereo.

Didn't want to play the radio.

Didn't want to read or go to the Roxy's Saturday night movie or watch TV.

Sat there as night filled his windows. Listened to the wind. Heard a lonesome train whistle.

Life is a conspiracy of cans and can'ts, thought Luc. *Of do's and don'ts. Of wills and won'ts. And suicide: Where does it get you but gone to where you can't even try to change what's coming?*

NEVER TELL

Alice loved the feel of the steering wheel in her hands as Wendy chattered in the shotgun seat while the radio played a lonely woman's song on that chilly November 17 Thursday night in '66.

She glanced at her best friend beside her:

How could anyone not love curly brown-haired Wendy who had a smile for everyone and a bod for Playboy? *How come she doesn't have a going-steady ring on her finger? Sure, she's got her year-younger drummer for their off again, on again, but damn is she worth so much more than that!*

Alice shook her head: *How much am I worth?*

She knew what guys wanted. Knew what she had. Knew about the whispers. Wondered where was the *who* she wanted deep in her heart.

Alice glanced out her driver's side window as they pulled away from the drive-in diner where Wendy worked every day after school until 8:00 and the end of the dinner rush—which usually meant a dozen burgers, one of which owner Mrs. Beryl Russo always made sure Wendy got.

Wendy *Thank you'd* every free burger. Often "took it home to eat."

Then there pulled out plates from her family's rental's cupboard. Sat alone at the kitchen table with her mom. Cut the burger in half so they each ate.

No take-home burger tonight, noticed Alice, who almost every weeknight showed up at 8:00 to give Wendy a ride home instead of a long walk alone through the dark streets of town.

Everybody knew that ride was an excuse for Alice to get out of the house so she could go "looking" and dragging Main.

Wendy *knew* that was ass-backwards: Alice made that nighttime drive to make sure Wendy got home safe, not to grab whatever freedom she'd get from driving her parents' car.

That night Alice didn't notice the headlights in her rearview mirror.

"Let's hit the Big Pink," said Alice.

"Why not?" Wendy grinned.

Alice turned the car off its homeward route.

The radio played an *enh* song by The Monkees, a TV-comedy show "rock 'n' roll band"—a strategy right down to the acceptable length of the actors' mop top haircuts to cash in on American teenagers' obsession with the British Beatles.

Fakery creating a "reality" TV show: *What harm could that do?*

Alice and Wendy drove past blocks of northside houses.

"Look!" Wendy pointed to a passing house.

"Coach Moent's place," said Alice.

"That's a lot of lights on," said Wendy. "And boxes. Like it's moving day."

"Moving in." Alice frowned. "That's the librarian Mrs. Dawson!"

"Why did she chop her hair?" said Wendy. "Dye it black?"

"Beats me. But that's her husband carrying boxes into Coach's house. He's lifting and loading where she's pointing."

"Heard her snap back to Principal Harris yesterday."

Alice's car passed that glowing house in Vernon's night.

"I guess Coach's wife took him back," said Alice.

"I miss my dad," said Wendy. "Wish he didn't have to travel so much."

"Yeah," said Alice, who knew hers was sitting in the big chair in their comfortable home not knowing about The Boogeyman.

Get out of my head! commanded Alice.

And *now*, The Boogeyman usually obeyed.

"There's my boss's house," said Wendy as the car rolled past Luc's aunt's bungalow. "I hope Beryl gets home soon. She's sagging."

They took a left at the corner where Buffy's house stood.

They were three blocks away from Buffy's on the street to the Big Pink when headlights turned the same corner they had. Winked in their mirrors.

The radio news came on:

An eighteen-year-old Arizona high school student told the cops he wanted to be famous like the Texas tower shooter as the reason he walked into a beauty parlor, shot and killed four women and a three-year-old girl. The news said he'd been planning a mass shooting ever since his parents bought him a gun.

"Meanwhile," said the radio news, "newly elected Republicans issued a joint press release condemning President Lyndon Baines Johnson's 'Great Society permissiveness' for the tragedy. Among the new Republican stars are first term Congressman Texas oil company executive George Bush, new governor of Maryland Spiro Agnew and California's new Hollywood governor Ronald Reagan.

"Finally in tonight's news, our casualty rate in Vietnam has risen to 7,657."

The weather report covered the hundred-miles-away Big City of Great Falls where a smelter's smokestack billowed toxic clouds into the Big Sky.

They passed the last turn before the high school.

Alice saw headlights in her mirror pull over to the curb.

"What's happening in the teachers' parking lot?" said Wendy.

Alice's headlights spotlighted four high school girls and Mr. Bundy.

Three of the girls were juniors.

"That's Janice, a freshman," said Wendy as Alice's headlights illuminated the fourth girl. "Looks like she's lost weight since she sang at Co-ed."

"Good for her," said Alice.

"I wonder where Bobbi Jean is. She's always in chorus practices."

They circled out of the parking lot for the five-block-long street from the Big Pink toward the STOP sign at the highway.

"Are you going to College & Career Night next month?" asked Wendy.

Alice shrugged.

Noticed headlights flick on in her mirror.

"My parents say *yes*," she said. "Me . . . *I dunno.*"

"I *dunno* either. My brother Ed's the smart one anyway. I got an aunt who has a dance school she needs help running in Denver."

A pair of headlights turned off the highway toward their windshield.

Wendy's voice softened: "You . . . *we* could both probably get jobs out there."

The look they shared made both their hearts swell, their eyes glisten.

"Look!" Wendy's words pulled them to their windshield. "That's Luc's car. Wonder where he's going?"

The two carloads of teenagers drove past each other.

"It's not where Luc's going." Alice nodded to Buffy's house as they, like Luc, drove past it. "It's where he's driving past to get there."

"Steve's coming home for Thanksgiving next week," said Wendy. "My brother's postcard says he's hitching a ride home with him even though Steve's at Eastern College in Billings and Ed is in Miles City community college."

"A postcard? Why didn't Ed call?"

"Cheaper than long distance."

Alice turned the car toward the viaduct over the hobos' train tracks.

Told Wendy: "Let's see if driving past Buffy's is all Luc's doing. We'll know if he swings around 'n' drags Main."

"Maybe he's got one of those Key Club things at the school," said Wendy.

"*Uhn*. Those guys. I mean, I like 'em even though they look so funny in their white shirts and ties on Thursdays. Kurt's like obsessed with racking up Key Club points for the national club while Wayne struts around as president. Who cares?"

"I like those columns Luc writes for the *Growl*," said Wendy of their high school newspaper. "They're weird but sometimes kind of funny."

"He's always got something to say. Too bad for him there's Steve."

Two teenage girls in the car purring over the bridge to the bright lights glanced at each other. Knew they both were thinking about Luc.

Chorused: "*Naw.*"

Grinned and turned left on to the Main drag.

Headlights rolling up over the slope of the viaduct followed them.

Wendy sighed: "It's so sad about Recie's Style Shop."

"What do you mean?"

"My dad says it's closing after Christmas. Says he's not got Recie to sell dress to anymore. It's harder than ever out there for traveling salesmen."

Alice let a pair of cruising sophomores be the first to honk.

Gave them a senior royalty *toot* back.

Told Wendy: "They're going to be us someday."

"They should be so lucky," said Wendy.

They laughed as they rolled under the turning-yellow stoplight on the east end of Main Street. The red light stopped the headlights in their mirror.

Alice followed the route for dragging Main.

Past the stoplight she'd made it through.

Past city hall where a cop car waited parked at the curb.

Past the city park.

A half block more to the railroad tracks crossing the highway headed east.

A pole of peeling white-painted X crossbars with *Ding! Ding! Ding!* bells and warning lights that flashed red whenever a train was coming waited on a patch of gravel at that edge of town.

Alice steered a gentle half-moon turn at the crossbars.

Drove back on Main Street's neon row.

Once she knew the car coming toward them had an adult man behind the wheel, she paid no more attention to it.

Saw Mr. Tom standing on the sidewalk in front of the Roxy with a long grab-pole changing the giant red letters on the movie theater's marquee:

FAHRENHEIT 451

Wonder what that movie's about? thought Alice.

She saw no headlights in her mirror.

Main Street is slow tonight, she thought. Even the cruising sophomores seemed to have gone home.

Kids these days, she thought. Laughed to herself. *Let's see if Luc's still out here and gonna hit the strip.*

She lucked out. Got the green light at the far end of Main Street. Turned around in the supermarket parking lot as Wendy was telling a story about how she caught Kurt goo-goo eying Sandi in Government class:

"Why don't boys just say what they mean and mean what they say?"

They found no answer as they rolled east on Main Street.

Alice spotted an unknown car parked at the turnaround point.

Out stepped a shadowed figure in a businessman's suit.

He lit a cigarette as Alice's headlights lit him for the girls to see.

"Do you know him?" said Alice.

Wendy shook her head *no.*

He motioned for them to stop.

Alice's heart thumped.

He's an adult. A grown-up to us teenagers. Dressed in a suit like he's important. We're safe in a car on the edge of town two blocks from the cop shop.

"Lock your door," she told Wendy as she pushed down her own knob.

He wore a smile as he walked to the passenger's side of the idling car.

Called out: *"Hey, Wendy!"*

Motioned for Wendy to roll her window down.

She did. He leaned on her car door.

"Glad I got you here," he said. "Figured I'd find you at work, but . . . Hey, this way I can still head home come morning. Lucky I know how kids roll.

"Hey you," said the man with tobacco breath to Alice behind the steering wheel. "Good to meet you, too, darling. Don't bother introducing yourself. I got your license plate. That'll do it for me.

"Bet you're wondering what's up, right, Wendy? Damn, girl, I'm here to tell you. My boss figured I'd figure out how and look at us: Here we are.

"Sorry about your dad not coming home for Thanksgiving," lied the stranger to Wendy. "Doubt he'll be coming to see you on Christmas either, but that ain't up to me. Ain't up to him either.

"You don't know, do you? My boss, the big *now call her Mrs.* figured that. That was kinda the deal that got worked out. But Mrs. Boss figures why should you have to wait until you graduate to know what's going on. The whole truth and nothing but the truth of your own damn life, right? Seems only fair.

"You know why your dad don't come home much? 'Cause he's your dad, but he ain't married to your mom no more. They're divorced.

"Even I gotta admit he's a handsome, charming son-of-a-bitch. Lucky, too. A traveling salesman. First time he walked into the Seattle clothing factory 'n' department store combo my boss owns from her dead rich daddy, she decided he was for her. Fuck that he was married. Fuck that he's—*Don't tell him!*—really *eleven* years younger than her, not *five.* And *fuck* that he loves your mother.

"Your brother Ed. Graduated high school last year. A healthy young man with a family that's got no money to help him get some school student defer-ment from the Draft gonna ship his ass to Vietnam. Bullet jungles. Landmines. Bar girls in Saigon who got razors taped between their sweet thighs.

"So after years of saying all kinds of *no* to Mrs. Boss who'd already made herself his major customer, your dad had to do what's gonna keep his son from getting killed in the war. Takes her deal. Goes to Vegas. Gets a quicky divorce him and your mom knew they had to get to keep Ed alive. Then he marries Mrs. Boss who ain't gonna die some *failure old maid* now. And in return, she pays for brother Ed to go to community college where he gets a student defer-ment instead of getting Drafted to death.

"Part of the deal is your dad gets to come back to this shithole from time to time like he's still on the road so he can play Daddy to you, hubby to your mom.

"But the truth is, he belongs to Mrs. Boss now. And she wants to make that clear to everybody who has to know—though not her country club crowd. For a private dick like me usually paid to crush union organizers, tracking you down to make sure you know the truth you're in . . . Well, easy-peasy."

He blew a cloud of smoke into the car.

"Now you go on. Appreciate what got done for you. And don't go stupid and rock the boat 'n' kill your brother."

He flicked the cigarette off into the night.

Climbed in his car. Disappeared toward Main Street's glow.

A thousand years roared past. Stars fell from the November sky.

Wendy's shattered face turned to her best friend behind the steering wheel: "Please, please, *please* don't ever tell anyone!"

Alice never did.

WHO YOU ARE

 od stood in the propped-open double doorways to the Big Pink's gym.
That polished wooden floor held fold-up tables boasting colorful pamphlets and catalogs. Folding whiteboard walls for some of the tables created booths.

College and Career Night.

Tod shook his head:

A year ago we were so broke and I was so whatever I wouldn't have come.

He saw his fellow seniors drifting along the tables of destinations.

There were table booths for state, county and the city governments. Mining companies from Butte and Libby. A logging company looking for muscle. The railroad heeded the invitation from the Chamber of Commerce with a booth that offered lollipops. The monopoly phone company showed up. So did the monopoly power company. Walt stood talking to a recruiter sitting there.

Tod saw Kurt directing his Key Clubbers helping C&C Night organizers move this, shuffle that, as their president Wayne stood jabbering at the table for the state university in Bozeman. Buffy ignored Wayne as she picked up a pamphlet from that school where Steve wasn't.

Tod saw five booths for the military:

Army. Navy. Air Force. Marines. Coast Guard.

Saw none of his fellow senior boys stopping at those tables to talk to the uniformed sergeants who'd been detailed to this out-of-the-way posting instead of, say, far preferable big time Missoula—

—even though long-hairs were popping up at the university there in spite of a Beatles-hairy and Beatnik-freaky guy last week getting the shit kicked out of him at the noontime university fountain by a dozen fraternity guys and football players while dozens of male and female students watched.

Motion caught Tod's eye: *Finally* someone walking up to the Army's booth. Mike Jodrey. Not laughing.

Guidance Counselor Stern walked past Tod. Saw him. Shook his head.

That scorn marched Tod into a gym of tomorrows like he belonged there.

All four of the state's land-grant institutions of higher learning were arrayed in a row of tables and booths, plus the state's two Catholic colleges and four community colleges.

Which one did Wendy's brother Ed go to? wondered her friend Tod.

And if he himself was going to go to any college . . .

Well, Tod gambled that for once, the money odds were even.

Maybe we're all just pinballs zapping this way and that, but thanks to some cosmic whoever *for letting my dad get a good job!*

That wasn't enough *for* every dream, but if someone like Tod didn't need to share what he earned with his family like Ed and other Big Pink students, many in-state-qualified Montana "kids" earned enough in their summer jobs to pay for a school year at most Montana public diploma factories.

"That's what my parents don't get," Luc told Tod that morning in the school library.

"And that's got Mr. Stern pissed at me. I got that National Merit letter, but my parents just found out I'm like seventeenth in our class of eighty-eight. The only reason I passed college math and physics is you can't give Laura Ross's kid brother anything less than a C because then you'd have screwed-up as a teacher.

"They all can't figure why I don't go after a rural small-town scholarship from the Chicago school where Laura's gonna graduate. But I saw our folks still having to pay money even with her scholarship. And if they're paying . . .

"If I pay my own way, I have my own say. Workin' since I was ten. Got enough saved now for a year at a Montana school. Figure I can get summer jobs that will pay me enough to cover each school year coming up.

"Plus . . . I don't want to go to Chicago. There I'd still be Laura's kid brother."

Luc didn't add: *Plus, the idea of any big city freaks me out. How would I keep myself from exploding out to see every face? Getting caught by every story?*

The tables for Montana institutions came toward the center of the gym. Before them were tables for colleges of Idaho, Washington and Wyoming.

Tod froze in his tracks.

Saw Gene laughing with Kyle and Gideon. Gene wore a tight sweater. His jeans fit *just so.* Tod's gaze followed those senior boys as they joked and laughed, shuffled past Montana college tables, pausing here, stopping there, moving on.

Gene walked alone to the booth for the biggest Catholic college in the state. Tod's eyes and face followed Gene's motion. Watched him—

A man's voice: *"What are you looking at?"*

Tod whirled.

One of the minders for the state of Washington's table stood outside/same side as where Tod stood. A man and a woman sat behind the table laughing, their eyes not on the shuffling past crowd or their bemused colleague.

He was a man in his thirties. Wore a suit like his male colleague.

But . . . *Tod couldn't name it* . . . the man standing there wore a suit of *different.*

He smiled like he knew exactly *who/what/how*—Tod had been looking at.

"Don't worry," the stranger told Tod. "Someday you'll get to look at what you want. My bet is you're not used to that here."

The stranger's nod took in the gym. Took in the town outside.

"So," said the stranger, "what do you want to do *when?*"

"When *what?*" said Tod.

"Yeah."

They both laughed. *I laughed*, thought Tod.

"What do you want to do after you graduate? How do you want to spend your days?"

Tod shrugged: "It's kinda dumb."

"Not if it's what you want."

"I got a job as a nurses' aide. And what I'm doing . . . I like helping people."

"You wanna be a doctor?"

"I don't have the time or the *get the grades* for that. Or the money."

"Have you done anything that might get you some kind of scholarship?"

Tod shook his head *no.*

"I'm selling schools in Washington here," said the stranger. "Plus chaperoning my colleagues."

The man and the woman sitting behind the table ignored *their* colleague. He nodded to Tod. The teenager took a few steps back as the stranger stepped with him for a discreet conversation in this gym of advertised futures.

The stranger shrugged.

"Back there on our table is a brochure for a nursing school. Great place to go to get a career helping people. But don't start there."

Tod blinked.

"Write to them. Find out what transfer classes they accept. Go to one of these cheaper-for-you Montana colleges that have those classes. Nail them, then transfer to the out-of-state and more expensive school with less to do to finish."

The stranger stared straight into Tod.

"Get out of this town. The nursing school is in Spokane. Lots bigger than here. A city. More kinds of people. Different kinds of people. And people who are . . . different. Even if they don't know how or what. Easier for them to live there. Easier to figure things out there. Easier to be whoever you are.

"And lucky you, I never go there. I live in Seattle. With . . . my buddy. I'm never going to see you again after you grab the brochure. So you're safe. But my gut tells me you need to find other *yous*. You already know about being lonely."

THAT MOMENT

Luc escaped from the Big Pink in the gray '54 before Last Bell that Tuesday afternoon in 1967. A pink slip rode in his shirt pocket.

On the car's shotgun seat rode the form for him to apply for a work-study scholarship at the University of Montana's School of Journalism where he figured he'd learn how to write news stories, short fictions, poems and a novel.

That's what journalism is—right? News stories and fictions.

Guidance Counselor Stern pushed the paltry scholarship on Luc. Said his whacky columns in the *Growl* might as well get him something.

When his parents heard "scholarship," they swelled with hopeful pride. They would have signed anything.

But they weren't happy about the opportunity being at the Missoula university for the same reason Luc thanked the stars it was:

Rumors said after the "hippie" beating incident, Missoula was starting to tolerate longhaired guys. Teachers who didn't wear ties. And . . . *attitudes* talked out loud. A "liberal arts school," whatever that meant.

Whereas the other university in Montana was at Bozeman. Crewcuts everywhere. Fraternity and sorority culture. An agriculture school. Business school. An engineering school. A U of slots for you ruled by invisible architects.

No way after Gorilla Harris did Luc want to go to a school of straight lines.

Plus, the Green Monster demanded to learn how to be better clattered.

The work-study scholarship chance sealed the deal for Luc.

That Tuesday afternoon, he needed to get a parent's signature on the application form, bring it back to school to have Stern send it in.

Luc logically should have gone to get his dad's signature. It only took two songs on the car radio to drive from the Big Pink to the trucking company.

But it was Tuesday afternoon. Luc's mom didn't go to her job at the county library until the night shift. And if Luc drove the gray '54 slow, the trip from the Big Pink might take four songs.

Luc's mom wouldn't be in any hurry to rush him out of the house and back to school. So he'd have time. Time he could steal from the clock of *supposed-tos*. Time he could *maybe* make his.

He found his mom ironing white sheets in the basement rec room.

The TV was on to keep her company. Unless one of her *stories* (soap operas) was on, she kept the volume way low, ignored what the screen showed.

"Be better to take this upstairs, sign it on the kitchen table," said Mom as she stared at the application Luc'd handed her. Climbed the stairs.

Luc glanced at the TV she'd left on.

A color show. About half of the shows on this new TV were in color.

His glasses' lenses rainbowed a show broadcast *live* from back east where high school had been out for a couple hours. That meant kids like Luc in the Mountain Time Zone couldn't watch the show unless they skipped school.

What he witnessed was a teenage music show: *American Bandstand*. Or maybe its clone: *Where the Action Is*. Shows where a suit-and-tied host played records while *oh so properly dressed* high schoolers *appropriately* danced. Sometimes a band played there "live" in the studio for the TV cameras.

The band now playing rock 'n' roll wore mandated suit jackets—

—but one of the all-guys group wore a tan leather fringe-sleeved jacket!

A cool-sideburns soul playing guitar leaned toward the microphone.

He's wearing a gray cowboy hat!

And their hair, *yes*, Beatles length but . . .

But it's their own look. Their own lives. Their own sound.

Guitars crying questions.

The drum's *bump ba-dump-bump* heartbeat.

And then, *oh then*, came a low-volume singer's voice Luc misheard rocking together with how *That Exact Moment* of Luc's life *felt*:

"Somethin's happening here . . ."

He rocketed away. He was in his home basement. He was everywhere all at once. Surging with the band. Alive in a new way as lyrics burned into his soul.

He didn't know the band was named Buffalo Springfield.

Didn't know the song was "For What It's Worth."

But he realized his life had somehow just changed.

LAST DANCE

May, a month that sounds like it's giving permission *to*.

Luc let Kurt and Wayne walk out of English class without him. Marin hustled past Luc to where Barbara was scheduled to walk. Gave Luc a grin.

Marin should have won the award for best short story in this class, thought Luc. *My winning story had been suspenseful, clear, descriptive. Marin's story had that too, but it had a heart and humor beyond what Luc had learned so far.*

Luc stepped into the hall thinking: *Learned to write or learned to live?*

Yeah, a voice in his skull answered. Luc grinned.

"What's so funny?" said Buffy as she came out of the classroom.

"What isn't?" said Luc.

You gotta do it or you'll always wonder.

Luc told Buffy's smile: "Would you go to Prom with me? It's our last one."

Relief brightened Buffy's face: "Sure! I mean, *yes!*"

He wore his black suit. His mom tailored-away the ankle cuffs so his pants became long enough. He wore a new white shirt. His dad's blue tie.

"Goes with your eyes," said his mom.

That no one ever sees behind the thick lenses of my glasses, thought Luc.

He picked Buffy up in the white '64 Chevy.

Didn't bother to wash it first. *It's the car I got.*

She walked out of her bedroom to her parents and Luc.

Her Prom dress was blue and sleek. The satin neckline scooped low on her creamy flesh—not too low for her parents, but *damn*.

She slid under the steering wheel to sit beside him.

He climbed behind the wheel. Shut the door. Turned the key.

The radio came on to a big city station.

Came the sound of . . .

Like a concert hall. Mutterings of the audience.

A bold crash of electric guitars. The drummer kicked in.

Then came the bold voices of the new Beatles album that shook the world.

"Oh my God, have you heard the whole thing?" said Buffy as the white car rolled them forward on the streets of their hometown.

"Dozens of times," answered Luc.

He'd bought the album at the new record store opened on Main Street by a woman two years older than Laura. Tables with bins of record albums. Walls hung with record album covers—old, new, known or not, didn't matter, they were there. Music for anyone to come in, buy and carry home.

Buffy shook her head: "Don't you wonder what it's about?"

"These days for everybody," said Luc. "Especially our generation. We were in high school or junior high when JFK got shot."

"If that's the start of us, then when does our generation end?"

Luc shrugged: "Maybe when the war in Vietnam ends."

On the way to pick up Buffy, the radio told Luc that KIA count was 12,235.

The *Sgt. Pepper's* album cover blew him away even without The Secrets. *With The Secrets* . . .

Luc went back to the Main Street music store after school the day after he'd bought and played the album over and over and over again.

Babbled so long and intensely to the store owner that—

"*Stop!*" Her hand pushed toward the bespectacled excitable boy.

The record company worried that the Beatles-controlled cover of their album might alarm influencers like Mrs. Sweeny, so the distributor passed along to record stores in outlying markets a list of the images crowded on the album's cover beneath the cover's strip of blue sky.

The 1967 classic album created a montage of history's important faces.

Or at least, of that era's heritage as defined by that rock 'n' roll band.

The Beatles somberly dressed in garish full color carnival band uniforms centered the cover. A cut-out of conservative suit-and-tied *them* smiling as they were when they hit American TV back in 1963 stood on their right side.

Flowers spelled out BEATLES at the bottom of the album.

Faces and figures in black and white and full color crowded behind and beside the Fab Four's mock Sgt. Pepper's band with its booming bass drum.

Luc's dream Marilyn Monroe in black and white stared out from the center of that crowd. So did other movie stars from the era of the Greatest Generation that fought World War II, parented the Beatles and their fans:

Come on up and see me sometime, va-voom Mae West and twinkly angel little girl Shirley Temple. Bette Davis with those eyes and Diana Dors—"the British Marilyn Monroe"—with platinum blonde hair and a strapless gilded gown.

Fred Astaire, the dance movies' star whose smiling lipsticked partners did everything he did only backwards and in high heels. Marlon Brando—who'd blown Luc's mind in *The Chase* movie—was pictured from a '50's black and white movie about a motorcycle gang where he answered the *What are you rebelling against?* question with: "What do you got?" Silent movie actor Tom Mix whose fame came from playing cowboys like Luc's grandfather had been. Laurel & Hardy, the comic buffoons of dozens of movies Luc'd seen at the Roxy. W. C. Fields who Luc couldn't remember. Luc did remember the album cover's Johnny Weissmuller as Tarzan and Jungle Jim set in an Africa that never existed.

The Beatles put World War I legend Lawrence of Arabia on this cover. Luc had seen the movie about him. And Karl Marx—*that* made Luc nervous. There was an image of a former British prime minister who fought for reform. Wild-haired genius Albert Einstein who changed what we knew about time and space. Carl Jung whose name Luc wrote down in his notebook to look up later. Explorer Dr. David Livingston ("I presume"). Boxer Sonny Liston who lost his heavyweight crown to another Black boxer who'd changed his name to Muhammad Ali in '64 when Luc was a sophomore.

Luc spotted the black and white gaze of singer Bob Dylan, but without the list, he'd never have recognized Dion, the brilliant singer of 1961's "The Wanderer" now struggling in 1967 to change with the times and not be cast aside as yesterday's oldy-goldy.

As they drove over the viaduct to the dance, Luc told Buffy: "How cool is it that they put a doll of a girl wearing a black and white striped dress that reads WELCOME THE ROLLING STONES."

"I wish we were welcoming any other band besides Mr. Bundy's tonight," said Buffy as the rise of the viaduct filled the windshield with the night's blackness and twinkling stars. "Everybody's so tired of them."

"Principal Harris," said Luc. "He knows what they will and won't play."

"What the hell." Buffy grinned: "We'll have fun."

She looked down below the viaduct through that night's car windows:

Lines of boxcars on railroad tracks that followed and fought the sun.

Shook her head more for all that than to send her words to Luc:

"I wonder if our grandkids—hell: our kids! Wonder if they'll even know who the Beatles are let alone all those faces on that album."

Luc's heart thundered: *Buffy said "our kids"! Grandkids!*

Of course they'd know the Beatles!

Hell, how could history or anyone forget what's going on now?

Then he remembered the river's fossils.

Luc shook his head as the car slowed toward the viaduct's STOP sign.

Buffy said: "You think maybe you're spending too much time on all that?"

"Guilty." Luc grinned. "But hey: I gotta uphold my reputation as a geek."

The car turned onto Main Street.

Buffy blurted: "Everyone respects you!"

The white car they rode rumbled over the town's pavement.

"Great," said the bespectacled driver who wasn't branded *The Wanderer*.

Wasn't Lenny Bruce either. That comic was on *Sgt. Pepper's* album cover.

Respect, thought Luc. *EXACTLY what a guy wants from The Girl Who He.*

He shook his head. Shook off all that. Right now, this night, he was driving.

What completely blew Luc's mind about that album cover was how many authors stood with the Beatles' crowd. Writers of fiction.

Don't even think about it.

Don't think about the drawer in your desk with those typed stories.

Luc remembered that list of authors.

Edgar Allan Poe, the man who invented mysteries. Aldous Huxley, who wrote *Brave New World* about future mankind who drugged themselves to live in a technological facade that sorted each beating heart into data points.

The author named William Burroughs rocketed Luc back to 1959's Easter morning after two teenagers' car wreck on a midnight highway outside of town. Just before KRIP radio announced that terrible news, they told their listeners that the Post Office had confiscated all copies of Burroughs's novel *Naked Lunch*.

Luc had read pictured H. G. Wells's *The Time Machine*. He'd seen the movie, too. The heroine was played by actor Yvette Mimieux whose belly button terrified people like Mrs. Sweeny. Luc grew up bombarded by another album author's stories about a girl named Alice who falls down a rabbit hole into a world of wonder and *watch out.*

Luc spent an hour at the Big Pink's library tracking down other authors pictured for *Sgt. Pepper's*. Poet Dylan Thomas. And not *one*, not *two*, but *three* Irish authors: poet Oscar Wilde, a playwright named George Bernard Shaw and a novelist named James Joyce.

The Big Pink's midnight-haired librarian Mrs. Dawson said Joyce wrote like a river. Helped Luc figure out last year's thick annual volume called the *Readers Guide to Periodical Literature* so he could turn pages and scroll his forefinger down a long list to identify one of the images on *Sgt. Pepper's* album cover: a writer named Terry Southern who helped create the black and white movie *Dr. Strangelove or How I Learned to Stop Worrying and Love the Bomb.*

Luc shook his head as he sat in the Big Pink's library.

I learned to be a projectionist watching that movie.

Now he pulled the white Chevy to the curb outside the brick building where he'd first gone to school. Turned the key. The white car's engine and radio died.

Buffy said: "An album like that. The Beatles. Is it just rock 'n' roll?"

Luc shook his head: "Now it's all rock 'n' roll."

He led Buffy toward their last Prom.

REVOLUTION

Luc and Buffy shuffled in a slow dance at the decorated grade school gym with the usual band of adults playing on stage.

They held each other.

Not—

—oh God, *not* so close as her flesh against his front.

But he felt her heat. Felt the friendship of her arms.

They'd barely stopped talking since they'd gotten out of the white car.

Luc smiled: They always had a lot to talk about.

The slow dance ended.

Buffy and Luc went back to their white paper covered round table and their side-by-side chairs to sit down. Catch their breath.

"There's Marin!" said Buffy. "With Barbara. They never come out."

"He wanted to give her at least one formal dance," said his buddy Luc.

"He's going to Eastern College next year," said Buffy.

Neither of them said *So is Steve.*

Though they both knew and they both knew they both knew.

"Kurt didn't come," sighed Buffy. "There had to be someone he could ask."

"I think he wants to," said his friend Luc. "But he's too shy."

"Too late now." Buffy nodded: "There's your other Key Club buddy Wayne over by the red punch bowl. Jabbering away. Who'd he bring?"

"A freshman girl who I hear he says thinks he's so cool."

Buffy frowned.

"Don't you hang out with him?" she asked Luc.

"Not so much anymore. Or Kurt either. You know, busy. Plus, the Pezzani family up on Knob Hill—my cousins. Lots of times I drift up there. Hang with Seba and his buddies from his class. Eat breadsticks."

"While you're eating breadsticks, Wayne's telling everybody how he got Principal Harris to get the Main Street clubs to cough up extra dollars to hire some guy he heard at Boys State to be our graduation speaker."

"E. Z. Daly. All the way from the Lone Star state of Texas to us up here just south of the border to Canada. He delivers a great speech."

"But why?" said Buffy. "It's just graduation. Nobody listens anyway."

"If you ask Kurt, he'll say it was part of a Key Club project to earn us points to get nationally ranked," said Luc. "If you ask me, now Wayne's used other peoples' money to get a connection for wherever he's stiff-walking to."

Luc leaned closer to Buffy.

She leaned closer to him.

"Want to know a secret?" whispered Luc.

"Only one?"

"Kurt can't find out about it. But you know that he *is* Key Club. Loves the accounting. Making things work. With the class, too, the secretary. Band. Other clubs and things.

"So a bunch of us Key Clubbers, we got together behind our president Wayne's back *and* Kurt's. Voted to give Kurt an 'Outstanding Student' plaque on Awards Night. Gorilla Harris will present it to Kurt. Not Wayne."

Luc shrugged: "You do what you can for the good guys."

"That's one of the things that's good about you," said Buffy.

"*OK, everybody!*" boomed Mr. Bundy's voice through the microphone. "You know what time it is! Come on up here, chorus!"

Bobbi Jean stepped up from her solo table with the other thirty-some formally dressed students who walked the same high school hallways as her.

Mr. Bundy smiled, slick black hair and looking trim. He waved his arms for three new songs from the chorus. His night gigs' band rested by their instruments. Two hurried off to go pee.

After three songs and applause, Mr. Bundy walked to the lone microphone on its silver pole pointing to heaven, pointing to hell.

"And now as you know," came his amplified voice, "we have traditions at formal dances. So let me—"

Bobbi Jean.

Grimly marching toward—*at* the microphone before Mr. Bundy could call her or anybody else's name. She wore a dress of her own, not the borrowed fairy tale gown. Her brown hair curled to her bare shoulders. She wore the fire red lipstick she'd loaned to Buffy in the GIRLS room *oh so long ago.*

She grabbed the mic pole. Pulled the mic free in her left hand, its cord trailing along the bare wood of the stage like a whip. Or a snake.

"No 'Blue Velvet' tonight!" she hissed into the mic as she stepped away from any graceful, appropriate grab by her teacher and conductor Bundy.

She kicked her high heels off.

The crowd gasped. Mr. Bundy stood frozen at the other end of the stage.

Then . . .

Bobbi Jean sang . . . *Was it a song?*

Melody. Some kind of heartbeat rhythm. Snatches of mystery lyrics:

"Breaking hearts . . . Breaking could be's . . . Breaking me! . . . Lying and lying . . . Taking and taking . . . And laying there lying! . . . Gave you me! . . ."

Bobbi Jean sang—*screamed*—that song no one but her knew.

Belted it out like a blues singer in a smoky night club until—

Her lone voice . . . stopped.

Bobbi Jean blinked at the crowd of her fellow students.

Her face was a plea of horror and fear, shame and anger, *oh anger.*

She didn't look at the stunned chorus behind her. The chorus where in front stood the wide-eyed, lost-weight younger girl from their co-ed duet.

Bobbi Jean dropped the mic.

BONK! on the stage floor amplified over the crowd.

She ran barefoot off the stage. Out of the paper-streamered auditorium of where she'd gone to grade school. Gone.

THE RIGHT KISS

Frozen silence filled Luc and Buffy's last Prom.

   Then a banker in the band struck an organ chord. Glared at Bundy until he came alive and shooed the chorus off the stage. One girl picked up Bobbi Jean's shoes. Dropped them on Bobbi Jean's lone table by her purse.

   The other adult musicians hurried back on stage to strike up a jazzy song.

   "*Wow*," whispered Buffy.

   She shook her head. "Bobbi Jean. I mean, what the hell?"

   Buffy sighed: "My guess is they're going to shut Prom down early."

   "Yeah, so . . . Ah . . . Look, *ah*, I'll be right back."

   He hurried through the dazed crowd.

   The nearest BOYS room was packed, and when you've got to go . . .

   Luc hurried down dimly lit halls he knew by heart. Hurried down the long hall toward the office where that principal once beat fifth grader Marin because he'd dared to stick up for himself and other Indian kids. Luc turned into the Pine-Sol bathroom. Snapped on the lights and *made it*.

   Flushed. Washed his hands.

   Could hear the sound of the Prom band still playing all the way down here.

   Snapped out the bathroom lights.

   Stepped out into the dimly lit hallway.

   Barefoot Bobbi Jean charged from the shadows into the glow from street-lights flowing through the big windows of the school's closed front doors.

   Charged to where Luc stood not knowing what to—

   Bobbi Jean hammered her fists into his chest.

   Again and again and again as he stepped back to block her blows.

She was panting. She was crying. She was screaming at him.

"Why? Why? Why didn't you kiss me? Freshman Co-ed. My one ever real date and . . . First time . . . Asked you. You. All you had to do . . . Dance with me right and . . . One kiss! That would have been enough so I wouldn't feel . . . So he . . . I could have known, could have . . . wouldn't have and now it's . . ."

They heard the band echo down the hall.

Her eyes softened as they took in the sight of Luc standing there.

"Just one kiss," she whispered.

Barefooted her way to the locked push-handle doors.

Slammed one open.

GONG! GONG! GONG! The Door Danger alarm blared through the school.

Bobbi Jean vanished out into the darkness.

Luc ran to the auditorium.

Fought his way through the *Move to the Exits Quietly and Calmly* crowd.

Buffy standing by our table! She waited for me!

Her jaw dropped as he hurried past her.

Luc scooped Bobbi Jean's purse and shoes off her table.

Hurried out with Buffy as *WOW-WOW-WOW!* the volunteer fire department engines screeched to a halt. They climbed into his parents' white car. Luc spotted a break in the pell-mell traffic—

—shot the '64 Chevy into a safe lane out of there.

They drove through streets they didn't really see.

Buffy stared at the purse and shoes on the seat beside her.

Looked at their rescuer Luc: "What will you do with them?"

Next day, Sunday afternoon, he drove twenty minutes west out of town to the oil refinery with its chimney that regularly blasted out methane fire and gas. He knew which of the six corporate houses was Bobbi Jean's. The curtains were drawn. He walked to that front door.

Didn't knock: *What the hell would—could—anybody say?* Left a brown paper grocery store sack with Bobbi Jean's shoes and purse on the front porch.

Drove home.

And Prom night, told Buffy *zero* about Bobbi Jean hitting him. Blaming him for . . . *For what?* Said nothing about Bobbi Jean fleeing. *Bonging* the doors.

"Somehow, I don't feel like going out to dinner," Buffy'd told him. "Is that—"

"Me either," said Luc. "Although there'll be a hundred stories told tonight at all the restaurants, at school Monday."

"Will any of them have it right?"

"No," said Luc.

Buffy believed him.

And Luc couldn't . . . It didn't feel right to try . . . He drove Buffy straight home. Walked her to her door.

She turned to face him. Stood right in front of him.

"Guess I have to say—Tonight was . . . I'm glad it was you I had to get through it with. So . . . *Thanks*."

Luc stared at who he saw standing there.

Leaned in.

So did she.

A kiss more than casual. But her lips stayed closed.

They said goodnight.

He waited until she got safely inside her house. Closed the door.

Walked to the car that got him here.

Turned the engine on and the radio off so it was just him and the road home.

Heard the night whisper: "*Just one kiss*."

GRADUATION

Donna sat in the old lady's beat-up car in the gravel driveway.

Come on, she told herself. *Do what you wanna do.*

"You oughta," said her boss Zelda as she lit a cigarette three days before in the hospital's file room that held their desks and stacks of ever more work.

Donna inhaled the smoke and fire of where she was.

No more being stuck in my parents' house. Got my own one room 'n' kitchen nook apartment. Paid off Doc Nirmberg.

Donna sat in the old lady's car next to her parents' house.

The sun crimsoned in the west that Friday, June 2nd, 1967.

Now's the start of something the 1967 newspaper she scarfed up in the hospital called: "The Summer of Love."

Yeah, thought Donna. *Right.*

"I'm telling you," Zelda'd said at work: "You gotta go."

Knock–knock on the file room's closed door.

"Come in!" yelled Zelda who was the boss for two more pre-pension years.

The opening door admitted a scruffy man wearing a tool belt.

"Not you!" said Zelda. "How many times you got to check our pipes 'n' ceiling?"

"Sorry," said the stocky nearing-thirty man. He had the jaw of the strong but the stance of the shy. "I gotta keep looking till I fix it."

He'd *twice* told both the women in this office that his name was Gus.

Office boss Zelda forgot about him as she turned back to her protégé Donna.

"So what if you aren't on that stage?" she told Donna as Gus stood on his portable ladder to run his eyes along the file room's overhead pipes. "You went to school with all them. You're already further along than they are. So go!"

Zelda stubbed out her cigarette. Picked up the next file.

Blink and it's three days later.

And Donna sat in an old lady's car in a driveway next to her folks' lives. Donna turned the key.

Cars surrounded the Big Pink. Filled both of the high school's parking lots.

Donna limped into her old high school with the dust from the road that got her here and a whiff of perfume from a sample bottle at the pharmacy where she'd picked up a prescription for the old lady. Donna wore her best dress—emerald green. Her best walking shoes.

This is who I got to be!

Who are you all going to be? thought Donna as she clutched the ceremony's printed program listing the names of all the graduates in "her" class.

She climbed switchback stairs to the balconies ringing the basketball court filled with gray folding chairs and a long dais for the high school teachers approved by Principal Harris. Neither librarian Mrs. Dawson nor Coach Moent had seats up there. The mayor sat there. Superintendent of Schools Makhem.

Members of the school board sat up there, too, but for 1967's ceremony, Luc and Kurt's fathers chose to sit with their wives in the audience and celebrate their sons' victory *together* rather than be on stage with their own glory.

Those two couples and more than a hundred other proud, dressed-up parents sat in the pulled-out-to-the-floor bleachers where they could watch their cap and gowned children parade in to their orchestrated seats.

Aunts, uncles, cousins, next-door neighbors, work and otherwise friends scattered themselves on the balcony seats along the horseshoe above the basketball court. A backless long wooden bench put Donna four rows above the railing around the edge of the court below.

Two high school girls stood beside their mother and three women sharing a bench with her. Donna recognized those three women as the Conner sisters: The youngest was Dory, in from the farm. Beside her sat Iona. Beryl sat on the far end—maybe out of politeness because of the cough she kept covering up.

Squeals from the two girls near Donna slashed through the bleachers.

"*Oh my God*, Mom, we are SO going downstairs to watch them walk in!"

"We gotta! I mean, *can you imagine*. We heard that they're actually going to let Bobbi Jean parade in with everyone else like—"

"Like she didn't go *whatever* at Prom!"

"She hasn't been in school since. Heard she's going to college somewhere out of state. But still, can you imagine? Knowing her now, she could go nuts and run wild in her cap 'n' gown and bring the whole place down!"

Knowing her now, thought Donna.

Knowing some version of what everyone in town "knew." The crazy song. Barefoot. Running away. Causing so much chaos someone tripped the alarms.

Knowing Bobbi Jean's happy country-girl face when their fifth grade teacher hooked them up to help then no-glasses Luc see the blackboard. Bobbi Jean who stayed her friend even when she landed in the A classes while lower family income "crippled" Donna got bumped down to the Bs. Or Cs. Bobbi Jean who somehow drifted away freshman year. Bobbi Jean who only days ago went . . . Who broke the rules. Broke free. And now had the guts to come to this graduation night to claim what she'd earned.

Donna rocked the rows near her with her loud voice: "*Fever!*"

The two teenage girls whirled to stare at the *woman* who used to be them.

"Up at the hospital," continued Donna, knowing the Conner sisters knew where she worked.

"Heard nurses talking," lied Donna. She pushed her voice as loud as she dared. "They said Bobbi Jean had a fever Prom night. But she didn't wanna not show up like she was supposed to."

Donna dropped her voice so every ear that had been listening to her before now strained harder to hear the confidentiality thus being revealed.

"The fever threw her off. Mixed her up. Made her try to do her best when she was confused. They're pretty sure she got the fever because . . ."

Donna paused to let her reveal hook every listener:

"They said she probably got fever crazy because of her period."

Nobody *but nobody* in town back then questioned anything about the mysteries of menstruation.

That secret dropped the jaws of the two still-in-school teenage girls.

Iona Conner *humphed*: "Been there. Being on the rag, you never know."

"*Oh my God!*" exclaimed one of the teenage daughters.

They ran through an exit to the stairs down to the basketball court.

How long will it take those two high school girls to spread their gossip? wondered Donna. How long before the Conner sisters had *the word* spread throughout the whole town? How long for *fever* to be the alibi for Bobbi Jean?

Don't know what you did or why, Donna telepathed to Bobbi Jean whoever and wherever she was now. *But I did what I could.*

The school band struck up the graduation processional.

Adults walked onto the dais.

Two lines of Donna's cap 'n' gowned peers paraded into the gym.

The crowd stood and roared—

—and there was Donna: Standing and cheering. Clapping. Crying.

About-to-graduates reached their last assigned chairs in the Big Pink.

Principal Harris moved to the lectern. Used the mic to announce: "You may be seated!"

The graduates and their fans obeyed.

Donna set her rump on the wooden bench above the ceremony.

Sensed *motion* changing her space.

There, sitting *not quite* beside her, wearing a blue shirt with a bolo Western tie and weathered but clean slacks, sat the carpenter/repairman Gus who kept walking into her cramped shared office at the hospital.

"Why are you here?" whispered Donna as amplified oratory echoed through this high school gym. "Is somebody in my—in the class a relative of yours?"

"Lost my brother in the Korean war. Dad got hit by a falling beam workin' a building in Great Falls. Only relative I have left is Mom over in Shelby."

Donna saw him sitting there. Looking at her. Seeing her. Talking to her. *Gus. His name is Gus.*

Donna heard him say: "Thought if you showed up, maybe I could give you a ride home. Or wherever you wanna go."

She heard herself whisper: "I've got a car."

Amplified *blah blah blah* faded into the background.

Gus shrugged: "So . . . Can I catch a ride?"

NOW IS WHEN

L uc sat behind the steering wheel of the white '64 Chevy parked with the motor running in the Big Pink's students' lot.

The car's windshield faced away from the high school.

The radio played WLS: 50,000 Windy City watts all the way from Chicago.

Where I'm not going, thought Luc.

Smiled and thought of Laura.

She's never *for real* coming home.

Does everybody have a hometown?

Luc stared through the windshield at this prairie valley town of twinkling streetlights coming up on midnight of the day he graduated from high school.

His eyes flicked to the rearview mirror. He stepped on the brake pedal. Red lights flashed on the school walls. Flickered in the locked glass front doors.

He took his foot off the brake pedal. Red lights vanished.

Gone is gone.

The radio played.

Luc'd ditched his graduation suit in his bedroom while his parents hung around the living room of the only house he'd ever lived in. Walked out to where his parents couldn't stop their smiles and the sadness in their eyes. *Of course* they let him take the car—the good white Chevy Impala, not the gray '54 Dodge. *Have fun*, they said. *Be careful*, they said. *See you in the morning.*

The graduation dance surprised him.

Most of his classmates showed up. But most of them left early.

Not Kurt.

And not Wayne, who Luc had seen strolling along Main Street that afternoon with the bigtime Texas graduation speaker.

In the rumbling darkness, Luc grinned: *Just being a good host, right?*

He saw Buffy at the dance. Talked to her. Watched her walk away. Like Wayne, she was going to the university in Bozeman next year. She brought Wendy to the dance because the drummer Wendy dated had other ideas. And where was Alice? The drummer's bandmate on guitar Andy and Cherie showed up together but didn't seem overjoyed about that.

My first real date, thought Luc as he watched Cherie.

But tonight, he had the white '64 Chevy.

In the school parking lot alone near midnight, Luc *Vroomed* the gas pedal.

He could go anywhere the car could take him.

The point of his last dance *ever* in the Big Pink was to celebrate it with the right music. Leave it . . . *not alone* or with Kurt who he'd made bring his own car.

As the DJ played songs, Luc'd spotted hope.

A freshman girl. Pointed black glasses. Kind of cool.

He asked her to dance. Two fast ones and then a slow tune where she circled her arms around this graduated senior's neck. Didn't pull him close, *but*.

Said *yes* to him taking her home. Walking her to her front door.

Leaned forward to give him a polite kiss.

Leaned back to say: "Thanks for the ride and good luck to you."

Hurried inside to the *never again* they both knew.

He drove away.

Drove damn near every street in town. Knob Hill where the Pezzanis lived. Where Steve's parents lived. Where the cemetery was.

He knew there were parties. Somebody's house. At the river.

He wasn't looking for them.

Was just *looking*.

I'm eighteen, he thought. *The ten o'clock curfew whistle doesn't control me now.* He drove along Main Street lined with parked cars outside the seven bars where he still couldn't legally go in for a beer, a jukebox for his quarter. He drove past City Hall where he still couldn't vote. Drove past the Draft Board office where he could sign up to fight in the war.

Well, except the Draft Board woman clerk took one look at Luc's near-sighted-as-hell optometrist report and stamped 4F on his file: physically unfit for military service. He was legally free from the Draft.

The radio news let any listener know the KIA count was now 13,193.

Luc drove over the viaduct. Wondered about hobos.

Where are we all going?

Missoula for me, thought Luc. The university there. Luc'd told Kurt he didn't want to list him on the university form as his preferred roommate.

Luc knew, *just knew*, he was going to get a great roommate. A guy who wouldn't mind the *clackety-clack* of typewriter keys or Luc's music from his stereo and boxed-up record albums.

Won't it be cool if he's Black! And from someplace magical like . . . like New York! I wanna know who other people are. What they think. How they feel.

He turned left off the northbound highway leading to another country.

Drove past Buffy's house.

Watched it slide past his open driver's side window as the radio played.

Just like a thousand times before.

Luc drove his ride into the nighttime deserted parking lot of the Big Pink.

Backed up the car toward where he'd been.

Now sat there staring out the windshield toward . . . *What?*

"And now here on WLS, it's the Friday Night Blast from the Past!"

The DJ in charge of that night spun an oldy-goldy record:

The Beach Boys' "Don't Worry, Baby."

A perfect song, thought Luc. Bragging. Bluff called. Risking all to claim real. Having someone who loves you. Realizing exactly *where* and *who* you are.

The song ended.

Luc reached under the driver's seat.

Shifted around behind the steering wheel to hold the pipe in his left hand while he tapped it full of the last of the grass. Smiled because he knew what to call it. Wondered if his dad would spot his lighter MIA—Missing in Action, a crucial new official term everyone his generation learned as at least 233 Americans were prisoners of war. Luc snapped the lighter's wheel. Flame flickered beyond his eyes in the rearview mirror.

Slowly, carefully . . .

Luc put flame to the outlaw fuel right in front of the Big Pink.

Drew fiery breath through the pipe, into his mouth—lungs.

Held it there.

Let out a cloud of smoke, wondered if cigarette aunts would smile.

Fed the pipe bowl another flame.

Second time he also caught the smoke, but only held it for a couple heart-beats before he coughed out to the open window night. Coughed again.

The pipe bowl was empty of everything but gray ash.

The tiny manila envelope: empty.

A lonesome train whistle drifted into the car about the radio's sound.

The perpetual wind here in his hometown blew away the smoked rope smell from his parents' car.

He sat there with the car rumbling fuel from dead dinosaurs.

Five songs.

He felt only like what he'd felt before. Wild and outlaw but . . . not *stoned*.

Someday, he thought.

How much of life is someday?

His glow-in-the-dark wristwatch read after midnight.

Luc released the emergency brake. Dropped the car into gear.

Drove off into the new day and the bed he knew.

CELEBRATE

R emember," ordered Mom as she plopped scrambled eggs, bacon and one of the new-to-Vernon English muffins on the kitchen table in front of Luc at 9:17 on the sunny Saturday morning of July 1, 1967, "it's a celebration."

Luc wore a white paper napkin tucked into the open collar of his short-sleeved white shirt. The clip-on black tie waited on his bed.

He checked the clock: *Lots of time.* He didn't need to show up for his summer box boy job at the Thriftway grocery store until ten A.M.

Was his boss who owned and managed that family store who told him he was getting off early that Saturday so he could "go to the river thing for Beryl."

"It's a family picnic," Mom told Luc that morning. "A celebration."

"Too early for Independence Day."

"Maybe not." Mom shook her head.

Sighed: "Beryl sold the drive-in and that's what we're celebrating."

Turned from the kitchen sink to see her son sitting at the table.

"Plus . . . she's gotta . . . Come August, they're cutting out part of her lung."

Luc stared at her.

"I don't know much more than that. Nobody does. Not even the doctors. But . . . But it's good they caught it now. So we're celebrating that, too."

Whispered: "Celebrating Beryl."

Went back to her mom voice:

"Now hurry up and finish your breakfast. I need the car. I called Teresa. When he comes in from the farm, Seba's gonna pick you up at 5:00 at the store. Ride you home to change clothes for the river. It's a family picnic. Everybody from the Conner clan for a hundred miles 'round is coming."

She dropped Luc off in the grocery store parking lot.

The other white-shirted box boy named Dennis rode up on his Japanese motorcycle. He wore glasses, too. Either the wind off the streets or the wind he made motorcycling the streets had mussed his brown hair. He dropped the bike's kickstand. Killed the engine. Swung off like a cowboy. Buttoned his white shirt. Clipped on his black tie.

Dennis was two years younger than Luc. Still in high school, now a junior.

"Friends" wasn't what Luc thought of when he saw Dennis. They'd nod. Share small talk. Who was going to shelve what in which aisle. Respond to the loudspeaker calls for a box boy to hurry to the cash registers, sack groceries for a customer and help them carry the bags outside to their car.

But Dennis had seniority on this job that was also his after-school gig.

That meant he got to deliver groceries to the whorehouse.

Drive the pickup truck full of sacks to the red stucco mansion of mysteries.

Dennis knew Luc was jealous. Let Luc know that *he knew* with a smug and a smirk and a smile whenever the loudspeaker call came for "delivery boy."

Plus, there was that afternoon when Luc and Dennis aproned-up to lug cold and squishy butchered quarter-cut beef slabs from the slaughterhouse's refrigerator truck into the grocery store's frigid walk-in meat locker and then hang blood-smelling *dead cow* on the rotating steel hooks.

There'd been a TV show the night before of stand-up comedy that featured a band called The Association that played a song Luc was singing that butchered beef day when Dennis called out: *"It's 'Windy,' not 'Wendy,' you idiot!"*

How many other song lyrics do I have wrong? thought Luc. *But . . . "idiot"?*

That Saturday morning as the body count in Vietnam reached 14,055, Dennis and Luc walked together into the store's metal-can atmosphere with local radio station KRIP on the store's loudspeaker system playing smooth and safe songs softly over the cart-pushing customers.

Was a good day at work for Luc. He liked bagging groceries. Creating architectures in brown paper sacks. Judging how heavy to make a sack for the customer. Joshing with the middle-aged women cashiers. Joking with customers. Helping people who lived in Vernon but who he'd never really known or talked to. Like they were from a layer of the town he didn't know. Packing the bags *just so* in the trunk of some customer's car and closing it with a satisfying *clunk*.

Plus, the store was *Ahhh!* air conditioned in that swelter of July.

Luc's buddy and cousin Seba Pezzani pulled his car into the grocery store parking lot at exactly 5:00. They loaded the car with four cases of chilled cans of Cokes and ginger ales for the picnic courtesy of the store owner who said: "You tell Beryl *hey* for me, you hear?"

Luc was clothes-changed and riding shotgun in Seba's car by 5:27.

They were halfway to the river when Seba said: "What's Beryl gonna do? The house and the drive-in next door: Did she sell them both?"

"Beats me," said Luc.

Watched a hawk circling a plowed field.

Dozens of cars filled the river's picnic grounds. Picnic tables circled grill stoves filling the trees and river air with barbecue smoke.

Luc and Seba slogged the cases of cans toward folding tables loaded with homemade food. Plates offering steaming corncobs. Hamburgers in buns on a platter that kept being refilled by the grill guys doing the only kind of cooking married men supposedly did in those days.

At the center of it all were the Conner sisters.

All four of them sitting at one picnic table.

Aunt Dory in from the farm. Aunt Iona. Luc's mom Cora.

And Aunt Beryl. The gravity pull for every eye.

Luc turned away. Heard a lighter's *Click!*

"What the hell," said Beryl behind him. "Might as well. Too late now."

None of her sisters knew what to say.

Luc told Aunt Beryl whose cocked high arm held a smoking cigarette about the store manager's *hey*.

"Tell him '*Hey!*' yourself," said Beryl. "I ain't no—"

Legendary jokester *her* braked the reflexive classic snapback.

Softened her voice: "Tell him *thanks*. And *sorry* if my drive-in 'cross the road from Thriftway was ever a bother. He won't need to worry 'bout that much longer. I think the new guy's gonna turn it into a laundromat soon as summer's over and the car hops don't pull in the cash, so all that'll be over."

She blinked at a vision of where her husband Johnny had lived and died.

Took a drag off her cigarette.

Let out the smoke and watched it drift away.

"What the hell doesn't get to *over.*"

"*You two!*" came Cousin Teresa's voice of distraction behind Luc and her son: "Get your burgers while we figure out what in tarnation is going on with . . ."

Everyone knew with *what tarnation* distraction didn't matter.

After burgers, corncobs and slices of cherry pie with the last of the cinnamon ice cream saved from the shut-down Whitehouse café, Luc and Seba met up with Aunt Dory's daughter Kate who was a year younger than Luc, Seba's age. She was a farm girl who went to school in Shelby.

"I gotta get away from all these people," said Kate.

Their trio headed into the trees along the shores of the Grady River.

"It's so low," said Luc.

They stood on a beach of gravel before an S curve in flowing water.

Kate took off her white sneakers. Stuck her toes in the water.

"Oh damn does that feel good!" she said. "It's hot as hell out here. But that means the river isn't cold, it's . . . *Oh yeah.*"

Like them, she wore cutoffs—short pants.

Kate stepped into the ankle-deep middle of the river. Scooted down so her legs and butt were almost covered by the slow-moving water.

The current *oh so slowly* pushed her butt over submerged rocks.

"*Wee!*"

Seba and Luc pulled off their socks and sneakers. Left whatever was in their pockets in a pile on a rock above all the others.

Luc put his glasses on the pile. Confronted a blurred world. Green trees. Blue sky. Silver blue river. Waded with Seba into the trickling water. They settled on their butts . . .

Let the warm push of the river water ride them over not-too-bumpy rocks.

Up ahead, Katie scooted around the high curve bend of the river. Had to push herself more with her hands to make the turn. Maybe twenty feet behind her and riding a shallow current along the opposite shore of gravel came Seba.

If I push/float toward the middle of them, going around the bend gotta good chance to catch up to them and the current—

Whoa! I can drop my feet and walk with the stronger rush to—

The river hole pulls Luc straight down underwater.

Gulped breath, feet kicking, touching rocks, push up—

Cramps hit his right calf. Then his left.

The rushing current whirls *can't use his legs* Luc into the hole.

Green everything swirling water in my nose can't hold my breath any—

Luc's head pops up from the river.

He pounds the water rushing him away from his cousins.

Time swirls.

Seba's grabbing me. Pulling me. Yelling and pushing/paddling: "Hold on, Luc! I got you! I got you!"

The red second hand on the black-numbered clock tick a half circle.

Now Luc's sitting in the river flowing below the top of his thighs.

His two cousins staring down at him.

Luc lifted himself off the rocks.

The three of them walked along on the gravel shoreline back to their stash. Loaded up. Walked into the trees back toward the "just a family picnic."

Kate said: "You two sure know how to show a girl a good time."

They stepped out of the trees to the park filled with celebrating relatives.

Luc knew time past. Knew he obeyed orders to help clean up. Filled cars with trash and treasures. Nodded. Grunted. Flowed with what others did. Found himself riding shotgun in Seba's car under a crimson streaked sky.

The radio played a song he knew like he'd never heard it before.

Seba stopped his car at the curb outside Luc's house.

Luc stared at Seba. At his cousin. At his friend. At *who.*

Out of Luc's mouth came: "I . . . I . . . don't know what . . ."

Their eyes drilled deep into each other's.

"*Seba . . .*"

"I know," said Seba. And he did.

Luc said: "*Thanks.*"

Seba got it. Nodded.

Luc got out of that car. Closed the door behind him. Watched it drive away on a hot July 1967 Saturday night.

THE TUNNEL OF LOVE

The Ferris wheel glowed in the dinner hour of the sunny blue sky Friday east of Vernon in July, 1967, at the Four County Grady River Fair & Rodeo.

Luc sat stopped at the top of the Ferris wheel. His seat swung back and forth. The sway of inertia. The soft breeze. The kicks of the grade school kids sitting on either side of him—all of them locked in by the restraining bar.

The kids' Gramma had spotted 'that nice young man from Thriftway' standing there looking at that wheel in the sky. She asked him the favor of herding Melisa and Tommy who barely reached the height line to take that ride.

"I'll buy the tickets," said Gramma. "But hell, I'm too old for that go-around."

Now stopped at the top of the Ferris wheel, Luc pointed: "Look, kids! You can see the town from up here."

Little Melisa whined: "Where's my house? I can't see my house."

"It's there," said Luc. "You just gotta look. And believe."

The Ferris wheel lurched.

The box they rode rolled forward in a down slope curve.

"Look!" yelled little Tommy.

A yellow cyclops eye freight train pulled out of town, *clackety-clacking* past the fairgrounds toward Chicago.

Luc saw the train—

—saw Buffy walking out of the four-story-tall white wooden grandstands that overlooked the racetrack and pens for bull riding, bronco busting, steer wrestling, calf roping and a clown. The grandstands also held rooms of exhibits. Tables of baking, sewing, pottery, art paintings.

And flowers, realized Luc like Sherlock Holmes.

The Ferris wheel *thunked* to a stop to let the riders in the box on the ground get out and get on with their carnival delights.

Buffy wore a light and breezy blue summer dress, not the shorts and blouses worn by most gir—*women* her age walking the midway of '*Hur-ray, hur-ray, hur-ray!*' carny booths to take your quarters amidst roller coaster screams.

Buffy's working her family floral shop booth in the grandstands. I'm stuck on the Ferris wheel and she's going to walk right past me!

Whoosh and the Ferris wheel rolled Luc's box forward two stops.

Can't see her. Has to be—

Whunk. The Ferris wheel stopped with Luc's box only one stop away from freedom. Little Melisa waved to Gramma. Little Tommy picked his nose.

Whoosh . . . Whunk!

The carny unlocked the bar holding Luc and the children safe.

Luc grabbed a kid with each hand. Hurried to Gramma.

Her darling grandchildren tugged at her for *what's next*. She thanked that nice young man: "Got you these."

Handed him two tickets good for any carnival ride.

He mumbled: "*Thanks.*" Stuffed them in his blue jeans pocket as he whirled this way and that. Pushed his glasses up his nose.

There!

Buffy walking toward the concession stands.

"Buffy!" he yelled.

She stopped as he ran to her.

"Where are you going?" he called.

"The payphone."

She nodded to a tall glass booth with a folding door and a bolted-in *black with a silver metal chord* and *slots for coins* phone. That booth stood as a lone soldier in the army of millions like it from sea to shining sea.

"Our 'free flower' promo ran out," said Buffy. "I'm supposed to call Dad when I'm ready to go home."

"Come on. Stick around. We can grab some rides. A freak show."

Buffy laughed: "I'm not going to go looking for your buddy the Geek."

She remembers the secret I told her about when me and Marin were ten!

"I think the Geek's history. Now they got a gypsy fortune teller."

"No thanks," said Buffy. "Are you out here alone?"

"Yeah." He shrugged. "I just . . . you know. Wanted to walk around."

"Have fun." Buffy turned to walk away.

"*Wait!*"

Buffy blinked.

"I still owe you a dinner after Prom!"

They laughed together as the Ferris wheel spun 'round.

"Come on," he said. "Bet you could go for a burger. And then I'll give you a ride home. Save you a dime for not having to call your dad."

"Oh, *well*, an offer like that . . ."

They settled on the Elks Club's food stand. An open on all sides wooden shack with benches and counters. They sat beside each other facing out the open window with the counter in front of them covered by their paper plates of greasy burgers and French fries, plastic packets of red goo labeled catsup.

They laughed. They ate. They watched the crowd streaming past.

He carried their empty plates, dirty napkins, empty Coke cups to the garbage can. Wet brown paper towels waiting by the counter's bowl of warm water, brought them back so they could wash their hands.

He wet-towel patted his mouth. She did, too.

"There goes my lip gloss," said Buffy.

"You don't need it."

"It's mostly a sunblock."

But she smiled.

They stepped out to the popcorn and black tar smelling midway.

"Come on," he said. "Walk with me. You can always go home.

"Hell," he added. "You can never really leave."

The payphone booth stood to her left.

Waiting for her.

Luc and the carnival midway waited to her right.

Buffy shrugged. Walked over the sticky black tarred midway beside Luc.

"I've got two free tickets," he told her. "We can go on the Tilt-A-Whirl. Or the roller coaster."

"With my Prom burger filling my stomach?" said Buffy. "I don't think so. Every year they have some special new ride. What's this year?"

He led her to it.

"*Really*," she said.

The Tunnel of Love.

An architecture of illusion. A flat-faced structure with a train track at the boarding platform that disappeared through a dark hole for a shorter ride than you felt. Ups and downs. Curves. You could see the rails where you used to be as you clattered forward. The bold *you* got caught kissing when the train clattered across an open balcony above the fairgrounds. You might be surprised. You could pretend to be surprised. You could care less. Keep on kissing. Brush your hair off your face. Smile.

Then right at the end—

WHOOSH! The five-car train emerged to swoon into a pool of water. Time to get off and let the next set of ticket holders climb on board.

"Hey you two!" yelled a voice they both knew.

Getting off the Tunnel of Love train. Laughing and waving: Alice.

With Fred by her side.

Fred who'd graduated with Steve the year before.

Fred home on leave after his first tour in Vietnam with the Marines.

Fred who stared at Luc and Buffy with cataloging eyes. Whose smile . . .

His smile was Fred's, but his face shaped itself with phantoms no one in his hometown could fathom.

"You two have got to do it!" Alice told Luc and Buffy.

Smiled with a mischievous twinkle in her eyes.

Alice said: "All they did is fix up the haunted house ride from last year!"

Her face went *wow*: "Maybe love *is* a carnival haunted house!"

Fred softened as Buffy and Luc told him how glad they were to see him. Knew they meant it. Knew they meant *glad* he wasn't KIA. Wasn't fucked-up, blown apart or scarred as shit. At least, not like they could see.

"Come on." Alice pulled Fred past their friends. "You've got the white convertible. I've got a hankering to show come-home you the stars up north."

They retreated into that hour long before the stars came out.

Luc whiffed *like burnt rope* shrouding the retreating couple.

Oh.

Luc smiled: *Marijuana—grass—has come to town.*

The carny running that ride shouted at the two rubes who were just standing there: "*You two getting on board or what?*"

Luc handed the carny his two free tickets.

He and Buffy climbed into the ride's last of the five built-for-two cars.

No restraining bar lay locked across their laps.

Strangers filled the four cars ahead of them.

The carny threw the lever.

The love train flowed through the tunnel.

Luc felt Buffy's bare arm near his. Weak bulbs hung on each side of the track so its riders had a sense there were walls, a path. Nameless music played. They rode past images of lovers. Caricatures staring at each other. A stolen movie poster of a plunging neckline Hollywood beauty not really resisting the coming kiss of the manly man brave and lucky enough to give it to her.

Rumble curve tossing Luc and Buffy that way together.

Rumble curving tossed them back the other way.

They held on to the handrail. Didn't crash into each other.

The train pulled them onto the platform above the midway for everybody to see. Luc saw faces glancing up at them. Wondered what they saw.

The train pulled them back into its tunnel.

Whoosh down the curved tracks. Swooping left as Bu—

WONGGGG!

A life-sized, black and white painted cardboard red lipsticked skeleton!

Springing up on the right side of the train. Hovering there for startled riders to notice but not know the hole near the skeleton's neck came from Fred's triggered *Semper fi* punch while Alice ducked with the push of his other hand.

One more curve and—

The love train swooped through the tunnel's hole of light.

Splashed in the pool.

Buffy and Luc got sprinkled. Dried as they walked off the train.

"Well," said Luc. "It was a free ride."

"Next time let's pay for something more," said Buffy.

Next time, thought Luc. *Next time.*

"Come on," he said. "Let's go for a ride where *we're* driving."

They walked the crunchy prairie grass parking lot to the waiting '64 Chevy.

Buffy opened the front passenger's door to ride shotgun *instead of.*

They rolled all the windows down beneath a scarlet sky.

Luc rumbled the white Chevy to life. The carefully tuned radio crackled with KOMA Oklahoma City.

First heard Bob Dylan's world changer on this station when I was running projectors at the Roxy, thought Luc as he steered the car onto the gravel road leading to the highway's red STOP sign. Realized that he'd started to experience songs he heard *today* triggering movies of some *yesterday*.

Damn! he thought: *Now I have yesterdays.*

Today's Luc clicked on his left blinker to head back to town.

Told she who sat in the shotgun seat: "We gotta drag Main."

He turned the white car with the two of them into the setting sun.

They drove past the three women's clothing stores. Both of the men's clothing stores. The general store and the JCPenny. The dime store. Both drugstores. The seven bars and two cafés. The corner barbershop. The whitewashed windows of the Whitehouse. The boarded-up bookstore. The dark windows of Doc Nirmberg's office. The bank where there used to be a bus stop. The state liquor store. Wayne's family's hardware store. The Roxy with its marquee naming the movie that was blowing minds all over America: *Guess Who's Coming to Dinner?* Luc loved that confronting-racism movie. Imagined going home with his Black college roommate who he was *certain* to get.

The Roxy, thought Luc as he saw its golden marquee in his rearview mirror.

How great is it that the Roxy is always there for dreamers to be together!

The west's red ball of sundown burned his eyes.

"I wish I could wear sunglasses!" he told Buffy. "Plus, they'd look cool."

"OK, yeah: *Gotta have the cool.*"

They both laughed.

"Then we're both so screwed," said Buffy. Meant it.

Luc looped the Chevy through the far end of the parking lot for the national chain supermarket. Scanned for cars belonging to his Thriftway job's customers.

Turned back onto Main Street. Faced where tomorrow's sun would rise.

"Now I can see clearly," said Luc.

"Good," said Buffy. "When are you going to Missoula?"

"That Sunday before Registration Week. What about you?"

"I'm going down to Bozeman for Sorority Rush, so earlier than you."

"Don't think I'm a fraternity kind of guy," said Luc.

"What do you mean? Any of 'em would love to have you."

"Yeah, but . . . I'm an *everybody* kind of fraternity."

He slowed the white car with doors to its spacious backseat driving closer to the swaying-in-the-wind stoplight clicking red to green.

Drove past the white crossed-X railroad warning sign where Main Street cruisers turned around or got ambushed by private detectives. Drove the two-lane blacktop east like they were headed back to the fair.

"You get better radio reception out here," he said.

Buffy said nothing.

Nothing for the drive to the fairgrounds entrance . . .

. . . that they past.

Their ride drove past the grain elevators where their friend died.

Rumbled up the slope out of the Vernon valley.

July 1967's car radio serenaded them.

Urging them to go to San Francisco where people wore flowers in their hair. Lamenting vestal virgins doomed by the coast. Warning them that the door mouse said: "*Keep your head.*"

The white car topped the slope out of the prairie valley and filled its windshield with a blacktop two-lane highway.

Buffy and Luc talked about the *whatevers* as they rode that road.

The white car turned off the highway at the Marias Massacre sign.

Stopped on a graveled turnaround.

The radio played.

The big sky filled with magic blue. The soft breeze through the open windows brushed their bare arms. All horizons were a far-off line.

Buffy turned in the shotgun seat with a puzzled smile:

"What are we doing here?"

"We've gone to Prom and Co-ed. Talked on the phone a million times. Shared nearly every class. You know most of my secrets and stories. I know all you told me, some you didn't. Known each other since seventh grade."

Luc took a deep breath of the magic hour air. Let it out.

"And we've never parked to make out."

Buffy looked across the car seat to her friend in glasses facing her full-on from behind a steering wheel.

Sprang across the front seat/landed with her head on Luc's chest, his right arm around her. Her blue dress slid up past her knees.

They both laughed.

Then . . .

Luc bent down to her upturned face for that kiss. A kiss that said *hello*, not *goodnight*. His left palm felt the soft flesh of her face. She turned more toward him/met his turn with her right arm around his shoulders holding them close. Their mouths soft and hungry. Open. The taste of her tongue. The scent of her flesh. The throbbing in his jeans. A soft moan from her.

"*My girl?*" he whispered.

She turned her face for another kiss.

Gave him another kiss in reply when again he asked: "*My girl?*"

Was it seven songs? Was it nine? His left hand slid up and down her blue-dressed side. Cupped her face as her right arm was inside that grip to lever it *just so* as she caressed his cheek, *back*. She was pulling back with an *oh so never seen before* smile in that graying light.

"We better go," she said. "I don't want my dad to worry."

Buffy sat up straight. Combed her fingers through her hair.

But didn't slide back over to the shotgun seat.

Nestled against his right side as he rumbled the Chevy around, over the gravel road, back onto the black ribbon of highway toward the glows of Vernon.

The darkness of night covered them.

He turned on the white car's headlights.

Turned right to *clump clump clump* over the railroad tracks crossing. Drove through the northside of town where she but not him had gone to grade school. Past the Thriftway where he'd go to work the next day. Turned left so his car yet again pointed down the road to the Big Pink. Parked illegally on the curb beside her corner house. Climbed out onto her family's grassy boulevard. Reached back. Gave her a hand sliding out under the steering wheel.

Say something! Say the right thing!

They held hands as they walked the eleven steps to her back door.

She whirled to face him a step before they got there.

Pulled his face down to hers before he could say anything—

—and *oh!*

That sidewalk kiss. Deep. Burning. Tongues. Joy. Rebellion.

Buffy pulled away and gave him a smile.

Swooped back to deliver a mere peck from her lips to his.

"Thanks for the ride," she said. "Bye!"

Dashed into the house behind the *thunk* of the closing door even before the echo of her words disappeared in that July night.

Luc stared at that closed door he'd seen a thousand times before.

Walked back to his car.

Climbed in.

Turned it on.

"And now out there in radio-land, give a listen to Linda Ronstadt telling us about traveling to a different drum."

Laughter burst out of Luc.

WHILE YOU CAN

I t can't end like this.

Right? Luc told himself Friday, September 1, 1967.

The summer of love is over and I'm leaving town in just two days.

He closed the driver's door of the gray '54 parked at the curb in front of his house as the clock ticked to the dinner hour.

The almost-autumn warmth felt great on Luc's bare arms after the air-conditioned chill of the Thriftway. His clip-on black tie bulged the heart pocket of his short-sleeve white shirt. He closed his eyes behind his thick-lensed glasses. Let himself *feel* his Right Now.

You can't just leave town without some special go-for-it farewell.

He'd already said his good-byes. To Aunt Beryl recovering in the hospital across the street and Gramma Meg in the same building's nursing home. To his other aunts. Kurt was chronicling every item he was taking to Missoula where he, like Luc, would go with his father behind the steering wheel. Marin had gone to the Gros Ventre Rez to see his relatives before heading to Eastern College. Stiff-walking Wayne'd called Luc the night before. Prattled on about how with his Boys State glory *and* being president of the now nationally ranked Third Place in small-town Key Clubs, he was *already* getting courted by *the right* Sigma's where All the Brothers went on *to.* Buffy had been *gone* from Luc since "*Bye!*"

Luc opened his eyes toward where the sun would soon set.

Saw *her.*

White-uniformed nurse's aide walking toward her car at the hospital curb.

Cherie.

Brown hair grazed her shoulders. She needed no glasses. Her muscled legs walked her toward where she wanted to go.

"Hi!" blurted Luc.

Cherie turned with the sinking sun behind her.

That light in Luc's glasses lenses didn't let him see her puzzled smile.

"*Hi*," said Cherie as he casually hurried toward her.

Words tumbled from him:

"School starts for both of us next week, the drive-in where I used to work is closing then, too, and I was wondering . . . You wanna go? Like, tomorrow night?"

Cherie gave him a spy's smile.

"To the drive-in," she said. The place he'd asked her to go on a date *oh-so-many* years ago before he ghosted her. "Tomorrow night."

September's breeze warmed their bare arms.

Cherie said: "Sure."

Let him know: "My parents are out on the farm."

Heart-thumping, Luc said: "I'll pick you up at 7:30. Before sundown."

TAKE THE SHOT

*O*h *yeah*: he took the white '64 Chevy, the cool ride for a Friday night.
Showed up at her house right on time. Parked in her driveway.

Got out and slammed the perfectly positioned driver's door.

Luc smiled at the thirty—*No: forty!* There must have been a *ga-jillion* high steppin', sweat-makin', deodorant-breakin' concrete stairs he climbed slow and easy to arrive at Cherie's front door.

That she opened at his knock.

A white blouse. Black slacks.

Brown hair curved along her smiling face.

Lips glossed pink for more than sun.

Brown eyes taking in his black V-neck pullover and blue jeans.

She *Yes!* slid in behind the steering wheel. Didn't flinch when he looped his right arm around her shoulders so he could better see as he backed down her driveway. He *casually* pulled his right arm off her. He had to shift gears with a lever on the steering wheel column, so his move was logical. *But*. Maybe she smiled. Maybe she didn't. His strong grip held the red steering wheel.

The obvious route took the white Chevy down the Main Street hill. Past his grade school. Past her Catholic St. Jude's K-through-8 elementary school Luc had helped Aunt Teresa and Seba clean some nights. They told him about the nunnery. About the brown brick Roman Catholic church and the long gray rectory beside the church that served as both home and office for the priest.

Luc steered the white car onto the viaduct.

Do it! Take the shot! Say it!

"Did you take French?"

"No, Latin," said the Catholic brown-haired girl riding beside him. "Why?"

"Your name. '*Cher-eee*.' In French, it means '*darling*.'"

"Really," she said. "I didn't know."

Couldn't stop a slight soft smile.

Yes! Smooth move!

They drove north of town to the drive-in.

Luc passed the ticket seller the money for that night's double feature he'd folded into his shirt pocket so he wouldn't need to awkwardly reach into jeans.

Drove to a choice spot on the packed sand rows pointing car windshields toward the giant white wooden screen.

Luc lifted the speaker from the pole outside of his driver's side door. The speaker's black cord hardwired into the theater's sound system let him hook it to dangle on the inside of the partially rolled up driver's-side backseat window. He turned the car off. The movie speaker's sound on.

Beyond his windshield rose the sixty-foot-high white plane of dreams.

The theater's watch lights snapped off.

Giant technicolor images filled the white screen.

Casual, gentle, put your right arm around—

Cherie snuggled in\turned her face up to his—*to their*—hungry kiss.

The movie's title hadn't even hit the drive-in's screen!

Kissing, she's kissing me back. Arms around me. Mouths open. Tongues. Kissing her cheeks, her neck—pulls me back up to her lips!

They didn't stop until the credits for that first movie rolled on the huge white screen and the drive-in's watch lights all snapped on so snack bar customers wouldn't step into any gopher holes.

Panting, Luc said: "Do you want . . ."

"I gotta visit the women's."

"I'll keep you . . . Walk you there."

Cherie pulled the rearview down so she could see her face. Wiped a smudge of pink lip gloss off her chin. Grinned to Luc. She slid out her door. He slid out of his. Walked side by side. Their hands close but not touching for others to see.

Don't let anybody notice the erection in my blue jeans! Make it go down! Make it so . . . So I can and so none of the guys will see when I try to go pee!

There was a line into the WOMEN's room.

Luc walked right in to the MEN's room where guys waited to do their thing. Luc washed his hands to listen to inspiring water trickle out of the sink faucet. Made it to the urinal. Made it/sighed *yes*. Washed his hands again. Patted down his longer than a Big Pink crewcut in the mirror where he couldn't stop grinning.

Walked out under the night stars.

She came out of the WOMEN's room with a smile. Hair brushed. Lips freshly pink.

They held hands to the car.

She scooted to the middle of the front seat.

The watch lights winked off.

The second *In Living Color!* movie filled the white screen.

They smiled as he put his get-in-the-way glasses on the dashboard.

'N we're there. Kissing. Hands holding my face. Arms holding my shoulders. Pressing against her in the middle of the street. Oh God! Oh yes! Left hand stroking her side. Right arm around her. Leaning closer. Our fronts straining toward each other. And . . . And . . .

And *slowly* Luc's left hand slid up her left side. Up her left front.

Filled his gentle palm with her right breast.

Oh God YES!

Kissing her touching her she's leaning back 'gainst car seat yes her right breast oh brush her left YES! and touching her moaning we're moaning and—

Wait! Be smart about it. About how.

Luc scrunched his left thumb and fingers into a sneaky bird's beak.

There! Easy! Soft! Don't rip her blouse!

Luc wiggled his bird's peak between her white blouse's straining buttons.

Yes! In! The feel of her bra cupping his palm. Smooth. Firm.

But then . . . *Oh then . . .*

The Power of Education kicked in.

I can't feel her nipple!

Bond, James Bond. Every book. Read 'em all and he ALWAYS finds 'n' touches her nipple 'n' she immediately goes wild with ecstasy And Then.

Luc felt himself leave himself.

Felt himself become a detective. A scientist.

The bird beak fingers of his left hand crammed between the buttons of her white blouse began to explore. To prod. To poke for. To find and thus to—

Cherie explodes off the car seat!

Luc frantically tried to pull his trapped hand out of her blouse.

She grabbed Luc's *Stuck!* arm.

Whipped it up and down like she was pumping him and—

Free! I'm out of the blouse! Didn't rip it. Didn't—

"Take me home right now!" Cherie leapt to the shotgun seat.

"Yes! Sure! I'm sorry! I'm sorry! Please, I—"

"Just get us out of here!"

Luc tossed the speaker out his window to crash on the packed sand—not hanging it back safely on its waiting pole, the kind of arrogance that angered him when he was janitoring this very drive-in theater.

He grabbed for his glasses on the dashboard above the radio—

—knocked his damn glasses to the floor beside her white sneakers!

Dove down to get them.

Cherie shrank away from his touch.

He whirled back up.

Bumped his head on the dashboard and the radio roared louder.

Raced the car out of the drive-in and onto the dark highway back to town.

Babbled with every spin of the car wheels:

"I'm sorry! I didn't mean to! I shouldn't have! Let me explain! I'm—"

"Just drive!"

He raced over the viaduct.

Past the Catholic church and school where she'd learned.

Cut left to turn into her driveway.

Cherie jerked her door handle.

Luc stomped on the brakes.

"I'm sorry!" he yelled. "Wasn't you! It was me! I shouldn't have. I—"

She slammed the car door shut behind her.

Charged her white sneakers up the thirty—*No: forty!* There must have been a *ga-jillion* high steppin', sweat-makin', heart-breakin' concrete stairs she raced up to get away from him. Threw open her front door. Slammed it BAM!

A great tumbling filled Luc's mind, his heart, his guts, his dreams, fears:

Oh, shit! What should I do now?

REDEMPTION

The next morning: 8:17 on a sunny September Saturday.

The Ross family home where any error might trigger the end of the world.

"What the hell!" said Mom as she turned from filling her husband's coffee cup to see her son walking into the kitchen. "You're all dressed for work. You should still be in bed. Sleeping in. You don't go to work on Saturdays until 10:00."

"Last day." *Don't lie*: "There's stuff to do."

"You gotta do what you gotta do," said Dad to his wife's skeptical Conner sisters' face. "Luc doing a good job is what's important, even on his last day."

"Lucky for you I got your orange juice squeezed." Mom handed him a glass from the refrigerator full of Vitamin C from Florida. "I'll scramble—"

"Thanks, Mom, but I gotta go."

Luc drained the orange juice. Rinsed the glass. Grabbed the keys for the gray '54 Dodge out of the counter's glass ashtray without asking.

Luc walked from the house to the gray '54 parked at the curb like nothing was wrong. The gray '54 faced the hospital across the street where Cherie'd mentioned her nursing home shift on Saturday started at 9:00.

Luc settled behind the gray '54's steering wheel. His wristwatch he'd checked with the time-of-day phone operator read: 8:21. The gray '54 spun a 180-degrees turn. The hospital filled his mirrors. He headed to the left-hand turn that would put him on the street across the railroad track to the northside and the blacktop street that left town as the highway to the north:

The logical route to the Thriftway grocery store.

And if Mom or Dad are looking out the window, they'll see the gray '54 at that Stop sign. See me make the correct left hand turn to Where I'm Supposed to Go.

Two blocks later, Luc caught a green light at Main Street.

Detoured a right turn instead of going straight toward the Thriftway. Snaked a backtracking circular path through the east side neighborhood to . . .

The nursing home side of the hospital hidden from his house a block away. He parked the gray '54.

Stepped out. Saw no one who'd care.

A white envelope burdened his every step.

The seal he'd licked at midnight looked intact. The Scotch tape strip he'd stuck over the sealed flap had a crinkle but that wouldn't matter:

No one could steam the envelope open like in a spy movie.

No nosy could secretly read what he'd written for one set of eyes.

Two pages—front *and* back—of blue ink, hand-printed sometimes lapsed into cursive lines penned by the dim of his flashlight as he sat in the bed of his dark room, ready in the "click" of his closed door to dive under the covers and feign sleep. No click ever came. But the words did.

> I'm sorry! Didn't mean to . . . Sure, wanted to BUT no
> shouldn't've . . . You're great . . . Honorable girl . . . Really,
> REALLY like you just not . . . I'm a . . . Leaving town tomorrow
> . . . won't have to see me . . . won't bug you . . . no calls or letters . .
> . Well, except this one and it's 'cause I gotta . . . Sorry! . . .

On and *on* and *on* and *on* for four pages.

Signed Luc. With his last name to make it *obviously* true. Formal. Legal.

On the outside of the sealed envelope he wrote CHERIE and her last name.

Now at 8:39 that morning, he carried the secure message into the nursing home. Smelled the "old people smell." Two white-uniformed women stared at the approaching spectacled teenager in his white shirt and black clip-on tie.

Luc reached across the nurses' counter to hand over the white envelope:

"Would you please give this to Cherie when she comes in this morning?"

"Oh," said a hatchet-faced nurse. "What do we have here? A love letter?"

"No, nothing like that."

Luc walked out to the sunshine.

Climbed into the gray '54.

Pulled away from the nursing home curb.

His watch read exactly 8:57 when he steered the gray '54 to the curb in front of St. Jude's Elementary School. Turned the car off.

He had one hour to do what he had to do *and* get to work on schedule.

Plenty of time.

Please don't let anybody notice our family's gray '54 parked here on Catholic block. Please don't let anybody ask why! Please don't get me crucified on my own cross of mistakes and make-rights!

Luc looked both ways as he hurried across the *Yes, empty!* street.

Walked past the Roman Catholic church where according to what Aunt Teresa once said, early Mass and Confessions would be over.

Hustled through the bushy yard to the gray rectory beside the church.

Three short concrete steps to a brown wooden door. A black iron knocker.

Knock. A discreet *Anybody there?*

Knock-knock. Louder. A more formal *Hello in there!*

Bang-bang-bang! Luc heard his call reverberate inside the rectory.

Sparrows flew out of a tree next door.

Shit! Have I missed my chance? Should I knock again or—

The brown door swung open.

A gray-haired man in an open and empty collared shirt and everyday pants frowned at the teenage boy who'd knocked.

"Yes?" said the gray-haired man.

"Father, you don't know me, but—"

"You're Don Ross's son, right?"

"*Ah*, right. Luc, my name is Luc. And we're—*well*, technically Methodist, so . . . But . . . I need to—Can I talk to you for a few minutes? Now?"

The priest frowned. Shrugged. Stepped back and gestured for Luc to enter. Shut the door behind him.

"We'll go back to my office."

The priest led Luc down a dusty hallway crammed with statues from nativity scenes as ruthless witnesses. Walls of paintings glared at the intruder.

Luc followed the priest into a crowded office. The priest edged behind a desk sagging with files, letters, an ashtray. Settled himself in the swivel chair. Gestured for Luc to sit in a wooden chair across the desk from him.

The priest opened the desk drawer.

Pulled out a pipe.

Pulled out a bag of tobacco.

Slowly, methodically, tap after tap filled the pipe bowl with tobacco.

Tap. Look down into the bowl. Pinch in another load.

Tap tap tap.

Tick tick tick.

The priest grunted. Positioned the pipe in his lips. Used a lighter to put flame to the bowl.

Puff puff puff whoosh an exhale of blue smoke.

The priest pointed the pipe at Luc.

"So, what can I do for you?"

"I've done something and I don't want somebody who's innocent to get blamed for it."

"OK."

"And . . . well . . . She's a Catholic girl."

The priest looked at him.

"OK, it's Cherie, Cherie Alston. And see, *well*, we went to the drive-in theater last night and we—*AND I*—went too far."

The priest blinked.

"I mean, not *THAT* too far. Just . . . I touched her breast."

The priest didn't move.

"I didn't make her let me. I mean, she kinda liked it. Was not pissed off—*Sorry, Father*—at me or made me stop and then came the second feature—*They run two, I used to*—So it starts and we're . . . We're going at it again—I mean, *you know*: kissing. Kissing really good. And I . . . touched her breast. She didn't knock my hand away or say . . . So I kept going. You know. James Bond kind of—*No, not there, no way!*

"She made me stop! Pushed me away. We raced out of there. I drove straight—and I mean *straight* to her front door and she got in *totally* safe."

The priest blinked.

Luc snuck a peek at his watch: 9:17. *Plenty of time.* He cleared his throat. Said: "So why I'm here now . . ."

"Yes," said the priest. "I've been wondering."

"See, I don't want her to get in trouble for me doing bad or wrong."

"*Un-huh.*"

"No offense, Father. But I've got a lot of Catholic relatives. And this is a real, *real* small town. Everybody sort of knows everybody—*You knew who I am!* And all the great people who go to your church—*like Cherie*—you know them. Know who they are and how they're doing, how they . . . talk. You know their voices."

The cramped office filled with smoke. With sweat.

"Look," said Luc. "My dad used to be a Catholic. And my relatives are. I lived here all my life. Know how things work.

"And I don't want Cherie to get in trouble with you and the Church when she confesses about what happened at the drive-in last night."

"Huh?"

"See, *yeah*, I know, I'm sorry and it's probably insensitive or whatever of me to even say, but . . . I know Confession is supposed to be secret. But I know in a town this small you probably know the voice of whoever it is on the other side of the confession shield thingy.

"Cherie's a good girl. A really good person. And when she comes in for her next Confession, tells you about something with her and a boy at the drive-in . . .

"I don't want her to get blamed for what I did. She's innocent. I'm guilty.

"So I don't want her to get . . . I don't know. Penance or punishment or chewed out, even though you're *technically* not supposed to know who's getting it. So I'm asking you—asking the Church, really—to *please* let her off the hook."

The wide-eyed priest's pipe went out.

Tick tick tick . . .

"Wow."

"Yeah," agreed Luc. "It's a *wow* I wanted to do right by, so here I am."

Tick tick tick . . .

The priest shook his head. Told the earnest young man across the desk: "Are you . . . You two . . . Cherie, are you going to be going out again where maybe . . ."

"Oh no, Father! Don't worry. I am outta here tomorrow. And when I come back for Turkey Day or Christmas . . . I'll be like, a whole different person. Smarter."

"Smarter would be nice," whispered the man of God.

Luc shrugged: "I got what I got."

"Is there any more 'got' that you got now?"

Luc shook his head.

"Well then . . . *Ahh* . . . I guess this is just . . . Last night. Chalk it up to . . . a mistake. People make them. You're leaving town. So I guess you should go on your way."

The priest stood. Led the young man back the way he'd come.

Say something respectful to ease the tension! thought Luc as they shuffled through the long corridor to the brown wooden door. *Say something polite.*

Luc nodded to what hung on the wall: "That's a nice painting."

The priest's hand on his arm stopped them dead in their tracks.

"Yes," said the priest. "There's an interesting story about that. You see . . ."

All Luc could see or hear as the priest rambled on and on and on was the red second hand of the universe ticking off his chances to get away.

But then . . .

BAM the brown wooden door closed behind him on the outside steps.

His watch read 9:41.

Plenty of time to zoom over the viaduct to work at the grocery store!

Luc dashed across the street to the gray '54—

—with a flat tire.

LAST CHANCE

AAAHHH!

Luc charged across the street.

His black tie flapped in the wind that always was and the wind of his mad dash. The image of the gray '54 with its driver's side back tire squished flat on the pavement filled his glasses.

Flat tire! Don't know how to fix a flat tire! Oh my God, oh my God, oh my—No, not God, pissed off because I just—

Can't run to a pay phone to call Gene or Seba—Then they'd know!—Can't call anybody for help. MY PARENTS, no, can't let them know I was/am here!

The trunk. Pop it open!

Yes! A spare. How do I get it out of there? Those bolts. Work that tire iron wrench thingy free. That must be the jack.

Jack in one hand. Tire iron in the other. The gray car's trunk wide open.

How . . . Where . . . ?

Luc dropped flat toward the ground—

OH GOD DON'T LET ME GET MY WHITE WORK SHIRT DIRTY GREASY!

Bam! His palms slapped onto the gritty street caught his fall. His legs shot out together like he was back across town doing pushups in football practice.

His black tie dangled to the ground like a *got you* cobra.

Is that the car's frame? Seba once said that's where to put a jack.

Luc shoved the heavy rusted brown metal jack under the car at that spot in front of the flat tire. Jerked the tire iron up and down and up and down.

Four jerks YES! The gray '54 lifted off the pavement.

The flat tire: *How high should I jack it?*

Off the ground. *Obviously.* Got it standing free in the air.

Luc slid the jack onto one of the wheel's nuts. Pulled to—

The free-standing wheel spun Luc staggering toward the hood of the car.

The driver's side mirror speared his ribs!

Didn't break it off! Didn't crack it!

Luc glanced at his white shirt: *No bad marks!*

Jack the flat tire down to hold on the ground. Grunt with muscle who the hell even knew he had. Pull the nuts off the wheel. Roll the flat tire to the open trunk. Switch it for the got-air-in-it spare. Race back to the empty wheel. Jack the car back up to get the spare tire on. Jack it down. Tighten every damn nut.

And it worked!

Luc threw the jack and the tire iron in the trunk.

Refused to look at his wristwatch as he roared away from the curb.

Why is it always this fucking gray '54 Dodge? What did I ever do to it?

Luc whipped off the road north.

Skidded the '54 to a stop at the employees' part of the grocery store lot.

Shoved into PARK. Killed the engine. Grabbed the keys.

Whirled out of the clunky door/slammed it shut.

Checked his watch:

Its visible-in-the-dark radioactive green hands pointed to 10:17.

He raced through the glass front door.

Saw the other box boy Dennis sacking Mrs. Mallette's groceries.

Dennis gave him a look: *What's going on? You're always early.*

Luc ran to the elevated office platform in the front corner of the store.

The manager son of the Thriftway owner looked up from a ledger—

—gave Luc a smile like nothing was wrong.

Luc yelled loud enough for every cashier, Dennis and even the butcher at the back of the store to hear: "I'm sorry I'm late!"

"Oh hell," said his boss from the elevated office. "Don't worry about it. It's your last day. You can pretty much do what you want."

RUN

Made it! thought Luc as he faced the front wall of windows to the world outside the Thriftway grocery store.

Made it through a slow September Saturday afternoon.

Made it to 5:14.

Just forty-six minutes to go before *done* with work, going home, *gone.*

He'd sacked groceries for customers. Joked with the cashiers who said they were sorry to see him go 'n' damn near made him cry. The white-aproned butcher saluted him with the flat edge of a carving knife when Luc went through the aluminum swinging doors at the end of the meat counter that led to the backroom storage area and walk-in freezer.

Now as he stood at the wall of windows in the front of the store, his white shirt and clipped-on black tie held no incriminating stains as he scanned the blue sky horizon of his Montana prairie valley hometown.

The treacherous thirteen-year-old gray Dodge smirked in the store's parking lot.

Fellow box boy Dennis snuck onto the boss's empty elevated office where local AM radio station KRIP filled the store with nightclub crooners and country and western wailers, *not* rock 'n' roll. Dennis spun the radio dial to the hundred-miles-away big city Montana station. Landed on them playing an oldy-goldy that was still the #1 hit song for American troops in Vietnam.

That song rocked Luc to his bones:

"We Gotta Get Out of This Place."

Hell yes!

All I've got to do is make it to tomorrow's road outta here!

Then today's wall of windows showed him white-uniformed Cherie getting out of a car in the parking lot.

With her parents.

And heading into the grocery store.

What if they're coming after me for what happened last night!

What if 'what's gonna happen,' the law maybe, what if that stops me from—

Luc ran to the back of the grocery store.

Through the silver metal doors where the boss had sent Dennis to stack crates of returned empty soft drink bottles. Then left the store before Dennis snuck back out to change the radio station. Now Dennis stopped what he was doing as Luc raced up to him in the back room smelling of butchered meat.

"Dennis. *Look*, I know you and me . . . We aren't exactly friends and just work here together and . . . But I gotta ask you a giant favor!"

Dennis blinked.

"You gotta go out there! I'll do the bottles. But you gotta go out there. Work checkouts so well, best box boy in history. Work 'em so hard nobody will call for all box boys. It's gottta be like I'm not even here. And you gotta do it right now!"

Dennis stared at the pleading face of two-year-older-than-him guy.

Stared at the face of Luc Ross and his Famous Good Boy reputation.

Hurried through the silver doors to the front of the store.

The store intercom system played rock 'n' roll Luc's ears wouldn't grasp.

He heard the *clank* and *clink* of empty soft drink bottles he crated.

Smelled dried sugary syrup. Whiffs of Coke. The sweat of his own fear.

Clank! went his world. *Clink!*

But no calls for box boys. No hubbub from out there *demanding to see.*

What did Cherie tell her parents that made them come to the store?

Sure, they could just be all food shopping for the farm, *but.*

Did the priest—

Oh.

Umm . . .

What if Cherie *doesn't* tell what happened in her next Confession?

Cherie in the Confession booth. Saying she's done. The priest who knows her voice and who she can't see clears his throat. *'Are you sure that's all? Isn't there something about you at the drive-in theater?'*

Luc shook off that fantasy.

When did the world go crazy?

Did it start with the murders?

With JFK and Oswald. With the four Black girls in an Alabama church. Three civil rights workers in a Mississippi bog. Uncle Johnny. With the KIAS in Vietnam of guys just like me: *How many were there now? How many on the other side?* A shooter in the clock tower of a university like where I'm supposed to go tomorrow *if.* And what happened on a snowy Sunday to that girl in my freshman year—*Becky, her name is Becky!*—that disappeared her? The Berlin Wall. Vernon's *Dr. Strangelove*'s missile sites. The smog that chokes the streets of Hollywood where Marilyn never got free before her murder.

Luc clanked and clattered, grunted and stacked, stared at those silver metal doors that could swing open in a heartbeat.

Is it just me that's gone crazy?

No, he told himself. *I've always been crazy.*

(*Shh: Nobody knows!*)

So it's gotta be more than just me.

I'm nowhere close to being the center of the world.

I'm just clanking and clinking and walking it like everybody else.

Lucky to be here at all.

You gotta do what you gotta do. Choose what you can. Hope you do it right.

Clatter and clank. The ticking clock.

He stared at the crates holding empty bottles in their final stacks.

The store loudspeaker: "*Luc Ross to the cashiers' counter! Luc, up front!*"

His stomach sank. His heart thundered. His mind emptied.

He pushed open those silver doors.

Walked to what sentence waited for him by the windows to the world.

Two women pushed grocery carts in aisle 2, one with an uncomfortable husband who looked like he'd never before been family grocery shopping.

The whiskey-sweat stinking alcoholic man from the city road crew with one untied work boot and a misbuttoned gray work shirt shuffled along the red and white cans of soup shelves with a lost look in his drooping eyes.

Luc saw no one in the elevated office where the radio now played KRIP.

Saw no Cherie. Or her parents. Their car in the parking lot: *Gone.*

The boss, two cashiers and Dennis stood up front.

"There you are!" said the boss. "Check the time. You're off the clock! Shift's over—hell, your summer job's done. You did it damn good. Wish you were stickin' around for another year of high school like Dennis here, but you gotta go."

The cashiers smiled their *See yas*.

Two cart-pushing customers rolled up to check out. Got taken care of by the boss and middle-aged cashiers. Shifts over, the two box boys walked through the glass doors to the parking lot outside in the warm evening air.

They stopped beside Dennis's motorcycle.

The smirking gray '54 Dodge waited across the parking lot.

"Someday you gotta tell me what that was all about," said Dennis.

Luc stared at a new friend he owed.

Told him the truth: "I wish I knew."

DAYDREAM BELIEVER

Sunday morning. September 3, 1967. Vernon, Montana. USA.

The gray '54 Dodge sat at the curb in front of the Ross house.

The white '64 Chevy sagged in the driveway.

The Chevy held cardboard boxes of records. Clothes. A half dozen books, including a Webster's dictionary with seven $10 bills hidden in its pages *just in case*. Luc carried his new first-ever checkbook in his blue jeans' back pocket. The Green Monster and Luc's portable stereo rode in the trunk buffered by his bags. The backseat held a tin of Mom's homemade chocolate chip cookies:

"For you and your roommate so he'll know you're the kind of guy who'll get care packages and appreciate you."

There were the things he left behind.

In his closet hung a black suit and clip-on black tie.

On its floor were *Don't throw them out, Mom!* stacks of *Playboy* magazine.

Miss August waited on top. She would receive more fan letters than any other Playmate *ever*. Her name was DeDe—and she looked it:

California bleached blonde with a cutie pie smile sitting on the edge of a swimming pool. Pink skin showing the untanned pale strap of a modest bathing suit top carefully put away so she could show her hefty pear-shaped naked breasts. She wore a bowtie-like yellow ribbon in her curled hair. One picture showed *prim* her on "a friend date" by the San Francisco Bay Bridge with a blue uniform and white-capped sailor who was about to be deployed to Vietnam.

She's who I'm supposed to want, thought Luc. *The just-out-of-high-school Girl Next Door who my parents would love. Always smiling. Waiting to be . . . possessed. And yeah, sure, she's . . . And yeah I'd like to . . .*

But I never wanted a cutie pie smile. Want a smile that creates itself. A person. A woman. Someone who is real and true. Who chooses and does.

They're coming, he told himself. *They're on their way.*

Please let one of them also be kinda crazy.

Thoughts of imagined her and Marilyn, not a cutie pie.

Luc wondered: *How long do we carry what we did and didn't?*

Handfuls of stupid mistakes. Laughs and tears. All the winds of love.

That Sunday morning Dad wore a sports jacket like he was going to work. Mom wore her nicest housedress.

They'd all stayed home the night before.

Luc packed the last of what had to be packed.

What about you? he thought as he picked up the green rubber toy soldier he'd found in the Roxy's projection booth. *Still crawling forward. Looking up.*

He tucked the toy soldier into his book bag.

Buffy was already gone.

So was Marin.

He wondered about Alice. About Wendy. Walt and Tod and Sandi. Surfer Zack. Gave *zero* thought to his once-upon-a-time best friend stiff-walking Wayne who was, like Buffy, already gone to Rush Week at the conservative other state university. Cousin Gene was trying out for football at his Catholic college. Kyle and Gideon were heading to state schools, too.

Kurt called to tell Luc he'd look for him after he got settled in "down there."

Always laughing Mike Jodrey was in the Army. Headed to Vietnam.

Big sister Laura called Luc on his last night at home. Used the person-to-person ruse for 'not here' Meg Conner. Answered when Luc called her back.

"You'll figure it out," she told him. "If not, write me a letter. Hell, call."

He heard her smile at his *thanks.*

Imagined the shake of her head after she hung up.

Church bells chimed the next morning.

"Well," said Dad, "we better hit the road."

Their trio stood in the gray living room.

Mom hesitated . . . Gave Luc a quick hug.

His first from her in . . . He couldn't remember how long.

She stepped back. Gave him a Conner sisters' friendly slap on his shoulder.

"Stay out of trouble, you dumb shit."

"Do my best," promised Luc.

He followed Dad out to the white car in the driveway for the four-hour ride off the rolling prairies and deep into the sky-carving Rocky Mountains to a university he'd never seen before.

Dad climbed behind the steering wheel.

Luc rode shotgun.

As the car backed out of the driveway, he said: "Can we take Main Street?"

That turn filled the windshield with the red stucco whorehouse.

They drove past stores Luc knew. Cafés. Neon bars. The Roxy theater where Mr. Tom was changing the marquee for a movie Luc'd never see. Doc Nirmberg's windows. The spire of the Catholic church and the Methodist loudspeaker hymns filling the air. They drove past the viaduct to the northside, the Thriftway, the drive-in restaurant Aunt Beryl owned no more, the road past Buffy's house to the Big Pink.

"Do you want to change the radio station?" asked Dad.

"*Naw*," said Luc.

Local KRIP reported the news. A US landing craft on the moon. A Saudi billionaire named bin Laden died and left behind a son who planned a future event called 9/11. America's Vietnam KIA total reached 15,837.

The two Ross men knew they'd lose their hometown station before they reached the mountains. Luc saw golden leaves in the trees of the town as his dad drove the highway headed south to the Grady River.

Luc shook his head:

The river gives you sink holes along with the fish you catch.

The rearview mirror reflected a glimpse of the Big Pink—gone.

The road rolled on.

Dad kept his eyes on the windshield as he said: "You'll do fine."

Luc stared at the blue sky.

Said: "Let's hope for something more."

TRAMPS LIKE US

A BUG IN YOUR EAR

Let me put a bug in your ear," the boss told Luc.

They stood in the oiled-earth "yard" for Vernon's city crew.

Monday morning. June 1, 1970.

Seven minutes after the job's *shape-up* started work at 8:00.

Spring blue "Big Sky" that Montana was famous for back then.

At 7:03 that morning, Luc'd sat at the breakfast table with his mom and dad. His parents' cigarettes smoldered. The kitchen countertop AM radio reported that the Vietnam war being fought by guys Luc's generation now claimed 43,784 KIAs—Killed in Action American troops.

At twenty-six minutes to 8:00, Luc couldn't contain his excitement. Nearly danced the few blocks from his home to his beloved summer job on the city crew.

He wore a red hooded sweatshirt. Brown leather laced work boots. Carried new buckskin gloves. His white T-shirt and blue jeans had wrapped him during his just-past junior year at the state university. They'd be rags by September.

And for the first time after two summers on the city crew . . .

. . . Luc wore contact lenses.

I can see better and I'm a better "see" for girls than in my yesterdays of dorky black-rimmed, Coke-bottle-thick lenses!

Luc's terrible near-sightedness made him certified by the Draft Board as 4F—"Unfit for military service" no matter what draft lottery number nailed him.

The cool city crew air carrying Boss Dave's "bug in your ear" words to Luc smelled of exhaust from vehicles burning dead dinosaurs.

God, I'm glad to be here! thought Luc moments before Boss Dave sidled up to him after passing out the day's assignments to the crew. The eleven adult men and Luc's two-years-younger buddy Dennis moved away from Dave and Luc. Maybe some of them knew *what's going on*. Maybe none of them did.

They were men. They had a job to do. They knew who they were in the eyes of this small town and the world. Most had loyal marriages. Kids. Some had aging parents. All had beating hearts. The city crew walked across the packed earth of civilization to their machines and trucks and most of them walked proud.

Luc'd gotten home for the summer on Friday.

What Happened Saturday no one in town but him knew.

Then came What Happened Sunday.

Now Luc blinked back to that June Monday morning.

Boss Dave and Luc stood in the city crew's yard filled with civilization's machines. Dump trucks. A frontend loader unattached to its backhoe. The giant yellow roller. The black-smeared and wired-together, thirty-plus-year-old, hot-oil-spraying "Black Beast" truck. The chipper box to clamp onto trucks' back ends.

The boss angled his head.

Luc followed him into the concrete boxlike office.

Wooden shelves and salvaged metal file cabinets. Empty folding chairs in front of a paper strewn desk backed by a boss's chair.

Dave jerked his head for Luc to take a seat across from the desk.

"Lloyd Mueler," said Dave from the boss's chair, correctly pronouncing that man's last name like a castrated donkey.

"Owns the smaller of our town's two weekly newspapers," said Luc.

"*Naw*," corrected Dave. "Think of him as *City Councilman* Mueler."

The City Council ruled their city crew paychecks.

"He hit me up 'n' told me to fire you from the crew," said Dave. "Was on account of that letter everybody knows you wrote 'n' got others to sign."

"But Mueler's *Vernon Times* didn't print it!"

"Don't matter. Don't matter that *The Promoter* printed it. You wrote it—hell, you thought it 'n' that's enough for Mueler. He wants you gone. Canceled."

Luc's life blasted apart.

Then that city supervisor. The boss of that city crew. The city employee whose job was under the thumbs of the City Council. The man who'd laughed a story to Luc about chasing Japanese civilians up the stairs of a Buddhist temple with a Jeep when he was part of America's post-WWII occupying force. The father of three kids he fed with a wife who could only work part-time. The first local citizen to embrace the National Rifle Association's shift from gun safety issues to gun political eroticism via millions of gun manufacturers' dollars. The high school dropout who used the US Mail to letter back and forth moves in chess games with strangers who always lost to this phantom David Rudd in a nowhere called Vernon, Montana. Dave who both outdoors and indoors wore a jaunty faded baseball cap. *That guy* Dave leaned across his *boss* desk:

"And I told that son-of-a-bitch Mueler that this is Goddamn America. It don't matter that I don't agree with you. Don't matter he don't like it. This is a free country. Our fucking flag. Said Luc can damn well believe any damn thing he wants and say any damn thing he wants and write any damn letter he gets any newspaper or whatever to publish. I told him 'Luc does his job' and that's all that matters to me, to the law, to our town, to some fucking God up there if there is one, and I wasn't about to fire you *no how, no way!*"

A soft breeze rattled the office window.

Luc wanted to cry with joy, pride, gratitude.

But the only words he found for his now-lifelong hero were: "*Thank you!*"

The chess master's smile knew what Luc meant.

"Now you know *what's what*," said Dave as he leaned back in his chair. "So get out there and get going. You got a lot of gravel to move and miles to truck."

NOW IS WHEN

Roaring engines soundtracked Luc across the city shop's packed earth to where three dump trucks waited backed up against the yard's chain-link fence.

"... *This is Goddam America* ..."

What better, luckier place could I be? thought Luc.

This hard-shoveling, back-breaking, machine-driving, broken sewer and water pipe fixing, road-building and pothole-filling summer job earned Luc enough money to pay for a year at the liberal arts state university in Missoula.

If I can pay, I get to say. That's one reason the city crew job meant so much. Plus, on the city crew, Luc felt like a full-on adult.

He'd worked since he was ten. Delivering handbills for the Roxy movie theater. Ages thirteen to sixteen filled his summer nights with being the Roxy's projectionist clicking cinema dreams at twenty-four frames per second. The flickering beam of light came like director Jon Luc Goddard celebrated, via Luc from *behind* the audience carrying *them into* the big screen and not the screen *into them* like TVs or some other futuristic beaming-out screens.

Luc grabbed any summer job he could get after those days of janitoring the drive-in theater north of town and nights sweltering in the Roxy's film-oil smelling projection booth abruptly ended.

Buckin' bales, sixty pounds of straw and sweat swung up onto a flatbed truck.

Driving a giant cabbed tractor to plow a farmer's fields surrounding the razor wire fence protecting an Intercontinental Ballistic Missile System site of "Minutemen" atomic-bomb-topped death rockets for the *any heartbeat now* nuclear war of mushroom clouds destroying all life on earth.

Being a pick and shovels gravedigger.

Luc worked his high school graduation summer as a box boy at the Thriftway grocery store. His buddy and now fellow road crew college student Dennis'd worked at that store, too.

But now we're here, thought Luc as he walked toward three waiting trucks. *Side by side with men working to sustain families and wives.*

There stood Jerry, the street foreman seldom without a smile or a gray work shirt and his decades-dusty, faded gray flattop cowboy hat.

Jerry stood by a new white dump truck and two scarred red trucks.

"Good t' see you back." Jerry grinned. "Which hulk you want to wrangle?"

"How about that red one? Seems like the one I worked last summer."

"Keys in the crank," said Jerry. "I'll take this white one. Get set up and give me a nod. I know you know the way, but follow me past the river. The gravel road's turn-off been narrowed down 'n' don't want you to miss it the first time.

"Hell," said Jerry. "Don't want you to miss it *any* time!"

Wonk!

Close the truck door. Adjust the seat best it can be for you. Check the long rectangle side mirrors mounted outside on the doors. The crucial driver's side mirror doesn't show what it should. Roll down the window. Reach out and muscle the mirror. Sit back in the driver's position. Again out-the-window adjust that side mirror. Satisfaction reflects back at you as you sit behind the steering wheel.

The right side, the gutter side mirror . . . Looks good enough.

The gearshift down by Luc's right leg had a red pull/push button below its round gear knob. The truck worked twelve gears with the left foot pedal pushing the clutch in and out to shift gears as the truck rumbled.

There were no seatbelts.

Luc cranked the in-the-ignition key to the right and *vroom.*

He glanced out his driver's side window.

Jerry behind the wheel of the rumbling white truck sent him a nod. Motored the white truck down the slope of the yard for Luc to follow.

Was three blocks of low-gear driving until they turned left on the two-lane blacktop US 2 highway as it passed from the city limits on the east toward Chicago where Luc's big sister Laura lived to west out of town toward Shelby and the intersection with one of the four-lane divided superhighways created to unite the country by savvy Republican president and war hero Dwight Eisenhower.

Luc opened himself to *the feel* behind the wheel of the ten-ton dump truck rumbling down that back street between the railroad tracks creating the northside of town and the back end of the bars, businesses and bullshit on Main Street.

West end of town. Pass the Dixie Inn. The Sullivan Motel. The truck stop. Luc shifting and steering. Getting better "wrangling" the truck with every spin of its tires. He rumbled the truck up the ramp onto the two lanes of divided highway empty for miles in his side mirrors. His windshield was empty except for Jerry once their two trucks topped the rim of the Vernon valley.

The border of their town passed their driver's side truck windows.

They drove past the country club golf course where the fairways were prairie and the greens were sand.

Their passenger side window panned past open fields to the blue sawtooth lines of the sixty-miles-away Rocky Mountains.

They drove past near-the-highway four giant metal rod frames of KRIP's AM radio towers. The low-bid city trucks held no radios.

Not that Luc wanted to listen to KRIP's country and western odes, acceptable ballads, lonely hearts or settled-adults love songs. His was a rock 'n' roll soul.

Luc drove past the farm fields he'd plowed around the missile site.

Drove toward the river now six miles beyond his red truck's windshield.

The highway rumbled his truck.

Vibrated him with the *what's*, the *why's*, the *how's* of Right Now.

Not what happened Saturday. Not what happened Sunday either or what he had to do this very night *because*. Not his packet of dreams.

The "bug in your ear" shook Luc as he drove Monday's truck.

GHOSTS IN YOUR MIRROR

hosts of *why* floated in the mirrors of the red truck Luc wrangled on an empty highway that "bug in your ear" Monday morning in June 1970.

Those ghosts swirled from a *gone* Tuesday morning twenty-seven days before, May 5.

That ghost Luc strolled to a class from his three-blocks-off-campus basement apartment he shared with Emil, another Vernon student a year younger than Luc, a high school classmate of Luc's cousin Seba whose house was the hangout for a crew of Vernon secret outlaws: When they could get it, when they thought they were safe, they smoked *lock you up* illegal marijuana.

But forget about getting stoned on grass. Or hooked by and on Norma.

The *why* ghosts in the rearview mirrors of Luc's first gravel run that Monday morning targeted him for stone throwers like editor/Councilman Mueler.

The mirrored ghost Luc in a vanished Tuesday scanned hundreds of University of Montana students his age as he walked across that campus. Boys and girls. Men and women. *What do those labels mean, anyway?*

A grim student Luc knew named Mark stood outside the Liberal Arts building door passing out flyers hand-rolled one sheet at a time off last night's re-purposed mimeograph machine in the Education Department.

"Hell of a day," said Luc as he took a flyer from Mark's hand.

Meaning the wonderful arrival of this wondrous spring morning.

"Yeah," said Mark.

Luc looked down at the flyer in his hand.

The world blew apart.

Four dead university students in Ohio. Shot yesterday by National Guard soldiers at Kent State University during a demonstration of twelve hundred citizens rallying against the US invasion of Cambodia expanding the Vietnam War.

STRIKE, proclaimed the flyer in Luc's hands that May Tuesday morning in 1970. A 2:00 P.M. rally in the football field of grass called the Oval that centered the Montana campus and ended at the steps leading into Main Hall's brown castle where the University President and other Powerful Positions had offices.

Come Stop the War! Strike! Shut our university down! PEACEFUL ONLY!

Luc rushed to the nearest box for the free student newspaper. The weekdays-only *Kaimin* was the major source of news for university students.

The newspaper's front page black and white photo showed a long-haired college age woman crouching with arms spread wide as she screamed about the face-down dead body of a male student crumpled on concrete by her feet.

That afternoon, Luc sat on the Oval grass with about three thousand fellow students, less than one-third of his university's total enrollment. The packed grass below his butt was hard. He smelled that living green mixed with the scents of sweat and fear, of tearful sorrow and rage, of hope and trying to believe.

The Kent State dead were just like us. Could have been us.

Norma sat beside him. Her two-years-younger freshman brown hair hung to her shoulders. Her lean form filled a tan blouse and faded blue jeans.

They faced Main Hall where microphones and giant music speakers and other electronic rigs loaned by rock bands created a podium.

Luc gazed past where protestors sat for anyone to see.

And film. *Say,* for the FBI or other badges of Uncle Sam.

Maybe a thousand other students stood outside the Oval. Filled sidewalks ringing the rebel space. They stood back to watch. Not be part of this event that might get them in trouble. Or that pissed them off with its politics. Most of those bystanders thought they avoided any *politics* as they stood on the sidelines and kept their eyes on the invisible bouncing ball of their promised tomorrows.

Speeches started.

The university president read a telegram he'd sent to the state's congressional delegation urging them to find a way out of the divisive war.

Protestors stood and cheered.

Student organizers took turns at the mic—

—including Vic, Luc's friend since they'd met in high school at the American Legion's week-long summer honors program promoting right-wing conservative patriotism education called "Boys State."

Stay peaceful, said all the speakers. No violence. Honor democracy. Remember the dead at Kent State and from the war. Stand up for what's right.

An acoustic guitar strummer performer sang 1930s Depression-era Woody Guthrie's "This Land Is Your Land."

Was 4:20 when this 1970 Missoula, Montana, demonstration ended.

Walking toward her dormitory, Norma and Luc fell in step with Emil.

"We gotta do something," said Luc.

"We just did," said Emil.

"I know," answered Luc. "And *that's* what we gotta do something about.

"*Home,*" said Luc. "Vernon. Most people there already think us longhairs and 'hippies' are bad. Now we've shut down the university. So we're gonna march on them, right? Commies trying to take over. Anti-Americans attacking our guys fighting in Vietnam. Trying to take over the world."

"I'm just trying to take over my own life," said Emil.

Norma mumbled: "Nobody gets to do that."

Luc said: "Emil, here's what we gotta do."

They left Norma at her freshman dorm.

Raced back to their apartment.

Made a list of every university student from Vernon.

Luc rolled a sheet of paper into his Green Machine manual typewriter.

"Dear Fellow Citizens of Vernon . . ."

He wrote four paragraphs about How We Are All in This Together. How We Are All Loyal Americans Who Love Our Country. How student protests at the university were about Americans being Americans. Reaching out to legally persuade our government to get out of the Vietnam War that had killed beloved young men from Vernon. The sorrow of the student protestors at Kent State. How "we" are not Communists. How none of us and almost every other anti-war protestor in the university at Missoula hated Russia and China's communism and loved America. How the protest was us trying to be citizens of America and honest, responsible children of our beloved hometown of Vernon.

Luc needed to type five copies of the one-page letter to get two copies relatively free of typos and his best pen-inked corrections.

Emil arrived with two buddies from Vernon.

Luc signed his name on the two final copies of the letter.

Then so did Emil and the other two Vernon students.

"You know the most important person we've got to get to sign," said Luc.

Luc and Emil lined up for dinner in the student cafeteria. Got three other Vernon students' signatures. Luc tracked down two Vernon students who lived half a dozen blocks from his apartment. One mumbled *no*. One signed.

The luminous numbers on Luc's wristwatch read 7:57 when he finally knocked on the front door of the Delta Gamma Sorority house.

Just breathe, he told himself as he waited for that white door to open and let him into the "good and smart girls" sorority.

The senior class Delta Gamma on that night's door duty let him in.

Sent one of her DG sisters to fetch who he came for.

Mary Kay. Vernon's virginal sweetheart.

If she signs the letter, then the rest of us can't be just crazy radical hippies.

Mary Kay nodded as her high school classmate Luc talked about how it'd be great if she'd help reassure everybody back home.

"We've got to make things better," she told Luc.

And signed.

Watched him fold each letter into white envelopes, one addressed to the *Vernon Promoter*, one addressed to the *Vernon Times*—both marked "Letter to the Editor" so it would be clear these letters were meant to be published for the two weekly newspapers' readers to see. Though a letter needed only one six-cent First Class stamp, Luc put two stamps on each envelope "to be sure."

He walked through the street-lit night with the letters safely tucked into the front waistband of his jeans under his hoodie so they wouldn't get dropped or fly away or get dirty as he hiked across a half-mile bridge over the river.

Walked up the steps of the marble-columned Post Office.

Dropped those two envelopes into the outgoing slot of tomorrows.

DON'T BACK DOWN

But what do we do now?"

Luc's mom stared at her husband and son as they sat at the kitchen table after lunch of tuna fish sandwiches that June 1 Monday in 1970.

"After you phoned 'n' warned us about the letter, your father checked with what it said in the next weekly *TIME* magazine, and the only thing you got wrong was the girl in the picture wasn't a student there, she was—"

"Doesn't matter now," said Luc's dad. "What's Mueler going to do next?"

The clock on the kitchen wall ticked.

"Whatever Mueler does," said Luc, "I won't back down."

"Do you hear anybody telling you to?" said his dad, who knew his parental powers had shrunk since Luc graduated from high school.

"I'm gonna call my sisters," said Mom.

Her three sisters. *The Conner girls.*

Their dead father'd dealt cards for a saloon in the winter.

Cowboyed from spring roundup to fall auction.

Their mother's polio legs confined Gramma Meg to her bed in the across-the-street-from-Luc's-house nursing home Where It Had Happened on Sunday.

The Conner sisters rooted the men they'd married in Vernon and its swath of prairie their family pioneered away from the blue-coated-cavalry-defeated Blackfeet nation in 1884. Conner sisters were legends of their own, always up for anything, middle-aged mothers and wives dragging along with them their agoraphobic, always-waiting-for-the-bad-shoe-to-drop sister Cora, Luc's mom.

"Let 'em know," said her husband. "But tell them not to spread the word.

"What time is it?" said Dad, looking at his *don't get him/still love him* son.

The kitchen clock filled Luc's eyes.

"It's twenty-five to 1:00," he said. "I've got to hustle to work."

Mom frowned: "What the hell? It's only a five-minute walk."

"I, *uh*, I got to stop at the Post Office. Mail something."

"We got enough God-damn letters to deal with today," said Dad. "I'm riding you to work."

Luc climbed into the shotgun seat of the white '64 Chevy Impala.

"So how's the city crew?" said Dad, driving the family's white car.

"Great," said Luc. "Same guys. Jerry. Arson. Floyd."

"What about your buddy? Is he back?"

"Dennis, yeah. He's in an engineering program at the state college over in Havre. They like to have him help Arson mechanic."

Dad parked across from the city crew's shop.

"Don't say anything about this to anybody," Dad told Luc. "Or if you have to, just say how Dave is a helluva guy, a great boss."

Luc nodded.

Turned to get out of the white car.

"Sit a minute," said Dad.

He pulled out a red paper and cellophaned pack of cigarettes. Shook one free. Pushed in the car dashboard's cigarette lighter.

Two crew members parked their cars against the shop's chain-link fence.

Those two guys saw the man behind the idling car's steering wheel. Waved.

Dad waved back.

Dave drove up in his boss's city crew white pickup truck. Climbed out.

Saw a father delivering his son to where he needed to go.

Nodded his baseball-capped head. Got the right nod back from the man behind the steering wheel. Walked into his own office.

Pop!

Dad lifted the cigarette lighter to flame the tube in his lips. Took in a drag. Let cancer smoke billow out of his lungs.

"Gonna be a City Council election come this fall," said Dad.

Couldn't stop the twitch of a smile.

"Now get out of here," Dad told his son. "We both got work to do."

MAYBE

Monday means *maybe*.

Maybe what happened last week won't roll us forward into an *oh-oh* now. Maybe I'll figure out *What's Going On* and *What to Do*.

Luc shifted gears as the June fields south of town filled his red truck's windshield. Sixth roundtrip that first road crew Monday. He passed the any-heartbeat-now Apocalypse missile site. Felt like a rocket blasted up out of that field he drove past and filled his truck's windshield with movies of Norma.

He'd noticed her on April 23, 1970.

A Thursday.

The day *after* he'd proudly marched with thousands of others for Earth Day. The day *before* his first star shine.

He'd seen her around. Her university library job meant pushing carts of books to reshelve in her designated area—the wilderness called "Popular Fiction."

Luc spent hours scouring those shelves for crime and spy novels he loved as much as Harper Lee's *To Kill a Mockingbird*, Faulkner's *As I Lay Dying*, A.B. Guthrie's *These Thousand Hills* and John Steinbeck's *East of Eden*. And, of course, *Stuart Little*, a mouse who chose his own life and loves in our world.

So Luc'd *seen* Norma's straight brown hair brushing her shoulders before. Seen her lithe frame. Her serious oval face. The firm line of her lips.

But that April morning, Luc *noticed*.

She was the kind of girl The Way Things Are said he *could* and *should*. But with a . . . a *tingle* of *something more*—and that tingle pulled his eyes to her.

She wore a classy dress from the back of her closet because her dorm's washers were broken. The dress ended above her knees. She wore no pantyhose.

She was standing between two shelves of novels. Reaching up on her flat shoes' tiptoes to push a heavy book into its place on the highest shelf.

That dress rose up high on her sleek *oh so shiny soft* perfect *woman* legs.

He savored her lean body. The curve of her bra-prisoned breasts. Her straight brown feminine hair brushing her shoulder blades.

She brushed her brown hair back from her face. Narrow brown eyes. Soft cheeks and a determined close-in jawline.

Come on, Luc told himself. *You can do it. Especially for tomorrow night.*

He strategically stacked his class copy of Hannah Arendt's *Between Past and Future* under two library crime novels. Strode to the valley between the shelves where That Girl grabbed her cart to push it and herself to *gone*.

Luc said: "Maybe I should apologize."

"For what?" Her voice came with a *show me* tone.

He raised his stack of books topped by two mystery novels:

"I keep weighing you down with books to put away."

She shrugged: "Gives me a job."

Her brown eyes glanced at the titles he held.

And she smiled: "I love Nero Wolfe. A fat genius detective who never leaves his house way back in New York city, and Archie, his smart-ass legman."

"You've got to be kidding me."

"Why would I—Kidding you how?"

"No, not you, the . . . the universe. I found a gir—*someone* our age who likes those kinds of books besides me! *Catch-22* and *Slaughterhouse Five*, sure, but . . ."

"I'm Luc. Luc Ross."

"Norma. Norma Peters."

Somewhere nearby a door opened and closed.

"I, *ah*, I better let you get back to work."

"OK."

He turned. Walked Away.

Turned on his third step. Marched back to *Norma, Norma Peters*.

"Would you do me a favor?" he asked her anxious face.

"Tomorrow night's special for me," said Luc. "That coffee house just off campus. A drama class is staging a one-act play I wrote and two others by other students. I wanna . . . Would you go with me?"

"Yes," said Norma.

Or maybe it was: "*YES!*"

GRAVEL ROADS

L uc muscled the red truck off the superhighway and onto a gravel turnoff before the crest of the Grady River valley. His truck rumbled over the gravel road.

Dust and pollen flowed into the cab but he kept that window open.

The smells of the gravel road and the nearby river made Luc smile.

He spotted the giant frontend loader in the wide graveled pit he pulled the truck into. Luc wheeled the back of the truck toward a giant plateau of gravel.

That June Monday afternoon at the river grotto, Luc climbed out of the red truck to watch fifty-ish Floyd wheel the frontend loader, scoop up a bucket of sand/gravel, rumble it to Luc's truck, raise the bucket *just so* and *just when*, dump the load for Luc to carry, then go back, *Jack*, do it again, five heavy dumps.

Floyd backed the loader away from the truck. Levered the bucket to the ground. Turned off the engine. Stepped out and off with a pack of cigarettes. Offered one to Lucas who shook his head *no*. Floyd struck match in the cool spring breeze.

"What time you got?" he asked the college guy.

Why doesn't Floyd check the watch on his wrist?

Floyd was almost equal to street foreman Jerry in the crew. Chief mechanic Arson was their practical equal.

The city crew was lucky to get Floyd, thought Luc. A great equipment driver. Sure, not as good as S.K. who right then was working the grader in town at the city crew's west edge of town mesa lot to mix gravel and hot oil. But Floyd drove with a smile for you and the job. S.K. rumbled machines for his own smiles. Floyd was a hard worker. Savvy as hell. Nobody ever told Luc about why Floyd quit the county crew to come work under Dave, but Luc knew that was a strange move.

There were levels of respect and pay in Vernon's public services crews.

The top of the heap were the crews working for the State Highway Department. Great pay and benefits. The newest and thus safest equipment. Dedicated tasks that wouldn't have a worker, *say*, plugging a broken water pipe in the morning and patching potholes in the afternoon like the city crew.

Akin to the highway crew came the gandy dancers who worked the railroad tracks that like the State Highway crews connected Vernon to the rest of the world. The overtime hours they worked sometimes made gandy dancing more profitable than being on the State Highway crew, but gandy dancing was a tough-muscles job.

Roughnecks who worked the drilling rigs searching for oil in the golden prairies made good wages but dry holes kept laying them off.

Knifed into the blue-collar ladder of Vernon near the top came the public utility crews. The linemen for the phone company. For the electric power company. The sniffers and sealers for the gas company.

Below them and the State Highway crew came the Martin County crew—a large contingent because Martin County covered more than three times the square miles' total of the five boroughs of New York city. Martin County crew's equipment was almost on par in quality with the State Highway crew. Less pay than the highway boys, but more than the bottom of the ladder in every way from respect to yuckiness of jobs of guys on the city crew.

We're the bottom rung, thought Luc. He loved that.

I'm city crew through and through, he thought in that river grotto.

There were private industry blue-collar workers in Vernon back in those June 1970 days. Farmers. Oil refinery workers. Truck drivers and mechanics at the trucking firm managed by Luc's Dad. Artisan carpenters, builders and home renovators like the father of Steve, Luc's high school rival for Buffy's heart. Plumbers. Electricians. Maintenance workers at places like the hospital and nursing home across the street from Luc's house. Postmen—

—*Gotta go to the Post Office TOMORROW!* Luc ordered himself that afternoon in the grotto with Floyd.

Luc raised his wrist: "My watch says 'bout twenty minutes to 3:00."

"Good," said Floyd. "I'm riding back in with you to coffee at 3:00 like we do. Jerry just rolled on ahead of you. I told him to meet us with Dave and the others at the Husky. You can dump your load after coffee, keep up the schedule."

The Husky: a gas station and diner on the west end highway of town.

Where I learned to drink coffee with and because of the city crew, thought Luc, smiling as he followed Floyd to the red truck.

"Look," said Floyd. "Do a favor?"

"Sure," said Luc.

"Jerry's wife Helen broke her leg couple weeks back. And you know Jerry."

The two men bouncing in a truck speeding on a gravel road grinned.

Chorused their mimic of Jerry: *"Had to laugh."*

"Well, Jerry ain't been saying that lately," said Floyd. "He says they're doing fine, but you gotta wonder. The wife took 'em over a casserole. Dave's wife did, too. But now he's saying they don't need nothing, *thank you very much*.

"My thinking is you just come back to the crew, sitting at the Husky around coffee, you tell him you heard about his wife. Ask how she's doing. He'll come back with *don't worry*—him being *gotta be strong* and Helen's Cheyenne pride—but that gives me the chance to slide in something like my wife is ordering my sorry ass to bring her over there for a visit, maybe bring a little eats. And then we'll be able to really see how things are goin' 'cause Jerry don't ever want to do the wrong thing or insult me in front of you and the rest of our crew."

"I get it," Luc told Floyd as they climbed into the red truck. "You got it."

Floyd grinned. Took a drag off his cigarette.

Luc flashed on what Norma'd proclaimed on their very first date.

A WARM THIGH

That Friday night basement coffee house. Glass candles on the tables flickered ghost shadows of the previous generation's Beatnik stars: Allen Ginsberg *Howling* with his shaggy black hair and Buddhist beard. Jack Kerouac staring at a lonely road for answers out of the guilt he felt for being alive after his beloved big brother died. Luc imagined a soundtrack for those ghosts. Jazz like Coltrane and *The Three Ms*: Monk, Miles and Mingus. Dave Brubeck. Vince Guaraldi. Folk singers: Joan Baez. Richard Farina. The Kingston Trio. Judy Collins. Fairport Convention. Bob Dylan. Joni Mitchell.

An empty floor "stage" in this underground café filled with round tables full of jabbering hopefuls was the only thing that tore Luc's eyes away from Norma.

She sat facing him. Her long brown hair hung in curled waves. She'd painted her lips a shinier shade of pink. Her tan blouse complemented her brown eyes that tracked Luc's every breath. White jeans tightly sheathed her long lean legs.

Luc'd driven his blue car the three blocks from his basement apartment to her freshman girls' dormitory's parking lot pickup slots.

Norma walked around Luc's four-door Dodge. Bent herself through the driver's door Luc opened. Slid under the steering wheel across the front seat—

—and stopped dead center on the flat front seat. Her narrow eyes faced the rearview mirror. Her taut breasts faced the dashboard radio. Her white-jeaned legs bent because of the transmission hump in the car's floor. She wore white sneakers.

She'd claimed her spot sitting beside Luc.

Who then knew she *knows*—she *wants* this to be a *date* date!

Luc grinned as he started the car.

As they pulled out of the parking lot, the rock station on the radio played "Woodstock" written by Joni Mitchell and sung by Crosby, Stills, Nash and Young.

"*Wow*," said Luc to Norma sitting shoulder to shoulder with him. "Wouldn't you love to have been there? August '69, just last year. 'Three days of peace and music.' A half million of us. Outdoors. Rain. Shine. Nighttime. Great bands and signers. They're our poets. Make our souls rock. Make us feel alive."

Norma sighed: "I'm never where something big happens."

She turned from the windshield of that night's streetlights road, her motion triggering Luc to do the same so they smiled at each other as she said:

"Except for now," she said. "Tonight's *huge* because it's your play!"

That night Luc drank his first espresso.

Knew not to order more: *A guy rushing to the bathroom is uncool for women!*

They sat at their table two rows back from the stage.

Talked the usual stuff. What's your major? What classes? Where you from? *Her* big city state capitol Helena where high school Luc once threw up on the soon-to-be Watergate crook governor's shoes. *His* small-town Vernon where ten-year-old Luc sugared the gas tank of a lawman's cruiser in the name of justice. Their hometowns were four-plus hours of highway driving away from each other. She said she liked his movie reviews in the school paper. They talked books. Both loved mysteries. Agreed that category was too confining and underappreciated:

"I mean," said Luc. "*Hamlet* is about ghosts, spies, murder and skulls!"

Norma smiled.

Luc shrugged: "With a little romance on the side."

Norma kept her smile.

Luc turned her on to thriller author Alistair MacLean who confounded Luc with how he'd keep Luc turning the pages.

So in the coming crazy months of that summer, Luc forced himself to read the same MacLean novel over and over, twenty-one times in a row—all while *WHOA*s slammed his city crew, while Buffy and Steve did what they did, while Norma ached to be who she hoped she was and Terry . . . Terry . . .

Around read seventeen, after going from *loving* to *hating* to *So Bored!* by finishing and staring over, Luc *finally* sensed how MacLean made his story work.

Technique, thought Luc. Figuring *how*, not just *what* after *inspiration* shoves you to *Go!* Like watching that hippie commune in the movie *Easy*

Rider learning technique through something called *Tie she* or *gee*. There must be thousands of techniques to do or create anything—*and I can learn some!*

"Your attention please! Our plays are about start!"

The tables around Norma and Luc held mostly students. Over there was somebody's proud mother who'd driven three hours and got a motel room to be there. Over there a dad watched the stage like a guardian angel. People moved their chairs. Turned them to face the floor's "stage."

Norma dragged her chair around their table to side-by-side with Luc.

Sat shoulder to shoulder with him. Crossed her white-jeaned legs.

The lights dimmed in the coffee house.

Luc let his left palm settle on Norma's white-jeaned thigh.

APPLAUSE

Applause filled that candlelit basement coffee shop after Luc's play about a doorman who spoke in rhyming couplets to residents pouring in and out of the apartment building who ignored him until finally he laid down and died.

Scene! Curtain (even if there wasn't one)*! Applause!*

Moments of such applause were the only times Luc's hand left Norma's white-jeaned thigh. Luc made sure the drama group's student director and cast taking their bows saw him wildly clapping for them.

Friends of the troupe swarmed the stage. A waitress solicited orders. Luc whispered to Norma: *"Let's leave."*

She led the way up the stairs and out into the starry night.

BOMB

Luc's heart pounded his chest as he stood in his yellow-walled basement lair with its desk and chair and narrow bed. A clothes bureau. A nook for his hangered shirts hiding its back wall where Luc scotch-taped *wows*: Newspaper articles. Cut-out cartoons. Pictures from magazines (but not from his *Playboys*). A black and white photo of Marilyn Monroe scanning a book in a Manhattan bookstore.

Roommate Emil was gone—

—per their Roommates Agreement.

Luc'd led Norma through Emil's bedroom. Pulled back the curtain separating the two rooms. Switched on his lights. She walked past him. He came in behind her. Closed the curtain.

Norma stood facing the bed he'd made. *In case.*

Turned to face him.

Luc cupped her face in his hands.

First kiss fumbled into *oh yeah.*

'N' then they're lying on the bed kissing. The curtained exit is on her side of the bed—

—but it's *not* where she's going!

His hands in her hair. On her face. Cupping her white-jeaned ass so they're loin to loin. Touching/cupping her breast. "*Oh!*" she says not "*No!*" His fumbles unbutton her blouse and lift her bra up/off/over her teardrop breasts and *Oh God!* Soft teardrop nipples. His fingers. His thumb. His deep kisses. '*Oh!*' she moans. Deep tongue-linking kisses as his right hand slides down to the snaps for her white jeans. Reaching in and—

Norma jerks back from Luc.

Her eyes are wide like she's about to cry. Her kiss-swollen lips tremble.

Say you're sorry you went too far! Get her home! Never see her again!

Norma's trembling voice: *"I love you!"*

FIRST TIME

*O*h my God! She loves you! First date! She's great *and not*. What do you do? What do you say? What are you supposed to do? Want to? Talk 'n' truth tell her 'n' no lies 'n' say you're *not there yet* crazy 'bout her SHE LOVES YOU, SOME WOMAN LOVES YOU LIKE THAT FOR THE FIRST TIME EVER and God you want her smile when/if she takes off white jeans and *What: We're both virgins!*

R-E-S-P-O-N-S-I-B-L-E

The woman sitting behind the cluttered office desk didn't introduce herself to the two university students who filled the two chairs in front of her. Desk woman looked thirty-something. Not old enough to be the students' mother. Not young enough to be as clueless as them. She wore a wedding ring.

Windows flowed morning sunlight into this downtown Missoula, Montana, private office where its lobby's front door read: PLANNED PARENTHOOD.

"Now," she said. "How can I help you?"

"We want to be responsible," said the young man with—*Yes, those are* contact lenses helping his eyes be piercing blue.

The young woman sitting beside him nodded her straight brown hair. Brown eyes. She wore contacts, too.

Miracles of science, thought the desk woman as the young man spoke:

"We . . . we're together now. A couple since last Friday and . . . We want to have sex but we don't want to get pregnant. So we've waited."

The woman behind the desk suppressed a smile as she imagined the agony and the ecstasy of these two bodies writhing on some clunky bed in a shit-hole apartment or in the backseat of a crappy car. Burning kisses. Ever-better touching. Tasting. Maybe even stroking *until*.

"We need birth control," said the boy.

"I want to go on the pill," said the girl.

"Are you over eighteen?"

The girl nodded.

"If you're at the university, the state legislature won't let the student clinic prescribe legal contraceptives. I'll call the doctor's office down on the second floor. See when you can get an appointment to get the pill exam. Maybe he has a few minutes to squeeze you in today. Few questions and he signs the prescription for you to take to any drugstore.

"Unfortunately, it takes a few weeks for the pill to kick in and be effective—and then it's almost 100 percent safe, as long as you take it every day. I suggest every morning before you brush your teeth so you won't forget.

"In the meantime, condoms—

"*No!*" The virgin shook her head. "I don't want my first time . . . No condoms."

The woman behind the desk recognized the relief in the blue eyes of the kid/man/guy sitting across from her. Knew he was thinking:

Thank God no condom! How do you get one of those things on WITHOUT?

"In that case," said the woman behind the desk, "we've got another good alternative, not as effective as the pill, but . . ."

She turned in her chair behind the cluttered desk. Her right hand lifted an aerosol can from a desk drawer. Her left hand pulled out a tan tube tapered on one end to a sloped tip and on the other end fitted with a screw-top entry hole lid.

The desk woman faced the young woman yet also spoke to her companion as they leaned closer to her rising-toward-them tan tube and aerosol can hands.

"Contraceptive foam," she said. "Insert it like a tampon, then plunge the foam in, put the tube away. But first, fill the tube like so."

Desk woman popped open the tan tube's top cap.

Inserted and locked the aerosol spray can's nozzle into the tan tube's entry.

Pushed in the aerosol can's button.

"*Ha-Choo!*" sneezed the desk woman.

Reflexes locked her grip down on the aerosol can's FILL button.

Roaring in chemical foam blasted apart the delivery tube!

Splattered tan spermicide all over the leaning-in young man and woman.

YOU GOTTA

Luc steered his blue car. Stunned Norma sat beside him while he drove them back to their everyday lives after a drop-in at the doctor's office and a stop at a pharmacy for the small boxes riding in a white paper bag on the shotgun seat.

Luc couldn't help himself: "*BOOM!*"

Norma whirled from the windshield to stare at him.

He grinned: "We're an explosive situation!"

She fell back into stunned.

"You gotta laugh," said Luc who felt a wisp of foam crusting in his bushy hair.

"Maybe, but . . . typical," mumbled Norma. "The glass isn't half-full or half-empty. The glass is cracked."

"*Hey,*" said Luc: "So we get—*we got* a new glass. And we know how to fill it."

His look birthed a skeptical smile on her public bathroom scrubbed face.

He said nothing about flecks of dried foam in her long brown hair.

Tenderly nudged her shoulder to shoulder as they rumbled across the Higgins Bridge over the river rushing through their university town.

TICK . . . TICK . . . TICK . . .

Why they waited until Friday night perplexed Luc for the rest of his life. Something about *easier for her to skip out of the dorm overnight* or *our one-week anniversary* or the movie he had to review or the test she needed to ace.

No reason *why* ever made sense to Future Luc (as Buffy liked to say).

Why didn't we just French movie run away "to" after that afternoon explosion? Any afternoon. Morning. My bed. On the table in the library.

But now it's *that* May Friday *first time* night.

They're standing beside his basement bed.

Lights on. Yellow walls. A record player. Stacks of albums. A clock radio shared its bedside table perch with a translucent tan tube and an aerosol can.

He tosses off his polo shirt.

Kicks off his loafers he'd worn with bare feet so when he stepped out of his blue jeans he wouldn't have to jump from foot to foot trying to get his socks off.

Norma wore a red dress.

Turns around to face the zipper to Luc.

Feels his fingers zzzz down her back.

Turns to face him. Lets the red dress fall to her feet.

Wears her best white bra and pink panties.

Oh my God what if she'd worn nothing under her dress except brave and bold?

She reaches behind herself. The bra tumbles away.

He shoves his blue jeans and white underpants down to his ankles in one powerful push while she peels her pink panties down to her ankles.

He cups her face. Kisses her like the first time/now *oh so better* were they.

On his bed, I'm on his bed oh kiss me want you to kiss me love you love you won't say it scare him his hands there oh yes there and finger there the hard throbbing of him no condom denying my feel and—

Norma pulls away from Luc on the bed.

Reaches to the nightstand. The can. The tube.

Makes it work. Puts the gear back. Lays her back on his bed's white sheet.

Spreads her thighs . . .

. . . Norma came back to *steady mind.*

Lay in the crook of Luc's left arm with her cheek resting on his chest. Listened to the *beat beat beat* of his heart. Felt her own rhythm.

"We did it," he said.

"Well, I'm not sure you actually made it all the way in the first time."

"But . . . the second time?"

"*Oh, yeah.*"

She snuggled closer.

"You know," said Luc, "there's a lot of foam left."

He lifted her face up to his kisses and she came to him with a smile.

Safe darkness covered them.

The clock radio blared on at 7:15 the next morning playing the song "Come Saturday Morning"—which it really was. A song by The Sandpipers about two lovers going away from who they'd been to some wonderful *new.*

"I don't believe it," whispered Norma as they snuggled.

Luc felt *epiphany* rock his world like . . . like a gong, or like . . . like . . . *Clongs!*

What you're doing. What you're thinking. What you're feeling. How you feel. What's happening around you on this street you're driving. What's happening in China. In Baltimore. What your buddy said last night. The woman walking the sidewalk beyond the windshield of the car you're driving flicks her wrist *just so* as the car radio's song chords all that together in a cosmic truth.

Or like being in bed with your *Who* and the radio plays a song about that. Call it . . . A *clong.*

He babbled his epiphany to naked Norma in his arms as they lay in his bed.

Norma felt him riding with wild horses.

The heat of his naked body.

The thumping of his heart that could, *oh yes* and would, he would love her.

She birthed a shy smile: "You'll always be like this, won't you?"

Their kiss shared their morning bad breath 'n' then it didn't matter.

"Emil spent the night on his buddy's couch for us," said Luc.

"I know," said Norma.

Luc's right hand smoothly stroked up her bare *shaved so well* right thigh.

She felt him shrug: "We shouldn't let his sacrifice go to waste."

They didn't.

Worked out *whens* for them to be with the foam.

Then *Oh Then!* came Earthquake Monday.

Three days before she was getting picked up by her parents to go home to Helena for a summer job in her dad's hardware store.

Luc was driving to his home in Vernon the day after that.

Norma met him at a bench on the Oval. Sat him down.

"I'm late."

Two words.

A double-barreled shotgun blast.

No no no and she shakes her head, too. What to do. What can you do? Chains on your body by bankrolled politicians. By churches that used to say it was OK but now oppose it and your freedom of religion. A female can't have an abortion even if she's been raped.

Luc flashed on if only he hadn't been right about Doc Nirmberg in Vernon back in his sophomore year when Luc got that phone call in his dorm room.

But now in this spring of his junior year . . .

He'd heard about a place in Oregon. Somebody in Billings or was it Butte? What about Canada? Less than an hour and a border guard wave away from Luc's hometown. What about. What if. Won't let her have to do it on her own. Be ready to tell your parents about a fake wedding you gotta go to *because*. Or wait: A university fellowship retreat that *will*. What about the road crew? *Gotta, we gotta!*

Thursday morning as that university year of 1970 slipped away.

The city's daily newspaper reported that a civil suit had been filed by relatives of Black Panther, anti-fascist and community activist Fred Hampton's family after the badges' gun-blasting raid in December '69 on Hampton's Chicago apartment shot Hampton to death in his bed. All the badges involved had already been legally absolved. Subsequent investigations revealed the still-secret-then-in-1970 COINTELPRO program created by the FBI's director-for-life J. Edgar

Hoover—a closeted "illegal" homosexual who persecuted other men for being like him—was key in the raid and that Hampton's death was essentially an assassination.

That unknowing Thursday in June 1970, Luc met Norma's parents in the freshman girls' dorm parking lot.

Nervous handshakes. Small talk about weather. The routes they all had to take. *See-yous* instead of *good-byes*. Car doors slam. Norma stares back at him through her receding family car's rear window. He felt time *tick tick tick* suck away his dreams like a vampire.

Friday afternoon.

Luc slammed the trunk lid closed on his blue car in a university street.

His own bags and boxes filled the blue car's backseat.

"Thanks again for doing this," said his friend Vic who was taller than him. Smarter than him. Luckier than him with women who *weren't*.

Vic frowned at his dark clouded friend.

"You sure it's OK? I mean—"

"It's just storing a box of books for you."

"But a big one. It's just that the Forest Service wants me on the fire tower like *yesterday* because the snowpack is somehow way less than last year so I don't have time to get home to Libby and . . ."

"I couldn't toss them. Keeping them is like holding on to an old friend."

Vic shook his head:

"I could put in my graduation papers. Get my degree now. Got enough credits. Don't even know if I want to come back for 'my—*our*—senior year.' I mean, my big chance is a longshot."

"You deserve it."

Vic stepped back with a deeper frown: "Forget about me. You OK?"

"The way our world's going, the way things are, is anybody OK?"

"We're not talking about *anybody*. We're talking about *you*."

Luc managed a smile.

Is that a goodbye or a hello? worried Vic. Knew it was both, *but* . . .

"I gotta hit the road," said Luc. "You take care."

He climbed behind his blue car's steering wheel.

Drove away toward the distant town he'd always called home.

Glanced in his rearview mirror.

Saw Vic standing there. Watching him go where they didn't know.

Dawn caught Luc in his first hometown summer 1970 Saturday morning.

In the house where I grew up, thought Luc. *Is grown up what I am now?*

His dad was working at the trucking company.

His mom got a call to meet her sister Aunt Dory across the street in Gramma Meg's nursing home cell.

The road crew job started Monday.

He was unpacking his past in his bedroom.

Luc muscled Vic's cardboard box of books of academic knowledge across the floor of his closet. The box filled half the left wall space under "dress" shirts and pants he seldom wore. A stack of thick magazines filled the rest of the wall space.

Playboys.

The most famous magazine of the era. Even illiterates knew its name.

And what it was:

The first "dirty magazine" to break out of the commercial and social shadows in America's post-WWII superpower era with some perfume of respectability.

A celebration of nude women in full color pictures.

Plus, *of course*, justifying important essays by big bucks journalists and great stories by famous fiction authors, cartoons *and* the star of every issue:

The centerfold.

An 21.5 inches long and 10.5 inches wide three folded sections full color pose of a nude "girl next door" Playmate.

That last Saturday of May 1970 morning was almost to the historic month when *Playboy* stopped obscuring the genitals of its nude photos and Playmates.

Luc's five-years-older sister Laura gave him a four-year subscription to *Playboy* for his eighth grade graduation present.

His parents insisted Luc "read" those glossy pages only in his bedroom.

"Just keep the damn things in the closet and shut the door," ordered his mother when Luc insisted on saving every issue and re-subscribing.

That Saturday 1970 morning made him push Vic's box into a place where it wouldn't disturb his family home. He stood up—

—tangled himself in his hung-up clothes—

—fought his way free.

Glanced down at the stacks of magazines.

Pulled a random one from a pile: March 1967.

Three years ago. I was a senior in high school. A geeky virgin.

He opened the magazine.

Let the centerfold flip out and open to its full length for the Playmate photo.

Her name was Fran. Her hair hued more reddish brown than Norma's. Her breasts were swollen twice the size of Norma's. But not as pretty.

Nude Playmate Fran wore glasses.

A caption said she was the first Playmate ever to wear glasses.

Norma wears contacts, thought Luc. And thus, glasses. Like me.

Now is Norma the only real woman I'll ever see naked for me? For my touch?

Luc shook his head.

Folded the centerfold back into the center of the magazine.

Flipped through the pages . . .

. . . stared at photos of a naked beautiful *almost* more angelic than erotic blonde with savvy in her eyes.

Luc glanced at the captions that identified the rising star actress as . . .

Sharon Tate.

Murdered less than a year ago. August 1969.

Charles Manson's "Helter Skelter."

Manson's cult broke into the Hollywood house where eight-months-pregnant Sharon was staying with friends. Killed all four of them. She begged them to let her live for the baby. They stabbed her sixteen times. Lynch-tying her with a rope.

Other innocents elsewhere died too before Manson and his cult got caught.

He scratched a swastika into his forehead during his trial. Grinned.

Cultists claimed the murders were to be a trigger for a race war that would lead to Armageddon and the triumph of their cult in a new time of peace and love like the Beatles who wrote the song "Helter Skelter" prophesied in secret messages sung in their records that only Charlie could hear. Some evidence indicated the killings may have been ordered by ex-con Manson because he'd been denied a deal to be a rock 'n' roll star and his cult hit team went to the wrong address for revenge.

Luc shook his head that Saturday morning as he stood in his closet:

Is this the world we—

WHUNK!

The front door flew open!

Seba! Seba Pezzani! Third cousin Seba. Who rescued Luc from a whirlpool hole in the Grady River. Seba's house was where Luc's crew hung out and Luc got to be part of Seba's family.

"Hey!" called year-younger Seba, a student at the private Catholic college in Helena where Norma lived. "Grabbed these from your mailbox."

Seba held out a half dozen envelopes to Luc.

End-of-month bills. Ads for the grocery store Luc's family didn't use but his buddy Marin's mother had worked for. *TIME* magazine. An envelope with a cursive blue ink scrawl addressed to "Luc Ross" with return address of . . .

Norma.

Luc whirled away from his friend/cousin Seba's puzzled face.

Hurried into the kitchen where the countertop radio broadcast the weekly "KRIP Swap & Bulletin Board" show. Ripped the one-page letter out of the envelope from four-plus-hours-away Helena:

"It's OK! I felt my period coming as soon as our car pulled out of the parking lot. I almost yelled for my folks to stop, but then they'd know something was wrong—I mean RIGHT! I got home and am racing this letter to the Post Office to get it to you in Vernon like you did with the Kent State letters so you don't need to worry! We're completely fine!"

Luc shot both his arms high in the kitchen air like a football referee proclaiming *"Touchdown!"*

Glanced at the family phone on the kitchen wall.

A long distance could have come yesterday and ended hours of fear.

But long distance calls are special. Guess Norma didn't want to alert her parents by spending a couple dollars on their family house phone or speaking where they or her brother and sister might hear.

Luc whirled back to Seba's puzzled grin.

Opened his mouth to shout out the whole story—

—Shut it: *What would his beloved cousin Roman Catholic Seba think about the abortion Luc now didn't need to scheme?*

I can't make him deal with that, thought Luc.

Seba knew Luc: "So I'm guessing you've finally got a girlfriend."

"Girlfriend?" Luc couldn't stop his smile. "Is that what she is? I mean . . . Girlfriend, that's enough. *Yeah.*"

The rest of that Saturday before What Happened on Sunday and then his "bug in your ear" first Monday back on the city crew was marvelous.

THE LUCK OF YOUR DRAW

That smell is old people.

Luc walked down the second-floor corridor of the nursing home. To get there that Sunday before his first day on the city crew, he'd walked around the outside of the hospital and came in through the nursing home's double glass main doors.

He could have walked through the hospital front doors on the other side of this block-filling tan brick complex where it faced his house. Maybe then he would have *seen*. But Luc wanted to enjoy the clean June air that Sunday before his *of course gonna be joyous* first day back on the city crew.

The corridor where he walked was a long green receding shaft of doors that only locked from the outside.

The clatter of plates in the dining room. Family members speaking loudly for weakened ears in the reception room. The door where he had to go was open.

There's a door like that waiting for all of us, thought Luc. *If we're lucky.*

He put a smile on his face. Walked through that one.

"Hi, Gramma!"

Meg Conner lay propped up in her nursing home bed. She wore a top chosen by a nurse's aide who didn't give a shit. Her wispy white hair curled around her saggy face. Her eyes were as steel as they'd always been.

"Well, guess who's back in town," she said as Luc patted her arm. "Mister *clickety-clack* on a typewriter. How come you don't write me no letters from school?"

"The newspaper letter was for you, too, Gramma." Luc pulled a chair closer to sit beside his mother's mother, the matriarch who'd repeatedly mocked and fondled his uncircumscribed genitals until he made her stop that fateful year of 1959 when he was ten. That revolutionary Sunday in 1970 when he was twenty-one, he stared at that old woman from whom he'd come now trapped and helpless in the railed bed of her nursing home cell. Said: "How are you today?"

"Still here," she said.

Frowned.

"Come me being *gone*, if you're gonna be writing, who's gonna tell you how it really *was* so's you can know how it really *is* for you and your *clickety-clacking*?"

"I pay attention."

"And then what?"

"Yeah," he said.

She led their laughter.

Luc sat there and listened as she grumbled about his aunts Beryl, Dory and Iona. How his mom Cora'd better bring over a new bouquet of purple lilacs from Luc's front yard cause the ones in that vase over there on the bureau were droopy and it was near the last of the lilacs season out there where "nobody ever takes me no more, even in a wheelchair."

Luc lasted half an hour of this and that and *grumble grumble*.

"Gotta go," he said.

His grandmother took a deep breath.

Softened her eyes and voice.

"Keep an eye on your Aunt Beryl. She don't seem so good after they cut out a chunk of her lung. Let me know so I don't worry 'n' you can do what I can't."

That *old people smell* sailed him back through the green shaft toward the dining room and the reception room where Aunt Iona once had ten-year-old him untie muddle-minded residents cinched into chairs by white dish towels.

Coming out of the reception room was a woman his mother's age steadying the arm of a woman Gramma Meg's age. The elderly woman was sobbing as she shuffled back to her room. The middle-aged woman was obviously her daughter.

The middle-aged daughter's sad eyes spotted Luc. Knew who he was a heartbeat before he realized she was the mother of his classmate Mike Jodrey whose laugh had filled the halls of their Big Pink high school.

Mike Jodrey.

KIA, Vietnam, May 27, 1969.

One year and four days before now.

Teardrops glazed the eyes of his grandmother when she spotted Luc.

Maybe the gramma knew who he was. Or not. His name didn't matter.

"*You*," she sobbed to Luc. "You're just like him. When are you going to go and do your duty? When? My Mike, he went and did and he now he's up the cemetery and you, you're here. When are you going to do your duty? Take your turn?"

Luc whirled in time and space. *Can't talk. Can't think.*

Mike's grandmother shuffled past. His mother threw Luc a sorrowful look.

The elevator down from that Sunday's hall went *Ding!*

Ring! went the phone in Luc's parents' bedroom Monday evening as the family sat down to dinner on that 'bug in your ear' day.

"Nothing to worry about," said Dad as he came back from the bedroom where the petroleum trucking company phone was. "A mix-up at the refinery."

Luc saw Dad hold back a smile as they passed the serving plates of pork chops, canned green peas and home-mashed potatoes.

"I was talking to Raymond," said Dad as they filled their plates. Didn't mention how or where he happened to be talking to that town mayor who owned the grocery store where Dennis and Luc had both worked before the city crew.

"He says Dave doesn't need to worry about Mueler bossing the city crew. I mentioned to Raymond how I'd chatted with your buddy Kurt's dad, him being the CPA who checks all the trucking company's books and being city treasurer, too, and how he agrees with me and the mayor about Mueler, too."

The grin broke free from Dad: "We don't have that to worry about now."

"Thank God!" said Mom as she plopped mashed potatoes on her plate.

"No," said Luc who'd showered and put on clean blue jeans and a pullover shirt after getting home from work at 5:09. "Thank you, Dad."

"No thanks needed," said Dad. "You do what you gotta and oughta."

"Yeah," said Luc.

Yeah, he thought.

He dried the dishes while Mom teased him by having the kitchen radio playing KRIP's "The Reverend Carl McIntyre" show with Amen Charlie praising the reverend's rants on how long-haired hippies, harlots and hellfire politicians were defying God's word by not doing exactly what Reverend Carl told them to do.

"See you later," Luc said to his mom, knowing his dad would soon follow him out the door to go back to the trucking company office on the northside where there was always work for him to do and thus be the boss.

That June 1 Monday evening his parents assumed Luc was going to his cousin Seba's hangout house. Or meeting up with his high school buddy Kurt who went to the same university with him but now walked a more Main Street path.

But no.

What other gotta and oughta can I do? haunted Luc as he drove away from his house. His hometown filled his windshield. His gaze rode in another dimension.

He parked his blue car at the grocery store where his high school buddy Marin's mom used to work and flash red lipstick smiles at frightened eyes who saw her Gros Ventre tan skin on a sassy woman. She'd left town with a man who promised her more and Marin—the true poet in Luc's class—now lived in a bigger Montana burg grabbing classes from the local college while running a bar that paid for him and his Vernon sweetheart who'd told him "I'm late" halfway through his freshman year at a bigger state college, dropped out of high school and married him, who loved her and the child they'd created in the backseat of his '57 Chevy.

Sliding glass doors *whumped* Luc into that grocery store.

He went to the glass-doored refrigerated shelves. Found what he needed.

"Miller High Life," said the cashier as she took Luc's cash and quoted the TV commercial: "'The champagne of bottle beers.' You sure you only want two?"

"Don't even want them," muttered Luc. Paid for a "church key" bottle opener. Walked his load back outside through the *whumping* door.

Miller beer was his drink when Luc could afford it and felt cool. In his heart and mind, the brew was the best he could get. Have. Do.

He drove up Knob Hill Road.

Glanced left at a house with a driveway filled with a car and a pickup truck. Steve lived there. Luc'd heard he was back in town, too.

We came home.

Luc turned right off Knob Hill Road onto a side street that ended in a black iron poled fence with its gates spread wide.

The Martin County Cemetery waited through those black iron gates.

Where I was a gravedigger, thought Luc as he drove through those gates. A thousand headstones. One-car-width roads between their rows.

The big blue sky sun hung low above western golden prairie horizon. The sawtooth snowy tips of the Rocky Mountains rose sixty-some miles away. Green grass colored that field of graves.

No other cars, he thought as he slowed his car to crunch over the gravel roads between rows of headstones: *I'm the only one here.*

Well, he thought as tombstones rolled past his open car windows.

He spotted wilted flowers on a grave.

Read the name on the red marble gravestone.

Stopped his car.

Listened to his engine hum. His tense breaths. His beating heart.

He'd turned the radio off when he'd left the house. Wanted only to hear sounds of his hometown as daylight faded. The breeze past his car's open windows.

Luc turned the car off. Grabbed the two beer bottles. The church key.

Stepped out with them to face the tombstone.

Stood there as the evening sun warmed his face.

"Hi, Mike."

The breeze carried his words away.

"I'm sorry!" whispered Luc. "I couldn't . . . If I could have . . . What I'm doing, all I can do is the protests. Find someone to vote for and . . . And all that, everything, it's too late. Too late for you. *I'M SORRY!*"

He shook as tears broke free from his eyes, his heart.

Caught his breath. Sniffed back his snot. Wipe his cheeks with the back of his hands each holding a bottle of cold beer.

"You got robbed. You got wronged. You and all the other guys killed or hurt or messed up fighting in Vietnam. Your families. The people who loved you. Who need to hear you laugh. Need to have you here to walk with them."

Luc used the church key to pop open the bottles of beer.

Set one open bottle in front of the gravestone.

Held the other as he stared at the name carved in rouge marble.

"Wish we'd been real friends. Better friends than just high school classmate friends. Wish I'd been . . ."

Luc shook his head.

Made himself take a long drink of cold beer he held.

"'Member that time you gave me a ride to school on the back of your moped? You stopped for the sign on the road. I shifted around behind you. You *vroomed*—and the moped shot out from under me! Left me standing there wobbling bowlegged on the street. Even when you were yelling at me for being so dumb, you were laughing. You were always laughing."

Luc took another swig of 'the champagne of bottled beers.' The best he could bring. All he could bring besides himself to witness. To face that gravestone.

A lonesome train whistle echoed through that field of etched stones.

The breeze swayed the flowers in the bouquet, the grass on the grave.

Sunset crimsoned the blue big sky.

Luc stared at where he was. Finished his beer.

Whispered: "I'll do what I can. I promise. *I promise!*"

Climbed back in his car.

Sat sobbing behind the steering wheel.

MAGIC HOUR

Luc drove out of the cemetery.

The sun had gone below the horizon but still lit the sky.

Three blocks away from the black iron gates in his rearview mirror, Luc steered through the left-hand turn to go down Knob Hill.

Knob Hill Road rolled straight down from the blocks of houses on the rim of Vernon's prairie valley. Past the concrete wall holding up a shale and scrub grass hill for a mansion its owner never built. Past the funeral home. The junior high school and the grade school where Luc went with Mike. With Marin. Donna. Kurt. Wayne. And from seventh grade on, Buffy. Plus year-older and way cooler Steve.

Steve. Buffy. Me. But it was really always only Buffy and St—

Steve. Standing on the curb of his family home's driveway filled with his dad's pickup truck and Steve's used car he'd driven off to college.

Luc pulled over. Put his blue car in park. Got out and stood within the gap of the idling car's open driver's door.

"Hey, Steve! How you doing? What are you doing?"

"Watching the world turn."

There was something . . . *odd* about the way Steve stood. Something about the way his eyes focused as they filled with Luc.

"You OK?" said Luc.

"What you see is what I got."

"*Ah* . . . Yeah. I heard you'd come back from school after Christmas break. Been working for your dad."

"College was taking me nowhere," said Steve.

Shrugged. "High number in the Draft lottery."

"You always were lucky."

"Nobody ever said luck wasn't part of the deal."

Steve saw Luc standing there in his car ready to go to his own somewhere.

"I hope you're doing great," said Steve.

He saw Luc glance back over his shoulder toward where he'd come from.

Shake his head: "Sometimes just *being here* is great enough."

The two young legally full-on adult men stood there as the car engine purred.

"I better head home," said Luc. "Been a helluva first day on the city crew."

Luc drove off down Knob Hill toward the distant railroad tracks.

Steve knew *exactly* which street Luc'd turn on to get where he wanted to go.

The streetlight on the corner across from Steve glowed.

He checked his watch.

Climbed behind the steering wheel of the car he had.

Drove to *exactly* where he needed to park:

The Fortress.

A four-story redbrick box filled a street corner and half a block of his hometown. Forget about the corporate logo and name displayed in giant letters above its precisely spaced identical second-story windows. Everyone called this majestic legal monopoly *Ma Bell*. The phone company—the only phone company.

Ma's forty-foot-tall wooden pole sentinels stood watch on nearly every corner of America in 1970. Lined its highways, city streets and back country gravel roads. Black rubber sheathed "wires" ran from pole to pole to houses and businesses and a million human-sized glass payphone booths.

Ma's poles of black wires linked phones hung on kitchen walls or set on business desks and bedside tables. Phones only rang when a call came, alerting whoever was there to pick up the corded receiver and say *whatever*.

Ma Bell was the only way Americans could reach out and connect with someone out-of-sight *right now*.

Ma Bell's local fortress rose kitty-corner from where Steve parked. He saw the front glass door with a buzzer lock to protect What's Inside. And maybe Who.

Then night filled the cool of that first day of June Monday, 1970.

The watch Steve wore on his left wrist read 8:47.

He climbed out of the car.

Crossed the street to the corner facing those glass front doors.

He looked east down this street that Luc lived on a few blocks away.

Figured Luc got home OK.

Steve's gaze followed the street toward the eastern horizon, the wall of the prairie rim circling the town where he'd been born. Low on that horizon but slowly rising shone a huge pale full moon in the starry sky.

Was only a year ago that humanity left footprints up there, thought Steve.

Where are we going now?

He knew the first two women dressed in mandated proper dresses and prim makeup who walked out of the telephone company's brick office minutes after 9:00. One was older, a schoolteacher Steve never had now in her summer job. The other woman with sassy dyed blonde hair had been two years behind him in high school. She saw Steve standing on the corner across the street—*Got it!* 'n' hustled the older woman toward their parked cars.

Buffy came last through the glass doors to the night.

Saw Steve standing there waiting for her.

Her light brown hair curled to her shoulders. Her smart eyes. Her slicked pink lips that said nothing as Steve walked up to her.

"Can I walk you to your car?" he said. Like it was a joke.

"Hi," she said.

"Hi back," he said. "I haven't seen you since before Christmas break. Your parents said you spent the holidays skiing."

Don't ask. Don't ask. Don't ask!

His words waterfalled to her.

"We're here now. You. Me. No high school. Beyond all that. I was an ass-hole to you a lot of times then. Cheated on us . . . because . . . because I could, I wanted . . . wanted to be *a guy* even though I wanted more to be *your* guy.

"That's all I want now. I dropped out of Eastern because that was never for me. You are. I know you got a year more down at the U in Bozeman to get your teaching certificate. *You'll be so great with kids!* You're . . .

"We gotta take a chance. *Please!* I'll show you. I'm not that guy I was before. I know what I need. What I want. And it's you. I'll move down to Bozeman. Get a job while you—"

"*STOP!*"

Buffy's dusky hair broke free from the work hairspray and whirled from side to side in the glow of the rising moon and the streetlight's glare.

Her face wanted to cry. Her face wanted to scream.

You gotta do this! Buffy told herself. *This is Today's Buffy. This who is true. This is who you gotta be to be Future Buffy like you want to!*

She kept her voice flat. Firm. Honest.

Can't give him a wiff of *maybe*. Can't do that to him. Hurt him like that.

You'll hurt him enough nailing him to the cross of NOW.

"I've got someone special," she said. "Was him I went skiing with. He's got a job working for the attorney general in Helena, but I see him all the time. Whenever we can. Talk on the phone every day. Every night. We both know . . . We both know where we're headed."

The night breeze blew over the flesh of the bare, empty arms.

Steve whirled into starless darkness.

Buffy knew she had to stand there. Let him say what he had to say.

What came from Steve was: "He's a guy going places."

"You are, too, Steve. But not with me."

She forced herself not to reach out to comfort him. Knew even a gentle touch of her hand on his arm would just bring him more pain.

He whispered: "I'll always love you."

Oh those words he'd once heard from her! She remembered the magic he'd made her feel. His scent. His smarts. Their laughs. Kisses. Her first touches. Him leaving her at her parents' door after countless dates, then riding off into the night to hook up with his crew of wild stallions.

Now she did what Today's Buffy had to do.

Said: "'Always' changes."

Walked away.

Got in her getaway car.

Drove off into the night.

THE DEAL

That night's full moon hung high above the small northern Montana town Steve heard Luc describe as: "Sixty miles west of the Rocky Mountains, thirty miles south of the Canadian border and a million miles from everywhere else."

Luc, thought Steve as he sat behind the steering wheel of his car parked in the driveway of the house he'd called home for his entire life. *Wish we'd been better friends. But him hooked on Buffy too meant NO. Plus he was a 'nerd' and I was . . . Sure . . . I was "cool."*

The night breeze whoofed past his driver's side open window.

Nobody ever said you being a joke wasn't part of the deal.

Reflexes snapped his gaze to the first-floor living quarters of this house where the driveway ended in a house-wide garage "the man of the house" had turned into a workshop for his home renovation and carpentry business.

The house's front door sent a shaft of light into the darkness surrounding where Steve sat in his car. The door closed behind the hulk of a stepping-out man.

The man's hand rested on the black iron railing as he walked down the steps to the driveway. He leaned on the car to stare at Steve behind the steering wheel.

"Enjoying the view?" he said through the car's open window. "I get it. Looking at that white wall of the pulled-down garage door is fun as hell."

Steve said nothing.

"So what else you doing out here?"

"Going nowhere."

"I've been there. It ain't worth the trip."

The man leaned off the car. Jerked open the driver's door as he did.

"Might as well step out and get a clean good look. Windshields get dirty."

Steve felt his body climb out from behind the steering wheel.

"Damn," said Steve's dad. "Look at the moon up there high in the sky. Just a while ago, it was hanging on the horizon like some giant glowing basketball. Now way up there, just looks like a pale golf ball. See the stars around it? That shining one is really the planet Venus. Steady reflected white glow instead of a twinkle. Planets be where people live and moons are what they see, but 's the stars that make the light. Big or small, see 'em or not, they're what we got. What we need."

The half-century-plus old man shrugged his shoulders—

—made them jostle against the arms of his dazed son standing next to him.

"So," said father to blinked-back son: "Where's the nowhere you're off to?"

"What difference does it make?"

"Well, your mom's big on visits if'n she can get off bartending down at the Sports Club. We love to take planes. Big old silver tubes lots better now that they don't use propellors like when you and your sister was kids. Sit down, buckle up and go. Course it's two hours driving down to the airport in Great Falls, but still, up there in the air, stewardesses bringing everybody their choice of hot meals soon as we take off . . . Damn nice.

"Course I'm a highway man myself. Getting to see where you're going as you get there. Choosing which turns to take. When to go, where to stop.

"So figure your Ma and me, it's like we're going with you 'cause you know we're gonna come see, so we're both just kinda wondering."

The night breeze brushed them.

The older man said: "I'm guessing things with Buffy didn't go where you was hoping."

"She's gone."

"No. She's always going to be somewhere. That's a fact. Like the moon."

"And I'm stuck here. Nowhere to go."

"Well, we all start from somewhere.

"You could get in that car of yours. Drive off going any which way. On the road, you might remember you got a big brain and big knowings in it—but still a whole lot of space you gotta fill up. That ain't always going to come no easy way like school. *Knowing* and *understanding* are hard. Hurt like hell sometimes. It ain't always our fault, but it's the *doing* with all that that counts.

"You say you got nowhere to go. But you're working and saving money for gas. Getting skills might earn you dollars where you park your car. You're helping me do bigger jobs faster 'n' keep up with the other guys so I got more money going into the feds' Social Security chest for when me and my lady cross the official line into *old*. You're helping Mom run the Sports Club down on Main Street, easin' her tired legs and that sore hip. You're seeing more of *what's what*.

"But standing out here staring up at that getting-smaller moon?"

Steve saw his father shake his head.

Turn and walk up the stairs to the front door.

Steve heard the front door of where he'd grown up click closed.

But not locked.

He looked up at the pale moon.

Nobody said the deal means you can't make your own light shine.

SCARLET WIND

Before sunset's ambush, Tuesday was another day of Luc driving the red truck ferrying gravel to and from the river grotto to the city sand lot.

And the dream.

No one at work said anything about the Kent State letter or City Councilmember Mueler, thought Luc when he left his house as soon as he finished drying lunch dishes and walked back toward the five-minutes-away city shop at 12:27, thirty-three minutes before he needed to be there at 1:00.

The Post Office waited one block away from Luc's house and three blocks away from his job. That one-story rectangle brick building with picture windows facing the sidewalk was a clean, well-lighted place. The glass front doors stayed unlocked. The entrance lobby had walls of mailboxes for rent. A corkboard hung with WANTED posters with photos of on-the-loose criminals. A second set of glass doors—unlocked from 8:00 to 5:00—led to the counter and clerks waiting to sell you stamps. Weigh your parcels. Pass you that Special Delivery letter from Aunt Martha's lawyer about why you weren't in her will.

"How you doing, Luc?" said the counter clerk as he took the unsealed manila envelope from the college kid in a white T-shirt, blue jeans and work boots. Put the manila envelope on a scale. Checked the address. Checked the nearby ledger of the brand-new things called *zip codes*. Tapped the keys of a bread loaf–sized adding machine. Pulled its lever *ca-ching*. Read its results.

"First class to the East Coast," said the postal clerk. "Gonna cost you . . . Well, a buck seventy-three. You could send it cheaper. Get it there, *oh*, three days later."

"First class please."

Luc reached into the unsealed manila envelope—

—pulled out its twin, a second addressed manila envelope folded to the size of the thin stack of white pages filling the rest of the first envelope.

"And would you put the same postage on this envelope, too?"

The second envelope he stamped was addressed to Luc at his parents' home.

Where I'll be for the next three months, thought Luc. Where an envelope could always find its way to him.

The postal clerk passed the second now postage paid envelope to Luc.

Who politely said: "I'll just step over there. Put it all back together."

Luc turned away from the counter. Stepped to a shelf table on the wall.

Hand-inked letters created his manila envelope's TO:

NOIR DAZE MAGAZINE

He'd gone back and forth about whether to send it to that bigger-than-an-adult's-hand paper monthly magazine in New York or to *Alfred Hitchcock's Mystery Magazine* or *Ellery Queen's Mystery Magazine*. Destinations like *The New Yorker* and other oh-so-intellectual or family-oriented magazines like *The Saturday Evening Post* were absurd longshots. *Playboy* was a fantasy.

He pushed the return envelope back into the send now packet.

Pulled out the first page of his short story:

Zen Green
by Luc Ross

The blonde leaning her ass on the kitchen table stared at Nick crouched in the hard chair where she'd ordered him to sit.

She'd scissored her peroxided hair too short to grab. Her red lipstick mimicked murdered-eight-years-ago Marilyn Monroe. Her blue eyes matched the sky outside this hulking apartment building in mountain valley Missoula, Montana. Her right arm dangled between her blue-jeaned legs where her hand coiled around the butt of a gun.

Nick knew the pistol was a Colt 1911 .45 semi-automatic.

Wondered if it got smuggled home from Saigon with a soldier of that eleven-years-and-still-going-on war.

She's not a student at my university, thought Nick. His hungry eyes would have spotted her amongst that vast herd by this April Wednesday of his third year. The factory line of Growing Up put her in his generation but her cobalt eyes were lifetimes older.

Someone's record player or radio somewhere in the building played "American Woman" by Canada's Guess Who, their hit rock 'n' roll song they were forbidden to play in their gig at President Nixon's White House.

The blonde with a gun dumped Nick's wallet. Found his student ID. His driver's license told her his real age and home-town of Shelby. She grunted at his fake "I'm twenty-one" ID that let him slide into bars. He'd outgrow needing it in eight days.

Her husky voice said: "What do you want with Shaughnessy?"

Her magnetism—plus the gun in her hand—pulled the truth out of Nick.

"Um, he . . . I ordered a nickel bag—$15. Paid him. A handful of grass as my going-home summertime stash. But he never delivered or called. So I came here to his place."

Nick couldn't stop himself: "What's going on?"

Her gun hand swayed between her legs.

"What makes you think you get to ask questions?"

That Tuesday standing in the Vernon Post Office, Luc folded the return-to-sender envelope into the mailing packet with his short story he'd finished typing the day before Norma'd said: "I'm late."

He passed the sealed packet over the counter.

Walked out into the June Tuesday for his second afternoon on the summer job on city crew.

Come five o'clock, street foreman Jerry walked up to him: "Might be something different tomorrow."

"What?" said Luc.

"Let's hope nothing. But me and Dave gotta check somethin' out."

Luc walked home past the Post Office.

Saw postal workers toss mail bags into trucks headed to the dispatching center two hours away in big city Great Falls.

Go! Luc whispered.

Knew he'd fail to stop thinking about his Zen Green story *until*.

But hell, he'd held out for six years until he realized Buffy was his *never*.

Now I've got Norma, he thought as he hand-over-his-heart stopped to watch Mr. Benson lower the American flag down the Post Office's white pole.

Norma loves me, thought Luc. Just *WHAM! Like I'd always hoped for—*

*—*but "hoped for" for me and Dream Lover.

Not *just* like the rebel erotic image on the Marilyn Monroe calendar hanging on the wall at the trucking company and haunting his heart.

Not *just* a savvy soul poet like Emily Dickenson or singer Joni Mitchell.

Not *just* like hero Rosa Parks who claimed her seat on the bus 'n' the hell with the Ku Klux Klan's burning crosses and White men's laws of racial hatred.

But someone with all of that who made him *WHAM!*

He was hooked on Norma. They had sex! She read books he liked and they had sex. She came to the war protests, movies and guest lectures with him. Sex. He really liked her. In a romantic way, too. She loved him. Was on birth control.

The postal clerk carried the American flag into the government building.

Luc walked up the short block to his house.

He didn't *exactly* know where he was going but he knew *Keep Walking*.

After dinner he walked down the front steps of his house. To get out. To just *go*. Drive his old blue car at the curb to Seba's house. Or Main Street.

Luc glanced at the hospital across the street from his house.

Wait! Is that . . . Is that Dennis's motorcycle parked at the hospital curb?

Is Dennis OK? Got someone in his family who—"

Dennis hurried out of the hospital's glass doors toward his motorcycle.

Hustling with Dennis came a their-generation woman.

Luc's eyes filled with her.

Who is she?

She straddled the motorcycle like a gunfighter.

Strapped on to ride behind Dennis.

He *vroomed* a *Whee!* Half-circle turn. Roared them off into the sunset.

Her midnight hair flowed free in the scarlet wind.

OBSESSION

Luc couldn't stop thinking about what came next in his short story *Zen Green* as he walked to work that next day's June Wednesday morning *before*:

"You've got the gun," Nick told the dyed blonde, cropped-haired woman. "All I've got are questions and a thundering heart."

"Where would Shaughnessy be if not here?"

"Nobody's on campus today. He barely goes to classes anyway. If it was night, he'd go to the Monk's Cave, the underground bar where cool bands play."

"But now is now," she said. "Wednesday afternoon. You knock on his door up here on the fourth floor. No answer.

"Then you either knew about or guessed stoner him kept a spare key hidden somewhere in the hallway. Found it in the fire extinguisher cabinet. Burgled his door and came in. You got skills."

"I read a lot of novels. You bonked my head with that pistol."

"Your Beatles long hair over your ears pillowed the clunk."

"You didn't wait to see who came through the door. So that gun barrel was looking for Shaughnessy's skull."

"Gee, why do I keep ending up with the wrong guy?"

"I've been busy with school."

"Zip it up, cowboy. This isn't your lucky day. So what am I gonna do with you?"

The apartment window above the street vibrated a coming-closer ruckus.

IN THE STREET

C hange of plans." Jerry strode toward Luc in the yard that Wednesday morning. "You and Dennis gonna be helping Floyd over t' could be a sewer leak.

"Floyd's better 'n' me on the backhoe," said Jerry. "Plus, there might be some overtime. Good for you and Dennis. But I got stuff to take care of at home so I'm outta here at 5:00. You got waders?"

"*Ah* . . . Just the work boots I'm wearing."

"You don't go mucking around in a sewer leak wearing what you gotta wear tomorrow. City Council won't spring for rubber waders for the crew, come up to your thighs, but Dave got a few guys round town to give him their old fishing ones. Arson's got 'em on a shelf in the garage. Grab a pair that fit good enough."

The gunwoman's chopped white blonde head motioned Nick to the ever-louder, noise-vibrating window four stories above Higgins Avenue—Missoula's "Main Street" crossing over a bridge to the commercial center of town.

He grunted the window all the way open over the wide street.

Worried that he was no stronger than your average hale bale bucking townie even with the pushups in Karate Club.

Why didn't I start sooner? he silently accused himself as the blonde with the gun stood and walked toward the window and him: *I'm only a green belt!*

Behind him, a long fall from the open window to the sidewalk flowed into the apartment that cool April afternoon air with the sound of marching feet.

"Turn around," she said, standing too far away to grab. "Face the window."

He looked out.

Saw Change that Would Save the World coming down the street.

Hundreds—*No!* Thousands of beating hearts! A wave of university students marching with fighting-up-the-work-ladder women and housewives. Gray-hairs. College professors. A used car salesman beginning to fear the exhaust of his job. Fraternities and sororities with names from the alphabet of Aristotle who Nick'd read in the half dozen political philosophy classes shotgunned through his whacky transcript that claimed he was a journalism major. People leaned out the windows of this block apartment building at the intersection of the river's bridge to the money side of town.

The gun barrel dug into Nick's spine.

The dyed blonde whispered in his ear: "Show me!"

Luc and Dennis sloshed shin-deep in muck. Floyd sat in the backhoe's cab keeping watch on the two crew members down in the nine-feet-deep, ten-feet-long trench. Dug-out muck made a truck-sized pile on one side of the trench.

"Should just replace the whole section of pipe," Floyd'd told them. "But *should* and *can* are two different things out here in the street."

Dennis grimaced as they pulled on their issued thigh-high green waders: "Smells like the whole town's got diarrhea."

"No shit," said Luc.

Dennis rolled his eyes.

They got to work.

Now two hours later, white T-shirted Luc and Dennis hunched over a manhole-sized pipe running lengthwise from one side of the trench to the other.

"Looks like the steel band sealed that gash," said Luc.

His rubber gloved hands held the yucked-up silver wrench they'd used to tighten the bolts on that circular clamp.

"How 'bout now you grab the shovels and toolbox?" said Dennis. "Haul it all up the ladder on the side. I'll hold it for you."

"If it sinks anymore in the muck, we'll have to heave ourselves out of here."

"Don't say 'heave,'" said Dennis.

Luc groaned from the joke.

Grabbed the gear they'd brought down into the hole.

Dennis leaned as far away from the ladder as he could while his muck-stained, tool-hauling buddy worked his way up the rungs.

Luc shoved the shovels, the silver wrench and the stained red toolbox across the pavement away from the open trench. Hoisted himself off the ladder. Stretched out with his stomach pressed to the damp pavement to—

SLURP-whoosh!

The far wall of this like-an-open-grave collapsed!

The flood of mud hit standing-in-watery-muck Dennis. Tidal waved around his trapped knees. His arms and body flopped and twisted like some blow-up giant sock puppet outside a car dealership.

Luc felt the wall collapsing beneath his lying-flat body.

Scrambled forward. Staggered to his feet.

Floyd swung the backhoe bucket down into the collapsing trench.

Dennis grabbed two of the bucket's teeth.

Floyd raised the backhoe's jointed steel arm.

Pulled hanging-on Dennis out of his thigh-high waders stuck in the muck.

Dennis rose out of the trench dangling from the backhoe's bucket.

Floyd whirled him toward safe ground and Luc's grasping hands.

SLURP/whunk collapsed the muck walls trench.

Lloyd scrambled out of the backhoe.

"You OK?" he yelled at Dennis.

"Y . . . Y . . . *Yeah*," said wide-eyed behind his black-rimmed glasses Dennis. Whispered "*Thanks!*" to the older man.

"It's the job," said Floyd.

He led the two muck-yucked coworkers over to a hose connected to a fire hydrant. Sprayed the two of them from head to toe in the warm June sunlight.

They walked back to the trench they'd dug that now had collapsed muck into truck-sized, shallow U-shaped impassable valley in this residential street.

"My waders are under all that," said Dennis.

"But not you," said Luc.

They rode Luc's truck back to the yard.

"You sure you're OK?" he asked Dennis.

"Besides my mind going a million miles an hour every which way? My heart thumping my chest even though now it don't need to? Yeah, think so."

"You wanna go to the hospital?"

Dennis smiled at his concerned friend.

"I mean," said Luc. "I hope you're fine—now and before."

"Before when?"

"I saw you coming out of the hospital last night. Is everything OK?"

"Oh yeah. I get allergy shots once a month. Rather than take off from work, the doc worked it out so I can get a shot from one of the nurses on night shift."

Luc shifted gears as they neared the railroad tracks cutting through town.

"Was that a nurse I saw you giving a ride somewhere on your motorcycle?"

"Naw, that's this college girl from Ohio. There's some new kind of program where juniors in their last college summer—"

"Like me," said Luc.

"Only she's way smarter. Gonna be a doctor. Students like her spend their summer working in small towns across the country where the hospitals and doctors can use a spare hand. It's like them being interns before they graduate. Gives them a taste of what they're facing. Make them sure being a doctor is what they wanna do before they sign up for all the work of trying to be one."

Their truck *bumpity bump bumped* over the railroad tracks.

"Good deal for everybody." Dennis's eyes scanned his hometown like never before. "Hospital pays for room and board. Course here that means she has to live in a hospital room and 'board' is whatever the cook is making for patients or the old folks in the nursing home. A few nights a week, she's gotta stay in and be like a backup for the night shift. Goes on rounds with the doctors. Sees patients with docs in the clinic. They gave her a stethoscope."

Luc clicked on the left blinker.

Downshifted to let the blue truck drive past the Post Office.

"So last night on your motorcycle, you were taking her . . ."

"Just a quick ride around town. She's pretty much cooped up there."

Across from my house, thought Luc.

Said only: "What's her name?"

"Terry Jones," said his still stunned friend.

Luc kept repeating that to himself all afternoon when he was back driving 'his' red truck to the river grotto: *Terry Jones. Terry Jones.*

He hurried home after work.

Saw no motorcycle parked in front of the hospital.

Showered. Told his parents the collapsing trench story but didn't make it sound dangerous. Didn't want them to worry about him being on the city crew. Wore clean blue jeans and his favorite pullover shirt after dinner.

Told his folks a truth: "Gramma asked for fresh purple lilacs off our bush so I'm going to cut some and take them to her."

Mom gave him a vase filled with water for the purple flowers.

The night duty front desk nurse smiled at vase-carrying Luc as he walked through the front doors *obviously* headed to the hospital-adjoining nursing home. She went back to her paperwork. Paid no mind as he turned away from that *obvious* path to walk down the corridor of hospital rooms. If she'd watched, she'd have seen Luc *obviously* merely pouring excess water from the vase into the water fountain on the wall halfway down the corridor of rooms for patients.

Luc glanced into the open doors on the first-floor corridor of the hospital:

There was a mom a year younger than him slumbering beside the hospital crib of her swaddled new baby.

There was a gandy dancer with his broken leg casted and propped up after a co-worker accidentally struck that leg with a sledgehammer.

He walked back the way he'd come. The front desk nurse didn't raise her head to see him walk up the stairs to the second floor, the *obviously to be delivered* glass vase of purple lilacs filling his hands.

The second-floor desk duty nurse was on the phone when Luc reached her level. Visiting hours ran until 8:00 and it was only 7:17. This nice young man who she recognized had *obviously* been waved to wherever he was going by the first-floor nurse so the phone-talking nurse paid him no mind.

Luc slow-walked down the corridor of open doors. Glanced into each room. Saw only Mrs. Robinson who was waiting to be taken via ambulance to a more sophisticated hospital in big city Great Falls for complex surgery.

Luc circled back to the water fountain exactly above the first-floor fountain. Positioned the nearly empty glass vase of thirsty purple lilacs in that upper fountain and re-filled the vase with a flowing stream.

Stepped back as the scent of the purple lilacs filled the hall.

From behind him came a woman's husky voice: "Are those for me?"

There she stood.

Her midnight hair fell past her shoulders from a widow's peak on her forehead. Her eyes were a blue he'd never seen. Her cheekbones were high. Her jawline was long and clean and *oh* her lips: Wide. Full. Smiling. She was shorter than him. Lean and curved and the AC chill of the hospital—

Don't stare!

The chill made her nipples stand up firm and large.

He kept his eyes on hers. Answered her ask: "I wish."

She blinked a quizzical smile.

"Hey," said Luc. "Everybody deserves good things. But these are for my grandmother over in the nursing home. I live across the street—summers, my folks house, I'm in school—the university in Missoula. Last year coming up."

"Me, too," she said. "Cincinnati."

Luc babbled his alibi: "Walking up to this level means I don't have to take the elevator up to my Gramma's second-floor nursing home room."

He shrugged. "No hurry to get to a room like that."

"That's why I'm here. So maybe people won't have to go there so fast."

"Are you . . . Terry Jones?"

Her smile sabered big city savvy: "So why and how would you know that?"

"Dennis. He's my summer job buddy on the city crew. I saw him give you a ride on his motorcycle last night. Like I said, I live right across the street."

"And just *who* is it living *right across the street* from me?"

"Luc Ross."

"Dennis didn't mention you."

"Why would he? But I've got a question."

Her gunslinger blue eyes sized him up: "Only one?"

"Let's start with a newspaper reporter question. How do you spell your first name?"

"*Ah*," she said. "That *is* the question. A *y* or an *i*."

"I got lucky," she answered. "*Me* is the question '*why*.'"

"Questions help set us free."

"If you ask the right ones. Get the true answers. Do something with them."

"I'm trying," said Luc. "I'm trying . . . *too*."

They both knew they both got the pun.

She nodded. Let her smile sparkle.

He pulled a branch with two purple lilac blossoms from the vase.

Handed it to her: "You'll have to put it in water."

She brought the cluster of purple leaves up to her nose. Closed her eyes. Breathed in. Her blue eyes opened as the lilacs lowered past her smile: "Thanks."

"So you live here in one of these hospital rooms," said Luc.

"If you ignore the smells and occasional moans, it's like a weird dorm."

"And you're all alone."

Neither of them blinked.

"No wonder you hopped on the back of Dennis's motorcycle for a ride."

"The motorcycle is loud. It's hard to hear. And windy."

Must have been memory that made her flick her head from side to side and let waves of physics float her midnight hair.

"You should see this town you're here to learn about," said Luc. "But next time, let's all just take my car."

WHERE WE ARE

The sounds of marching in the street below filled the fourth-floor apartment as Nick shuffled to the window.

"Stop!" said the fake blonde behind him.

The gun pressed into his back. Slid down his spine.

"I'm gonna pull the gun away. Count to ten, then turn around."

Heartbeat ten slowly circled him to face her.

She stood by the window. Her white sneakers were braced for a killing snapshot. Her relaxed gun hand pointed at Nick's groin.

The crowd below came closer to pounding this block's pavement.

She nodded her white blonde skull out the window.

Her husky voice said: "Tell me what's gonna on."

Luc's blue car shotgun seat door *Whunked!* shut behind Terry.

She wore a white blouse. Black slacks. A face full of *show me.*

He stood in the open driver's side door of his car parked at the curb outside the hospital's front glass doors that sunny after-dinner Friday.

Kept a cool smile: *She's in my car!*

His shrug told Dennis to pick his seat—in the back.

Dennis calculated *best choice* and came up with the driver's side backseat. Sitting right behind Luc but with a sight line to Terry's left profile: The waterfall of her black hair. Her high cheekbones. Her clean jawline. One corner of her smiles. The flicks of her eyes—and *sometimes* them looking back to see him.

Whunk! shut the car door of Dennis's best choice.

Luc slid behind the steering wheel.

Whunk! shut his driver's side door.

There were no seatbelts.

He keyed the engine to life.

Reached into the heart pocket of his short-sleeved shirt.

Pulled out his *oh so cool* aviator sunglasses with dark mirror lenses.

"There's a pair of sunglasses for you in the jockey box," he told Terry.

She pulled out the dark lenses in a curved frame that fit her fine.

Luc glanced in the rearview mirror where Dennis sat in black-framed glasses like Luc wore before he got contact lenses.

"Let's go see where we are," said Luc.

"We gotta show her the city shop!" said Dennis. "What we do. The yard."

The blue used car motored away from the curb.

Motored past the Post Office.

Where's my Zen Green story? wondered Luc.

They climbed out of his car parked at the city shop.

Terry stood looking through the chain-link fence.

"You two drive those big machines?"

"Dennis runs the roller. Right now I'm a trucker. I know how to work that car-sized frontend loader, but the big one with the glass cab? *Naw.* I usually work the spreader, that long yellow steel trough that gets hooked on to the back of a truck. A shovel guy. Dennis, they also got him helping out Arson mechanicing in the garage. He's got the knack, plus he's studying engineering."

Terry turned to look at blushing Dennis.

"A math and science guy," she said. "I made it through the math I gotta have for med school but numbers aren't my thing."

"They help us get where we're going," said Dennis.

"Where do you guys go in those trucks and things?"

They drove *bumpity-bump* over the railroad tracks to the northside.

Parked at that barricaded packed earth rectangle in an American street.

Luc and Dennis tag-team told her wide eyes the cave-in story.

Terry shook her head: "You got anything a little more normal?"

Luc sent a smile to Dennis's curious face in the rearview mirror.

Drove northside streets.

Luc hit his left blinker at the last stop sign before leaving town.

Dennis grinned into the rearview mirror.

The windshield filled with miles of golden prairie beyond this five-block canyon of ordinary houses.

Luc turned his head to the corner house flowing past his open driver's side window when they were three blocks away from their destination:

Buffy's house. A simple square golden cottage.

How many thousands of times did I drive past it? Looking. Hoping.

Yesterday's dream receded in his driver's side mirror.

Ahead, on the left end of the canyon rose the fence for the football field.

While ever closer on the right side of their route loomed . . .

The Big Pink.

Luc drove a slow circle turn in the student parking lot. Parked facing the football field. Further away waited railroad tracks full of brown boxcars.

They watched a distant train roll past. Heard its lonesome whistle.

"*Um*, can you two do me a favor?" asked the woman in the shotgun seat.

"*Name it*," said Luc as Dennis said: "*Sure.*"

Terry took a deep breath.

"Show me the whorehouse. I've been working the clinic when the . . . the women up there get taxied in for their weekly VD checkups by Dr. Schenck. He's the county health official and . . . And I wanna see *where.*"

Where, thought Luc as he steered his car out of the high school parking lot.

Where Dennis used to deliver groceries from the store the mayor owned when they worked there as box boys.

Where I never went, the whorehouse run by my Uncle Johnny before he was murdered long after I was a clueless ten-year-old pawn in a foiled attempt to help one of those women escape from this town and his control.

They rode through the northside of houses.

The whorehouse waited a heartbeat north of the city line. A two-story rouge box with closed-blind windows.

In Uncle Johnny's day, customers had to take his taxi here. That let him keep control—and pocket a few extra bucks as well as launder profits from the biz. That also let his customers keep their privacy from raucous teenagers brave enough to circle the building to its backlot parking spaces despite the risks of Uncle Johnny, the straight-razor-toting madam or Vernon's cops.

"This is it?" said Terry as Luc slowed their ride past the whorehouse.

She shook her head: "Right out in the open. And Nixon is our law and order president."

They followed the gravel road past the whorehouse to the city dump past the rim around the Vernon city valley. Lost seagulls swooped over gorges the city crew garbagemen filled with whatever Vernon's citizens dumped.

The blue car circled back down the gravel road to town.

Terry looked past driver Luc to the passing whorehouse.

"Did you guys ever notice how this whorehouse box is on the same color spectrum as your 'Big Pink' high school?"

"You see things like that, too," said Luc, who'd never made that connection.

"A doctor's gotta see before she can fix."

"Or write the stories in your head," said Luc. "I mean, prescriptions."

Terry's wraparound sunglasses looked his way with a quizzical smile.

Their car *bumpity-bumped* over the railroad tracks.

Took a right on Main Street.

Dennis pointed from the backseat: "There used to be a bookstore there. And an ice cream parlor called The Whitehouse."

"What happened?" said Terry.

Luc said: "Nobody in town wants to give all that a name."

They drove past the Roxy theater that would forever shut its doors in the first year of Donald Trump's presidency. The Roxy's marquee that warm June evening in 1970 advertised a World War II commando adventure movie released four months earlier that had finally made its way from big cities and packed suburbs to the watching eyes of small-town theaters.

"The Roxy's showing *Catch-22* in a few weeks," said Luc. "Great book."

Terry whispered a catchline from that fictional saga that became a factual National Security crisis forty-three years after that June Friday night in 1970:

"Where are the Snowdens of yesteryear?"

Luc and Terry smiled at each other.

The rearview mirror showed Dennis staring straight ahead.

His reflection silently screamed *I gotta read that book!*

Luc turned his mirror sunglasses to reflect the stores passing by on his side of the street. A men's clothing store. Another woman's store. Storefront offices. The Sports Club. The Alibi. The Tap Room. The Capitol Café.

The brick building with a deserted office's two darkened windows.

Don't tell her about those windows, thought Luc as he drove past a bank's giant digital clock tower. The decades that abandoned office was Doc Nirmberg's. That former frontier doctor and mayor's medical practice by the 1950s was almost solely selling illegal abortions to women who rode the rails and roads from as far away as Seattle and Chicago for their choice he protected with sheer will and a shotgun leaned against the medical office wall.

Badges never knocked on his door for crimes the whole town knew about.

Luc blinked the memory of the autumn of 1968 when he was college sophomore living in a two-bed dorm room.

A black rotary-dial phone hung on the wall by the door.

Rang.

"Hello?" he'd said.

A college woman's voice on the other end of the line: "Is this Luc Ross?"

"Yes."

"I got your number out of the student phone book and . . . You don't know me, but you're supposed to be a real good guy—"

YES! Finally! Some woman out there wants to . . . to like me!

"—and you're from Vernon."

Realization hit Luc in one knockout punch heartbeat:

"Don't go to the doctor up there! He's old. Shaky. Keeps a sheepdog in his office. I'll help you find some other place. Other doctors. I heard about some place in Oregon and I'll—"

Click.

She hung up.

A week later, just before 1968's Thanksgiving break, the University of Montana's student newspaper published a story about a *name-protected* UM coed who'd gone to a doctor in Vernon for an illegal abortion, then *barely* made it the four-hour drive back to Missoula and the student health service that *barely* saved her from bleeding-out after that terribly botched procedure. The paper didn't name Doc Nirmberg, but now the whole state knew *where* if not *who*.

Luc never told anyone about the phone call.

Doc Nirmberg closed up shop before that Christmas's snows.

Luc blinked: If Doc Nirmberg'd still been around 'n' not a shaky senile old man when Norma was late—

Don't. Think. About. Norma.

From the backseat, Dennis said: "I like that book you gave me, Luc. Terry, it's called *Steal This Book* by Abbie Hoffman. He was one of the guys in the Chicago Seven trial, the protestors who got charged for the anti-Vietnam war riots at the '68 Democratic presidential convention."

Terry's sunglasses reflected Luc behind the steering wheel.

"So you're one of those guys," she said.

"I'm my guy. Always been a rebel for *yes*."

"I read Camus, too," she said.

"As a pre-med major?"

"A doctor needs to grasp the big picture."

"Are you getting a grasp on Vernon?"

"Ask me another time."

The car rolled toward the low-hanging sun.

They showed her the giant sand and gravel mesa on the west edge of town. The triangle row of mixed blacktop waiting its turn to make a road to somewhere.

"Just looking at all that work waiting to happen makes me thirsty," said Luc. "How about we go all *high school* and get Cokes at the Tastee Freeze?"

In five minutes they were the third car in the line looping past the server window of that whitewashed square box of the ice cream parlor's successor.

Mission Accomplished, thought Luc, mimicking a TV show as his left hand steered the blue car out of the service line.

His right hand held a large plastic cup of fountain Coke:

One shiny quarter, twenty-five cents. With a free plastic straw.

Everyone paid for their own.

Luc chose the left-hand turn out of the service lane and toward the two-lane blacktop highway running on an east-west line. Railroad tracks ran parallel to and on the other side of the highway. Parked sidetracked boxcars name-branded stars of American commerce: *The Santa Fe. The Great Northern.*

Luc swung the blue car onto the highway toward the setting sun: "Detour."

He steered his blue car onto the just-out-of-town ramp for the interstate highway north.

The open window warm breeze of Terry's ride floated her midnight hair.

Dennis's smile hid his trusting wonder of where they were going.

Luc exited for the town's black pavement runway airport where a single engine plane was tethered. The hangar doors were closed. So was the office.

He circled past the airport.

Took the two-lane blacktop highway toward the town just over the hill.

Stopped on a graveled pull-off above the drive-in movie theater.

"I used to janitor this place," said Luc. "When I was young."

"What are you now?" said Terry.

Dennis sword thrust his words between the two pair of sunglasses locked on each other: "Whatever we are, we're not *kids*."

They stared down at the drive-in's brick concession stand. The graveled waves of parking spots beside concrete poles cabled with speakers. The sixty-foot-tall white screen where a golden eagle once nested.

The radio played The Beatles singing "Let It Be."

"*Wow,*" whispered Terry.

Her right hand shook the plastic cup of icy-still, half-drunk Coke.

A sly grin came over her face as the Beatles sang.

She shifted in the shotgun seat so Luc and Dennis could better see her.

Terry stuck her lidded Coke's plastic straw up her right nostril.

Her left forefinger pinched her left nostril.

And she sniffed.

Bubbles whispered in her Coke.

Terry jerked back with a laugh and a choke.

Luc said: "*Ah* . . . Are you OK?"

"Why'd you do that?" said Dennis.

She whipped the sunglasses off her incredulous blue eyes.

"The Beatles!" she said. "Their first movie made when Luc and I were in what: freshman year of high school?"

"*A Hard Day's Night,*" said Luc who'd had to get his come-from-Chicago-university sister Laura to drive him ninety minutes down to Great Falls to see that black and white, rock 'n' roll movie because *no* it was never coming to the Roxy.

"Yes!" said Terry. "Don't you remember? The scene where one of them snorts from an open bottle of Coke. Both nostrils. A couple times.

"I think it was John Lennon." Terry named the Beatle gunned down by a psycho assassin on a New York sidewalk ten years after that 1970 car ride.

"Snorting Coke," said Luc. "I never got that joke."

"It wasn't *Coke* coke he's miming snorting," big city Terry told her new small-town friends. "It was cocaine. The drug. The narcotic."

"I've never heard of it," said Luc in 1970.

Dennis nodded in agreement.

"It's a white powder coming up right behind LSD and marijuana now," she said. "Rock stars. People who remember our parents' Charlie Chaplin black and white silent movie when he's stuck in a shaker of salt that was really cocaine. The hip crowd in Greenwich Village. Hollywood. San Francisco."

She shrugged.

"I had one of those *mumble mumble* professors. Lectured us *wanna be* docs about street drugs. Said cocaine was legal once. Marijuana, too. Heroin is a lie that enslaves and kills your patients. LSD can fuck up their brains big-time. But he mumbled about those two movies like he knew more than he should. Mumbled he was pretty sure cocaine that gets smuggled across the Mexican border was going to be legal someday soon. Marijuana, too. Said we had to figure out how to treat all that and other dangerous intoxicants like tobacco and booze."

"*Wait!*" said Luc. "Smuggled up from . . . The movie *Easy Rider!*"

His companions nodded *seen it.*

"Two 'heroes' from our generation smuggle white powder up from Mexico. The limousine gangster outside an airport as planes roar over sniffs it and pays them. I've always thought they were heroin smugglers! And that made no sense! Made them despicable villains, not rebel bikers who end up murdered just because they aren't like everybody else. But if it's cocaine they're smuggling—"

"—then they're doing what some savvy people think is OK," said Dennis.

"*Wow,*" said Luc as cars turned off the highway to crunch down the gravel driveway to the drive-in's cashier's booth. "The mistakes you make about the things you think you know."

"Yeah," said Terry. "*Wow.* And I've never even tried marijuana."

Luc and Dennis froze as they sat in this June's idling car.

Carefully avoided looking into the rearview mirror that held their images. Luc drove the car back into town.

They drove the backroads. Followed the highway east of town to the fairgrounds by the giant gray grain elevators.

Tumbleweeds bounced on the packed sand of the fairgrounds' midway. Only the wind filled the giant white bleachers overlooking the horse track and empty animal pans and stage for musical acts.

Next month this complex of peeling paint shacks and creaky red barns would host the Four County Grady River Fair & Rodeo.

Now . . . Only the wind.

The blue car left the fairgrounds to turn east on the highway and head further out of town, up over the rim. Pulled into two highway rest stops for Terry to read historic marker signs:

"The Oily Boid Gets the Worm" celebrating the gushers from oil wells drilled all through this Hi-Line area since the 1920s.

"The Marias River Massacre" exactly one hundred years before when US Cavalry troops slaughtered two hundred Blackfeet Indians.

Luc turned his headlights on as the three friends drove back toward the sinking sun and the town that sheltered them now in 1970.

Corner streetlights winked on as Luc swung a U-turn in front of the hospital's front door. Parked in front of Dennis's motorcycle.

"*Phew,*" sighed Terry.

Shook her mostly empty Coke cup.

Her right hand lifted her straw for all to see in the streetlights' glow.

"Another movie," she said.

Her voice deepened to a respectable businessman giving sage career advice to a college graduate like they all would be soon: "*I've got one word for you.*"

"*Plastics,*" quoted Luc from *The Graduate.*

"What kind of future is that?" mumbled Dennis who'd seen the movie, too.

"Guess we'll see." Terry put her borrowed sunglasses in the jockey box.

Gave her two new friends a grin.

"This has been fun, guys. Let's do it some more."

Luc said: "I've got a . . . like a family thing this weekend."

Don't call that a lie.

"It's Earth Day," whispered Nick as thousands of people marched in the street below the window. "The first one ever all around the globe. You didn't know that?"

"I've been busy living what I got."

"Look out there. Look at that crowd. It's bigger than the Moratorium march against the Vietnam war last October. Marched over the same bridge. And that was huge! Yeah, mostly university students. Our generation. Fraternity guys who marched wore coats and ties to show the world we aren't all stoned-out hippies or communists. I wore my red hoody I'll recycle to the road crew.

And sunglasses! For the first time I had real sunglasses because I got contacts that—

"And I don't matter!" he said. "That Moratorium march was about getting us out of the Vietnam war. Albert Camus, he—"

"I know Camus," said the woman who'd dyed her hair blonde. Nick told her anyway:

"'A true rebel says yes, not no,' said Camus. That's what's going on out there. What went on with the Moratorium. People saying yes to better tomorrows for the whole damn planet."

The blonde with the gun shook her head: "You poor fools."

THE BUS

Norma stepped off the bus.

Made it, she told herself at 9:57 that Saturday morning.

Shook her head: *Of course there's no bus all the way to him.*

Her brown eyes scanned the sparse crowd in the Great Falls bus depot.

"Earth Day," said the blonde with the gun.

She shook her head with a sad crimson smile.

"You with your marijuana. Shaughnessy with his cash.

Those marchers down below with their banners about forests.

Don't you get it, cowboy? Earth Day is all about the green."

She looked Nick up.

She looked him down.

"Step wide and step away from the window," she told him.

"Go over to that rickety table. Open the drawer."

The crowd rumbled closer to the street below the open window.

Nick wondered if their noise would drown out a gunshot.

He stared down at What He Saw In The Opened Drawer.

Stared back at the blonde with the gun by the open window.

She raised the .45 to point it at his heart.

Clicked back the killing hammer.

Off-the-bus Norma wore her brown dress that primly ended at her knees and matched her eyes. A perfect meet-the-parents outfit.

Her shoulder-chained black purse carried lip gloss. Her contacts case. A wallet with cash from her summer job at her dad's hardware store. Her driver's license. That month's birth control pills pack hid in an interior pocket.

The exploding spermicide tube.

She shuddered with the memory.

Saw *him* standing there.

Bright happy smiles pulled them together for a kiss.

"I'll grab your bag," said Luc.

She swung the canvas bag looped to her shoulder: "I got it right here."

"We've got ninety-one miles to cover in two hours," he told her. "My mother insists on making lunch for us and they eat at high noon."

He grabbed the canvas bag. They ran toward his car.

Not the backseat for her bag BECAUSE! The trunk!

He slammed the trunk lid closed.

Checked his watch: 10:07.

He'd matched the time it showed with Ma Bell's Time of Day phone number he'd called that morning. Plus he'd wound his watch, his right forefinger and thumb spinning the SET knob on the watch.

He had 117 minutes to walk Norma into his house and his mom and dad's judgmental gaze.

Norma claimed the front seat beside Luc as he jumped behind the wheel.

He pulled her close. Their lips knew. His left hand slid up her smooth just-shaved legs. *No pantyhose—Yes!* Pushed her dress higher until that sheath closed her thighs with its tightness. His hungry hand cupped her breast.

Norma broke their kiss: "Don't we have to beat the clock there?"

Luc's blue car rocketed away from the big city bus station. Sped to the four-lane interstate highway ruled by Montana's legendary "no daylight speed limit."

Luc drove *pedal to the metal.*

Norma sat beside him.

The windshield they faced rivered speeding past prairie and checkerboard farm plots and barbwire-fenced brown and black cows.

The car radio played the rock 'n' roll station of the big city they'd just fled.

Songs about winners and losers and locked-outs like me, thought Norma. *He knows songs. I have to learn more songs. But now I'm with him. I am.*

The blue car trembled as Luc pushed it to its limits.

"Wish I lived in Shelby," he mumbled.

Norma frowned: "Why?"

"It's closer."

The radio announced it was 10:47.

The highway sign read: VERNON—59 MILES

Norma said: "We've got plenty of time."

"*Um . . .*"

She waited.

Waiting was what she knew how to do.

What she'd been doing since their white jeans date when the touch of his hand, his scent, his wild mind, his wanting her rocketed her to *love him*.

Waiting for him to say it, too. Come be with her all the way.

Luc glanced at her.

"I'm thinking . . . We've got time. We could pull off on this gravel road. A grove of scruffy trees. We could . . ."

He smiled as she watched: "We could try out your new pills."

"You've been thinking about this all along, haven't you?" she said.

"Haven't you?"

Norma's lips smiled.

His foot pushed the gas pedal toward the floor.

There!

He turned onto the dusty road toward his Vernon city crew's gravel grotto.

Roared his blue car to a stop in the grove of trees. Turned the car off: *Can't risk letting the battery die by playing the radio and strand us out here.*

"Backseat!" Luc whispered after a deep kiss.

He whirled out the driver's door. Leapt into the backseat where Dennis had ridden yesterday but today, today was *today* was *NOW!*

Norma slid out of the shotgun seat. Jerked open the backseat door. Pulled it closed behind her as she crawled into the open arms of Luc who'd already tossed off his polo shirt.

Kissing Fumbling Touching . . .

Norma scootches off her respectable white panties. Tosses them over to the front seat. Luc pulls off his blue jeans. Unzips her dress. Pulls it off her shoulders. Helps pull her arms up 'n' free of her bra. *Who cares where it falls.* She's in his arms. He's holding her breasts, kissing them *there . . . there* Oh!

"Hurry!" she whispers. "We can't be late for your parents."

Flat on her back on the car seat as they wiggle and figure out how to lay him between her thighs 'n' she reaches down to guide *OH!*

If the radio'd been on, they'd've finished in one song.

She'd sighed. Moaned. Wondered *when/if.* Never let out an *I love you.*

But he knew she did. And knew she fevered his heart.

They scrambled back into their clothes.

Norma leapt out of the car.

Her tan hair flowed back into place touching her shoulders.

She closed her eyes.

Smelled golden prairie she could not see. Felt the wind on her bare arms.

Opened her eyes.

The blue big sky lined a horizon far, far away.

This is where he comes from.

The breeze swirled a whiff of her sweat and *maybe.*

Norma jerked a tissue from inside her purse.

Used it to rub away the wetness *down there.*

Hoped she'd rubbed away the scent of the crime.

Let the wind bounce that white tissue away across the golden prairie.

Jumped into the car. Leaned against Luc as he drove the gravel road to highway to bridge over the Grady River highway to Vernon.

Luc drove the opposite direction on the Main Street drag than he'd piloted the evening before with . . . with other passengers in his car. Took a right turn on a route to his house that didn't drive past the hospital across the street.

Shit! The family's white '64 Chevy Impala filled the driveway alongside the east side of the house. *Dad's home early from work for lunch because.*

Luc turned his blue Dodge into the narrow concrete walled driveway.

Parked on its upward slope behind the white car—

—and *almost* out of view of the hospital's front doors.

Norma and he had to squeeze between car and concrete walls. He got her bag. Slammed the trunk. No one stood at the hospital doors to hear that *clunk.*

Luc led Norma up the front stairs. Past the two blue spruce trees. Up the front porch visible from the hospital sidewalk. Threw open the front door and led "his girlfriend" into his childhood home as the town's high noon whistle blew.

Mom paced in the kitchen.

Dad sat at the kitchen table.

White bread tuna fish sandwiches waited in front of the table's chairs.

Dad stood. Offered his hand to Norma: "Right on time."

"'Bout time," said Mom. But she grinned. Gave Norma the Connor family classic pat on her shoulder. Smiled: "Come on in, kid."

They all sat down around the kitchen table.

The kitchen radio played KRIP's blend of acceptable pop and country and western music that filled the gaps between the by-the-numbers conversation.

Norma did great.

Answered questions. Her dad's hardware store. Her little brother and sister. Life in Helena, the state capital where she'd lived her whole life. Labeled herself as an English major. No thank you, one glass of milk is plenty. These homemade chocolate chip cookies taste amazing.

Asked questions. Got invited to visit Dad at the trucking company that afternoon. Luc silently vowed *not* to let her see the bare bulb lit corner where the calendar showed naked against a red curtained Marilyn Monroe.

Now I know about real sex! thought Luc.

Well, I know something. Want to know more. Do more. Everything.

"Norma, swing up to the library," said assistant librarian Mom who worked that Saturday afternoon's shift. "Luc spent damn near his whole life from reading books from up there."

"Plus staring at the screen in the Roxy on Main Street," added Dad.

"And don't get us started on him and his sister Laura buying records," said Mom. "Or him sitting there in his bedroom thinking on my time."

Dad said: "You kids going to go to a movie tonight?"

Norma glanced at Luc sitting beside her at this table.

"We don't know yet," said Luc. "She knows Emil. We might meet up with him up at Seba's house."

The queen of Luc's home said: "*Ah.* Be good for her to meet Teresa."

Mom told Norma to come downstairs to Luc's 'star' sister's pink bedroom.

"Actually," said Mom as she clunked Norma down the twelve stairs to the basement, "besides family, it's only ever been you staying down here."

Dad called out his farewells.

"*Wait!*" said Luc. "I gotta move my car."

He felt his father's puzzled eyes on his back. Pulled his blue Dodge out of the driveway. Let it idle across the street with him behind the steering wheel. The rearview mirror captured the hospital's reflection. Dad took his time to fire up the white family Chevy. Back down the driveway. Luc was parked out of sight up there before Dad had even turned the corner at the end of the block.

Mom was demonstrating to the college girl the mandatory steps of *how to wash the dishes* when Luc came in through the back door.

Mom walked out the front door to the library at fifteen minutes to 1:00.

The weight fell off Norma's shoulders.

She stared at *why* she came here: "How'd I do?"

"Great!" said Luc.

KRIP radio played the parents' generation's Jersey boy Frank Sinatra.

"Now what?" said Norma.

Luc took her hand.

Led her into his blue-walled bedroom where his boyhood cowboy drapes hung over the two windows—one north, one west.

His mother *as always* had made his bed with tight precision.

Norma stood holding his hand. Stared down at the taut bedspread.

Luc whispered: "All I got to do is lock the outside doors."

"Really," said Norma with an inflection Luc couldn't label.

"This's been my dream for years. Doing it here. In the bed I grew up in."

She looked at him.

He added: "Doing it here with *you*. Another first for *us*."

Her slicked pink lips softly smiled.

"OK," she said. "But afterwards, I've got to take a shower or everyone we meet will smell.

"You, too," she added.

He whirled to lock the doors.

"*Wait!*" yelled Norma.

He froze.

"Get the bath towel on my shower rack downstairs. Spread it out where we'll . . . Under us where . . . So we don't leave any stains on your bed."

He ran through the house doing *musts*.

Back into his bedroom. Handed her the towel from the shower rack.

She'd turned down his bedspread and blanket. His white sheets glowed stripes of shadows from the sunlight through his venetian blinds. She flipped the towel open like a picnic blanket atop the bottom sheet.

They hurried. Finished.

Caught their breath naked side by side in Luc's bed of dreams.

Then—

—like two carefree lovers in a new wave French movie—

—she chased him, laughing with him as they raced naked through his parents' house down to "her" pink bedroom with its shower they shared. Touches and soap. The rain they chose.

They shared that towel to dry off. Stood naked in front of each other.

If she noticed his re-enhanced interest in her, she chose to say nothing.

If she didn't notice, he didn't want to pressure her.

She dressed in *those* white jeans and a summer top:

"Your parents will get that me wearing that dress was for them and now the everyday clothes are for everyone else."

They hurried upstairs. Re-made his bed.

Norma walked behind Luc through the gray carpeted living room to—

"SHIT!" yelled Norma.

Luc whirled in the kitchen doorway.

Norma stood locked in place. Her right hand cupped her right eye.

"My contact lens just popped out!" she yelled.

"Are you sure? Let me check your—"

"No! Stay there! If it's on the floor, if you step on it . . ."

Her good left eye scanned her clothes. The gray carpet stretching out before her. She shook her head.

Luc crawled around her. Found nothing on the gray carpet. Checked her right eye. Confirmed that her contact had fled.

"How?" he said.

"I don't know how! Stuff like that is always just waiting to happen.

"Didn't bring my glasses," she muttered. "Hell, I never wear them."

Luc said: "Buddy Holly tried contacts, but he couldn't work his guitar pick."

Her stone face told him to stick to the crisis of *now*, not ride wild horses back to the life and times of a rock star icon who died in a snowy plane crash back in 1959.

But . . . But maybe he was trying to distract me. Cheer me up.

She asked to use the family's phone.

Called Directory Assistance. Got the number and called her hometown optometrist. Ordered a new lens. Called her parents. Apologized for the cost. Hung up. Asked Luc if she could pay for the calls. His answer swept her up into his hug of *No*, of *It's OK*.

"Sorry," she said for the dozenth time.

Make a joke of it: "Guess I'm only gonna see half of what's going on."

"That's more than a lot of people ever see."

"We better go," she said. "Your parents . . . They're waiting."

He led her out the back door to the blue Dodge in the driveway. Backed out and took a long circular route so they only drove past the back end of the hospital.

Parked at the county library a block away.

She said squinting let her see OK with her one equipped eye as they walked through the library's glass doors.

His mom offered to take time off from work. Run home. Vacuum the living room. Dump the bag onto newspapers to pick through what got sucked up.

"No, please," said Norma. "Gone is gone."

Luc led her through the aisles he'd roamed to get to her. The science fiction shelves. The nook for "mysteries." Showed her the Dashiell Hammett anthology that led him to discover Montana's history of corruption and political murders.

As Luc turned to lead them out the door, he glimpsed the head librarian give his mother a nod of approval.

Ten minutes later he stood beside Norma in the cargo bay doors of the trucking company as his father pointed at vehicles and trailers waiting in there.

Luc listened.

But his gaze secretly focused on the glow of a lone bulb in the darkness:

Marilyn

"Now it's just us," he told Norma when they slid back into the blue car.

Grinned as he keyed the car to life.

Felt himself driving the same tour of his life and town he'd given yesterday evening to . . . to someone else. The Big Pink. The city crew shop. The whorehouse.

She shook her head as they drove past that rouge stucco box: "In Helena, we've got Big Dorothy's right on our Main Street called Last Chance Gulch. A quick drive from the state capitol building. You wonder how all that works. How the money flows."

He said nothing about his uncle Johnny.

Drove past the dark windows of Doc Nirmberg's hollowed-out Main Street lair. Said nothing: *Why bring up the scare they'd won?*

Drove east of town to show her the fairgrounds. The highway's tourist stop signs for oil field riches and massacre of innocent citizens.

Checked his watch: 4:16.

Time for a Tastee Freeze Coke and then home for the big dinner his mother told them she'd planned with the precision of the Ross family's rigid schedule.

His parents were home by 5:15. Dinner was on the table at precisely 6:00. Luc was standing beside the kitchen sink with a white dish towel in his hand at 6:29 waiting to dry the last of the dishes Mom was washing while her son's squinting girlfriend watched.

"*Knock-knock!*" yelled Aunt Dory as she led Aunt Iona into their sister's house where they knew her husband had gone back to work at the trucking company, same as every night.

His aunts scanned Norma.

Kept their poker face smiles until she told them the *whys* of her squint.

"Ah hell, kid," said Aunt Iona. "Shit happens."

"Ain't that the truth," said Aunt Dory.

Their sister Cora wrang out the dishrag in the kitchen sink.

"Come on, Cora," said Dory. "These two got better things to do than hang around with us old farts. Besides, Gramma Meg's falling asleep earlier now days."

Luc said: "She's worried about Aunt Beryl's lung surgery."

"Beryl's working her one lung just fine," said Dory.

"I think Gramma Meg's eagle-eying Beryl's thing to avoid thinking about her own clock," said Luc's mom Cora.

"*Naw*," said Iona. "She brags about how tough she is from polio and the strokes. Joked 'bout how she'd let the janitor climb on top of her 'n' get a cheap thrill."

Oh-oh. Dory saw the frozen face of her nephew's girlfriend.

"Go on now, you two," ordered Dory. "Get out while the getting's good."

Luc drove the blue car past the hospital and into Saturday evening's sun.

"Where are we going now?" said Norma.

The car's AM radio crackled "KOMA's fifty thousand watts all the way from Oklahoma City!"

The DJ spun some song on his turntable that she knew Luc would know.

Luc walked her from the blue car through an open garage on the side of a Knob Hill house.

In without knocking on the kitchen's side door.

Emil! I know him. Luc's ex-roommate. That other guy must be Seba.

"Well hey there, kid. I'm Teresa. You hungry? Here, have a breadstick."

Adult Teresa jabbed a breadstick straight at the white-jeaned college girl—

—who had only one fully functional eye.

Norma lunged for the breadstick.

Missed—

—plopped her hand on the old lady's left breast.

Emil and Seba jaw-dropped staring.

Luc paralyzed in his sneakers.

Gray-haired Teresa focused dead-ahead at Norma:

"Hell, kid," said Teresa to the stranger whose horror-stunned hand seemed glued to her breast. "Those jugs dried up a long time ago. Stick to the breadstick."

Luc machinegunned the story of the fugitive contact lens.

"So Norma's kind of like . . . double vision."

A chorus of *Ohs* drowned out radio lyrics about how a hard-working coal miner owed his soul to the company store.

Teresa swept Norma and Luc to the kitchen table with Seba and Emil.

Luc sat beside Norma.

Grinned. Passed a bowl on the table closer to her: "Have a breadstick."

Within the sound of her chewing, softly beneath the radio's song and ten feet away, Teresa clattering around in the open kitchen, Norma heard:

Luc casually ask Emil: "So?"

"Gonna go down to Missoula next weekend. Look for next year's apartment. See my big sister. The guy she's dating."

"Same guy I'm thinking about?" said Luc.

Emil's nod was slow and strong.

"You know," said Luc.

Emil nodded.

The volume of the three college men sitting at this kitchen table rose as they back 'n' forthed stories while Teresa scrubbed a black iron pan in the sink.

Luc touched Norma to stand. Led her back the way they came.

She thanked Teresa. Apologized again. Complimented the breadsticks.

"You want to take some with you? No? OK, but you come back anytime, kid. You don't need troublemaker Luc here to walk you in."

Wasn't even eight o'clock yet when the blue car drove away from Teresa's.

Norma blurted: "I'm sorry if I—"

"You did everything right," interrupted Luc behind the steering wheel and shoulder to shoulder with her. "And hell, we all got a good laugh."

Norma's monotone answer as she stared straight ahead: *"Yeah."*

They drove down Knob Hill where Luc didn't spot Steve outside his house.

"Not much left to see in this town," said Luc as the street they drove put them at the red STOP sign where Main Street's "back street" became the two-lane state highway that followed the path of the sun.

He turned left.

The same route he'd driven all week hauling gravel.

Only now Norma rode beside him. White jeans. Tan hair blowing in the breeze of the open windows. Face staring out the windshield with no questions.

As their radio played rock 'n' roll in that Saturday's sinking sun.

The windshield filled with the highway rolling toward the hill to the river.

Luc spun a right hand turn off that road.

Rumbled onto a well-cared for gravel road.

The gravel road circled around to the other side of a chain-link fenced field with concrete humps that blocked the highway's view of the parked blue car.

Sunset pinked the windshield glass filled with the sawtooth blue horizon Rocky Mountains sixty miles away beyond rolling gold prairie.

Norma stared in the car's rearview mirror.

The chain-link fence. Tall metal light poles. Concrete with locked doors.

"That's a missile site," she said.

"The end of the world." Luc shrugged. "Got to live for today."

Norma looked this way and that. Couldn't see the highway beyond the missile silo. Thus knew the highway couldn't see them. See her. Right? *Right?*

She stared into the face of the man who brought her here.

"I love you," she whispered.

"And I'm right here with you."

Truth, that's precise truth! rose through Luc as they surged into their kiss.

A pile on the front seat. Her white jeans. His blue jeans. A blouse. A polo shirt. Polite underwear. The car's engine purred so the radio'd stay on and *Oh!* The backseat. Naked her. Naked him.

His sitting spine pushes against the backseat. Her naked back bends to face him as she straddles him like she read in a book. Reaches back and down behind her. Fills his eyes as she *oh yes there* she guides, as she captures his hardness. She grabs the ridge of the front seat. He reaches around. Caresses her breast.

Norma flips her long tan haired head up.

Her wide-open, double-vision brown eyes fill with the setting sun.

There:

Hanging down over the windshield.

The rearview mirror captures crimson *reflections*.

Norma sees her own panting face.

Behind her, Luc's eyes-on-her-bare-ass ecstasy she pushes onto him.

Down onto on top of him. Getting—*taking* that choice.

Reflections capture the scene out the back window behind Luc.

Watch lights snap on atop the chain-link cage around The End.

Reflections show she's *yes* not alone in that darkening night.

With him, he's with her 'n' he's *oh so him*. Right behind her. Deep in our togetherness. Don't worry! Don't worry! He's following her *toward* as she bounces her ass and dreams on him. He's thrusting into *us* and *yes* she first time ever *oh Oh AHH!*

The burgled apartment's opened drawer held two things:
- A cheap cigarette lighter from a gas station.
- A marijuana cigarette. Call it a reefer. A joint.

"Toke up, cowboy," said the dyed blonde with the cocked pistol.

Nick blinked.

"You think if I get stoned, you can control me better."

"Let's say you're going to get what you came for."

He had to laugh: "It's just one joint."

The gun in her hand weaved from side to side.

The dyed blonde said: "Fire it up."

Nick obeyed.

Sucked in a long stream of smoke. Held it. Whoosed it out.

The gun weaved.

He took a second hit. Then a third.

Told her: "If this is good shit, I'm at my line."

He held the smoking joint out to her.

She cocked her head.

"What's mine is yours," he said.

"That's not either of ours," she answered. "It's the only dope in here. No money either. Not even a dime for a payphone."

Her ruby lips curved a smile.

"Put the joint on the windowsill."

Nick did.

Watched its trail of smoke flow in the air above the street now full of protestors putting their feet on the street for a better, safer, survivable world.

He stepped back to his side of the window.

She stepped to hers.

Kept the cocked gun zeroed on him in her steady right hand.

Her left hand picked the joint. Painted its white roll-your-own cigarette paper with her lips' color of blood. She inhaled the smoke. Held it with strong lungs. Let that long slow cloud slide out from between her ruby lips.

Flicked the joint out of the window to crowd below.

Uncocked the .45.

Let it dangle down by her thighs for a lightning snap-up.

Told Nick amidst the shouts and murmurs from the street below:

"Now listen up."

DEAD LETTERS

The blonde woman with the gun standing on the other side of that Wednesday afternoon's open window to Hope's Passing Parade shook her head at Nick:

"This march. Your dope stash. Shaughnessy. It's all about the green."

His stoned eyes whirlpooled her as he said: "Not for you."

She shook as she stood in a time and place that wasn't hers.

"Why . . . Why would you . . . What makes you think that?"

"I didn't think. I felt. And now you told me I was right."

She calmed herself.

Waved away what he'd said like it didn't matter:

"This life we got now. This world. It's all about the green. The moolah. The money. Not the trees. Not illegal grass dreams—or hell, any dreams.

"Right now, the green is shifting all over big buildings in big places. The green will build up phony organizations with righteous-sounding names about the planet. They'll always have a 'common sense' solution or paid-for phony science backing up their 'fuck yous' to the good people marching out there. Greenbacks are sliding into congressional election pockets to the limits of the law. Thank God we at least got the pretense of that limit and letting the public see.

"Money is flowing into law firms and lobby shops in Washington so they can let the big boys dodge the gutted-out laws they already got paid to get written.

"All those lawyers and lobbyists. They know the green they're stuffing into their pockets comes from them helping bad guys.

"Polluters. The who-gives-a-shit about earth, we rich can build and seal ourselves in domes to beat the sky while all of 'yous' bake or freeze outside. Those lawyers and lobbyists tell themselves they're successes. Well respected. Good people. Family people. Love their kids. Their cute dog. Give to all the approved 'n' virtuous charities. Think they're just doing their job. Just following orders."

"Like guards at concentration camps!" said Nick.

"And a bunch of those people our age marching down there in the street are going to career themselves into just like them and pretend and lie to themselves and for the assholes they're marching against today.

"You gotta look for the green," said the blonde. "Focus in on it. Like zen."

"Like breaking boards in karate."

She pulled back: "Karate. Good to know."

Shit, shit, shit! thought Nick. Keep your shit together!

"But this," he told the blonde with the gun. "You. Shaughnessy. And now me who took a risk and's trying not to lose. This isn't about any green for you. So why are you standing there by the window with a gun in your hand?"

L uc sat in the scruffy gold chair delegated to his bedroom.
Saturday afternoon sunlight filled his two windows open for the mowed grass heat of June.

Been six days since Norma rode a bus back to where she came from.

And here I sit. Spiral notebook on my lap. Pen in my right hand. The radio playing songs from people who know what to say.

She knows you're a writer. Knows you love to send letters. Postcards. She can see the mailbox from her family's front picture window.

What can I tell her in a letter?

How I promised Mike Jodrey's grave?

That's between me, Mike, the Universe and Our "Real World" where KRIP radio today said the number of Americans like Mike KIA'd in Vietnam now stands at nearly 44,000.

How I rode the chipper box on the rear end of a truck backing over a hot oil slicked street frantically shoveling out gravel/sand?

I could tell her that. Or half the reasons for Cal the Bull's nickname.

How Gramma Meg broke down crying about dying for two hours?

Who isn't crying about dying?

But talking about that isn't for a "girlfriend" letter.

Don't even think about what that label means!

How—

No.

NO.

Last Tuesday evening. Second day after Norma was gone.

Luc strode through the hospital's front doors.

Smiled at the front desk nurse who tossed back a *not foolin' me* smile.

He pushed the button for the elevator:

Ding! Those silver doors released him out to the second floor.

No one stood watch inside the second-floor wraparound counter desk.

The corridor of hospital rooms telescoped like a mine shaft.

The sinking sun lit the window at the far end of the shaft.

He walked pine-scented disinfectant gray tiles toward that sunset.

Luc stopped at a half-open door.

You're there. Here. Where you wanna, where you gotta be.

'Hospital quiet' he knocked on the door . . .

. . . that swung all the way open.

Terry. Midnight hair. Piercing blue eyes. Quizzical smile.

"I didn't expect to see you here," she said.

"Guess I'm just one of those things who happens."

"Then I guess you better come in."

She waved him in as she stepped aside.

A blank gray-walled room with a street wall of windows.

A single bed, rails lowered. Dresser drawers. Suitcases in the closet beneath hangered clothes. A white medical jacket on the closet door. Textbooks on a table. A lone chair. One corner held a battered guitar case.

Luc said: "I like what you've done with the place."

Laughed with her.

"Maybe they could lend you couple paintings to hang on the wall," said Luc. "Classic Vernon art. Paintings of cows. Cowboys. Indians getting chased. Riding proud. The Rocky Mountains where the snow on top never melts."

He frowned: "What does your Ohio look like?"

"Steel mills. Tall buildings. Rivers. People busting their asses working."

"I can picture that. Them."

"My folks earned enough to live on the dirty river's good side of town."

"Glad you got lucky."

"Me too or I wouldn't have gotten here."

"Luck got us all get here."

"Plus hard work," she said.

"And choosing."

Her window was open over the street where Luc lived.

The wind blew. A meadowlark chirped. Some engine died.

"I've got an idea," said Luc.

"I bet you always do."

Heard himself say it out loud:

"Can't help it. I want to be—I am a writer. Can't stop swirls of ideas. Images. It's like one of my uncle's needing to chase whiskey. Or. . ."

Or Marilyn Monroe naked against a red velvet curtain.

OH MY GOD: DON'T SAY ANYTHING ABOUT ANYTHING LIKE THAT!

Blew away that image by saying: "My sister."

Terry's thick and wide lips frowned at the change of subject.

"Laura. She lives in Chicago. We went back to visit her couple years back. My first big city."

"*Wow.*" But a *wow* without condescension.

"We all start somewhere," said Luc. "Anyway, she took us to the museum. I fell in—"

Don't say that "L" word!

"There was one painting by a guy named Edward Hopper. A night scene looking into a diner. A couple men and a red-dressed woman sit at the counter. Watch the white uniformed counterman work. It grabbed me. Real people as art. I bought a poster the size of a pillow."

They both flicked their gaze to her bed.

"You could borrow it. Tape it up on one of these blank gray walls. Might remind you of your big city life. Home."

"A painting of loneliness and night? I've seen pictures of that painting. And I've seen those nights."

Luc blurted: "Or we'll find something. . . cheerier."

"*Yes! Please!* But I want something else, too: Show me what you write."

Man's voice in the hall! "Me, too."

DENNIS!

"Hi!" said Terry.

Grinned as she waved Dennis into her room with her and Luc.

Who realized: *The engine I heard parking outside her open window.*

Dennis tore his eyes off his friend Luc who he hadn't expected.

Dennis smiled at who he'd come to see.

"I figured I'd check in on you in case you need anything," he told Terry.

"Good to know you guys are watching out for me," said Terry.

The two local souls shrugged together.

Shared a smile that said *oh so much.*

Luc said: "We're just—"

"*What's going on in here?*" snapped an adult woman's voice.

A white-uniformed nurse glared in from the hall.

"Never mind," she snapped. "I don't want to know what I don't gotta know.

"'N' right now, *Terry*: Grab whatever you need. We got an ambulance coming in from a car wreck between here and Shelby 'cause we're closer."

Terry snatched her white jacket off the closet door handle. Scooped her stethoscope off the textbooks' table. Flashed a smile at the two young men.

"Sorry, guys!"

Then she was gone.

Luc and Dennis stood there.

Oh so *not* staring at each other.

Luc shrugged: "She seems OK."

"Sure. Yes. She's fine."

The wail of an ambulance siren came closer through her open window.

No one sat behind the nurses' desk to watch them leave.

Their smudge reflections stared back at them from the closed silver doors of the elevator crawling them back down to the first floor.

A silent trip.

DING!

The elevator doors slid open.

Somehow they walked out of that box shoulder to shoulder.

Strode past the reception desk to the double glass doors to the world.

Luc stepped aside.

Dennis's face twitched as he walked outside first.

Luc walked Dennis to his parked black motorcycle.

"So . . ." Luc smiled. Shrugged. Said: "See you tomorrow."

Didn't look back as he walked across the street to his family home.

And now it's Saturday, thought Luc.

With me sitting in my bedroom. Pen and notebook and nothing to say to Norma who's supposed to be my girlfriend and What She'd Said.

It's logical, *hell*: She probably expects I'd be penning her letters.

But you've gotta tell the truth. If you want to wrap your arms around something true, you gotta tell the truth.

And truth isn't just what you say. Truth is also in what you don't say.

Luc stared at the virgin blue-lined white page in his notebook.

Oh by the way, Norma, there's this summertime girl my age named Terry who lives across the street from me and who I'm . . . who's . . .

He closed the notebook.

Knew he'd never open it to write Norma letters that summer of 1970.

Wish I knew what to say, thought Luc. *Wish I knew what to do.*

The blonde with the gun stared at Nick's stoned face.

"I don't give a shit about Shaughnessy. Or his green of any kind—'cept now for what he owes you, 'n' that's 'cause I'm too soft for my own good. I never met the dude, but he left his student ID on the wooden crate he uses as a bedside table.

"And I found a Polaroid color photo in his dirty laundry pile. Him naked from the waist up. Spoofing for the camera. Electric hair but not so long as to piss off cops. Looks like he escaped from the insane asylum. Gotta be at least six feet plus what, five inches? Going from lanky to chunky. Being stoned all the time leads to way too much chocolate ice cream."

Chocolate ice cream tantalized Nick's tongue.

He felt the swirl of now. The marching charging crowd below the open window. The woman who Camus said 'yes' to dying herself blonde. Ruby lips. A gun in her hand and her eyes trapping him with their equal bores.

"Then if it's not about Shaughnessy and it's not you all zen about the greens of him, a guy you've never met and don't know, why bust in and set up an ambush in his apartment with your gun?"

"It's not about him. Or now even you."

"Yes it is," knifed Nick.

She ignored what he said.

Raised the pistol in her hand.

But passed aiming at him. Pointed its bore toward heaven.

"It's about the two guys he's meeting today. They're going to kill him."

PARADES & PROPOSITIONS

Marching, charging feet clomped past the window in the street below the dyed blonde with the gun.

"Shaughnessy's meeting with two guys today and they're going to kill him?" said Nick.

Don't want to know! trembled Nick. But he had to ask.

"How do you know?"

She wouldn't look at him.

"Are you trying to save one of them from doing what will scar his life forever? Like a brother or. . . or a boyfriend you. . . love?"

The cold, flat sound she made sounded like "Hah!"

Her blue steel eyes locked onto his.

"You're going to kill them," whispered Nick. "Why?"

"Because of that movie."

Here's the question," said Luc's dad as he faced his wife and son standing in the living room at 9:07 in the morning of 1970's Fourth of July.

Don Ross wore dark pants. A white shirt. A sky blue sports jacket.

He held out a bright red necktie.

"*Red, white and blue*: Too much?"

"Whatever you think," said his wife Cora. "People watching the parade will either get it or they won't. Either way, they'll see you roll past."

"What do you think, Luc?"

Mom blurted: "Hell yeah, ask him. After all, he's why you're doing it."

"Not really. Been wanting something like this too long to wait anymore. I miss being on the school board. Doing a job for the town *right*.

"This is America," proclaimed Dad. Gestured with the hand holding the red tie. "People are supposed to be able to be whoever they want to be."

"*Hah*," grumped Mom.

She felt her husband's glare.

"You know I'm on your side, Don. Forever. Plus, you deserve it. Everyone knows that even if they won't vote for you."

Don Ross turned to his son:

"What do you think, Luc? You're a kind of *in politics* guy."

"The atom bomb blasted apart *private space* being distinct from *public space*, the Greeks' *polis*," said Luc. "Now everything and everybody's *in politics*."

"Damn," said his mom. "You're really working that university BS."

"Working my life, Mom."

"Like we aren't?"

She knifed him with her eyes.

"All you kids nowadays. Your and Laura's generations. First ones getting a good public education like the government promised for everybody in your *polis*. All that reading 'n' writing 'n' thinking stuff. Learnin' what gets written by whoever owns the damn typewriters. 'Liberal arts' to help everybody figure out what to do 'bout the money machines the Big Shots got other kids wrenching together. Eisenhower said making all of us 'book smart' would make us all 'life smart' so we could beat the Russians 'n' Commies 'n' Nazis 'n' now the damn Chinese and get better at staying alive from those flying saucers.

"But now look what that book learnin's done. Made you smart-asses. Made you ask questions. Mouthing off and marchin' your smart asses 'bout the war and what gets done down South with the negroes. And now that *whoop-tee-do* Earth Day *whatever*.

"The Big Shots'll figure that out. Fix their mistake. Make sure kids who come after you go back to only learning one kind of thinking: *How to do jobs the bosses want done* and *how to buy what they're selling*. Tap the keys and pull the levers on them big guys' cash registers. Hell, you'll probably end up helping screw your city crew buddies and the rest of your Conner family that don't got 'good education'—just like it's always been done.

"And *polis* my ass. It'll be *policing* all our asses."

Horror filled Luc's face.

No, she can't be right! We're . . . The country . . . Learning is making it better for everybody not just. . .

"Forget all that tomorrow stuff, Luc," said his dad. "Tell me about today. Is the *red, white and blue* too much?"

Luc blinked his focus back to his father.

"First off," said Luc, "you're going to be riding in a *white* convertible."

"Up front in the passenger's seat," said Dad. "And *yeah*, it's conned out of Alec by his son-in-law Ben so he could cruise like a big shot. Now the car's eleven years old. Ben's angling to get the company to buy a new one, but Alec and I aren't budging. I never rode in the damn thing in any of the parades before now, no matter 'bout its hung-on 'tax deduction' signs about Marshall Trucking.

"But today," said family-owned Marshall Trucking's *chief executive officer*. "Today I'm riding up front in the passenger's seat. Waving to everybody. Showing them *who's who* and *what's what*."

"You're riding American flag colors in a white convertible," repeated Luc. Added: "My guess is only a few people in the crowd are going to get it."

"But it'll make an impression on them. Stick in their minds."

"Yeah. And what they'll see is you wearing a boss's sports jacket which won't bother most people. But you wearing a tie—any color tie—especially when it's gonna be almost ninety degrees out there at noon—a tie makes you look like some Main Street *thinks he's a hotshot*. Plus, you're all cinched up."

"So I'll stand out," his dad told him.

"But maybe not like you want. You're riding a company car."

Cora shrugged: "Ray's gonna be riding the City Hall float. Probably gonna wear some shirt and pants like he was sitting at home watching TV."

Luc said: "Just like everybody. Only he's the mayor. For years."

"That asshole Mueler you're gunning for," said Mom. "Bet he's gonna be riding the City Hall float with all the other city councilmen and Mayor Ray."

RING!

The house phone rang on the wall in the kitchen.

Mom said: "I'll get it!"

Dad looked at his son who'd help trigger him to this moment.

"I'm going with the red tie. Show patriotism. It's the Fourth of July."

"Luc!" yelled his mother. The extra-price long cord let her hold the answered phone away from her. "It's for you."

Luc hurried into the morning coffee-smelling kitchen.

His father hurried into the bathroom mirror.

"Hello?" said his son into Ma Bell's machine.

The voice in the phone pressed against Luc's ear said: "Hey, it's Vic."

"You're supposed to be on a fire tower!"

"I'm standing in a phone booth outside the Forest Service's smokejumpers school outside of Missoula. Quit the tower Thursday 'n' yesterday they brought me down. Let me stay in the smokejumpers' barracks till tomorrow."

"Is everything OK?" Luc asked his friend.

"*Yes* and *no.*"

Luc's heart thumped harder. "Give me the *no* first."

"My dad . . . My hometown of Libby. He works—worked—at the asbestos plant. The big thing in town. Office team manager. An office, a door and a desk.

"Back in '59, they—the company—started manufacturing some asbestos thing called vermiculite for buildings. The whole town . . . There's like a sand feel in the air. The company calls it 'nuisance dust.' They've known for years workers are getting sick but *so what, shut up.* Uncle Sam looks the other way.

"Piles of nuisance dust all around town. Down by the railroad tracks. Giant tin roof sheds. Vermiculite gets piled there to be loaded onto trains. Us kids used to swing on a rope over the dusty piles. Sometimes fall in. Or hell, let go.

"There've been rumors about asbestos and vermiculite and . . . and how it tears up people's lungs who breathe it. Are around it.

"My dad . . . was never a smoker, but lately he's been coughing. Drove all the way to Great Falls to see a doc who wasn't Libby local. Last week his X-rays . . .

"He's got lung cancer.

"Tomorrow, Sunday, the folks are gonna pick me up here. He quit the company. Put their house where I grew up on the market. Moving to Billings. Hundreds of miles away from *nuisance dust.* There's a good doctor and hospital there. My mom's sister, she's there, too. I'm gonna help them settle in."

"*Oh Jesus, Vic!* What can I do? What—I'm so sorry!"

"Thanks. They hired movers to pack up our house in Libby. Told me to never go back there. But it's where I grew—"

Robot Woman's voice cut into the conversation: "*Your three minutes are up. Please deposit more change if you wish to—*"

Luc heard Vic's coins clunk into the payphone.

"Hang up and call me back collect," Luc told Vic. Saw his mother in the living room frown at hearing that. "Save your quarters."

"Too late."

Vic's laugh over the phone sounded real. But hollow.

"Hey," said Luc. "I mean it. Whatever I can—"

The world rocketed Luc to where he *really* was.

"*Vic*: You grew up there. Golf club star. Catcher on the high school baseball team. Walking the . . . Car windows open . . . Swinging on that rope . . . If nuisance dust gave lung disease to your dad and lots of other people in Libby, are you OK?"

"So far, so good. Their new Doc told them I should get a chest X-ray every year from now on. Guess maybe now Cari can really see she broke my heart."

"Her loss."

"Now maybe not."

Don't go back to talking about horrors and HIM!

"So . . . When I asked you before, you said no *and* yes. Tell me about the *yes*."

"Was almost a *no*. Told my folks I was putting in for transfer papers to Eastern College in Billings instead of for early graduation. Then cram for a teacher's certificate there so I could get a job case they need money or me helping with Dad.

"But even just me saying that damn near killed Dad. He said he'd kill me if I did that. If I didn't take the *yes* that came in a telegram to their house in Libby."

Silence filled the phone receiver pressed against Luc's ear.

He lightened his tone. "So what's the *yes*?"

"The Fellowship to NYU to study with Hannah Arendt came through. I start in September. Tuition is free. Extra grants help cover things like where to live. I get two round trip tickets home. Well, to where my folks will be living."

Luc heard his friend's usual lightness come back into his words.

"And *hey*: If I ever get homesick, I'll just go for a walk. Watch what's going on where they're shipping tons of vermiculite and asbestos all the way from Libby to New York city to build something called the World Trade Towers."

Those two young men on that 1970s phone laughed.

Didn't know about thirty-one years later 9/11 horrors that included 400,000 first responders, volunteers, attack escapees and survivors, people inside that warm September's open windows NYC apartments getting savaged by toxic *nuisance dust* air blasted from those terrorist destroyed buildings.

"So the box of books you're storing for me," said Vic. "Gonna bring back to Missoula for me. I can't . . . there's nowhere to . . . Sorry, I—"

"Fuck your books."

"I was hoping you were having a better summer than that."

They laughed.

Friends who found each other out there in the big wide world.

"Don't worry about your box," said Luc. "Long as it stays hidden by my *Playboys* in the closet, my folks won't care if I leave them here until we figure out what to do with them."

"Are we talking about the *Playboys*?"

They heard each other chuckle.

Vic's voice slid into wistful distraction: "Gotta remember whose orgasm you're having with *Playboy*."

He sighed: "I better go before Ma Bell's Miss Robot Of 1970 cuts us off. I'll write you a letter when I get settled in the Big City. And again: Thanks. See you."

"See you," repeated Luc.

Hung up the kitchen phone on the wall.

See you. Please let me see you. Keep seeing you!

"Your dad left," said his mother.

"And you're going down to see the parade with your three sisters. That way people can see you four and let that make 'em maybe see Dad a wink more."

"You coming with us?"

"I'll be there. But I've got other plans."

"Bet you do," said his mother with a smile.

Terry was chatting with the nurse behind the first-floor reception desk when Luc walked through the hospital's front glass doors at 11:15.

"Right on time," she said.

She wore jean shorts that bared her legs halfway up her smooth white thighs. A light blue T-shirt boasted black letters across her breasts:

Juncta Juvant

"I hate being late." Luc frowned at her shirt: "What does that mean?"

"*Strength Through Unity*. It's my university's motto. A sorority gave 'em out when I went through Rush. I didn't join any of them."

"Me either."

She frowned at his face as they walked through the glass doors.

"Something's bothering you," she said.

"What do you know about lungs?"

"What's wrong?"

He told her as they walked down the alley hill toward Main Street.

"I'll see what the textbooks say, but I don't know enough."

"I'll take what you got."

"You actually give a shit about people."

"And you don't, Miss—"

He let her see him stare at her chest: "—Miss *Juncta Juvant* coming all the way out here to the edge of nowhere to learn how to save their lives?"

"*Nowhere* is always *somewhere* and where I—*we* are now is where it's at."

He shook his head to birth a smile for her cobalt blue eyes.

"Come on," said Luc. "Let's hit the parade."

That Fourth of July 1970's sun beat down eighty-eight degrees of midday heat on the people-packed sidewalks from one end of Main Street to another.

Luc knifed through the crowd.

Weaving alongside him came Terry.

Hometown Luc kept saying *hi* to people. Nodding smiles. Seeing friends and neighbors' eyes flick from him to the midnight-haired woman with him. *She's not from around here.* He glimpsed his high school buddy Kurt who worked a summer job at the pharmacy. They waved. Knew they now walked different streets *but still*. Luc wished his classmate Marin with or without his high school sweetheart wife and child were there. He saw Steve standing by a parking meter amidst the crowd in front of the dime store. Glanced toward the flower shop owned by Buffy's parents. Saw her not.

"There he is!" said Terry.

Dennis waited anxiously near the corner barbershop with its red and white spinning spiral pole. Waved them across the barricaded empty pavement Main Street to the sidewalk under the shadowing movie marquee of the Roxy.

Finally, on that Fourth of July, "now playing at the Roxy" was *Catch-22*. Terry broke away from Luc to share greetings with Dennis.

"Wait!" said Luc. "I just realized . . . We gotta go back to the other side of the street. Stand right at the curb. Passenger seat side of the car floats."

WHOOOO! went the *loud enough to cover the whole town* noon siren.

"*Come on!*"

Luc grabbed Terry's hand.

The three of them surged across Main Street between two parallel sidewalks lined with eager waiting eyes now seeing a trio of laughing and running youngbloods racing across the parade's path.

From the west end of Main Street came the sirens of Sheriff Wood in his cruiser and the three red volunteer fire department trucks. The *tramp tramp tramp* Honor Guard of veterans in military uniforms that came out of their closets for parade days. The Honor Guard carried the flags of Vernon and Montana flanking the out front and center *red, white and blue* American flag.

Shuffling behind the Honor Guard came the high school band—

—or at least all its students who were in town for the summer. The band trombones and trumpets blared with a big bass drum BOOOM! BOOM! BOOM! Five baton twirlers pranced out front of the blaring band. Tossed their batons high into the air. Two batons got caught.

Luc. Terry. Dennis.

They watched from the curb at the cracked concrete sidewalk passageway leading up from Main Street to the county jail and below the two dark windows of the former frontier doctor/mayor's closed abortion offices.

Grinning firemen threw candy off their passing save-your-life trucks.

Men in Shriner's red fez hats zipped go-karts through the parade. Also tossed candy to the sidewalks of scrambling and grabbing children.

Floats slowly rolled past. The Elk's Club. The Masons. Moose and Lions and Kiwanis. A flatbed truck with waving 4H grade-school-age kids holding heifers and a pig the science of evolution let them selectively breed and love and blue ribbons triumph with before the slaughterhouse sales.

Both banks had floats.

Really, a pickup truck and an antique car, each barely decorated but carrying the presidents who threw out smiles. But not candy.

Then came the City Hall float: a flatbed truck with waist-high sideboards.

Mayor Ray leaned dead center on the truck cab from the flatbed. Made him easy to see. Easy to wave to everybody, not just one side or the other.

The town's eight city councilmen. The elected clerk and recorder. The voter-chosen treasurer. All men. All White. All working the backend flatbed like a shuffle game. They'd step to the left side of the truck. Wave to the people standing on that side of Main Street with the dime store and liquor store. Jump across the flatbed to grab a space facing that side of Main Street with the First State Bank, the Capital Café, the Tap Room and those dark second-story windows.

Councilman and weekly newspaper owner Mueler grabbed that gap.

He wore a 1950s hat. His trademark bowtie. Suspenders over a white shirt. Smiled at the passing sidewalk.

Blinked.

Saw two long-haired freaks and a beautiful girl who thus had to be dumb and given her age, probably pushy against her pre-ordained place and doing stuff like no girl ever did with him 'n' *shouldn't*, shouldn't until 'n' unless.

Blinked again.

Mueler *recognized*.

Kept his cold stare on that Luc Ross radical no-account as the float of who's got the official power in town rolled on toward the dawn end of Main Street.

Luc never broke gaze with Mueler.

Never gave him the satisfaction of more than a stone hard *see-you* smile.

The float for the oil refinery west of town went pass Luc and his crew.

Then came a truck with its back end filled by . . .

Women in dark dresses. Gold pins on their chests. Some were Gramma Meg's age. Others were younger. And a few—

There rode Mrs. Jodrey. Mike's mother.

The banner read: "Goldstar Mothers of America."

Moms and dads and Kids Who Knew waved from the curbs as the Goldstar Mothers drove past. Held their hands over their hearts. Sent *be strong* smiles.

The Goldstar Mothers.

Each lost a child to America's wars for freedom.

Fourth of July 1970 notched 44,259 KIAs in the ongoing Vietnam War.

A respectful distance behind the grieving mothers crawled giant tractors and combines from the nearby farm implement company.

A float from a church group.

The float for local AM radio station KRIP blasted out upbeat country and western songs from a portable DJ setup on a flatbed truck. KRIP's most popular DJ spun hand-sized black disk 45 rpm records while shucking and jiving in his chair. The station's ultra-modern technology broadcast LIVE! so people driving on the highways out of town could hear the parade coming out of their car radios.

And then . . .

Luc stepped off the curb to look down past the line of floats.

There! Ahead of a few other commercial floats and the end of the parade created by horseback posses of Stetson hats, snap-button shirts, pristine cowboy boots and poofy calico dresses. Ahead of the not-smiling but proud to be here to *represent* riding tall members of the Blackfeet nation from their reservation give or take an hour's truck ride away toward the setting sun.

Amidst the floats before all that . . .

A white convertible. Top down. Doors draped by—

WAIT!

The white convertible: It's stopping!

The front passenger door swung open.

Got slammed shut by Luc's dad who fancy quick-marched around to a couple steps ahead of the white convertible's front bumper—

—and started walking.

The white convertible had no choice but to drive its parade behind him.

Why look! That's Don Ross. What's he—

Oh! He's waving his red tie. Pointing to his white shirt. To his blue—

Oh yeah! Folks all the way on both sides of the street *get it.*

Look at him! He's making a funny face to show how hot he is all dressed up like that. Shuffling along like a one-man presentation.

Yeah, he came out of the trucking company's convertible where he's the boss 'n' everybody says he's a good one. But this feels like . . . like something more. Like him being his own man. Marching right in front of all of us. Hiding nothing.

The gigolo who's driving the white convertible. He ain't from around here like Don. His smile looks stapled on.

Don's walking past his son. Good kid. Long hair *but* road crews with Dennis and *whoa:* Who's that with . . . Well, with either Dennis or Don's son.

Oh, she's the summer gal helping out up t' the hospital and nursing home! Good for her, lucky for us.

Ha ha! Look at Don all-comic actor like gaping *What the hell?* up at the Roxy marque for *Catch-22.* Don't matter if you don't know whatever the hell it is but it's funny seeing him do his thing about it.

Looking at him walking in our parade. Showing up for us.

"Way to go, Dad," whispered Luc.

Dennis looked at Luc.

Gave him The Nod.

Luc leaned toward Terry.

Leaned close to her puzzled face so only they heard what he said to her:

"We've got an offer for you."

The dyed blonde's face held Nick's gaze as she drifted away.

"Great night, right. Finals are over. Your long black hair shines in the lights of the bar where everybody goes, so it's safe, right? Two guys talking about their motorcycles. Their cross-country trip. Buying shots. And suddenly it's like a freedom dream come true. You riding on the back of the motorcycle. Black hair flying in the moonlight. And it's just like those rebel heroes from our generation in that movie Easy Rider but no, oh no, you won't get shotgunned to death by freedom-hating Americans. You won't be so lucky.

"The motel they roared to as you screamed for them to stop, let you off, let you go. 'This is the ride you wanted, bitch!' They grab you. Slap you. Knock you into the motel door. Then through it.

"Then . . ."

Nick cried as he realized "then."

"Heard them talking after . . . Before they threw me out knowing it was my whiskey-smelling word against the two of them saying 'she wanted it.'

"They were drunk-talking about how they were going to grab some guy in Missoula named Shaughnessy who thinks he's bringing a ton of college kids' cash and gonna walk away with a wholesale shitload of grass to retail back to them. But those two . . . They'll take him on a ride that ain't gonna end up as nice and 'go home' as it did for the bitch huddled in there on the bathroom floor.

"After the hospital, the no-show cops, I cashed in everything I could. Bought a plane ticket here. Looked up Shaughnessy in the phone book. Got in here to wait and got stuck with you."

"You're going to kill them," repeated Nick.

"Yeah," she said. "But what am I gonna do about you?"

"No," he said. "What are we going to do?"

BUSTING GLASS

"What are 'we' going to do?" the dyed blonde repeated back to Nick. "You think your vote matters? Where do you think you are? You're in the real America, Nick with the fake ID. It's all about the green and who's got the gun."

July 16, 1970.

A Thursday.

A day like any other day in America.

"The Benevolent and Protective Order" of Elk's Clubs with thousands of local chapters like the one on Luc's Main Street nationwide voted overwhelmingly to deny membership to non-Whites.

A vote in the Boardroom of Acceptable Beauty revoked Miss Montana's title and chance to be crowned Miss America because she refused to stop being seen with her *hippy-freak long-haired un-American*-looking brother and they both opposed the Vietnam war where our KIAs kept creeping up from 44,000.

A mom in Iowa scheduled her day around being able to sit down in front of the living room's box TV set to watch that evening's summer rerun of a half-hour comedy set in middle-of-America Minneapolis where the *Not Married! Cool job!* heroine throws her cap up to the sky and swirls with joy.

Screen watchers in 1970 had only two chances to see any TV show:

One, stare at the screen when the show came on precisely on the half hour or hour. Many shows featured commercials for, *say*, a famous laxative.

Or *two*, follow the same one-shot/nonstop-only rule whenever the show played as a one-time summer rerun.

That Thursday in 1970 started like any day on the Vernon city crew.

Luc gunned the red truck back and forth to the river.

The gravel/sand packed truck lugged Luc up a hill past the city's round outdoor swimming pool filled with July's splashing children. Drove two blocks to the city crew's sandlot plateau on the high up west edge of town.

He was daydreaming about Terry smiling.

Envisioning Norma staring.

Thinking about the one-room "furnished" apartment that shared a bathroom with the apartment across the hall that he'd sublet in his university town from a divorced friend of his family. A private room for him. His first *ever*.

With a bed.

Drove his truck of *now* remembering a short story in a science fiction anthology called *The Machine Stops* written by E. M. Forster way *way* back in 1909. A doomsday saga: Humanity is linked into a giant "Artificial Intelligence" thinking machine that dictates how they communicate and what they do.

Luc wrangled the red truck to the crew's sandlot plateau where—

What the hell?

There sat the empty smeared-oil-stinking black street oiler truck. Held together by welds, wires, duct tape and hope. Decades of oil spray and splashes blacked every inch of the perpetually rebuilt truck except for its cracked windshield and smudged windows. The back end held a black tank with a top hatch secured by a jangly lever. Luc couldn't remember how many hundreds of gallons of boiling black oil the tank held. The tank's rear was a platform of spigots to spray hot oil onto a road as *stick'm* for the blacktop or half-sole covering.

The Black Beast slumped on its tires in the middle of the city crew's sandlot with its high mesa of sand/gravel. Slumped there all alone and empty.

Where's Arson who drives the Black Beast?

Where's Cal the Bull grinning in his oil-smeared coveralls he wears when he rides the rear end sprayer and works levers to let hot oil flow or no?

Luc steered his red truck off Test Hill's north-south street.

Glanced to his left.

His hometown stretched out below him.

Second Street ran a straight line down a steep slope past blocks of homes for families. Some had dogs. Random cars lined the sidewalks.

There!

On the plateau of the city crew's sand/gravel field.

From inside the high-up cab of the giant yellow frontend loader:

Street foreman Jerry waved his gray cowboy hat.

Gestured for Luc to dump his load on the gravel mesa.

Then those two city crew members stood by the slumped Black Beast.

"It's shot again," said Jerry. "Arson tried jumping the battery. Fiddled with this, fiddled with that. Couldn't do any more here. 'Sides, he got a call on pickup's radio. A big water leak. He 'n' Cal took off.

"But we came up with a plan.

"I'll back the frontend loader up to the front grill of the oiler. We'll chain it there but not so tight that you won't be able to steer the truck."

"Me," said Luc. "Chained to you."

"We'll take Second Street down near a straight line all the way to the shop. Park the son-of-a-bitch close to the garage bay doors. See if Arson can bring it back to life one more time."

"Dr. Frankenstein," said Luc.

"Whatever," said Street Foreman Jerry. "Can you smell it? That hot oil? Damned if they didn't just fill the tank up to the brim.

"Remember: You're chained right behind me. I'll keep looking over my shoulder. You got problems, wave. I'll slow it down until you tap your front bumper up against me. We brake to a stop.

"If your foot brakes need help, pull up on the hand brake. Or put it in second gear. Pop the clutch out like going downhill to start a car. That will either start the truck or the transmission will lock the wheels, skid you to a stop."

"Got it."

They positioned the yellow frontend loader. Worked the chains.

The Black Beast's driver's door closed Luc inside the broken machine.

Have to try it for myself. Push in the clutch. Turn the key.

Nothing. Not even a *grrrr* of the engine trying to start.

Sigh. Make sure the gearshift is in neutral. Handbrake off.

Send your left *thumbs-up* through the driver's side open window.

Beyond the windshield rose the yellow frontend loader with Jerry in the up-high cab. Heard the engine roar on his giant rear tires and low front steel bucket machine.

Here we go.

Two chained-together massive machines crawled to the top of the long deep slope down Second Street.

Easy, we're going easy. The gentle pull of the chains wrapped around the in-neutral-gear black oiler moves that dead machine you're driving.

Feel that? Just rolled over the crest of the street, starting down . . .

Going faster now.

Push your right foot down on the brake pedal—

—hit the floorboard without an ounce of resistance.

Jerk the handbrake.

Comes up as smooth as if it wasn't there.

Push in the clutch pedal. Slap the gearshift into second. Pop the clutch.

Clankety-clinkety clumpity!

Sounds from under the rolling-faster-now truck carrying hundreds of gallons of 228 degrees hot oil.

Glance in the driver's side rearview mirror:

Poles and chunks of metal broken off under the truck tumble to the street between rubber tires.

Faster, steer the runaway rolling-ever-faster black oiler.

Keep lined up on Jerry's frontend loader.

One chain snaps!

The windshield speeds closer to Jerry's yellow machine.

Crash!

The Black Beast slams into the rear end of the frontend loader.

Bounces Jerry whirling to see—

The oiler's front bumper *and* grill tear off/up fly-back—

The windshield shatters in front of your face.

Shards of glass shower. *Blink!* Shake them off.

Steer!

Crash into the frontend loader again/bounce back.

Jerry speeds up to match/blend calm the speeding from behind Black Beast *CRASH!*

Bouncing back and forth in the black oiler cab. *Keep steering!* Line up with Jerry. The truck doors clatter back and forth, shut to open.

Wait. That . . . Hear that up-top clattering?

The hatch cover:

Has it popped open? Is boiling hot oil splattering out on top of the cab and into the cab where you're bouncing around like a puppet?

Each side of these city blocks you're careening down are filled with houses. Children run out to the curbs to see what's crashing toward them.

Don't lose control 'n' let the Black Beast race to the curb hit little kids splash them with hot oil!

Can't jump out to safety/don't hurt the kids/steer *steer STEER!*

WHAM!

The front end of the runaway oiler crashes into the back end of the frontend loader a heartbeat after Jerry slams the front bucket to the ground and hits the frontend loader's brakes as hard as he can.

Slams you against the steering wheel.

Truck bounces back—

—rebounds into Jerry's skidding/slowing machine.

Crash inertia and the tanked sea of the shifting oil flip the truck onto its rear tires. The oiler's front tires pop up off the road. Rolls the Black Beast angle-up onto the shuddering/stopping frontend loader.

Throws you back against the seat.

Angles your face to blue sky through the shattered windshield.

BAM!

The oiler slams down on all its tires.

Shudder/stop/settle.

Jerry leaps out of the braked and bucket-down loader.

Throws open the Black Beast's driver's door.

"Are you all right?"

Breath, catch your breath!

Yes I'm alright! Not burned! Broken! Dead! Not killer of kids! Or anybody!

Then somehow . . .

Luc's standing on the street staring at crunched-together machines.

Other crew members lock them together—*really* lock them together.

He's riding with Dave driving the city crew's white pickup.

He's standing in the yard.

"Luc," orders Dave. "Go move those trucks. Switch their parking places."

Luc did it. Drove again. Less than an hour after he'd—

Oh.

Your downward grin shows pride for your job and boss who wanted to be sure he was OK. *Could—would—had* moved on from not dying to still driving.

"Five o'clock," said Dave. "Quitting time."

Luc walking out of the yard with the crew.

Walking out as Dennis asks if he's OK.

Telling him: "Made it here alive. We both did."

Walking on the sidewalk past the Post Office.

Walking the opposite side of the street in front of his home.

The white Chevy in the driveway. Both parents home.

Shower. Dinner. Books to read. Radio. Your record player with albums of poetry called songs. A boxed TV screen waiting to beam images into your mind. Friends from high school across town. The Roxy.

You stink of sweat and fear. Of oil. Filthy white T-shirt and work blue jeans.

Now is now and what is now.

Your brown work boots choose the sidewalk past your home.

Up the steps to the hospital's glass doors.

Through them to the air conditioned cool. The desk nurse knows where you're going. You do. You don't. *Does anybody ever know where they're going?*

Fuck the elevator *machine.* Take the stairs.

Down the second floor's mine shaft corridor.

Stand in her open doorway . . .

Terry. A surprised smile brightens her face.

Her husky voice: "*Hey you!* I didn't expect to see—"

She blinks.

Luc's standing there in his work clothes. Filthy white T-shirt. Faded and stained blue jeans. He always cleaned up before coming to see her.

His face is a mess.

She takes a step closer. "Are you OK?"

A friend's ask. A medical ask. Her scanning blue eyes.

"I . , . I'm OK."

"*No,*" she said. "This isn't you."

"Is now. Lucky me. I could have been—Road crew."

"Come in." She gave him a glass of tap water. "Sit."

You slump against the wall facing her hospital bed. Slide your back down the blue walls until you're crouching on the floor, knees up to brace you.

She's fighting urges. *Come closer to comfort* or *give you space?*

She sits on the bed.

Asks: "What happened?"

And you tell her. Tell it all to her as the clock *tick-tocks* this time you got.

"Do you want me to take you to the ER nurse? Have her check you out?"

"Naw, I'm . . . I'm fine."

"*Sure.*" Her lips go firm, then she said:

"What do you do to relax—when you're *fine?*"

"I don't . . . Relax, I mean . . . How can you? But . . . Doesn't . . . Sometimes it makes me surge. Makes me feel . . . Feel all sorts of things, but . . . Music."

"Me, too. Makes my brain think without getting lectured to. You know, like . . . I don't know . . . Leonard Cohen."

"Who?"

"You're kidding me."

She slides off the bed.

Walks through the pine disinfectant smelling hospital room.

Picks up the guitar case. Snaps it open. Pulls out a guitar. Sits on the bed. Her legs cradle her steady. Her right foot dangles down the side of the bed. Her heart-side hand holds the guitar neck. Her right hand strums the strings over the magic hole. She plucks. Tunes.

Takes a deep breath.

Softens her husky voice.

"*Suzanne takes you down . . . to her place near the river . . .*"

And you're there.

There. *Here.* And it's *real.*

Sitting on the floor of a hospital room. Back pressed against the wall. *Alive.*

A dream woman on a bed strumming her guitar to share poetry with you.

Watching hearing being floating in the magic of *there*, of *then*, of *now*, a flow *oh* a timeless flow right up to the last guitar strum of Leonard Cohen's—

"KNOCK KNOCK!"

Standing in the hospital room's doorway.

A pudgy middle-aged woman in a white uniform carrying a tray.

"I waited out there until you was done," says the kitchen staffer to Terry as she carries the tray to the table.

Now the room smells like oiled-Luc, pine disinfectant *and* macaroni and cheese.

"You were done, right?" says the woman wearing the white uniform as she looks at that nice girl from Ohio and Luc Ross from across the street and the Conner clan. Wasn't his dad a hoot in the Fourth of July parade?

"I mean," said the kitchen aide, "probably best if you're done. I could hear you making your song in the hall where the signs say QUIET.

"Plus, take it from me: Tonight's dinner's better than it looks, but you gotta eat it while it's hot."

She beamed at the two people who were young enough to be her kids.

Luc muscled himself up off the floor.

Terry set aside her guitar.

"Gotta go," said the kitchen aide. "More trays to deliver."

Luc and Terry.

Standing alone in that *oh so quiet* room.

Staring at each other.

Until he told her *a* truth: "I better get going, too. Go home."

Made sure her cobalt blue eyes were locked on his: "*Thanks*."

She shrugged safety: "What are friends for?"

No answer to that question came.

Her other words came just before he walked out her door:

"See you tomorrow night."

"There's gray duct tape under the kitchen sink," said the blonde with a gun. "Afterwards, an anonymous phone call to the cops sets you free."

"I'm not a guy you want to wrap up and I don't think you'll shoot me if I say no. There's a bunch of sides here—Shaughnessy, the two sons-a-bitches bikers, you, me, John Law and whatever passes for Judgement Day."

He shrugged: "I appear to be standing next to you."

"Why?"

"I can't just walk away. I couldn't save you from . . . before. I guess I want to save you now from your worse self somehow, someway. Can't tell you any more than that. Knowing 'why' shit like that, hell: I haven't graduated yet."

"And it's not just because you like blondes?"

"It's always all about the choice. Blonde or not is just one choice. The bottom-line choice here is saving the better part of you from shooting itself to shreds. You've already been ripped and hurt like you never should have been."

She whispered: "I was a virgin."

"You still are," he told her. Shrugged. "Me, too. Because I wouldn't lose it once by being a 'drunk girl' less violent version of those two guys. Nobody's ever really told me yes."

"Don't look at me for that."

"I'm only looking for you to be the better, safer, best you."

"Yeah, well, sometimes we never find what we're looking for," she told him. "So what are we going to do? And where the hell is—"

She whirled to the window before the word "Shaughnessy" got born.

Nick stared out to that outside world filling with marching, charging feet crossing over the bridge.

They whirled to each other. She said what they both realized:

"He's a green salesman hustling green to make more green and out there is a river of rebel-yes people with hope and happy in their hearts who are customers waiting to score green and pay up front!"

The gun snapped up and locked on Nick.

MAGIC

"We go now!" shouted the blonde with the gun. "You go with me. I won't wanna, but you try to stop me, try to run, try to karate me . . . I'll try to only shoot you in the ass."

The gun flicked toward the door to the herd in the street.

Nick ran out of the apartment.

The blonde with a gun ran right behind his ass.

That *running wild* July Friday in 1970 startled Luc when the new full-time hire grinned his way into the morning shape-up.

Everybody shook the new man's hand.

When it was Luc's turn, he and Jed Fuller shared smiles and names.

His son 'n' me were—are—friends, thought Luc. *Same high school class. Now I'm working as kinda equals with the father of a kid from my "bygone youth."*

Shit! "Bygone." I'm only twenty-one. When did my youth become "bygone"?

Boss Dave said: "Luc! Go show Jed the hook-ups for the spreader."

The yellow box linked onto the back of a truck's slowly rising cargo-box full of sand to spread on hot-oiled streets that Luc "bossed" with one or two more furiously shoveling-sand souls.

Jed's work boots shuffled beside Luc across the packed-sand, revving-engines, gas-fumes yard to the unhooked rusted yellow spreader.

Luc asked how Jed's son was.

"Doin' great." Jed grinned. "Got his paper from a community college 'n' landed a good job down in Billings. And National Guard. He's gonna be tickled as hell to find out we're workin' together now."

Jed's talking to me man to man, thought Luc. *Not to some "kid."*

Luc felt his heart whisper *Yes!* and *Thank you!*

Jed glided stocky smooth across the yard of his new job. Wore a crunched down, brimmed sun-protection hat, a faded denim work shirt, blue jeans, short gray hair. Luc showed him the pressure-triggered clamps that hooked the back of the spreader onto steel crossbar centered on the dump trucks' rear bumpers.

Walked Jed to the back of the red truck.

Showed him the rear bumper steel crossbar.

Jed who'd come to the city crew from a local construction contractor who'd had to let him go or let the whole business fail said: "Gotta be a tricky hookup."

And then . . .

. . . through the gas fumes, the roar of truck engines, the soft west wind . . .

. . . looming behind them came Sam Kraeger.

"S.K.," as the crew called him.

"S.K.," as he spotlighted himself in his *tell you why and what* pronouncements from his post as the crew's chief operating engineer.

S.K. rose himself amidst the duo of the new guy and the college kid who'd been in the same high school class as S.K.'s daughter and new guy's son.

"Look here." S.K. marched the duo to the truck's driver's side rear window. "See, what ya gotta do is pick a point on the spreader reflected in here."

S.K. tapped the mirror.

"Then as you back up, line up with that point."

Jed stood tall and studiously stared into the mirror where S.K. pointed.

"Oh yeah," said Jed. "I get what you're going for."

"Should lock you in place," said S.K. "Unless you can't handle the truck, 'n which case if I'm workin' close, grab me and it'll get done like it should."

"A man's gotta appreciate all the help he can get," said Jed.

S.K. grunted.

Royally marched off toward the giant blade-on-the-ground grader.

Dennis walked up to Luc and Jed before they could say anything.

Nodded a smile to Jed, asked Luc: "We all set? I mean, for tonight."

Jed laughed: "You two young'uns figure out life. I gotta get the truck up to the mesa and get my gravel and sand load and go where we gotta go."

As Jed walked away, Luc told Dennis: "We're set."

Thirty minutes later, Luc found himself "set" with the empty chipper box on a northside street of houses that had been cleared of parked vehicles so Arson and Cal the Bull could ride the borrowed-from-the-county hot-oil-spreading truck to paint the graded smooth blocks a steamy, sticky black.

From one block over came sounds of S.K. grading that bumpy street as smooth as any man-machine combo could get it. Just ask him.

Coming around the far corner behind the chipper box came the red truck with Jed behind the wheel. He turned the gravel and sand-loaded heavy truck through a 180 back-around, aimed the rear bumper at the chipper box . . .

Clinked into the clamps with smooth perfection.

Luc looked up to the truck's open driver's side window.

A co-worker to co-worker grin that said it all passed between Jed and Luc.

Jed raised the truck box so its load could tumble down to fill the chipper box and get spread over the oiled street the truck backed down. When the truck bed was empty, Luc stopped the vehicle's backward crawl, unclamped the truck and waved good-bye to Jed. Saw a savvy man's arm wave back through the open driver's side window.

Boss Dave rolled up in his city crew white pickup just before noon when the chipper was between refills.

"Get in," he told Luc.

Dave sneezed as he drove them two blocks over to an ungraded street.

"Probably hay fever or a damn summer cold, but whatever, it's what the hell and might make me not good as you at it. 'Sides, you're one of the best."

Dave parked the white pickup. Sneezed.

As they both stepped into the city street, Dave pulled out two meter-long, copper and brass welding rods, round and slightly thinner than a pencil. One end of each rod had been bent ninety degrees into a hand-width handle.

Excitement trembled Luc: *Witching rods!*

"Between useless city maps and the gas company's paperwork just to ask a question, let alone get an answer, normally'd be few weeks before we can do whatever we can do on this street that don't seem to be doing so bad, but Mayor Ray says we gotta get 'er done—or something done—now."

Dave sent Luc a sly grin as they walked to the street's gutter.

"And definitely before election time."

They faced the middle of the road.

Dave passed the metal witching rods to Luc.

"Get what you can," said the boss.

Luc held the rod handles in his closed no-gloves fists that he kept snug against his white T-shirted chest. The rods stuck straight out from his chest like railroad tracks from his heart flat and level with the ground.

One slow step at a time, Luc walked toward the other side of the street.

The rods moved when he'd gone three steps from the curb.

Began to spread apart.

Three steps later, the rods turned as far away from each other as they could so that they made a line *almost* parallel to and in the middle of the street.

Luc took a step . . .

The rods eased their spread.

He stepped back to where he'd been and the rods swung apart.

A collaboration of physics and magic.

The physics:

Luc's upright body became an antennae for subterranean electrons freed by pipes containing flowing water or natural gas (if the gas pipes were not swathed). Once the electrons reached the rods in his fist, the rods' copper conductivity split the electrons into negative streams that needed to be on opposite ends of the rods' straight line pole singularity made by Luc holding them close in his fists. The tips of the rod swung wide to create a straight line when they and their antennae were on top of one of those pipes buried under the street.

The magic:

Some people made better antennas than others.

Some people somehow couldn't be antennas.

Luc was a great antenna.

"Don't figure it'll be a living for a shirt 'n' tie college guy like you," road crew boss Dave once joked.

"I'm not a *get tied up wearing a tie* kind of guy." Luc smiled back at him.

"We'll see," said the boss.

That late morning July Friday in 1970 heard Boss Dave yell to Luc.

"Hold it there!"

Dave walked to the middle of the street.

Used a can of blue spray paint to mark a line on the road exactly beneath the stretching-out-into-infinity line created by the spread-apart witching rods.

"Got it," said the boss. "Just in case, keep walking it to the next sidewalk."
Luc did.

Two steps from the curb, the witching rods spread wide again.

"Shit!" said Dave as he blue spray painted another line. "Wish I hadn't been right 'bout how busy this damn street is."

He led Luc back to the white pickup.

"What are we—*you*—going to do?" asked Luc.

"It's what I—*we*—done today," said chess master Dave with a wink in his words. "Folks'll see the blue lines and know we're on it. Even if it takes a few days for me to figure out the *hows* and *whats* and clearances."

He climbed behind the steering wheel of the city's white pickup truck.

"'N that oughta make Mayor Ray happy." Dave sneezed as Luc settled in the shotgun seat. The boss nodded to the houses on both sides of the street. "Somebody 'round here complained to the mayor. Now today, they got city crew blue lines in the street for everybody to see. 'N' eyeballs logging you being the one out here workin' it for the good of these folks, gotta admit that don't hurt."

Luc knew the *hurt* meant politics beyond the mayor's moves.

Maybe Boss Dave's *hurt* meant Mueler's attack on Luc's job.

Maybe chess master Dave's *hurt* meant Luc's dad's still officially secret after the parade campaign for Mueler's city councilman seat.

'Maybe' don't matter when you're out in the street, thought Luc as the white pickup roared him forward to next.

By that afternoon's 4:11 when Luc and Arson figured it was time for the crew to roll the equipment back to the shop for the weekend, they'd re-paved almost half a dozen blocks.

Dennis rode his open seat atop the giant yellow roller he slowly guided in overlapping laps to seal the just-paved streets.

S.K. leaned against the giant grader with its scrape-the-streets clean blade resting on the road just across the intersection to this *where the action is* block. Luc saw the smoke of S.K.'s cigarette rising to the oil-smelling blue sky.

Jed's engine-off truck'd lowered its emptied cargo box but kept its hook up to the yellow chipper box so it could ferry it back to the shop. Jed sat behind the steering wheel in the open-windowed cab breathing in the summer afternoon's air of his first day on the new job.

Two recent high school grads who'd gotten lucky with their Draft numbers and been hired by Dave to help Luc on the chipper box "for a month or so" had already caught a ride back to the shop with the boss in his white pickup.

Luc was making sure the shovels wouldn't fall out of the chipper box during the journey when a rusted green car parked across the street where Dennis had rollered the new road. The rusted green car's driver's door opened.

Out stepped Mayor Ray.

Who owned the grocery store where Dennis and Luc worked that wild summer after Luc graduated from high school three years before.

Mayor Ray was a husky man in a summer shirt and slacks and scruffy loafers. He wore a crunched-up businessman's hat.

Everybody in town knew that image.

Everyone with any smarts could see the steel in his eyes.

Mayor Ray waited until the giant yellow roller driven by Dennis passed between where he stood and the red truck and yellow chipper box across the road.

Walked over to Luc standing at the back of the truck: "Thought maybe I'd catch Dave over here when I heard your engines rumbling."

The machine rumbling came from Dennis's giant yellow roller going back and forth in the street. Luc figured the roller was on its last, straight down the middle of the road lap before Dennis guided it back to the shop.

"He had to go take care of something else," said Luc who'd been a good employee at the grocery store turned into a good *but* problem employee on the city crew. "You doing OK? Anything we can help you with?"

Mayor Ray grinned: "Dave's your boss, not me.

"But you can tell him I seen good work you an' him started over t' the other block. Blue stripes. Tell him I got a *thanks* call. He deserves you telling him 'thanks' for me."

The mayor shook his head at this young man he'd known all that long-haired, college cowboy's life. His mom was one of the Conners he'd grown up with. Son of a man who . . . Well, everybody respected Don Ross. Ray liked him, too.

"You, *you* were just doing your job," said Mayor Ray.

But grinned.

"Now go on with what you gotta do."

The mayor pulled a pack of cigarettes from his shirt pocket, flipped one free and used a lighter he oh so publicly bought from a church fundraiser to put flame to the white paper death tube held in his lips.

Luc turned to the chipper box hooked onto the back of Jed's red truck. Knew it was locked on tight. Felt Mayor Ray's eyes watching him make sure.

Luc straightened up and turned to face Mayor Ray—

—just as S.K. huffed and puffed there from hustling over from the next block.

"Hey, sorry, 'scuse me, Ray!" huffed S.K. "Think I could please maybe get a light from you?"

"You need a cig, too?" answered Ray as he exchanged *done* nods with Luc.

"Naw, thanks, but I'm fine. I'm fine. I got it."

What the hell, thought Luc as he walked around the back of the truck. Luc heard the click of a lighter as he climbed into the truck's shotgun seat. *S.K.'d dropped a lit cigarette to rush over here . . . to get a light?*

Something made Luc close the truck's door as quietly as he could.

Driver Jed frowned at Luc's face.

They turned to face the reflections in the truck's driver's side mirror.

Saw Ray turning away from S.K.

"Wait—I mean—Can you give me a sec for a thing?" S.K. said to Ray in hushed tones that the fading sounds of Dennis on the yellow roller didn't hide.

S.K.'s reflection looked both ways.

Tossed his just lit cig to the street he'd helped build.

"My daughter," he said to Ray as quietly as he could. "It's . . . That . . . Her husband's an asshole. Ain't never around. Never brings home enough money for her 'n' the kid he . . ."

S.K. glanced both ways.

Jed saw that and roared the truck engine to life.

But still coming through the truck's open windows:

"I know she's got quite a bill run up at your grocery store. Know you usually cut off credit for . . ."

S.K. shoved both hands in his front pockets.

Pulled out a bundle of greenback bills, maybe a few dollars, likely more from a man who Luc knew liked to show off the cash he got to carry, a bunch of $20s or at least some $10s.

S.K. held out the wad of cash to mayor and grocery store owner Ray.

"Could you do me a favor? Put that on her bill? 'N' let me know if'n she gets in deep again? 'N' don't tell her? She ain't never been good with knowin's anyhow."

Jed slammed the red truck into first gear. Let out the clutch and rolled it carrying the yellow spreader away from two men standing on a new road.

The driver's mirror showed Ray take the wad of cash from S.K.

The truck was traveling as fast as Jed could let it to get away from those two men and their *wanna be secret* none of them would ever tell.

The street to the railroad tracks filled the truck windshield.

Jed said: "I'll be damned."

"Won't we all," replied Luc.

Thought about the coming night.

Hoped he was wrong about being damned.

OUTLAWS

The outlaws converged that July 1970 Friday after dinner.

Luc, Terry and Dennis stood on a prairie hill looking beyond the river valley below. Smelled prairie grass gold. River trees' green. Luc's secondhand blue car waited parked behind them. A warm breeze stroked their bare arms. The sun hung above the distant horizon.

"We can't get caught," Terry had insisted. "Forget about prison. They'd never let me be a doctor and I can't, *I won't* lose that."

"These are our days," Luc'd told her. "We have to choose what part of them we wanna be. Besides, don't worry: Dennis and I, we've got a plan."

The two of them picked her up at the hospital at 7:00 o'clock that Friday night. They all wore good blue jeans. Luc's pullover shirt was black. Dennis wore a blue button-up short-sleeve. And Terry . . .

Terry wore a crimson blouse and zero lipstick.

Just three friends innocently hanging out on a July Friday night.

They drove seven miles to the river and a gravel road turnoff usually only used by the city crew. Parked on the hill. Saw dozens of empty miles every which way they looked. Could see if any dust cloud raced toward them over the gravel road.

Terry'd asked about the *to and fro*.

"If we two 'good boys' get stopped and somehow busted, tell them you didn't know what us locals were doing," said Luc. "You got stuck with us."

"Will you two—*we*—be alright?" she asked. "I mean, able to drive?"

"Don't worry," said Dennis. "We know our limits."

Now on the hill facing the aging sun, Luc pulled out the gas station lighter and a hand-rolled joint.

"My guy got 'em from his guy who sells 'em already rolled. Lucky for us. I've never been able to roll a joint. I'm a water-pipe guy."

"I'm a whatever I can get kind of guy," said Dennis.

"And I'm the twenty-one-year-old woman who's never tried marijuana."

"Welcome to these days," said Luc.

He stuck the joint in his lips. Bent to cup his left hand around it as his right positioned the lighter. Dennis shifted his body between Luc and the breeze. Terry got it. Moved closer to make a trio huddled against the wind.

Click! A quivering flame. The white papered joint blazed.

Luc took a deep hit.

Coughed as he held the joint out to his friends.

Dennis politely nodded to Terry.

"You go first," she said.

He did. Coughed.

Handed the joint to Terry.

She held it like she'd seen cigarettes on TV and in the movies. In bars. By girlfriends who sucked in tobacco's cancer with a thousand lipstick smiles.

"Don't just exhale it. Breath it in and hold it long as you can," said Luc.

Terry held it for four seconds before smoke burst out of her coughing lips.

Luc and Dennis each took another hit from the burning-away joint. Each held it in far longer than Terry.

She took another hit—inhaled deeper, blew it out a bit later and softer.

Luc glanced at the joint.

Offered it to her again: "Have your next hit before it gets harder to hold."

Hit number three held on to her longer than her first two.

Came out coughing and coughing.

Luc took the joint from her shaking hand.

Looked at Dennis: "Can you take it down to the nub so we don't waste?"

Luc got a *yes* nod.

Took his own last hit deep and full.

Passed the joint's burning stub to Dennis who inhaled while letting it burn right down to the flesh of his holding-it fingers.

Dennis pinched out what was left. Held that nub toward Luc.

"Bury it," said Luc.

Dennis heel-kicked a hole in dusty prairie sod on top of that river hill. Dropped in the remnant of the joint. Stomped to flatten that grave.

"*Um,*" said Luc: "I've got two more joints."

"No," said Terry. "Not for me. And for you . . . We gotta drive back to town."

"We know the way," said Dennis. His smile floated beyond.

"Do you feel . . . anything or different or . . . whatever?" Luc asked Terry.

"Just the wind. It's shifted."

Her midnight hair floated.

Luc assured her he was OK to drive.

Nine minutes later found him staring out his windshield as his blue car hummed over a highway hill toward Vernon.

Terry rode beside him.

Where Norma rode *when.*

Dennis created Terry's choice. He'd called shotgun. Didn't want to be a backseat man that *whoa* night as he felt sunset's shimmering waves.

Terry said she felt safer between the two of them.

The radio crackled the hundred-miles-away AM station playing a song rising up the charts: Crosby, Stills, Nash and Young's "Teach Your Children Well."

That *oh yeah* grin hit Luc.

Teach our children well, he thought as his stoned surge expanded him while driving a fast-moving car on a narrow highway. *Will we do that?*

Driving north.

Whoa! The mouse Stuart Little drove north to find the bird he loved!

Luc clicked on his right hand turn signal for the Vernon exit.

An *exit* to let you *enter.*

Wow went through Luc as he rumbled into his hometown.

They cruised past the Husky truck stop and café where he and Dennis took workday coffee breaks with their crew. Past the Tastee Freeze for *yum* soft swirl chocolate ice cream and cold Cokes for cruising high schoolers scanning out their car windows for who they wanted to be.

Do any of us ever get past searching for who we want to be? he thought.

The radio played. Terry rode beside him. Dennis rode shotgun.

"Shouldn't I feel something by now?" said Terry.

"Sometimes it takes a while," Luc said as the blue car let him steer where they went. "Or hell, it took me five or six tries to get stoned."

"How are you guys?"

"*Oh yeah*," said Dennis.

Between the movie *Beneath the Planet of the Apes* playing at the Roxy and the six other bars, Main Street was a-hopping that Friday night. The only empty parking space they found was in front of the Elk's Club with its café and bar.

"Smooth," said Dennis of Luc's city-crew-worthy parallel parking.

They climbed out of the blue car parked in the coming night.

Car doors slammed. Luc checked to be sure he put the keys in his jeans pocket. Checked again as his Three Musketeers walked the sidewalk toward sundown. Passed under Larson's Clothing flat awning above the sidewalk.

They walked the same line they'd ridden in the blue car.

Luc. Terry. Dennis.

Dennis *whoa'd* at the pavement on Main Street he'd once-upon-a-time sculpted by driving the giant roller over a fresh level of blacktop.

The buildings on Main Street posed beyond what Luc had ever seen.

Terry kept looking for other familiar faces—

—found hers reflected in the tinted blue glass of the pharmacy.

But I'm still not stoned! I am—I'm nearly a medical professional and I know I'm not intoxicated. Except maybe by how wonderfully weird it is being on this small-town Main Street far from Cincinnati! And by . . .

By friends like Dennis.

And like Luc whose house she'd see out her bedroom window every day.

Music blared through the Alibi bar's closed door.

Step inside to its chattering crowd. A band playing. Whiffs of perfume. Hairspray. Aftershave. Workweek sweat. Clouds of cigarette smoke. Fumes of beer as bartenders pull spigots to pour golden waterfalls into chilled mugs.

Luc smiled: *Nobody's gonna smell dope on us!*

He led his crew through the crowd of familiar yet *different* faces. Middle-aged couples. High school classmates with questions in their eyes. Some'd stuck around. Some of them went to college. Were still in it like him. He saw Steve talking with an older married couple. No Buffy.

The band finished a song as Luc and his crew reached the edge of the three steps down to the dance floor and a jumble of tables where—

An empty round table way at the back of the Alibi's dance floor!

Luc knifed his way through the shuffling crowd. Claimed that hard wooden circle. Cajoled a third chair from the next table as Dennis and Terry joined him.

"I'm not twenty-one," said Dennis. "But I've got a fake ID."

"Like that's gonna work in your hometown," said Terry.

The harried middle-aged barmaid blew a wisp of hair off her face and wrote down the order from Luc for three cold bottles of Miller Beer.

"A cold mug of tap's cheaper," said the penny-counting barmaid to these kids paying for college.

"But first round, let's go with the best," said Luc.

The barmaid blew that damn loose strand of hair off her face again. "*The best?* Don't go believing everything them ads say."

But she hurried off to fill the order, no IDs asked for.

Luc announced: "I'll buy this round."

"It's some sentimental thing," ventured Terry. "You're not just stoned."

He shrugged. Smiled.

The drummer clicked his sticks *one two three* and the band played.

They were a local group. A band of middle-aged guys. Fathers. Husbands. Only one bachelor: Mr. Bundy, the tenured high school music teacher.

Am I just stoned? thought Luc as he watched Mr. Bundy pull the microphone closer to where he sat pounding the piano keys.

Bundy's looking . . . Black hair getting silver, still lean and chiseled, but . . . Somehow he seems . . . more anxious than when I was in high school.

Nobody in the Alibi bar that July 1970 Friday night—hell, nobody in the whole town—knew that Mr. Bundy'd groomed not one, but three successive Vernon high school girls for sex, including Luc's first-ever date Bobbi Jean.

Bobbi Jean was one of the two who'd survived and rejected suicide.

She wasn't in the Alibi that night.

Neither was the other survivor who'd dropped out of high school, left town.

Bundy's band advertised their gig that July night as "new songs and old hits." They played standards for the WWII crowd. Threw in 1960s pop songs where Bundy was often the lead singer, just like he was in the few new songs they'd pulled off of 1970s radio to be ready for that year's high school dances.

And that night, while Zen Green was working its way in New York, the great American author of Luc's generation—a guy his age named Bruce

Springsteen—was rocking with his band Steel Mill at the Jersey Shore bar called The Stone Pony.

Asbury Park, New Jersey's Stone Pony. Vernon, Montana's Alibi Club. A thousand other bars and nightclubs across America. Soaring music. Faces. Twirling bodies.

Luc held out his right hand to Terry: "Dance with me."

And she did. Shuffle rocked dancing without touching to a fast song like most customers on the floor. A few holdouts to time's passage held hands and swirled dancing the 1950s jitterbug or the cowboy two-step.

The fast song ended.

The drums whisked the quintet into a famous slow song.

Luc raised his arms.

Terry met his stance. Her left hand around his back like his right was on hers. Her right hand softly filled and held his left hand. Her arms didn't weigh on him: She merged with him. He smelled the warmth of rose-scented midnight hair that flowed with their together steps and the rhythm of the music.

He ached to hold her closer. To feel the push of her breasts. The brush of the front of their jeans.

But he waited: Her choice. He waited. The band played.

They could have said anything to each other. No one else would have heard. But they didn't. He looked at her and smiled. She sent a soft smile back.

The song ended.

They stood staring at each other on the mingling dance floor.

"My turn!" Dennis grinned as he stepped toward them.

Luc walked to their table with its three waiting half-empty/half-full bottles.

The band played another slow song.

Dennis's holding her. She's holding him just like me.

The band launched into a recent Rolling Stones hit: "Under My Thumb."

On the dance floor, Terry told Dennis: "Great song. But not me."

She led him back to their table.

They finished their bottles of Miller High Life.

Ordered mugs of the cheaper bar beer to be polite, pay for their table.

"Rather have another toke," whispered Luc.

His two remaining joints were in a sealed plastic baggy taped to the inside front of white underwear shorts under his blue jeans. *Wait: Is that funny?*

"Not that some of us need it," he added to Terry.

Dennis grinned.

"High or not," she said. "It's a fun night. Thanks."

Her two male escorts relaxed in their chairs.

Turned to check out the scene by the bar and—

Reality slammed them.

Oh shit! No! We're stoned!

Marching into the Alibi came their street foreman gray cowboy hat Jerry. Waving off an offer of a drink.

Spotting—

Clomping straight to the round table at the back wall of the dance floor as the band played some song Luc and Dennis couldn't hear for the imagined *clunk clunk clunk* steps of road crew Street Foreman Jerry's boots coming to get them.

"Am I glad to see you guys!" said the man in the gray cowboy hat.

He smiled at Terry: "I'm Jerry. Great to meet you."

Luc said: *"What's wrong?"*

"Wrong? Hell, more 'n' half the world, but it's all good here. My old lady got her cast off's afternoon an' after dinner she told me to stop hanging around. Get the hell out of the house. Let her make it around on her own 'stead me and our kids eyeballing her all the time. 'Go see what's going on around town and don't come back until you do.'

"I had to laugh," said Jerry. "And get out of there like she said."

Stoned Dennis said: "So there's no water leak? Or sewer? Or emergency?"

"Hope to hell not," said their boss on the city crew.

Terry felt her two stoned companions fall away from fears.

"Hey, Luc," said Jerry. "I just ran into your old man.

"Don was confabbin' with a couple Main Street guys over cups of coffee in the Husky so I let them all be. Had a cup. Drove my pickup down Main Street with the windows open 'n' heard the music. Spotted a parking place and here I am.

"Hard to hear anything when the band's playing," he said to the trio of young'ns. "Gonna get a beer so's my old lady will smell it on my breath and know I did what she said."

He nodded his gray cowboy hat to Terry: "Gotta tell you, you grabbed a couple of wild ones here, but they might turn out not so bad."

Walked away as all three of them felt his grin.

The band played an electric guitar ode to hopeful broken hearts.

And *Oh then!*

Forget about the Roxy's movie about what happened after we finally succeeded in fucking humanity into a global horror show and who took over.

The star movie that Friday night played in the Alibi.

Lights! Camera! Action!

The bandstand. Five adult guys rocking drums, electric guitars, a keyboard like radio stars. Songs catchy and classic—all with a beat, a flow.

The dance floor. Swirling red and blue waves projecting from the bandstand. Hometown couples spinning and shuffling with the music.

And centering the screen of then and there:

Terry

Lucas   Dennis

Three dancing souls on the spinning-colors crowded dance floor.

Terry fast dancing with Lucas. Their bodies gyrating apart from each other. Their hearts thumping to the same beat.

Lucas spinning/dropping into a song's final chord *Ta-dah!*

Ta-dah gesturing Dennis to slide in and take Luc's place with Terry as the band kicked into the next song.

And the next. And the next. And the next.

Songs fast and slow. Doesn't matter. Terry dancing with one or the other of them. Waves her arms. Shakes her long black hair in the spinning lights and swinging music. Grinning. Laughing out loud. *Oh, yeah? Oh, no. Oh yeah!*

Luc and Dennis stun the ring of regulars dancing past:

Look! Those two college guys are dancing with each other!

The long black-haired gal with them laughs and struts her solo.

The whole world swirls colors of joy.

"We gotta take a break now!" announced Mr. Bundy as the band left the stage. Waitresses scurried to the round tables for drink orders.

Everyone in the Alibi heard the night's ten o'clock whistle blow.

Curfew for the minors the three of them were no longer.

"Still," said Terry: "I'm on weekend duty starting at eight in the morning."

They walked under the dark starlit sky on the Main Street sidewalk.

Drove off pressed together in the blue car's front seat.

Luc pulled the car to a stop at the sidewalk to the hospital's glass doors. Jumped out into the corner streetlamps' glow. Held the door open for Terry. Dennis was a stoned blink slow. Still vacating his shotgun seat as she slid under the steering wheel. Stood on the street beside Luc.

Who reached into his jeans' back pocket.

Pulled out and handed to her a folded sheet of white paper.

"Since you asked."

She frowned.

But took it. She took it.

Smiled as she walked around the front of his car.

Smiled as she walked not too close and past where Dennis stood.

Called out to both of them: "Thanks! I had fun!"

"*Even if,*" said Luc.

They all laughed as Terry walked to the glass doors. Dennis and Luc stood guard. Watched her as she thumbed the door buzzer. The warm wind blew. Her ebony hair flowed. Trees swayed on the hospital's newly mown grass.

A white-uniformed nurse walked the inside hall to the locked glass front doors. Opened them for the kind-of-an-intern from Ohio.

Terry waved goodbye to the two Montana young men on the sidewalk.

The night rolled on.

And WHOA, the gunpoint grass's stone hit Nick as he stepped out of the apartment building and into April's cool sidewalk facing a passing crowd of faces he knew even if he'd never met them.

Oh wow! Cosmic!

He'd never met the cropped blonde woman with the gun following his every step either!

What a day. Man, don't call it "Earth Day."

Call it Everywhere Day.

He glanced behind him:

She'd pushed the safety-cocked .45 down the front of her blue jeans. Let the too-big green Forest Service shirt cover it but the gun was still an easy grab.

Her left hand on his shoulder pulled their two bodies together.

Her breasts pillowed his back.

The gun in her pants pushed his spine.

"Find Shaughnessy in this crowd! He's six-foot-five, scraggly Beatles haircut. You know him and I don't. But I'm with you. Just a whisper or a shot away. Don't try to karate me to escape. These heartland people aren't like the don't-do-nothing crowd in New York that let a woman get murdered. They'll save me from you. Don't you yell for cops. In this crowd, my gunshot would sound like fireworks. Nobody expects to hear or be caught in the middle of a shootout."

Her gentle push moved Nick off the curb and into the river of believers, her right behind/beside him. Protestors grinned, waved greetings and solidarity.

Nick stumbled in the shoulder to shoulder crowd:

Wait! rocked inside Nick's skull. *Up ahead! At the front of the parade just reaching the bridge! Is that—*

THE BIG RIDE

April glowed on the thousands of Earth Day marchers filling the main street to the bridge over a river running.

In the crowd, Nick walked tippytoe to see over the heads of those in front of him and the woman with the gun.

That wasn't Shaughnessy. It was one of the beanpole guys from the basketball team walking beside one of the football team's stars, scholarships but not salaries for the two of them who helped bring in wheelbarrows full of green to the university.

Nick'd lived next door to the football star in Aber Hall their freshman year. Shawn Cosby was his name, and he'd been a leader in the Black Student Union with its seventy-six members—every Black student at the University of Montana except two, he told Nick.

The day after a white supremacist sniper gunned down Rev. Martin Luther King on a Memphis motel balcony on Thursday, April—

{Hey: April, just like this first Earth Day!}

—April 4, 1968, and whoa: Shawn and the BSU marched in to the university president's office, demanded a Black studies program, and ironically, had a brilliant Black preacher visiting from Chicago sitting out in the hallway, qualified and waiting to say yes to such a Montana offer.

Nick shook his head.

The crack of one rifle changed the world. Ended a brilliant and important life. Led Nick to stand in a circle of UM students in the wide grass Oval at the center of campus in quiet vigil of remembrance and hope. And MLK dreams.

The blonde with the gun walked beside/behind Nick now.

All around the two of them marched faces and forms.

Humans just like me, thought Nick. *Does she see them?*

Is she only looking for the two monsters she plans to kill?

R *emember this Four County Grady River Fair & Rodeo.*

"They say 'the third time is the charm,'" said Terry as she sat between Luc and Dennis in the blue car idling at the far end of a full prairie parking lot.

"Who's *they?*" asked Luc in that July Saturday's evening sun.

Nobody answered.

"Look at us," said Terry as she sat beside Luc. "The first time we hid on a hill seven miles from any eyes. Second time we parked on that west edge of town empty lot for your city crew. Houses could see us. But we didn't get busted either time. And I didn't get stoned either time. And now—'third time is the charm'—we're surrounded by a herd of cars that could all honk to summon the cops."

The radio played Three Dog Night's song "Mama Told Me Not to Come."

"*Clong!*" groaned Terry and Dennis, beating Luc to the punch.

"Hope not," said their friend who'd drilled his concept into them.

"Roll up your windows," said Dennis.

"Is this what's left over from last time?" Terry bent over to put her face between the car's steering wheel and driver Luc.

His lighter snapped the half of a joint her lips held.

"Yeah," said Luc as Terry filled her lungs. "It wasn't a roach."

"Is now," said Terry as she sat up between the two men on the front seat of the blue car and passed the burning ember to shotgun-seat Dennis.

He grabbed a hit—quickly crushed out the glowing ember in his fingertips.

"Don't worry." Luc held the sandwich-sized plastic bag in front of the radio where they could see what was going on. "I've got one more."

Terry shuddered: "I can't believe you tape that inside your underpants!"

Dennis laughed.

"So yes or no?" said Luc. "Remember: I haven't any kind of hit."

"*Ah*," said Terry. "Fair is fair and this is *The Fair.*"

That woman from Cincinnati shrugged: "We've come this far . . ."

The last joint made the rounds once. Twice.

Terry waved her hands as Luc offered her the joint for round three.

"My lungs need a break."

Dennis gave Luc the *gone* smile and an *I'm cool* shrug.

Luc stubbed out the joint.

Dropped it into the plastic bag.

Terry covered her eyes as she whirled to Dennis: "*I can't look!*"

Made it easier for Luc to re-tape the baggy under the front of his white underpants but *carefully* not blocking the necessary opening folds.

He turned the car off.

The three of them climbed out.

Terry went out Dennis's door like any regular passenger.

Luc and Dennis fanned the blue car's open doors:

Smoke *out.*

Evening prairie air/crunched dirt/distant popcorn/parking lot smells *in.*

Closing car doors *clunk.*

Three blue-jeaned outlaws stand in front of a sunlit old blue Dodge.

Stand tall like three gunslingers out of this western prairie's movie myths.

The Four County Grady River Fair & Rodeo spreads out before them.

The grandstand's walls glow white in this night.

Luc. Terry. Dennis.

Walking from the prairie into civilization's lights.

Past the displays of farm machinery. Past barns and corrals for cows, pigs, chickens, sheep who 4H kids lovingly raised for the slaughterhouse.

Past the grandstands.

Onto the midway.

Carny games.

The whirl of rides.

Loops of a roller coaster with screaming kids.

A merry-go-round of plastic horses on steel poles to up and down you right back to where you started.

"Damn, Luc!" said Terry. "I almost forgot."
She pulled a creased white sheet of paper from her back pocket.
"I *got it*," she said. "And I really liked it. Made me get you guys more."
Stoned Dennis blinked: "What are you guys talking about?"
Terry handed him the folded piece of paper:

Home Hotel: Summer, '68

We tore the old whorehouse down
yesterday. Fire scarred and long
deserted, only bums were sleeping
there, lying on rusted bed springs
(Room Rent Absolutely in Advance).
Only kids laughed in the square rooms
sounds that once cost a dollar
now free. Trespass is also illegal
and this law the sheriff enforces.
Scavengers and former tenants
had salvaged what useful brass
and iron there might have been.
There's no gold here, Emily.

We started in with pick and axe,
tearing planks and tar paper from
the third story roof. Dump trucks
go north to the junkyard, the road past
the pink, third-generation Hillside Ranch,
half the size and outside the city limits.
a dozer and five men against plastered walls.
All our tools, all our machines
broke on the stiff wood beams,
so the boss and the others, drunk
and mad, splashed gas on the floor
and finished what the first fire started.

                                        Luc Ross

That white sheet of paper and black-ink-typed words filled Dennis's eyes.
She'd said: "I got it."

Dennis *got it*, too. *Hell*, he'd been *there* in the poem's reality. But . . .

Carnival lights *blinked* him.

Nearby laughter pulled his face toward a partying trio of gir—*women* his
age walking the other way from him and this year's main attraction.

With *her*.

Maybe it was the carnival lights highlighting the crimson shade in her
hometown auburn hair. Maybe it was her holding-back soft laugh. Knowing
she was like he'd been two years ago: Scared *but*. Headed to college to let her
life grow. Same college as him. Maybe all that's what caught his eye.

But what he *saw* was her looking back at him.

Seeing him.

Smiling at—Smiling *to* him.

She's the real her, not a stoned me.

Dennis whirled to Luc and Terry.

His friends. Who were older than him. The same age. So many *sames*—
—but *not* like him.

"Hey, guys!" said Dennis. "I'm gonna—I gotta go check in with those . . .
I'll catch a ride back to town with them or whoever."

Their stunned expressions made him smile.

Feel a warmth in his heart.

"*Hey*: It's the fair," Dennis told them. "The carnival. You two go on. This
year's special attraction is dead ahead."

Then black-framed glasses and honest-grin Dennis quick-walked through
carnivalgoers to three women standing by the Tilt-A-Whirl.

He smiled at the other two wide-eyed with wonder women.

Softened his face toward the shy crimson auburn haired *her*.

WHOOSH as screams of joy and *wow* rushed by on the Tilt-A-Whirl.

Dennis spoke only to *her* with the crimson auburn hair: "Hi, Barbara."

She blushed. Her lips trembled.

"Why didn't you call me 'Barb' like everybody else does?"

"You deserve your whole name from me."

WHOOSH went the Tilt-A-Whirl.

Staring at the two of them from across the flowing midway, neither Terry nor Luc needed to hear whatever those words were that the carnival drowned out.

"I think we better move on," said Luc.

"Are you sure we haven't just seen this year's special attraction?"

They laughed.

Walked shoulder to shoulder to the end-of-the-midway white dome of light.

A handful of seventh grade boys scurried toward them.

Didn't even notice that *way* older couple as one of *the guys* blathered:

"You should have seen it! *Like*, a totally round building, right? You get your ticket. They tell you to go in and stand with your back against the wall.

"Then you hear an engine whine. Whining louder and faster. The wall behind you spins everybody around in a circle. You're spinning faster and faster! You can't even MOVE you're pressed so hard against that spinning wall!

"And then . . . *THEN* the floor drops away! You're spinning around a black hole! But you don't fall in because spinning fast like that, the wall has got you!"

"*Wow!*" said one of his buddies.

"What do they call it?" asked one boy as they hurried past Luc and Terry.

THE WALL OF DEATH

olored carnival lights and sounds swirled around Luc and Terry that *oh so special* night while thousands of miles away in England, across the Atlantic Ocean from Zen Green's New York struggles, a guitar virtuoso and genius author Luc's age named Richard Thompson was wowing audiences with his pioneering folk rock band Fairport Convention years before he'd write a stunning song about life's carnival rides named like the one Terry and Luc now faced.

"*Umm*," said Terry as they stared at where they arrived. "I don't know if I'm stoned or not, but you are and . . . You heard those boys so . . . Will you be OK *if*?"

"Will anybody be OK *if*?" Luc smiled. "Come on. Let's take a chance."

A carny led them and their fellow ticket buyers into the circular dome.

Terry grabbed Luc:

"Grab a spot so we face each other across the middle of the circle!"

They *Pardon me!* and *Sorry!*'d their way through the other ticket holders to place their backs *exactly there* against the wall.

Luc stared straight across the empty circle.

Terry smiled back at him. Her midnight hair hung loose by her shoulders. Her white blouse and blue jeans rode her curves.

rrr*RRWHINE!*

Magnetizing me! Pulling me back against the curved wall. My arms flat against the wall, too 'n' faster faster can barely—But yes, *yes I can smile!*

And see.

See across the circle—

—as reality's floor drops away from my feet.

See Terry.

Midnight hair splayed against the whirling wall like a web.

Her arms trapped against the wall like me. Her body . . .

Her body forced against the same curved wall as his.

Her eyes are wide. Her face spinning into another world *Oh!*

Stoned Luc had never felt so trapped and helpless and surrendered.

Let go. Oh let it all go.

Time. My wheres 'n' whats 'n' whys 'n' who . . . who . . .

Who I am is going round and round in space 'n' time and . . .

And is this spin of the Wall of Death what life's all about?

Then all thoughts spun away from him.

All he could *do* was spin with the circle and *be*.

'Round and 'round and 'round . . .

Until . . .

The hard floor rose beneath his feet.

His arms drooped.

Across the circle: Terry's blue eyes.

Their world stopped spinning.

Left them staring at each other across the circle's void.

She's grinning and—

And maybe she's stoned, thought Luc.

They met in the middle of the circle as the carny ushered the other ticket holders out to the midway lights.

"Dizzy," she said as she looked up at him. He steadied her arm. "Don't know if it's . . . Wow, *The Wall of Death* but it makes you feel a new kind of alive!"

They walked outside to the warm July night.

Knew better than to look for Dennis. Faces rivered past them. Carnival lights. Strings of colored bulbs. They smelled pink cotton candy. Heard the grandstand's loudspeaker announce the name of a cowboy straddling a snorting bull in a pen while waiting for the gate to blast open for his chance to make it to the bell. Laughter. Shouts. *Whoosh!* went the Tilt-A-Whirl. "*Hurry, hurry, hurry!*" called a carny summoning an audience for the gypsy fortune teller.

Terry wide-eyed Luc's face.

"This is . . . Can we get out of here? It's too—too much."

"And not enough," said Luc.

"Yeah." She said *yeah*.

They marched past the white walled grandstand. Past the Ferris Wheel raising its cars of eager seers and feelers in circles through the night. Past . . .

Buffy.

Walking out of the grandstands. A handsome stranger holding her hand.

Buffy saw Luc and the full-lipped, ebony-haired woman with him headed to the parking lot and some car that would take them away.

Buffy smiled at Luc. Caught his *back at you* smile.

Both couples walked on their separate ways.

Parking lot prairie crunched under Luc's sneakers.

Under Terry's.

She went to the passenger's side of Luc's blue Dodge.

Claimed the safe distance shotgun seat as he slid behind the wheel.

"Where do you want to go?" he asked the image reflected in the windshield.

"I want to hear music. Not . . . Not any place like the Alibi. Like from one of those stations that you can only get in your car radio."

Luc keyed the blue Dodge to life.

The radio crackled static.

Some 50,000 Watts city in that night played the poetry of those days.

Luc drove them out of the parking lot.

Over the gravel road to the STOP sign where it met the two-lane highway.

He turned right. Toward where the sun would rise. Away from the lights of his hometown. Toward the rim of the Vernon valley to the higher land prairie with better radio reception. A lone dark highway, the two of them in his blue car.

They topped the rim.

Drove past the "Oily Boid Gets the Worm" tourist attraction sign.

The Marias River Massacre sign and pull-off waited three miles ahead.

Where I drove Buffy that fair night of the Tunnel of Love, thought Luc.

Now he turned left on a different gravel road.

Terry said: "Those lights up ahead on the prairie."

"A missile site," said Luc.

Didn't say: "Like the other one with Norma/*DON'T THINK ABOUT HER!*"

His tires crunched the gravel road as he stopped the car.

Security lights flooded the barbed-wire, chain-link fence, two-concrete-bunkers missile site up ahead and off to their left.

Wait. What . . . Shimmers in the windshield?

Luc turned off the car's lights.

The dark horizon far beyond the Armageddon lights flowed with waves of green and blue and rose shades of light no human palette ever matched.

"Northern lights," whispered Luc.

"Come on," he said. Turned off the car. The man-made music died.

He stepped out to the gravel road.

Heard Terry open her door. Step out into the gravel with him.

They met at the front of the car.

Stared at the distant northern horizon.

"I've never seen them before," said Terry. "I—"

"Wait! Listen!"

Then she heard it, too. Too soft to be a rumble. Too solid to be a wind.

"They do that," said Luc. "Not very often, but . . . They create some sound with the flowing lights off the arctic snow that's always gonna be there. We see and hear what our sun makes just . . . just because that's the way it all works."

"We get to be here," said Terry. "We . . . We gotta feel all this."

Was it three or was it thirty heartbeats later?

Terry said: "Are you still stoned?"

"On everything out here, *yeah*. On the grass, *naw* not really."

"Me either. And this is . . . This is wonderful."

He looked at her.

She looked at him.

Looked away as he ripped the plastic bag out from his underpants.

His gas station lighter lit what was left of the last joint.

He passed it to her as the black starlit sky shimmered its horizon.

Two more hits each.

Her white sneaker heel kicked a hole in the gravel road.

Terry dropped the smoldering roach in its grave. Stomped dirt atop it: "Don't want to start a fire."

She closed her eyes. Drew in a deep breath of everything.

Coughed *from* and still smiled.

Her arms rose like the ballerina she was when she was *just a kid.*

Her white sneakers floated her on the gravel road under the night sky. She twirled. Saw it all: The glowing ground lights to end the world. The stars of forever in the dark umbrella sky. The whispering color lights of *now* on this gravel road's horizon. The parked car that got her here. The man who drove the car standing there with her under a shimmering aurora night sky of stars.

They stood face to face in front of the hood of that car.

The July night warm on the flesh of their bare arms.

A soft breeze stirred her midnight hair.

"We . . . we have to be here," she whispered. "Remember forever."

"We are here," said the man staring down into her blue eyes. "We can't just turn away from this moment, this . . . all this."

She watched him breathe in her every word: "But all this will be gone from this in a few weeks. Days. Minutes."

"Yes," he said. "No."

The flowing whisper of northern lights.

His hands cupped her face.

Her hands cradled his neck.

Lips magically knowing. Merging. Burning. Electric.

Until she pulled back.

Stared into Luc's eyes.

"I have a boyfriend," she whispered.

"I have a someone," he whispered.

The breeze on their flesh. In their hair.

No whispers from the fading waves of light.

Terry said: "We had to do that."

Luc said: "We had to *everything* that moment."

"Poetry," she whispered. "A ballet."

His heart pounded against the cage of his ribs.

"Take me home now," she said. "Or where home is supposed to be."

"Are you sure?"

"I'm the doctor."

She chose the safely distanced shotgun seat.

Their car doors slammed.

They drove the gravel road to the night's two-lane blacktop highway.

They drove back to town.

As the radio played.

Reported the KIAs in Vietnam now numbered 44,484.

The blonde with the gun led Nick through the marchers.

"Excuse me!" "Sorry!" "Looking for our friend." "You seen Shaughnessy?" "I heard some guy in the crowd is selling weed."

They got smiles. Frowns. Nods. Don't-be-pushy glares.

"Get to the front of the crowd!" she hissed at Nick. "If he's in this mob, he'll have to go past us!"

They burst into the banner-carrying front rank just as that first wave of marchers stepped off the bridge past downtown's Wilma movie theater where Nick spent many of his entertainment dimes. But since he was a storyteller even if nobody knew it, him going to movies to learn their how and why was actually work.

That he loved.

As he turned with her in the middle of the street to face the crowd streaming around and past them, he flashed on the first movie he saw at the Wilma, POINT BLANK, where gunman Lee Marvin persuaded beautiful blonde Angie Dickinson to keep the creepy man Lee wanted to confront "occupied" until Lee could show up. And. Whoa! That vision bent Nick's mind. *Now I'm the trapped-into-helping blonde and she's got the gun to nail the bad guys!*

Just like always, Nick told himself. *Man or woman, we're all trying not to fuck up.*

Nick blinked in the cool April Wednesday sunshine of the crowd: Does everybody sometimes feel like they're in a movie?

"Damn it!" said his real (dyed) blonde with the gun standing beside him. "If only we had those things on that TV show *Star Trek*! Tricorders! Hold them in your hand, click them open. Better than regular wall phones! If we all had those . . . We could call Shaughnessy!"

The crowd streamed past them.

Tick-tock, went the watch on Nick's wrist. *Tick-tock.*

STREETS ON FIRE

Was it three, was it five, was it all the minutes in the world later that Nick and the gunwoman beside him saw the end of the crowd crossing the bridge to where they stood in the middle of the street like poet Gary Snyder's riprap rocks in a mountain stream.

She turned to look at Nick.

His eyes filled with her.

They whirled. Pushed their way forward through the marching crowd.

"He's gotta be here somewhere!" she said as they excused and bullied their way to the front of the crowd hundreds of yards and dozens of city blocks away.

The crowd turned right on the main intersection of downtown Missoula's main street. Headed down that wide avenue toward the other main bridge across the river that Nick had laughed along the night he first got stoned. This wide, protestor packed avenue ran past the Greek columned Post Office speakers and banner holders and microphones lined the Post Office's high marching marble steps above the avenue filling each direction with protestors. Nick led the dyed blonde out to the edge of the marching crowd between two parked cars on that city avenue to where gawkers stood on the sidewalk with a commitment to do nothing more than watch and Mind Their Own Business.

Nick and the blonde gunwoman slid along storefronts creating green for their owners and staff. The cops had patrol cars parked crossways at that edge of the protestors' route on the avenue.

Crowd control. Not expecting any trouble from these hippy-dippy tree-huggers who weren't like the probably Commie war protestors on other days' marches.

The dyed blonde "wanna kill" woman followed Nick across the first intersection before the Post Office. Her eyes frantically skimmed the crowd. She knew he was doing that with her, too.

Nick led her along the wall of storefronts.

Only two more blocks to squeeze their way through before the Post Office and the heart of Earth Day's champions.

They detoured around barricades blocking that intersection.

They made it to the middle of the side street. The crowd to their right.

Nick felt the dyed blonde freeze.

Turned and saw her looking away from the crowd of protestors gathering to hear speeches about how they were saving the world.

Saw her eyes locked on two blocks further up this side street.

Saw that intersection corner.

Saw a couple police cars parked there on the right-side corner of that street's intersection, blue-shirted city cops standing around shooting the shit, stationed there "in case" some ten-code sent them charging down to the peaceful protestors as an anti-riot force.

Saw the left-side corner of that intersection.

Saw two parked Harley Davidson motorcycles.

L uc set Vernon city streets on fire that last Thursday in July 1970.

He started his first fire on Second Street South.

The same street that almost killed him in the runaway Black Beast.

His first arson came with the help of a fellow city crew member.

Cal the Bull and Luc drew pothole duty in that morning's shape-up.

A hay wagon ran over Cal's head when he was nine. Left him needing hearing aids. Glasses. Crunched him to a simple mind. He was a squat squinty

man in his mid-forties shuffling through life with a side-to-side gait on that
July Thursday.

Cal always wore tan khaki shirts and pants. Lived with his aging mother
and under the watchful eye of an older brother who managed a highway
department crew. Cal'd been on the city crew since he was nineteen and doc
pronounced him as fit as he'd ever be. Dave's predecessor as boss figured he'd
give Cal a chance. Give his family a little help with their bills.

Of course Cal couldn't drive.

But he got to ride the back of the Black Beast. Work the lever to oil slick the
streets passing beneath his boots. Breathing that *noir* mist made mask-wearing
Cal feel alive and worth something. He'd work a water or sewer break dig. A
pothole patch crew. Always showed up on time.

Plus, he was strong as a bull—half the reason he earned his nickname.
He muscled wrenches. Lifted. Toted. Pushed. Pulled. His favorite job was
to dig up a street with the heavy, body-shaking, arms-aching *rat-a-tat-tat*
jackhammer.

"You gotta see," crew members told Luc his first summer on the job when
the Home Hotel's arson fire created a poem. "Then you'll know we ain't joking."

Sure, thought Luc. *Let's trick the newcomer to the crew.*

Then one day that first summer when the crew's budget was low, Luc and
Cal got sent to the sewer lagoons east of town to chop weeds growing around
the shorelines so they wouldn't clog up the lagoons' connections.

Plus, Cal and Luc were thus demonstrably *not* idle on the taxpayers' clock.

They swung their scythes back and forth, back and forth, back and forth
all day long until Luc's arms could barely swing themselves.

Cal never faltered.

Never said much.

The most social Luc ever saw Cal be was on payday. Boss Dave passed out
envelopes with their checks. Then about half the crew would drive across the
railroad tracks to the Oasis.

The toughest bar in town. Hell, toughest for four counties around. Honest
men and women working blue collars for Main Street and The Man. Sunburnt
gandy dancers who kept the trains rolling through America. Wildcatters off
oil rigs pumping fuel into the fortunes of a few and warming everyone's air.
Low on dollars but high on hopes good souls. Troubled souls looking for a

fight to prove their worth. Looking for a fight to flee their own pain. Dreamers slumped on barroom stools. *The hell with my husband* lipstick wives. Trolling husbands.

That first Home Hotel summer with a new paycheck in his blue jeans' pocket, catching a ride with one of adult crew members but knowing he'd solo walk back across the railroad tracks and home in time for his mother's dinner curfew of 6:00, Luc in his thick black-rimmed eyeglasses stepped into the Oasis as a nineteen-year-old "good boy" minor who could not legally drink or be served alcohol.

Gorilla bartender Rose wore her brown hair short. Loved the bar's *break 'em up* baseball bat. Rose knew Luc by sight and rep. His dad was a Main Street boss but a good man. His mom was the softie in the kick-ass Conner sisters. Rose also knew the law said their son was way too young to belly up to her bar.

But Luc walked in as one of the city crew. Rose plopped a boilermaker in front of him like all the other hardworking payday souls in her care: a frosty mug of tap beer and a shot of bar whiskey.

And that was that.

From then on, Luc was a some kind of grown man in the streets of Vernon.

Just like Cal the Bull who sat grinning on a stool with his boilermaker in front of him and guys he worked with every day on either side. Pretending he could hear the song playing on the jukebox and knew what it was talking about. He'd earned his way there and knew it. Knew he was a real person on a stool.

Cal kept his grin all through his years on the city crew.

Kept his grin even on that iconic chilly first summer day when Luc and he were chopping child-high weeds around the sewer lagoons.

Don't think about the sewer smells. Just swing the scythe. Do the job.

Was after meeting the crew for morning coffee at the Husky. *Several* refills on a chilly summer's morn. Back to the sewer lagoons. *Swing, swing, swing.*

About 11:00, Cal pulled his left wrist up to his thick glasses.

Squinted at the wristwatch he'd bought with his own money.

Looked at Luc: "When you gotta, you gotta."

Cal stepped to the edge of the pond.

Fumbled with the front of his brown khaki pants.

Luc realized he *kinda* had to go too, so . . . *Why not?*

Was an hour until lunchtime back in town.

Besides, peeing in the sewer pond seemed efficient.

Luc unzipped. Pulled out his *Gramma hates it!* uncircumscribed penis. The nearby sound of Cal's flowing stream inspired his own bladder.

He casually glanced toward Cal . . .

. . . learned *THE TRUTH.*

There stood Cal. Holding his full hand away from his pants.

Call it a firehose. Call it a python. Call it a *ginormous* penis.

Shy and simple Cal who could barely talk to any non-relative female.

Hay-wagon crushed Cal who no woman ever gave that *Hmm* smile.

Cal had the hugest sexual organ in the world that back then told every man that *bigger* made you *better* and more wanted by and successful with women.

That's the other half of why he was Cal the Bull.

Cal the Bull and Luc set the first street on fire together.

Cal and Luc started their potholes hunt up "the top" of that street that last Thursday morning in 1970's July. The west end of town. The city gravel and blacktop plateau. They'd filled two buckets with oil at the city shop's yard. The buckets dangled on the open-ended red cargo truck Luc drove up to the plateau.

Luc shook his head as he rumbled the truck toward their destination.

Terry. Norma. Going-going-gone summer. WHEN. IF. WHAT.

He ached and surged at the same time. *Yes. No. Don't. Can't. Could. But.*

Luc piloted the small frontend loader on the plateau with novice skill that would have made Floyd shake his head. But smile. Luc's dumps filled the truck's box with three coffins' worth of sticky blacktop.

He and Cal rode down Second Street from its 12th Avenue border.

The same street the Black Beast almost got away and killed me.

Luc spotted a pothole at the 11th Avenue intersection.

Now we're two blocks from where I chased my rolling away empty car on my first real date ever.

He shook his head.

We all have places that made us who we are.

Luc remembered that sophomore year Prom. Cherie. Who later wore a white uniform as a nurse's aide. Worked in the hospital where—

DON'T THINK ABOUT TERRY!

Cherie Cherie Cherie who I took to the drive-in theater for my get-out-of-town *gonna* and then 'confessed' our lustful fumbles to her Catholic priest.

Luc shook his head.

Do we all do stupid shit like all that? Do we ever stop?

Luc and Cal's tattered broom swept dirt and debris out of the paved street potholes. One of them would dip another *rescued by the garbagemen* broom into a truck-hung bucket of oil as warm as that July day. He'd "paint" the inside of the swept pothole with black oil. Then the two of them shoveled blacktop from the truck's lowered tailgate to fill the pothole. Level it as best they could.

Bang their flat-edged shovels on the road to knock off sticky blacktop.

Shove the shovel handles into the metal loops on the side of the truck. Climb in. Slam the truck doors. Drive on.

There are always more potholes.

That Thursday morning, the red truck stopped for three before they reached the corner of Second Street and 8th Avenue.

The beautiful brick house on that corner lot belonged to Bill Stewart, a wealthy farm implement dealer. A vast green lawn surrounded the three-story brick house. Their spacious garage meant no cars parked at the curb.

Luc hung out in high school with the house's son and heir Carl who'd never been comfortable with that future. After the first fill-the-Army Selective Service draft lottery awarded him the number five, Carl dropped out of the university and volunteered. Was "*in the Army now, not behind the plow*" as that old song sang.

But thank God Carl wasn't assigned to Vietnam! thought Luc as he parked the red truck on the centerline beyond the pillow-sized pothole on the road just past the corner of the Stewarts' brick house and green lawn.

Cal the Bull liked to paint the potholes.

He swirled the black oil to prep that pothole that July Thursday morning.

Luc was three shovelfuls of blacktop dumped into the pothole by the time Cal'd rehung the oil bucket on the truck and shuffled over with his shovel bearing heavy blacktop off the truck, dumped it in the pothole.

Their shovels shaped the blacktop.

The last cloud from that dawn's soft rain floated away in the blue big sky.

Soon the sun would dry the damp and gutters.

Cal banged his shovel on the road.

Thick sticky blacktop still clung to his shovel blade after that whack—

—and he was Cal the Bull!

Luc banged his shovel blade on the hard pavement.

Only a few crumbs fell off the hefty clog of blacktop on his tool.

He sighed: "I'll get the gas."

SOP as Americans in 1970 liked to say. *Standard Operating Procedure.*

What you pick up sticks to you.

Shoveling blacktop coats your shovel blade with blacktop. That clinging blacktop makes the shovel heavier. Makes the shovel blade less functional.

Ergo: Get the blacktop off the shovel blade.

A tiny splash of gas on the shovel blade. A burning match dropped onto smeared-on blacktop. *Whump.* Two heartbeats of flame on the shovel blade heats the blacktop. Weakens the oil's adhesion. *Bam!* You knock the shovel blade on the street. Blacktop falls off. Flames snap out.

Voila, as the French say: A clean shovel that now works like it should.

Luc turned away from the now packed and sculpted pothole.

Turned his back on Cal as the Bull laid their two burdened shovels flat on the street beside the pillow-sized, shiny blacktop-filled pothole.

Luc pulled the ten-gallon gas can out of its rack on the truck.

Cal squinted: *Was that another pothole across the street?*

He shuffled away from the shovels to take a closer look. His back was to the just-filled pothole near the two shovels on the ground—

—as Luc set the gas can down on the street. Moved the shovels further away from the pothole to the downward slope of rain-damp Second Street that ended in the sidewalk gutter in front of the Stewarts' big bucks brick house.

Luc leaned both shovel handles against his chest. Backed his work boots as far away from the touching-the-ground shovel blades as he could. Unscrewed the metal ten-gallon can of gas. Tipped the wobbly can above the shovel blades.

Damn! thought Luc. *That's lots more gas than I wanted to spill.*

He screwed the gas can closed. Moved it away from the shovels.

"Ah shit," he mumbled.

Said loud enough for *looking-the-other-way* Cal to hear: "I forgot the matches!"

Luc hustled back toward the red truck's cab.

Cal turned from his search. Saw the shovels lying beside the gas can as Luc *who forgot* reached the red truck.

Cal shuffled to the shovels as Luc jumped into the truck's front seat.

Luc rummaged in the truck's glove compartment.

Cal saw the waiting gas can. Knew what to do. SOP.

Luc found the glove compartment's free matchbook from the Husky.

Cal leaned the two shovel handles against his chest like Luc had.

'Draw me!' read a profile of a curly dark-haired woman on the matchbook.

Don't think NOT THINKING about Terry's lush lips/the curve of Norma's—

Luc shut his eyes.

Thus did not see what the truck's rearview side mirrors reflected:

Cal the Bull lifting the gas can off the road. Unscrewing it. Proudly *strong like bull* tipping the open can high above the two damp blacktop shovel blades.

Whoa! thought Cal. *Big splash.*

Cal laid the shovels on the street.

Luc tumbled out of the truck as Cal carried the gas can toward the truck.

Ran past Cal who was *obviously* just moving the gas can far away from the shovels Luc had over-soaked.

Luc lifted the shovel handles. Smelled the gas he'd splashed. Ripped a match out of the *Draw me!* packet. Struck the match to flame. Tossed it tumbling burning down to the soaked shovel blades.

Whoosh!

An ankle-tall fire snake rushed along the stream of gas floating on the sloping, rain damp streets to the curb in front of that corner brick house—

KA-WHOOMP!

A wall of blue and orange flame roared up from the sloping gutter.

A wall of gas-stench flames as tall as Luc's jaw-dropped and wide-eyed face.

The roar in his hearing aids whirled Cal around to see.

"Whoa, Nellie!" he cried.

The heat of the wall of flames he faced blasted Luc.

Do, what should I gotta do GOTTA DO SOMETHING!

A screen door slammed on the other side of the wall of flames.

WONK!

The wall of flames vanished.

Left behind a half block long stretch of sloping blacked curb.

"Luc!" yelled a middle-aged woman in an expensive house dress from where she stood on her corner brick home's green front lawn.

She waved her hands: "Should I call the fire department?"

"*No!*" yelled Luc. Waved back at his friend's mother. "Everything's OK!"

Don't come look at your curb! Don't see that blackened line of concrete!

"We're all done!" he yelled at her.

Big smile. Send her a thumbs-up.

Mrs. Stewart shrugged. But that shrug meant OK. She sighed: *This town.* She headed back into her unharmed corner brick home.

"Come on!" Luc yelled to Cal.

Grabbed the shovels. Tossed them into the truck's open back end box of blacktop. Scrambled behind the steering wheel. Keyed the engine.

Cal jumped into the shotgun seat.

Luc roared the truck away from the scene of the crime.

They said nothing to nobody when they parked back at the shop for lunch.

"What the hell," said his mom as she plopped white bread, mayonnaise and canned tuna fish sandwiches on the kitchen table in front of her husband and tale-telling son. "Shit happens. 'Specially to us Conners. Remember when you were ten and you and your Aunt Iona set Main Street on fire?"

"Forget about *then*," said Dad. "This is *now*. You burnt the curb in front of *Bill Stewart's* house?"

"Yeah."

Dad turned to his wife: "What's his wife's name?"

"Mary."

"You two are friends, right?"

"Our boys are friends. She and me don't have any beefs. Don't see her much. They're Catholic. And money like we ain't. Plus, she's a homebody. Like me. 'Cept I got my sisters who drag me—"

Dad tuned out his wife as he whirled from the table.

Pulled the phone book out of its drawer in the kitchen counter near the hanging-on-the-wall black rotary dial phone. Flipped pages. Squinted as he ran his finger down the lines of fine type. Found the number he wanted. His lips moved silently repeating it so he would remember all of the four digits he spun around the rotary dial as his other hand held the phone receiver to his ear.

His wife and son in the kitchen with him heard one buzz in his ear.

Two buzzes.

Three—

"Oh, hi, Bill! It's Don Ross . . . Not much, just checking to see how's it going with Mary after this morning's little surprise with your son's buddy *my son* and the city crew . . . Really, hell of a deal. Have to drive by and have a look. Just glad my guy was there to make sure nothing big or bad happened. How's your son—"

Dad deliberately coughed like a cigarette smoker would—

—whipped around to face his son. Held his hand over the mouthpiece.

Luc *got it.* Whispered: *"Carl."*

Dad *harumphed* as he took his hand off the mouthpiece.

"Sorry about that. How's Carl doing? . . . Good. I'll let Luc know . . . Anyway, let you get back to your lunch and Mary. Maybe we'll grab a cup of coffee someday down at the Chat 'n' Chew . . . Yeah, I'd like that, too. See *ya.*"

Dad smiled as he hung up the phone.

Sat back down at the kitchen table to finish his tuna fish sandwich.

"What the hell?" said Mom as she poured herself another cup of coffee and sat down at the kitchen table where her men were finishing their lunch.

"I don't know Bill so well," said Dad. "Business now and then for the trucking company and his implement shops, mostly—Doesn't matter.

"*What matters* is our buddy Councilman Mueler keeps suckin' up to him. And even though the Stewarts are Catholics, us three guys're all Republicans like most good folks."

Luc said nothing.

"But Mueler's out on the right-wing edge. Not sure he's even smart enough to be a Nixon man. I don't know where Bill is. Never mattered much before.

"But Bill swings some weight in town. Come November, he could talk up Mueler. Or *maybe* he could talk up me. Or almost as good, keep his mouth shut and say nothing 'bout either of us. Today me checking in to be sure his wife and stuff are OK after my son set his street on fire—"

"Just the gutter of his curb!"

"*Whatever, wherever,* I let him know I care and that things are straight. And come next couple days, probably first of next week since today is Thursday, turns out I'll have to be up to Main Street. Most likely he'll be up t' his implement warehouse. Closer to the Husky, but there we might run into Luc and the city crew so I'd rather not. Call him first 'bout that coffee we been talking about at the Chat 'n' Chew. Have a friendly sit down. Tell him nothing 'bout what's coming. But give him my attention like he deserves. Listen."

Mom said: "So this is how it's gonna be from now on?"

She glared at Luc: "Guess you and your dad just dropped a match on Main Street."

Dad shrugged away her glare: "You gotta take the chances you get. And as long as Luc keeps setting the streets on fire . . ."

Luc grinned: "I'll do my best."

He *between you and me* told Dennis about the first fire after lunch.

Said nothing to nobody about the second fire he lit with his dad.

Luc and Cal the Bull spent the afternoon shift filling potholes blocks away from any blackened curb.

Shuffled into the cramped office to fill out their timecards kept in metal slots hung on the wooden wall with the rest of the crew.

Dave sat in his boss's chair behind the desk. Chatting. Laughing.

Called out: "Hey, Luc! I drove the white pickup 'round town 'n' saw you two did a good job on the potholes today. And a *fucking* great job keeping your shovels clean. Plus burning off any fungus on the curb of a rich man's house."

Jerry and Floyd, Arson and the rest of the crew laughed and snickered.

Luc threw out his hands. Took a deep bow. Laughter filled his face.

He knew everybody knew everything—and it was alright. *Thanks, Dave!*

Cal the Bull knew, too. Got the joke. A joke that he was an OK real man.

Luc kept that smile even as the Rev. Carl McIntyre pontificated out of the kitchen radio his mom controlled while they did the dinner dishes.

He hung up the dish towel (properly).

Headed to his bedroom with his stereo, records and a new novel.

His third streets of fire came with a *knock-knock* on the front door.

Firm but . . . but soft. Hesitant.

Luc swung open the curtained windows main door . . .

Terry stood on their concrete front porch.

She shrugged. "I knew your doorbell doesn't work."

"Hi! I . . . You . . . Glad to see you. Come in."

"*No*, I . . . Dennis came in for his shot. I heard you had another city crew adventure. Thought I . . . Wanted to come by and see if you're OK."

All of that was true.

And they both knew it.

He stepped outside to the porch without asking her.

Shut the doors behind him.

"You OK?" he asked her as the sinking sun softened her midnight hair.

"Why wouldn't I be?"

She smiled: "Thanks to you and your old boss at the Roxy, I got two movie posters hanging on the sad bare walls of my hospital room. *The Apartment.* If ever there was art with irony . . . But with red *brighten up the room* background and a happy couple hurrying away. Then on the wall behind my bed hangs *Easy Rider* with that motorcycle rebel looking out at some new American horizon."

"Like you," said Luc. "Coming here."

"*Here* is just where the program sent me."

"*Nah.* You took a chance on this town. And . . . And who was—*is* here."

They each looked away.

"Lucky me," whispered out of her.

She blinked. Shrugged.

"I mean," she said, "the *Easy Rider* poster's background is colored like the sun. Yellow brightens up the hospital gray. Plus it . . . We shared about it."

Don't ask about 'we,' thought Luc. *Could 'we' just be her and me?*

"You wouldn't have liked the few other choices Mr. Tom at the Roxy gave me. I couldn't find one with a sea or ocean background."

He hated that necessary lie. There'd been a beautiful poster with an ocean view: *A Summer Place.* A young love movie everyone knew. That poster shows a couple near their age staring into each other's eyes. Holding each other. Kissing.

I didn't dare give that to her!

Terry said: "You going to hang onto the *Easy Rider* after I'm gone?"

"Hang on and hang it up in my new wherever."

"Will . . . Will you think about this summer when you look at it?"

"What do you think?"

They both looked out at the street and houses beyond this porch.

Spun back/burst out together:

> Luc said, "I oughta—"
>
> "We should—" said Terry.

They both laughed.

Looked each other in the face.

"I don't mean to . . . You want to go for a ride in my car? Talk?"

"Talk, yes. Car, no. Walk."

They marched down the steps.

Turned right on the sidewalk toward the sinking sun.

Strolled side by side past his car that could have cocooned them. Carried them somewhere private. Kept them close.

They walked past the hospital doors across the street.

The window of her bedroom.

Luc let her choose when they reached the end of the block.

She kept going straight.

The houses of First Street South flowed past them.

Luc's heart beat harder than his steps. His stomach was tight.

"We haven't seen each other since the fair," she said.

"The Wall of Death."

"That's not what I mean." She shrugged. "Or maybe it is. We spun around. The floor fell away. But then . . . Now that ride is over."

They'd reached the corner for the brick fortress of Ma Bell.

Where Buffy works, flashed through Luc. Faded away.

Now he walked side by side with Terry as they followed the sun.

Their hands dangled between them. Close. Not touching.

"We were stoned," she said.

"Yes.

"Congratulations," he added.

She couldn't stop the smile he saw with one of his sideways glances.

You gotta, he thought. *You oughta. It's why we're walking now.*

"The kiss," he said as they walked on.

"Yes," she said as they stared straight ahead.

"Don't get me wrong," she said. "It was . . ."

"*Wow.*"

"*But.*"

"So many *buts.*"

They had to laugh at his accidental pun.

They could do that. Share that.

They kept walking. Reached the corner across from his junior high.

She nodded to the tan brick building: "So that's where you grew up?"

"I grow up everywhere I go," he said. "*Doing* not just *being*. "Choosing . . ."

"Choosing what's right," she said. "What works. What lasts."

"Whatever all of that means," said Luc. "Will you be able to write a prescription for that when you're a doc?"

Terry sighed: "*Physician, heal thyself.*"

They turned and walked up the street toward Knob Hill.

Luc saw Steve's house ahead. Smiled.

He pointed to the right.

Led Terry up Second Street into the sun.

"My boyfriend was jealous of you even before," said Terry. "Back when he first phoned me and I told him about you two guys. He zeroed in on you."

"Why?"

"Must have been something I said. What did you tell your girlfriend?"

"Nothing about anything in all this summer of us. It's too . . . special."

He stared at the row of houses where a Shirley he knew once lived.

"What do you tell your boyfriend now?" came out of him.

She shrugged. "Nothing. No ambulance for him to hear.

"Sometimes long distance making it harder to connect and communicate with someone is a good thing," said Terry.

They walked up the evening hill she knew he'd once almost died on.

Plus the fire that morning.

"I hate liars," she said.

"And we both hate *being* a liar," said Luc.

She hmphed. "Together again."

They stopped at the corner across from the Stewarts' brick house.

Luc pointed to the blackened curb.

"Your fire left a mark," whispered Terry.

She stared straight at his face. "But it's gonna wash away someday."

"You mean like your song Suzanne at the river?"

Terry whispered: "Sometimes a song is just a song."

She turned. Walked back the way they came. Sunset warmed her back that July Thursday in 1970. Sunrise waited beyond the small-town streets she faced.

They walked past the Methodist church.

Saw the altar awaiting promises through God's front windows.

Walked on.

Walked past the courthouse where justice was whoever wins.

The library sat on their left as they walked toward the hospital complex one block dead ahead. They were on the back end. The nursing home side full of trembling men and women with wispy gray hair webbing *remembers and forgots*.

"Your grandmother is in there," said Terry.

"Yeah. Gramma Meg."

"Did she love her purple lilacs?"

"Who wouldn't?" said Luc.

Terry said nothing.

They walked to the sidewalk in front of the hospital's main glass doors.

Luc's home and the car they hadn't taken were across the street.

They stopped.

Faced each other just out of reach.

The planet Venus rose in the dusky blue sky. As always, first to light.

"This is the walk I gotta walk," said Terry from Cincinnati.

"I get it," said Luc from these streets of Vernon.

"So are we all good?"

"We're *some* kind of good."

"But we'll . . . You'll still come and see me? Hang out? Dennis and you?"

"His fair night ended up with him moving on with Barbara."

"But you?"

"I'm right here."

They smiled.

She turned and he watched her walk up the sidewalk to the hospital doors.

She's turning back and . . . !

Terry waved and walked through the glass doors to *wherever*.

Luc felt all his streets burst into flame.

They made a triangle in the parked-cars-lined side street.

Nick and the dyed blonde gunwoman standing in the middle of the road.

A block away on the right corner waited the cops.

Across the street from them on the left corner waited those parked outlaw motorcycles.

Together, Nick and the blonde whispered: "What now?"

WHAT YOU DON'T KNOW

Earth Day, 1970. An April Wednesday afternoon in what passes for a city in Montana. Downtown where the green grows.

"Testing! Testing!" blasting from a microphone from around the corner of the Post Office to its marble steps where thousands of demonstrators' eyes and ears focused. Up off a block away at the next intersection, right side, three cop cars and twice as many blue-shirted badges and holstered .38 revolvers of law and order while left side of the street, visible at that corner, wait two black motorcycles.

Down the block, their backs to the public scene, stood Nick and the dyed blonde gunwoman.

And WHOA!

Racing around the motorcycles' corner like an Olympic sprinter came . . .

YES! Six-foot-five-tall, electric hair flying in the wind, arms a-pumping, blue-jeaned legs whipping out as far and as fast as they can, a face of "OH, SHIT!" came Shaughnessy.

And he's turning away from the cops. Racing toward Nick's team. He's a block away. Half a block away.

Whipping—

—well, chugging around the corner after Shaughnessy come two black leather, road-jacketed men. They braked their boots by their bikes: Roar after him or run or split up?

Nick and his partner raced to intersect Shaughnessy. Ran
between two parked cars to the sidewalk on that side of the road.

Ran toward the fleeing man.

COLLISION! Shaughnessy bounces them away from him.

Blondie crashes into Nick and they hit the concrete sidewalk.

Luc shook his head in the grocery store's after-dinner parking lot:

"*How did I not know this?*" he asked his high school classmate Gideon.

"Hell, how does anybody know anything?" answered Gideon.

They stood in the parking lot of the Thriftway grocery store where Luc and Dennis once worked as box boys.

Luc's mom sent him to the store to get what she forgot.

Life sent Gideon there.

Gideon. The wittiest guy in Luc's high school class of eighty-eight graduates—

—the same count as the number of keys on a piano.

Gideon who'd both gotten Luc *first time ever* drunk at the 1964 Montana Republican Party state convention, then rescued Luc after he hungover threw up on the (eventual) Watergate crook governor's shoes.

Gideon who Luc'd accidentally discovered had spent his *growin' up* years fighting off his stepfather's beatings of Gideon's mom and younger sister.

Gideon who made sure to keep his quick smile and wry *How you doin'?*

All those images in Luc's eyes shimmered with The Big News.

"You got married?" said Luc. "I mean—Congratulations and . . . And Julia, she's a . . . a *wow* and smart like you and . . . When? How?"

"I had a thing for her in high school. She missed me after I graduated. I went to Western 'cause, *you know*, the Draft and what the hell else was I gonna do. She graduated the next year, came to Western and there we were. Like we'd always been. And like we'd never been."

He laughed: "What else were we going to do, right? We get each other.

"And in case you're wondering, *no*, we didn't get knocked up—*though we practiced damn hard at it!*"

Both young men laughed.

"Come last spring, we didn't want to be stuck being students. Wanted to be out here doing real life. Dropped out. Came back to Vernon to start over.

Justice of the Peace'd our asses. Together wherever. I grabbed a job with Horner's concrete company. She was gonna take a job at the bank, but that rich boy asshole president started hitting on her even before she'd signed the papers, so now she's working for the clinic. We rent a place on the northside. *Our* place."

"I'm blown away!"

"Yeah, I figure you're blowing a lot of that smoke some of us like."

They laughed.

Stood there in the parking lot of the store where you bought what you needed to live. Held brown paper sacks of groceries in the crooks of their arms.

Luc'd bought his with a check from his parents.

Gideon'd bought his with a check from his marriage.

He watched Luc fumble for what to say.

"Hell." Gideon smiled. "Now all this out here is up to you to fix, college guy. I just bring home the groceries. You get a chance, stop by. If not, see you around—*unless one of us has too much of that smoke in our eyes!*"

They laughed. Got in separate cars. Gideon drove away first.

Luc drove over the viaduct above the train tracks out of town.

Wow.

His car radio played the hit theme from a recent movie about a US Mobile Army Surgical Hospital (MASH) in the Korean war that was still technically stalled in a cease-fire.

Call that helicopters' movie a comedy, *sure*, but call it a mirror on the war still being fought in another cut in half Asian country called Vietnam where on that Wednesday evening, Aug. 5, 1970, the KIA score of Americans like Luc and Gideon reached 44,592.

No one was home when Luc walked into the kitchen with groceries.

As usual, Dad'd gone back to being the boss at the trucking company.

Or maybe he was out taking subtle steps toward the city council.

Mom was supposed to be across the street with her sisters visiting Gramma Meg in the nursing home attached to the back end of the hospital.

Sure, the reason Luc walked out his front door and crossed the street was to tell his mom he'd gotten the groceries and put them away.

Sure, the urgency of that news was why he took the straightest route to Gramma Meg's room:

Through the hospital's front doors. Into its lobby—the desk nurse didn't look up. Luc climbed the stairs to the second floor. No nurse on duty at the second-floor desk. He lingered in the smell of pine ammonia. The silence of those halls.

You can't. You want to so bad but . . . but . . .

Luc retreated through the wooden double doors into the nursing home.

He heard the drone of the TV in the recreation room beside the dining room.

Heard the chatter of his aunts coming down a right-hand turn hallway.

The forty-plus hatchet-faced nurse behind the desk had worked there for years.

She gave him a sly grin. Her voice held a razor's edge.

"Looky here, it's Luc, 'the guy with the gotta.' I seen you working who's on the other side of those doors. Good thing I'm not younger. Seems you got a thing for girls who work at the hospital. Remember when you dropped off your love letter for our nurse's aide Cherie way back, *what*, day you left town for college?"

Her razor-edged voice cut loose questions he hadn't realized until now.

"It's good to see you, too," he lied.

Leaned on the ledge of her desk.

Stared into her eyes.

"Where *is* Cherie?"

The nurse blinked.

"She fucked up her life like you wanted to," countered the nurse who lived alone in a cheap house. "Got pregnant her first year down at Eastern—and her a biology major! Doc Nirmberg was on the way out, but she'd probably never done that anyway, being Catholic and all. She married the guy. Lost her scholarship. But folks say she's taking classes. Workin'. Got a son she loves the hell out of.

"I always figured she'd end up with that Andy fellow from her class. They were a thing after she dumped your ass. But the Draft got him. Last I heard, he's trying to keep *his* ass from getting killed over in 'Nam. Heard that his commanding officer told him something like: 'You're going home in a box, pothead.' But he ain't here yet."

Luc shook his head.

"When he is, I want him walking and playing the guitar like he used to."

Luc turned toward Gramma Meg's room.

The nurse behind the desk called out to his back: "Hey!"

Luc turned back to face her.

"When that someday comes that I'm gonna be on the other side of this desk 'n' in one of these rooms, you gonna come see me?"

"You never know," said Luc.

Gave her his back and that lie they both knew as he walked away.

Mom stood beside the bed with her sisters Dory and Iona.

Gramma Meg seemed shrunken under the bed's white sheet.

Dory beamed: "Why look! Here's Luc!"

"Hi, Gramma."

The wispy white haired woman stared at the latest arrival.

"You're . . . you're Cora's boy. Got some weird Bible-y name."

"Luc," he said. "But we spell it differently."

"I bet," said Gramma Meg. A smile curled her lips. "You're a Conner."

Luc's mom leaned toward her bed-ridden mother: "He knows his *who*."

The aunts took over. Talking loudly about this. About that. About "Remember Ma?" And "Who was it who let our horse Zeke loose down the house that time when the sheriff tripped over himself chasing Zeke?" "How you doing?" "What can we get ya?"

Luc eased out of the circle of Conners around a hospital bed.

His mother Cora turned to watch him go.

Watch him shrug.

She shooed him out with a quiet whisk of her hand and smile of *thanks*.

For coming to see Gramma Meg like she asked? wondered Luc. *Or thanks for something else I did? Or . . . Or will do in the future.*

This nursing home's nurses' desk stood empty.

Luc pushed through the wooden double doors into the hospital.

She stood silhouetted against the second-story lounge's picture window.

He walked straight toward her.

Saw another empty nurses' front desk.

We're all alone in sundown light and the scent of pine disinfectant.

Terry saw his reflection in the picture window to infinity.

Turned and they stood face to face only two arms' lengths apart.

She wore her medical white jacket. Her stethoscope hung around her neck.

Awe filled her face. Her lips were parted like they wanted to shout in these QUIET hospital halls. She shook her head. Stared at Luc like he was a spirit.

Her whisper was soft. Incredulous. For herself as much as for Luc.

"I got to . . . They let me assist in a baby being born! . . . That's . . . You don't get to do that until med school and . . . And the duty nurse roared off with the ambulance and they needed . . . *They needed, they trusted, they wanted me!*"

She blinked.

Truly saw him standing there. Gave him a personal smile.

"They let me cut the umbilical cord before the husband came in. A little girl. Seven pounds, three ounces. Her dad had been so nervous his cigarette smoke cloud was as thick as LA's smog.

"They . . . They named the baby Anne."

Luc smiled: *"Anne as in A as in your first one."*

"You get it, don't you," she said. Not a question.

"I'm just glad I get to be here. For it. For you."

"Guess we're both pretty lucky."

Exploding through those double doors to the nursing home came the razor-tongued nurse. She quick-marched to those two young *so whats*.

"Come on, *baby doc*. The ambulance is pullin' up. They got Roy Overton strapped in there. Shot himself in his head, stupid asshole. Got a family and a job. What the hell could be so wrong he figured to blow his brains out?"

She blinked.

She stabbed her forefinger at those two lucky still *growin' ups*.

"But don't either one of you go saying 'suicide' to nobody. Maybe Roy was smart enough to have an insurance policy. Let's hope all around.

"Now come on!"

The nurse whirled toward stairs down to the ambulance bay.

Terry told Luc: "Gotta go!"

"You'll be great!" he called out to her *going, going, gone.*

Luc walked out of the hospital's glass front doors.

A blue shingled roof, white-walled house waited across the street.

Zero small-town traffic.

He started to cross the street.

Stopped.

Stood in the middle of the street staring at August's sundown.

Felt himself bathed in the cooling summer orange light.

Gideon a married man. Gramma Meg shrinking under a white hospital sheet. Mom's *thank you*. A baby crying as its umbilical cord gets scissored. A cocked pistol to your skull. A "Gotta Go."

Sundown sank lower in front of Luc.

The coming-out stars of night twinkled.

And Luc sensed some coming dawn.

Shaughnessy bounced off the scramble on the sidewalk.

Raced toward the shuffling crowd of protestors.

Their pavement-shuffling feet and the blasting out for blocks microphone overwhelmed all ears.

The Vision grabbed Nick as he pressed against the facing up front of the blonde trapped on the sidewalk.

He grabbed the gun from her waistband.

Scrambled to kneel behind yet lean his shooting right arm on the trunk of a black '64 Chevy. Safety clicked back. Hammer clicked back. Sights locked on.

Nick shot past the end-of-the-block gathering of cops.

BANG! BANG!

The plate glass picture window of the closed bank behind the cops shattered. Alarms rang. Cops drew their .38 revolvers because those were gunshots from somewhere, bullets zinging over their heads.

The two bikers froze by their machines at the alarm.

Saw the cops drawing their guns.

The right hands of the bikers came out from under their black leather jackets with pistols they blasted toward the cops.

Who shot back.

The bikers crashed down. Shattered thigh bone. One eye lost.

Two painful shuffles to old age in the state prison for attempted murders of police officers.

Nick stuffed the .45 in his jeans under his shirt. Grabbed the stunned blonde's hand. Raced her to the crowd of protestors as those Earth Day sounds drowned out the wail of approaching ambulances.

ALL THE ONLYS

Nick and the dyed blonde scurried away through the crowded sidewalks. Saw ambulances race toward what they'd left behind. Turned like any 'innocent' normal person would to see the bloody chaos.

She whispered: "How . . . how bad do you think it is?"

"We'll have to wait for the morning newspaper to find out."

They reached a tree-lined, old-homes neighborhood. Turned left toward downtown Missoula to walk past family dreams-come-true of owning a home amidst such gentle green wonder.

They walked side by side.

"I've got to get out of this town," she told Nick.

The only thing he could say out loud was: "Do you want the gun?"

"Neither do you," she said. But smiled: "Nice shot."

"Just give me a chance."

She looked away from him.

Looked at the old homes with new families.

"Think either of us will ever live in a place like this?"

"I can't think about that now," he said.

"Yeah," she said. "Me, either."

Three steps later, she said: "Do you have a car?"

"Yeah, but it's way back across the river. I walked to Shaughnessy's so I could join the Earth Day march. 'Cause I believe. Still. Even. Course, my car keys and driver's license are on Shaughnessy's kitchen table."

She laughed.

"Let's hope you get your $15 back, too."

Her ruby lips made a grim red line.

"Does this town have a taxi?"

"I'll take you wherever you want to go."

"That's too far a road. For you. For me. I—we both got things to do."

He walked her to the taxi office around the corner from the Wilma theater. The dispatcher called for a taxi to make an airport run.

That man behind the counter said: "This time of afternoon, there's only the plane to Denver and one to Seattle takin' off."

The blonde who didn't have a gun in her pants only smiled.

The taxi pulled up outside.

*W*HUNK! socked the August Friday morning air as Dennis slammed shut the hood on the red truck in the city shop yard.

Street Foreman Jerry and Luc stood there waiting for his verdict.

"The fan belt should hold now," said Dennis as he climbed off the red truck's front bumper with a tool belt around his waist.

The yard smelled of sand and exhaust from other gas burning machines. Their engines grumbled and roared. Distant crew members readied their day.

Foreman Jerry's weathered gray cowboy hat nodded: "Or at least hold until you go back to college and don't need to worry about it no more."

The three men laughed.

Jerry said: "By the way, ain't you leaving us real soon?"

"A week from today," said Dennis. "Friday the 28th. The next Tuesday is September 1st and I gotta be back at school then."

"Sorry," said Jerry.

He turned to Luc: "What about you?"

"You still got one more week after Dennis leaves to put up with me."

The gray cowboy hat shook from side to side: "*Damn it!*"

They all laughed.

"We'll miss you guys," said Jerry.

His gray cowboy hat turned from side to side with a sly grin.

"Gotta ask," said Jerry. "That night in the Alibi. You two with Hospital Gal. I had to laugh. But now . . . Is one of you hooked up with lucky her?"

"She's great," said Dennis. Shrugged a grin. "But her and me are just friends. I've got . . . Well, Barbara and I . . . But Luc . . ."

Luc's two coworkers stared at him.

"We're friends," he quickly said. Shrugged . . . *something.* "I haven't seen her in a couple weeks."

Sixteen days, he thought. *But who's counting.*

Sixteen days. Fifteen nights. Staring at the windows of her hospital "dorm" room where he'd helped her hang movie posters. Where Suzanne took him down to the river. Where Terry might be looking out to see his house.

Sixteen days of him walking around to the back end of the hospital where the nursing home's front doors took him straight to Gramma Meg. Sixteen days of not thinking where else his steps could take him. What his eyes could see. What he might touch.

Only—*Only?*—hanging out with his buddies like Seba and Emil up at Teresa's. Driving around looking for what's going on that always turned out to be nothing much. Sitting in the high school parking lot one night when Emil admitted he had one joint left and *what the hell, toke up.*

Hanging out with himself. Hung with himself. Listening to rock 'n' roll albums on his stereo in his room. Consuming novels from the library. Staring at the TV screen flipped to one of the five channels. Sitting alone amidst an audience of moviegoers. Feeling their faces rainbowed by stories like he dreamed. Riding solo behind the steering wheel listening to scratchy radio stations from far away mythical places. Driving everywhere and nowhere in his hometown.

"Well," said Jerry that dangerous Friday morning in the city crew yard, "smart guy like you, figure you know what you're doing. Catch you up at the gravel pile. Damn near got the banks of the lake us and the county made shored up. Dennis'll ride the roller packing down what you bring."

The giant yellow roller bigger than the red truck waited for Dennis across the yard as Jerry walked away toward a white pickup.

Dennis waited until Jerry was out of earshot.

"*A couple weeks?*" He shook his head. "At the fair, me and Barbara saw you two side by side walking out of the Wall of Death. Did you piss her off?"

"No! We just . . ."

The atomic bomb kiss in the moonlight by the end of the world silo's glow.

Luc shrugged: "We both decided . . . realized . . . We're just *not.*"

Dennis shook his head.

"'*Just*' and '*not*.' What are they getting you? Me and Barbara, we're going for all the *just* we can, whenever we can, wherever we can."

He blinked.

Stared at his friend.

Whispered over the machines roar:

"You don't just wanna fuck her. You'd already have made that move. Won—or lost and walked on. She's got you living and dreaming somewhere else. And I think you took her somewhere else, too."

Inspiration rocketed Dennis.

"I got it!" he said. "Barbara's curious about Terry. If we pick you two up to go riding around for maybe 'one last time' *in my folks' car* . . . After I drop you off . . .

"Or drive you to some kind of place you two wanna go, too. Hell, I'm loaning you the backseat. I mean, what else is summer for besides bossing the steering wheel and going into the backseat?"

Dennis grinned at Luc.

"It's Friday. I'll set it up for tomorrow. Saturday night."

Especially after what happened sixty-nine minutes later, how could Luc say no?

The next day, Saturday, as the sun hung in the west.

Luc checked his watch as he stood in the living room: 6:51.

Said he'd pick me up at 7:00. When—how—will he pick up Terry?

She's just across the street. Just across the damn street.

Showered. Clean shirt and blue jeans. Sneakers. Teeth brushed. Twice.

Check your watch: 6:53.

Dad's voice from the kitchen table: "Luc! Come here!"

"I'm—"

"It'll just take a sec. And it's more important than whatever you're waiting on tonight. It's not like you're going to be late for a movie at the Roxy. If you are, you'll just miss—What is it they call it? *Previews of Coming Attractions.* And hell, I got that for you right here."

A white piece of paper printed with a government form of three paragraphs with two close blank lines lay on the kitchen table.

APPLICATION TO APPEAR ON ELECTION BALLOT

"All that blank space at the bottom is for twenty registered voters' signatures you gotta get for the application to be accepted," said Luc's dad. "Keeps crazies from clogging up the ballot.

"What do you think?" he asked his son.

"Can I sign? I registered to vote up here 'cause it didn't seem fair to the folks in Missoula even though I'm there nine months of the year."

"I appreciate that, son. I really do. But I don't want to have anybody from our family's signature except your mom's. That shows she approves and won't be any trouble 'cause she'll be the first one to sign so everyone can see. Plus, with what went on before, you signing seems a little too *personal*, about us, *not* about the rest of the town."

"When's your deadline?"

"September 15."

"Oh hell, you'll make that with no trouble."

"I know. But I'm gonna get what I need starting now, then hold it until I see what Mueler or somebody else might be doing to get that seat on the city council."

BEEP!

A car horn from the street out front of the house.

"That's for me!" guessed Luc. "Good luck. If there's anything I can do . . ."

"Just don't get into any trouble or . . . or into any more controversies before the election in November!" called out Don Ross to his son's hurrying away back.

The front door slammed.

Don didn't know if his son had heard him—*really heard* him or not.

The risk you take with kids, he thought. *Do what you can. Then so do they.*

Savvy Dennis had flipped a U-turn to park his parents' car in front of Luc's house on the right side of the street and facing the legal direction of west.

That meant the car's back door at the curb was behind the shotgun seat.

Luc saw and open-windows heard turned-around-in-the-whole-front-seat Barbara excitedly jabbering to . . .

. . . to Terry. Who sat behind driver Dennis. Sat by the door. Left the middle stretch of the backseat empty. Safe.

Luc opened the back door behind the shotgun seat.

Got a flash of a *Hi!* from Barbara who whirled to babble her interrupted story to the woman she barely knew sitting in the backseat behind Dennis.

"—*and then*, see what happened yesterday morning was these two guys here were working out at the lake with a big dam they built north of town so this place won't get flooded like it did back in '64 and then *my guy* here . . ."

Barbara turned to touch her hand to driver Dennis's blushing cheek.

". . . he's up on top of that big yellow roller that's like . . . *like three times as tall as this car.* Got a seat on it. Levers 'n' such. And Dennis is riding up there. Bouncing around. Packing down the dirt levees around the lake's shore.

"But suddenly . . . *The earth moved!* The ground under the roller starts to crumble an' sink and that God-damned yellow giant rectangle of steel starts to tumble sideways to the lake!

"But *my guy*," says Barbara, leaning closer to the older girl from big time Ohio, "my Dennis is so *fucking* smart and quick! He leaps off the *high* side of the tumbling-sideways roller! Flies off to land on the dirty prairie 'n' gets a little sprain on his wrist—Don't worry, his hand *oh yeah* works just fine! If he'd panicked or been stupid, jumped off the other side—the easy side to jump off—then hell, the flipped-on-its-side roller might have crushed him! Or at least tossed him into the lake on top of boulders and muck."

She grinned as she brushed her fingers through Dennis's hair.

I can feel that, ran through Luc. *Imagine that. But from . . . from who?*

Dennis smiled at the girl scrunched around on the car seat beside him. "Now that your story's done and Luc is sitting in our backseat, can I drive on?"

Barbara grinned at Terry.

Gave a knowing smile to Luc.

Turned to settle on the front seat beside Dennis. Their shoulders touched.

"*Oh yeah*, drive on," she said. "I just wanted the world to know how cool you are and how lucky I am that you're still here."

Her grin to Luc in the backseat filled the rearview mirror.

"No thanks to you," she joked.

"I just drive the truck," came his reply.

"Where are we driving this car now?" said Terry.

Said it staring straight ahead, at and past the back of Dennis's head toward a windshield she could barely see.

"We'll cruise a last look at this summertime town," said Dennis. "We're all leaving soon. Oughta see and get from it everything we can."

Barbara nodded toward the west end of town.

"Let's get Cokes from the drive-through at the Tastee Freeze," she said. "People'll see us and say that's what we did tonight."

"We were *real* thirsty," said Dennis.

He and Barbara laughed.

Tight smiles lined the faces of Terry and Luc.

The car rumbled over those small-town streets.

Terry said: "Seems like you two are always almost getting killed working your city crew jobs. Does that happen all the time?"

"So far, least once a year for me," said Luc.

"I don't come so close as Luc. He's on the street more. I spend a lot of time helping Arson working in the shop's garage. But I've been there. Hell, twice this year! Remember me getting jerked out of the collapsing sewer dig?"

Terry shook her head as they drove past Ma Bell's castle.

"What about the rest of the crew? The full-timers. The adults who aren't just there for the summer to pay for college?"

"They risk it all year long," said Dennis.

"Welcome to the street wages world," said Luc.

They drove past his junior high and elementary school.

The rearview mirror caught Dennis glancing at his backseat passengers.

Above the turned-low car radio, everyone heard him say: "Life's short."

Terry stared past the rearview mirror to the windshield.

Told the universe: "You gotta live it every day. No such thing as time-outs."

Luc said: "Every beat of your heart."

The car tires rumbled on the city street the crew had fixed.

Terry sat across the wide backseat from him at her own window.

Barbara snuggled shoulder to shoulder with car driver Dennis.

They all sent quarters into the Tastee Freeze serving window for plasticized paper cups with straws of Coke.

The rearview mirror showed the staring-there eyes of Terry, Dennis and Luc as memories filled their plastic straws.

Dennis drove over the viaduct to the Big Pink high school. Stopped his parents' car in the empty student parking lot like before. A visit of nostalgia that Barbara didn't know about or share.

The radio played some song.

Announced American KIAS in Vietnam had climbed the charts to 44,749.

Barbara looked at Dennis not saying anything about The Plan(s).

Thought: *Sometimes you gotta do it 'n' be the boss to get what you wanna.*

Suggested: "So let's do a couple more laps around Main Street—"

"—so your folks might hear that's where we were," interrupted Dennis.

"*Then* . . ." Barbara let her words trail off.

"Then," said Dennis, "there's two, *well*, two places we can go. One's a gravel road way out north of town that's kind of . . . Kind of maybe better for just Barbara and me. But we're totally fine going to the other place out east of town on the road down behind the road sign for the Marias River Massacre."

Where I took Buffy the summer before college for our one time of kissing-only passion, thought Luc.

The radio played half a song before anyone said anything else.

Barbara told the two backseat faces on either edge of the rearview mirror: "We'll go wherever you want."

Terry cleared her throat.

"I better get back to my room in case there's some emergency," she said.

Dennis and Barbara chimed in together.

Dennis: "*Sure!*"   Barbara: "*That's fine!*"

Luc said nothing.

The car rumbled over the viaduct.

Rolled down Main Street one more sundown time to be seen and reported.

Luc didn't look to see what movie was playing at the Roxy.

Kept his face staring straight ahead toward the windshield past the empty shotgun seat at whatever movie was playing there and here.

Didn't look at Terry sitting *way* across the backseat from him.

Dennis parked at the curb in front of the hospital's glass front doors.

Luc's legal residence waited across the street.

Terry leaned forward from the backseat to squeeze both of Dennis's shoulders with her soft white hands.

"You take care of yourself," she told the driver who brought her here. "Don't go getting in some city crew mess that sends you here at the hospital before you get out of here to college. And in case I don't see you again before we both leave town . . . *Thank you!* For being my friend. For taking care of me. For rides on your motorcycle. Letting me practice poking you with a hypodermic needle. You're a great guy."

She faced only Barbara sitting beside the driver.

"And I wish I'd had a chance to get to know you," big city/college star *her* said to the years-younger smalltown girl.

Laughed: "But speaking as a 'medical professional,' you're sitting next to a good man."

She opened her backseat door to get out.

So did Luc.

That car drove away. Left them standing on the sidewalk with no more good-byes said out loud. And while it was headed east toward the highway past the fairgrounds to the Marias Massacre sign, Luc knew Dennis's car would steer to a secluded spot on a gravel road north of the town far past whatever was showing on the drive-in movie theater's giant outdoor white screen.

"Young love," said Terry.

"If that's what it is," said Luc.

"Which is the *what*: '*young*' or '*love*'?"

"Yeah," said Luc.

They turned and faced each other for the first time that sundown.

She said, *she knew*: "You're not leaving town yet."

"Neither are you," he said, *he knew*.

"So . . ." Terry shrugged. "So this isn't our good-bye."

"I hope not," he whispered.

She walked to the glass doors out of this setting sun.

The dyed blonde without a gun turned to the man who had it as they stood on the sidewalk by the cab waiting to take her to the airport. Her smile shimmered from her heart to her head:

"Sorry about your summertime stash."

"I'm still high enough now. Wishing . . ."

"Yeah," she said. "Wishing. Me, too."

She shook her head. Whispered: "Can I ask you a true favor?"

"Yes. And yes. All yes."

"Will you kiss me? I want to know if . . . I want you to be the first man after. Who I choose."

He cupped her face with his hands.

THE LONG RIDE

Oh that kiss!

Right out there in open on a Montana street during the first ever Earth Day.

Nick felt her ruby lips against his like a trembling line of determination and . . . and then hope as those ruby lips softened.

He felt the fire of their kiss. Hoped oh hoped she felt it, too.

And felt safe.

Nick knew not to let his tongue penetrate her.

Not now. Not yet.

Maybe . . . Someday?

They pulled apart.

Saw each other.

"Thank you!" she said. "For that. And for stopping me from doing not-me."

"My pleasure," he replied. "My dream."

Wondered if her smile meant she also felt some *maybe*.

She climbed in the back of the cab.

Didn't look back as it carried her away.

Nick felt the gun hidden in his blue jeans' waistband.

Tuesday.

September 1, 1970.

Dennis was back at his university.

Luc took a day off from his last week with the city crew.

Took the day off to drive Terry eighty-nine miles to the airport to her Ohio.

Her boss, the chief of medicine for the Vernon hospital, asked *her* to ask *him*—who was *obviously* a friend of hers—because while the doc's wife had time to home-bake the chocolate cake with vanilla icing for Terry's going away afternoon *hoo-rah*, Mrs. Doc had too much to do getting their two girls settled in grade school to spend four hours driving back and forth to get that nice gal student down to the Great Falls airport to catch her flight back to where she belonged.

"Remember," Luc's father warned him at breakfast. "Drive safe. Drive legal. Don't get into any trouble. Don't make any trouble."

"'N' say good-bye from me to *what's her face*," said his mom. "I get them mixed up."

The way she looked at Luc made him wonder if she knifed him with savvy sarcasm or was she really confused.

Or both, he thought. *Like me.*

No, NO: I know where I/we're going.

He helped Terry pack his gassed-up blue car parked in front of the hospital at 8:11 that Tuesday morning after her last "free" breakfast.

Terry had two suitcases. A huge traveling purse. Her worn blue jean jacket tied around the waist of her black slacks. She wore a dark blue blouse. Soft pink moisturizer that was most definitely *not* lipstick! Her shoulder-length midnight hair hung loose.

Bags in the trunk.

Her traveling purse plunked on the front seat between rider and driver.

Car doors slammed.

Luc keyed the blue car to life.

The radio came on:

KRIP playing some *I'm a kick-ass cowboy in my good times bar* song.

Not even close to a clong, thought Luc.

He turned to look at her.

She turned to see him.

They'd barely made eye contact since he showed up at her room.

"That rolled-up tube is the *Easy Rider* poster," she'd told him there. "The poster of *The Apartment* is folded up in my suitcase. I'm taking it."

She'd shrugged: "Call me sentimental."

"You'll have to give me that phone number."

He carried a bag of hers in each hand while he followed the natural swing of her half-mooned black slacks down the pine ammonia scented hospital hall.

Now in the motor-purring car, he turned to meet her blue eyes.

"Those sunglasses are in the jockey box."

He kept his smile on her as she claimed what she'd worn before.

They put their sunglasses on together.

She saw herself reflected in his sunglasses' mirrored lenses.

Can he see himself like that in my wraparounds? she wondered.

"We gotta drag Main one more time," he said like they were high school teenagers. "*Hey*: it's on the way."

They drove past his legal residence.

She turned to watch it and its two front lawn pine trees slide past.

Asked: "Do you miss this place when you leave?"

The blue car slid past the Elk's Club. The men's clothing store with both business suits and snap button cowboy shirts. The whitewashed windows that used to be the ice cream parlor and the next-door bookstore.

"Place like this, it never leaves you."

The Roxy movie theater slid past on their right. Pulled Luc to a smile.

"I had the poet Richard Hugo for a creative writing class. A bulldog of a man. A bombardier in WWII. In a plane that got shot down. Semi-pro baseball catcher. Worked on a Seattle factory line for Boeing. Now he's Richard Hugo."

"He got to grow into who he had to be."

"Anyway, Hugo once told our class that a few certain places have a powerful essence you can't escape. He'd been living in and absorbing Montana for a handful of years by then. He went around the table. Asked us where we were from. Nodded to the answers. Came to me and I said: '*Vernon.*' '*Yeah,*" he said. '*You know what I'm talking about.*'"

"I've never read Hugo," said Terry.

Her reflection in the windshield smiled.

"But I've read one of his students. And whatever *that* is, you got it."

"*Naw,*" said Luc as they turned onto where the town's backstreet became the highway. "It's got me."

Luc drove his blue car the same route he took with the city crew's trucks.

Past the Conner reservoir—in reality, barely a pond of prairie hills runoff with two clinging to life trees. His family, the Conner side, they'd lived there while there were still free-range cattle drives for his grandfather to cowboy.

The blue car sped up and over the lip of the Vernon valley.

Drove past the four brand-new red and white steel girder towers for KRIP.

Luc spun the car radio's channel-changing dial.

Landed on the best Great Falls rock 'n' roll station as the blue car sped past the Minuteman missile silo where doomsday waited and where Norma . . .

Don't think about Norma. About that. All that. Just drive.

The radio played its on-the-half-hour news bulletins: France's atomic bomb tests. Rubber bullets fired for the first time by British forces in "the Troubles" of Ireland's civil war. American KIAs in Vietnam still climbing the charts.

Their car crossed the bridge over the Grady River that watered the town behind them. The river they'd watched while trying to get her stoned.

Drove past the gravel road turn-off to where city crew trucks got their fill.

Checkerboard brown and yellow farm fields flowed past their side windows.

They merged onto the four-lane interstate highway.

Terry shook her head.

"Thanks for doing this. I know . . . This ride . . . Hard for both of us."

"What do you want?"

"To get where I'm going," whispered Terry.

"A doctor's white coat. Stethoscope around your collar."

"You'll be clacking a typewriter keyboard."

"The keyboard will be clacking me."

"'First, do no harm,'" she whispered from the oath she'd work night and day to be able to say with "Doctor" before her name.

Miles rolled beneath their wheels.

The radio played.

A road sign:

GREAT FALLS—57

"Less than an hour," she said, not bothering to check the speedometer on this highway in a state where there was no daytime speed limit.

"Gotta say thanks again," she said. "For being there for me. For being a friend. For . . . Hell, I guess for being you."

"That last part is maybe not the best choice but the one I had."

She stared out her side window at the rolling-past world.

Stared at the driver of the car she rode.

Triggered his glance back at her.

"We did the right thing by not doing anything else," she said. "Well . . . A kiss is just a kiss."

"Every kiss is what *it* is."

She stared out the windshield.

The blue car rolled under an overpass for a highway running toward the horizon of mountains. The road sign arrow pointing that direction read Missoula.

"That's where you'll drive to go back to the university."

"Yup."

"Drive careful."

Luc sensed her smile as she said: "Say *hi* for me. But not to her."

"Tell your boyfriend turns out he had nothing to worry about."

"I'll figure out something else that isn't a lie."

Car wheels on a paved highway.

"How are we for time?" he asked her.

"My plane doesn't leave for . . . For a little more than three hours."

That's when they saw the highway billboard:

• STARLIGHT MOTEL •

ACROSS THE HIGHWAY FROM THE AIRPORT

CONVENIENCE • COMFORT • LOW COST

Neither of them said a word.

"Big city" Great Falls filled their windows.

The tan brick smokestack from a smelter rose above everything.

Their wheels rumbled up the highway EXIT marked AIRPORT.

Luc pulled to a stop at the curb in front of the airport's sliding glass doors. Empty cars waited in the short-term, long-term and rental car parking lots. A pigeon pecked at the sidewalk that held no other people. This was a small airport between major destinations where flights were spaced far apart. The few runways held no winged escape machines much of the day and most of the night.

Luc whirled, blathering out of the driver's door:

"I got your suitcases put 'em here 'n' go park the car to go in wait with—"

Terry met him beside her bags on the sidewalk.

"Leave them," she said.

Looked past him.

He turned and looked there too:

The Starlight Motel waited across the highway from her plane's 129-minutes-away boarding call.

"No words," said Terry with shining blue eyes.

Her midnight hair flowed in the airport breeze.

Her hands cupped his face.

Their hungers knew *oh how they knew* to burn with that last deep kiss.

As it was *now*. As it was *then*. As it was *forever*.

Her lips broke free.

Her forehead leaned against his chest under his chin.

His hands cupped her shoulders. He held her close.

The heaven flesh smell of her midnight hair.

She stepped away.

One last look at him.

Walked her suitcases through the airport's sliding glass doors into *gone*.

Luc found her borrowed wraparound sunglasses on the dashboard inside his car. Put them back in the jockey box. Drove to the airport's exit.

To the right waited the highway running toward Helena and Norma.

Across the highway waited the Starlight Motel.

To the left ran the highway toward . . . *Where? Home?*

Luc spun the steering wheel to the left and stepped on the gas.

> Nick walked across the bridge over the river he'd marched with fear and hope in his heart with thousands of other women and men just like him. Now he had the bridge to himself as he walked across its quarter-mile arch to go reclaim his IDs and keys of Who He Used to Be.
>
> He stopped.
>
> Looked at the river below him rushing from here to where.
>
> His aviator sunglasses reflected the sinking sun.
>
> He looked left. He looked right.
>
> Slid the .45 out of his pants.
>
> Let it fall into the river.
>
> The last of the marijuana cloud set him free.
>
> He stared over the river beyond zen.
>
> Had to grin.
>
> THE END

ZEN GREEN by Luc Ross

LAST DAY

Now you give me an earful," said Dave the boss to Luc.

Jerry. Arson. Cal the Bull. All the other city crew members except the early-off, early-on garbagemen shuffled with them on the yard that after-5:00 September 3 afternoon.

"Your last day," said Dave. "Like they say, your check is in the mail."

Everybody chuckled.

A train whistle blew through the blue sky of that warm Friday.

"So what are you gonna put in my ear?" said Dave.

"Not enough *thank yous*," said the college bound crew member.

Luc smelled the yard's oil-packed earth. Sand. Gravel. Gasoline for the big trucks. The frontend loaders and backhoes. The treacherous roller. The oiler truck on loan from the county. His sweat breezed into that cloud of *got 'er done.*

Dave said: "We gonna get to have you workin' with us next summer?"

Supposed to be my senior year now, thought Luc. *Go and get gone to $.*

Images of Vic dodging a yellow New York city taxicab blew through Luc. He answered Dave as everyone in the crew filled his actual vision:

"Tell you the truth, I don't really know."

"Just find out before *we* gotta know," said Street Foreman Jerry.

"Deal." Luc grinned: "You're the boss."

"The hell I am," countered Jerry. "Dave is."

Jerry shook his gray cowboy hat head: "You college types. Think you everything and you don't even know who the boss is."

Everybody laughed.

Luc shook everybody's hand.

Shook Dave's hand last.

Their nods said everything.

The crew walked out as the gates to the yard got locked.

All of them climbed into work-scraped pickups or dented cars.

Except Luc.

Don't look back, he told himself as he walked a block and turned the corner toward the Post Office two blocks away and one more block before Luc hit home.

If you look back—

THERE!

The Post Office parking lot.

A car parked all by itself way down at this 'far' end of the parking lot.

A man leaned against the hood of that parked car. Faced the street. Watched Luc walk closer where a thousand eyes had seen him walk before.

A 1950s businessman's black hat. Glasses. A red bowtie tight on a short-sleeve white shirt. Gray slacks.

Lloyd Mueler.

City councilman. A news media owner—even if it was only the second-best weekly paper in town. A community influencer who thought freedom meant you getting to do what you're told. Told by *loving America as it supposedly was* him.

Luc could have stayed on his side of the street.

Could have made Mueler call him over. Walk on by or step up *if and when*.

Gunfighter Luc strode across the street.

Work sun faded red hoodie. Oil stained white T-shirt. Filthy blue jeans ready for the rag pile. Scuffed brown work boots.

Luc stopped in front of the asshole leaning on his car.

Stared straight into his lens-covered beady eyes.

And waited.

"You happy now?" Lloyd Mueler stood tall. Tipped his face up so his hat brim didn't hide any of this traitorous college boy's smart-ass face.

Luc only gave Mueler a smile.

"You got what you wanted," snapped Mueler. "The damn taxpayers kept giving you checks all summer long. Let you drag your dumb ass around town and get a tan for all them slutty hippie girls to go '*Ooo!*' and '*Ahh!*' You're getting out of town in fine style come Sunday, I hear."

Don't blink, thought Luc. *So glad I'm not wearing my sunglasses!*

Mueler shrugged. His lips made a tight smile.

"You got what you wanted. You won. And now you're gone. Money in your jeans. So now there's no reason for your dad to come after me. Get his ass kicked running for my City Council seat."

"*Oh my God!*"

Luc startled the man who'd come to ambush him.

"I'm so sorry!" said Luc. "You've got it all wrong!"

"Wha . . . *What?*"

"My dad. Don Ross. Ex–school board member. Boss of a couple dozen people who think he's great and say so. And that trucking company! Why, it's hooked into all the suits and ties on Main Street. Even if they all don't agree with everything about Dad, they aren't going to shake their pockets or run their mouths or move their polling booth pencils against him.

"My dad. Don Ross. He's not doing anything because of *you*. Whatever he's doing, he's doing it to do *right*. For all of *us*."

Luc shrugged.

Pulled the small-town move. A Conner move.

"Most of the people around here been saying they wish you were the kind of guy who'd do that same thing.

"Too bad," said Luc.

Turned and walked away into the evening sun.

Naw, motherfucker: I'm not looking back. You *watch* me go.

Luc walked with a smile on his face.

WINDSHIELDS

He beat his dad home.

Knew Dad was working the streets *his* way.

Mom clattered pans in the kitchen to get dinner on the table exactly at 6:00 so the world wouldn't blow up.

Luc walked into his bedroom.

Found what Mom had left on his carefully made bed.

Mail for him.

Two arrivals:

- A thick, double-handful-sized green envelope delivering that month's *Playboy*.
- A manila envelope lined with Luc's carefully inked words.He grabbed the manila envelope. But he already knew.

Tore it open.

Pulled out his short story ZEN GREEN.

Double-spaced lines on white paper.

And on that title page . . .

An old-fashioned, hand-stamped verdict:

REJECTED

Plus an angry pen's blue ink scrawl:

ARe you Fucking KIDDING?!!

Luc slumped back into the padded gold chair facing his bed.

Tossed his short story next to the green-sheathed *Playboy*.

Outside his open window warbled a meadowlark.

Unseen plates clumped on the kitchen table.

Least they read it, thought Luc. Hated it so much they went above and beyond. Went personal: *BAM!* Stamped by hand. Said "*Fuck you!*" Not just some form-printed rejection slip.

KRIP radio in the kitchen kept Mom company by playing country and western star Patsy Cline singing "Stand by Your Man."

Luc blinked.

Forget about *Noir Daze* and their fuck you. If he re-typed the savaged first page . . . If he went to the Thriftway grocery store or . . . *Or to the drugstore!* Buy two new manila envelopes *and* in the drugstore's magazine rack, find a copy of *Alfred Hitchcock's Mystery Magazine* or Ellery Queen's or . . .

Luc's eyes landed on the green sheath hiding his new *Playboy*.

Where all the post WWII big name fiction authors went.

Any—all—of those magazines have their address printed on some credits' page. Don't have to buy them at the drugstore, just write addresses down in a notebook 'n' not get caught by the clerk, and I got . . . I've got . . .

He ripped *Playboy* free from its censorious green sheath.

Oh the feel of those slick pages!

On the cover stood a . . . A girl? A woman? Looked like a college co-ed. Straight blonde hair tied with a headband. Raising her right hand up in that era's two-fingered V peace sign created by the anti-Vietnam war protestors. She wore a scooped neck pale blue top like you could see walking the streets of your hometown. Strapped over her left shoulder hung a buckskin bag that could have held books *and* lipstick. Dark eyes. Slick pink smile.

One headline around the cover girl announced an article called "The Abortion Revolution." Other headlines announced a national survey of college students' attitudes on "today's major issues." Promised a pictorial spread featuring a nude blonde German actress famous for comedy movies. Boasted about that month's fold-out Playmate as a Radcliffe college bound ballerina.

No fiction authors made the cover that month.

Maybe no other prose-slinger is fictionalizing "today's major issues."

Like ZEN GREEN.

He had to, *just had to*, flip the magazine open. Let the Playmate triple-page spread fall out in front of his eyes. Skim four pages of Elke Sommer's pictorial.

Search for—*found* the magazine's business address.

Won't be able to mail it until the day after I get back to Missoula, but come that Monday, I can walk to the Post Office and then across the bridge to campus.

Luc walked from his room to meet his parents in the kitchen.

Told them about the gunfight showdown in the Post Office parking lot.

Dad said: "Guess I'll turn in my petition next Monday."

Mom said nothing.

But she cut Luc a second slice of apple pie without him asking.

Friday night.

Last Friday night in the town where he legally lived.

Luc drove up Knob Hill as the sun set outside his rolled down windows.

Chose not to go see the ghosts in the graveyard.

Besides, they rode with him anyway. Especially Mike.

Luc glanced left.

Saw Steve carrying a gym bag to his car in the driveway of his house.

Luc steered his car to park on the wrong side of the street in front of Steve.

"Hey, man," said Luc. "How are you? Where you going?"

"That's always the question." Steve gave his friend a smile. "Met an artist who lives over in Kalispell. Gonna spend the weekend with her. Wish me luck."

"Always," said Luc.

Drove away. Rearview mirror watched his friend open his own car door.

Like Dennis, Seba and Emil were back at their colleges. So was Luc's cousin Gene, last season playing football for the Catholic college in Helena. Where Norma lived. Gideon and his new marriage waited across town, while Gideon's buddy Kyle lived in Hawaii doing whatever you did in Hawaii. And Marin, Luc's first buddy to be a father, poet Marin and family were way east of here in Havre where Dennis went to college full-time while Marin took classes and ran a bar. Luc didn't know if his two childhood friends Wayne and Kurt had left town for their official last years at college. They all knew they now all walked different streets—and forget about politics: Luc's stoner path made him an outlaw.

Luc parked in front of Teresa's house.

As always, walked into the open garage and through the kitchen side door.

"Well how the hell are you kid?" said Teresa. "Come on in, sit awhile."

At Teresa's kitchen table. Where once also sat Norma.

He and Teresa talked about this. Talked about that. Talked about nothing.

"Getting dark out there," said Luc. "Better get home and start packing."

"Well, hell, kid. See ya when I see you."

Luc drove the other way home. Down the hill behind the courthouse. Past the library. Past the front of the hospital where he saw a second-story window and knew the room behind it was nobody's home.

Nobody was home at his house either.

Luc figured Dad was at work (as usual) and Mom was out riding around with some of her Conner sisters (as usual).

As usual, he thought.

Smiled with thoughts of Steve.

Held the wall phone's black receiver against his left ear as his right finger spun the four numbers he still remembered by heart.

"Hello?" answered a father on the other end of the line.

"Hi. It's Luc Ross. I was just wondering . . . Is Buffy there?"

"Oh hi, Luc! Didn't know you were still in town. Buffy . . . She left a few days ago to go to . . ." Her father cleared his throat. "She was stopping in Helena for a few nights before heading on to school at Bozeman.

"*Umm* . . . You got a message I should give her?"

"*Naw*," said Luc. "Just me checking in. She knows all I've got to say."

He hung up that phone.

Thought: *Helena—Again! Wonder if she'll run into Norma?*

He laughed: *Two strangers in the same dream.*

Saturday afternoon he went to the nursing home to see Gramma Meg.

She grumbled and mumbled, ordered and complained.

Caught him staring at his wristwatch.

"I'll be dead the next time you see me," she said.

Twitched a timeless smile.

Patted his hand when he touched her shoulder in a Conner *good-bye*.

"You sure you got everything?" said his mom the next day as she stood beside Dad facing Luc in their kitchen with its back door leading out to the driveway and his gassed-up, baggage-filled blue car with its Martin County license plate on that fine Sunday morning, September 6, 1970.

"Yeah," said Luc. "My buddy's box is in my closest beside—"

"Besides your *don't throw them outs*," said Mom. "How's he doing?"

"When Vic called last week, said he was doing fine in New York. Homesick. Worried about his dad who's holding his own. Reminded me to vote *yes* for calling a Montana state constitutional convention in November's election—a chance to shake off the Copper Collars of big corporations who wrote what we got now."

"You just be sure to vote in the election," said his dad. "For whatever."

The man of that house and town grinned: "And for *whoever*."

Shoulders squeezed. Good-byes spoken. Parents walked their son out to his blue car that he'd bought with his own money to drive to the university that his summer road crew job and a few scholarship pennies let him pay for himself.

They waved as he backed out of the driveway. Turned left at the corner.

Gone.

Have to drag Main Street.

Church bells rang.

Luc drove past the Roxy with its screen for heroes and villains.

Took the road, *oh* he took the road he drove with the red truck to haul city crew gravel. The rode he drove to take Norma to her bus. Terry to her plane.

He topped the valley rim.

Rolled past KRIP's radio towers.

His rearview mirror filled with the Big Pink high school—

Blink and it was gone.

So too was the missile silo.

He spun the dial to the distant radio station of rock 'n' roll.

Crossed the river bridge.

Knew he'd lose all radio contact when he turned into the mountains.

The radio broadcast the news:

Smog and air pollution were sickening millions of Americans, especially in big cities like Hollywood. Earth Day organizers had a dozen plans but only one would see success, the Clean Air Act negotiated in Washington, DC, by Republican President Richard Nixon and Democratic Senate Majority Leader Mike Mansfield from Montana on the last day of that year of 1970. But on rolled the polluters, their hired hotshot hitters and suckered dupes in the public plus their victims of today and tomorrow. On too rolled the Vietnam war managed and escalated by Nixon and his foreign policy murders-scheming, coup-plotting, secret bombings, lying guru and future Nobel Peace Prize winner Henry Kissinger that on that Sunday'd created 44,910 American KIAs.

The radio played "Long as I Can See the Light" by earth-voiced, military veteran John Fogerty and his band Credence Clearwater Revival.

Luc flashed on Terry who'd ridden beside him listening to that radio.

On Norma who had too and somehow would again.

Luc felt his blue car rumbling over that long gray highway.

The roads we take.

The roads we don't.

The roads we've yet to see.

Gotta hope we pick the right windshield.

ART

ACKNOWLEDGEMENTS. RESPECT. THANKS.

Wondrous souls inspired and supported this work. A muckraker respects sources, so a score of them leave only their shadows here. To chronicle this era requires recognizing poets who came out of car radios, authors, artists and creators cited and credited in this historical fiction and again here.

Tori Amos * The Animals * Rick Applegate * Hannah Arendt * Joan Baez
The Association * The Beach Boys/Brian Wilson * The Beatles
Buffalo Springfield * Rich Bechtel * The Box Tops/Alex Chilton
Lenny Bruce * The Byrds * Michael Carlisle * Jessica Case *
Chief Heavy Runner * Patsy Cline * Leonard Cohen * Judy Collins
Credence Clearwater Revival/John Fogerty * Crosby, Stills, Nash & Young
Ken Davis * John Dos Passos * Bob Dylan * Fairport Convention
Richard Farina * William Faulkner * Peter Fonda * The Four Seasons
The Four Tops * E.M. Forster * Frank Fuller * Deborah Gage * William Golding
Bonnie Goldstein * Desmond Jack Wolff Grady * Jane Grady * Nathan Grady *
Rachel Grady * The Guess Who * A.B. Guthrie * Woody Guthrie
Dashiell Hammett * Claiborne Hancock * Joseph Heller * Floyd Hildebrand
Abbie Hoffman * Buddy Holly * Dennis Hopper * Edward Hopper
Richard Hugo * Danny Kessler * The Kingsmen * Harper Lee *
Dennis Long * David Lynch * Alistar MacLean * Ron Mardigian *
Joni Mitchell * The Monkees * Marilyn Monroe *
Jerry Murray * Jack Nicholson * George Orwell
Alan Pulaski * The Rolling Stones * Julia Romero * Linda Ronstadt
Isabella Rossellini * The Sandpipers * Frank Sinatra * Michele Slung
David Hale Smith * Sonny & Cher * Gary Snyder * Terry Southern
Bruce Springsteen * John Steinbeck * John Stewart * Rex Stout * Don Stratton
Roger Strull * The Supremes * Richard Thompson * The Temptations
Paul Vineyard * Kurt Vonnegut * Dick Voorhies * The Wall of Faces
E.B. White * Holly Wilson * Josh Wolff * David Wood

ABOUT AUTHOR JAMES GRADY

James Grady's first novel *SIX DAYS OF THE CONDOR* became the Robert Redford movie *THREE DAYS OF THE CONDOR* and Max Irons's TV series *CONDOR*.

Born and raised in Montana where his family settled in 1884, Grady has received Italy's Raymond Chandler Medal, France's *Grand Prix Du Roman Noir* and Japan's *Baka-Misu* literature award, two REGARIES MAGAZINE short story awards, and been a Mystery Writers of America Edgar finalist.

He's published more than a dozen novels and three times that many short stories, poetry, been a muckraker journalist and a filmed scriptwriter for movies and television.

In 2008, London's DAILY TELEGRAPH named Grady as one of *"50 crime writers to read before you die."*

PUBLISHERS WEEKLY compared him to Larry McMurtry for Grady's 2024 novel *THE SMOKE IN OUR EYES.*

In 2015, THE WASHINGTON POST compared his prose to George Orwell and Bob Dylan.